Sarah Mason is a full-time writer and lives in Cheltenham with her husband and her West Highland Terrier. Her first novel, *Playing James*, won the Romantic Novel of the Year Award 2003.

HIGH SOCIETY

Clemmie Colshannon's life appears to be on a fast track to nowhere — having lost her job and her boyfriend on the same day, she's retreated to the bosom of her family in Cornwall to recover. Fortunately, life *chez* Colshannon is never dull. Clemmie's brother, Barney, is in love but won't tell anyone who with; her mother is in the middle of a production of *Calamity Jane* and won't come out of character; and sister Holly, who is a reporter on the *Bristol Gazette*, needs a big story before her editor sacks her. But when a colleague from the *Gazette* goes missing, and Clemmie stumbles across a clue as to her whereabouts, it's not long before the drama turns into a crisis and the whole family is forced to flee to the south of France . . .

Books by Sarah Mason
Published by The House of Ulverscroft:

PLAYING JAMES
THE PARTY SEASON

SARAH MASON

HIGH SOCIETY

Complete and Unabridged

CHARNWOOD
Leicester

First published in Great Britain in 2004 by
Time Warner Paperbacks
an imprint of
Time Warner Book Group UK
London

First Charnwood Edition
published 2005
by arrangement with
Time Warner Book Group UK
London

The moral right of the author has been asserted

British Library CIP Data

Mason, Sarah
   High society.—Large print ed.—
Charnwood library series
1. Love stories
2. Large type books
I. Title
823.9′2 [F]

ISBN 1–84395–872–4

Published by
F. A. Thorpe (Publishing)
Anstey, Leicestershire

Set by Words & Graphics Ltd.
Anstey, Leicestershire
Printed and bound in Great Britain by
T. J. International Ltd., Padstow, Cornwall

This book is printed on acid-free paper

In memory of my dear father.
With all my love

Acknowledgements

Firstly, enormous thanks to my wonderful husband who has been simply amazing.

As always, my grateful thanks to my brilliant editors, Jo and Tara. Tara for her help on the early part of the book and Jo for all her work on the finished product while battling with the deadly combination of deadlines and my crapness. Thank you for being continually good-humoured and encouraging.

Many thanks to everyone at Time Warner for working so very hard and for their great support.

A huge thank you to my agent, Dinah, for not only being a brilliant agent but also for her friendship and support throughout an eventful year. I appreciate it greatly.

And to my mother, the most courageous woman I know and without whom I wouldn't have been able to write this book.

Friends and family. Well. The least said the better. But my mad sister-in-law, Tasha, is roaming the London Underground absolutely determined to sign someone's book whether they like it or not.

1

'Bonjour Madame!' I greet the lady behind the desk and put on my most charming smile. It always does to treat these ladies well. Some of them have the power of a small country.

She looks up from her work, peers at me over the top of her half-moon glasses and sniffs slightly as though she can smell my Englishness. My smile falters a little. I mean, I have been in a police station in England before. Once. So although I'm not exactly a hardened criminal, I do have some idea of the form. But do they do things differently in France?

'Mon frère est ici . . . ' I start haltingly in my GCSE French. The problem with GCSE French is that you have to fight a constant urge to ask people their name, how old they are and where they live before you can get down to the brass tacks of any problem. 'Il est . . . er . . . em . . . ' I'm trying desperately to find the word I need. I trawl through my limited vocabulary. It's no good, there's nothing that vaguely matches it. So I try the English phrase.

'UNDER ARREST.'

It doesn't seem to fool her; she looks at me blankly. I try it again, this time with a French accent.

'ARRESTE.'

'Il est en état d'arrestation?' she queries.

This sounds vaguely right so I nod.

1

'Qui s'appelle?'

'Il s'appelle Barney Colshannon.'

'Attendez là bas.'

She gestures to some chairs by the wall, so Sam and I duly wander over to them and sit down.

Of course, I blame my mother for all this. She had just received Morgan the Pekinese's pet passport and suggested we all nip over to France for the weekend to see if it was working. He is a rather old and smelly dog with no teeth left in the front of his mouth and will pee on anything if you leave it in the middle of the room. I'm not quite sure what he is thinking when he tries to bite other dogs, he must be under the impression he can suck them to death. Anyway, despite being adored by my mother, Morgan and I have never quite seen eye to eye, so why we couldn't have just popped him on a cross channel ferry and waited to see if he came back I simply do not know. However, the pull of some French bread and cheap booze was simply too much for us and we all readily acquiesced.

My mother always makes France sound absolutely delightful as she is a bit of a Francophile at heart, but her version is solely based on Gérard Départieu and some adverts she did for the French tourist board back in the eighties which involved her getting pissed on Bordeaux. According to her, France is just one big bit of cheese with plenty of wine and a few ooh-la-las thrown in. Not a police station in sight. This is a clearly inaccurate opinion because here I am in a French police station with no cheese, no wine and certainly no ooh-la-las.

We had all split up this morning to go our separate ways. I wanted to look at the shops, Barney went down on the beach and as Sam has the only real job out of all of us, he had to make some work phone calls. Sam is Barney's best friend. He has been since we moved to Cornwall about fifteen years ago and hence he's always been a presence in my life. I popped back to the hotel after my little shopping sortie (didn't buy anything as I am stony broke but that is another story) and the receptionist there gave me the message about Barney. I immediately went to get Sam because he is a lawyer and I was under the misapprehension that he might be of some use, and then we headed for the police station in double quick time. So at this precise moment my parents are sitting in a little café somewhere in Le Touquet, expecting us to turn up any second but nonetheless having a raucous time and probably some cheese too, blissfully oblivious to the fact that their son has been arrested. Whereas I, by virtue of my French GCSE, sit here (which just goes to show that too much education can be a bad thing), with Sam who is busy smiling at some girl across the room.

Sam leans over and whispers to me, 'Excellent French, by the way.'

'Thank you.'

'I particularly liked the ARREST thing.'

'I couldn't think of the word in French.'

'Saying it with a German accent was nothing less than a stroke of genius.'

'It was a French accent,' I spit out between

3

gritted teeth. God, he is maddening.

'So tell me what the lady at the hotel said again?'

'She just said that Barney had been arrested for assault. He apparently broke some poor bloke's arm. My brother wouldn't assault anyone!' Barney is quite frankly the sweetest individual alive. He wouldn't come out of his room for three days when he accidentally killed the class hamster by tripping and falling on top of the shoebox as he was carrying it home for the weekend so you can imagine the tough sort of individual we're talking about.

'It does seem a bit strange.'

'A bit strange? Sam, you're the bloody lawyer. You're going to have to make them release him.'

'I am not a sodding criminal lawyer.'

'But Barney wouldn't hurt a fly!'

'You just said that he broke someone's arm!'

'Do you think they're mistreating him?' I ask in a whisper, with a terrible picture of Barney in shackles thrust into my mind.

'Clemmie, we're in the middle of France, not a war zone.'

An officer walks out of one of the side doors and comes up to us. He looks a bit scary and stern with a dark moustache and I can feel my knees starting to go with fright. He rattles something off in very rapid French which just sounds like 'Blah, blah, French blah, Barney Colshannon, acute accent, blah, blah, catch the word for arm, blah.'

I glance over to Sam, who looks none the wiser either, and then ask the officer to repeat

4

what he's just said more slowly, which he does. I throw in the occasional question and so does he. He then asks us to follow him.

'What did Inspector Clouseau say?' whispers Sam as we go through the side door.

'He asked if you were here to represent Barney, I said that you were and I was going to translate. He then said that Barney had been charged with assault. This bloke was apparently standing on the pavement, cleaning some dog poo off his shoe, when Barney came along and hit him with a chair.'

'A chair?'

'Yeah, from the café next door.'

'Why would Barney hit him?'

'I don't know. Apparently the bloke had never laid eyes on him before.'

The building reminds me a bit of a school and the officer leads us up to a door, which he opens to reveal some very tatty furniture and a very fed-up Barney.

I rush over to him. 'Barney! Are you okay? Did they hurt you? Don't worry about anything, Sam will sort it out.'

'Clemmie, I can only say 'two beers' in French. I don't think that's going to get us very far. Are you all right, mate?' says Sam.

'Oh, I'm fine.'

'Barney, what on earth happened? Why did you hit that man?'

'I thought he was being electrocuted. He was holding on to the electricity line which went into the café and shaking all over.'

'So you hit him with a chair?'

5

'A plastic chair. Yes.'

'He was cleaning dog poo off his shoe.'

'Was he? Well, he was doing it pretty vigorously, he was jigging his leg all over the place. It looked like he was convulsing.'

'So . . . ' says Sam slowly. 'A man was cleaning some dog poo off his shoe and you thought he was being electrocuted and smacked him with a chair.'

'That's right. And then out of nowhere this police officer swooped down and arrested me and carted me off here.'

'I hope your French is up to this, Clemmie,' murmurs Sam.

Christ. I haven't got a clue what the verb for being electrocuted is.

★   ★   ★

A difficult half an hour follows, where I have to act out being electrocuted, we make phone calls back and forth to the hospital and it's ascertained that the man in question was indeed holding on to something but it turns out to be the telephone line into the café. On occasion the police officers' faces start twitching. Luckily the man doesn't want to press charges so Barney is released. Sam and I are hustled back to the waiting room and told that Barney has to complete some paperwork but will be joining us shortly.

'Well, thank God for that,' says Sam. 'And thank God you speak French.'

'Sam, I had to act most of it out. I'm sure they

kept asking me questions so I'd have to carry on. At least they're not charging Barney.'

'None of them could keep a straight face, let alone charge him with anything.'

'He can be a bit loopy sometimes, can't he? Oh, that poor man. We'll have to send him some flowers.'

'We'll ask which hospital he's at. Your parents must be wondering where on earth we are, they've been waiting for ages.'

'I'm going to have the largest drink you've ever seen once we get to the restaurant.'

We descend into silence and turn our attention to the French waiting room. The magazines are in French, the TV is in French and the posters are in French. No surprises there but still very boring. Sam must have come to the same conclusion. He leans over, 'So, what are your plans?'

'To get to that bloody restaurant as fast as possible and order some booze and cheese.'

'No, I mean for the future. Are you going to stay in Cornwall for a while with us?'

I have just returned in a fairly disastrous fashion from an around-the-world trip and am living with my parents at the moment until I decide what to do with my life. My parents live in an old house in a small village near the north coast of Cornwall which is a pretty nice place to live. The constant stream of tourists, or grockles as we like to call them, can become irritating in high summer but anywhere that invented clotted cream must be okay. The village itself isn't too chocolate-boxy. We have a smattering of thatched cottages which the weekenders have bought up but we're also an old-fashioned working village and lucky enough to boast a pub and a shop. We have the best of both worlds as the north coast beaches are but a short drive away, as are the moors of Bodmin in the opposite direction. All prime Daphne du Maurier country. Of course you can't mention Daphne without Sam and Barney squinting their eyes and saying *Jamaica Inn* in wild pirate accents with a lot of me-heartiness about it. They spent ages the other day trying to make me say it and laughing a lot.

My career is sort of on hold as it came to an abrupt and traumatic halt, hence my round-the-world odyssey, and now I am currently working in a small café in Tintagel to tide me over until I decide what to do. And I am useless at it. Really bad. I can never remember what any of the dishes come with. Chips, baked potato, new potatoes, mash, salad or seasonal vegetables, and you'd be surprised how annoyed some people can become about it too.

'It's just the work thing.'

'Yes. I can see your point.' Sam leans over and pats my knee. For a second I feel almost comforted, until he follows it up with: 'I mean, I didn't want mashed potato and you told me it came with chips.'

He's very lucky I don't have any of the implements from said café with me. This is the thing about Sam. He's just like a brother but more irritating. For instance, I had been looking forward to a rhubarb yoghurt all of last week. I had hidden it behind a jar of olives in the fridge, even though no one in my family likes rhubarb, but when I got home on Friday Sam had eaten it. He apparently does like rhubarb. Now, that is irritating.

We sit in silence for a second, and I'm still brooding about my rhubarb yoghurt when he asks, 'I don't remember you being this good at French at school.'

'Hmm?'

'I don't remember you speaking French this well.'

'I learnt most of it on my French exchange. The parents of my exchange partner were really sweet with me and sat down every day for at least an hour putting me through my paces. Of course, I didn't think they were very sweet at the time.'

He frowns. 'Your French exchange? When was that?'

'God, you must remember! I was sixteen! Bernadette spent most of her summer with us wrapped around Barney.' And good for Bernadette as she will never find herself sitting in an English police station because she never learned a word of sodding English.

'Oh yes! I thought that was Holly's French exchange partner.'

'It was probably quite difficult to tell as she never spoke to either of us.'

* * *

We drive back in silence to the restaurant, manage to find a parking space and then stroll

9

towards my parents who are sitting contentedly at a table and basking in the sunshine. My mother is wearing her Jackie Onassis black glasses, which almost cover the entirety of her face, and a large hat. A complete overreaction to a mere fifteen-degree temperature rise but she says that after being in Cornwall for the winter she often stands in front of the microwave with them on.

Family outings aren't normally so quiet but Barney and I are the only ones around at the moment. I have three brothers and a sister who was thrown in at the last minute (I think she was a bit of an accident as there are only ten months between us). My mother is a stage actress, quite a good one too. She does the odd bit of telly and a few minor film roles but generally prefers the stage. When she's in the middle of a run she tends to partially adopt the character she's playing, which makes life very challenging when you're trying to have a conversation over breakfast with Lady Macbeth without plunging her into hand-wringing hysterics.

Of course, when she's finished the run and on a well deserved rest, her natural thirst for drama slowly asserts itself until she'll throw herself into a room with, 'That was your Aunty May on the telephone,' accompanied by much arm-throwing, head-tossing and gazing into the distance. My father says she's almost like that insurance company except she will always make a crisis out of a drama.

My mother stands up and waves when she spots us, nearly taking out a waiter's eye with her cigarette. 'Darlings! We saved you some cheese! Where on earth have you all been?' We weave our way through the other tables and when we reach her she kisses us all firmly on both cheeks.

'It's a long story, Sorrel,' says Sam, taking a seat.

'Cheese?' proffers my mother as I pull out a chair and sit down. 'That one smells but tastes ambrosial, that one is fabulous and only Morgan likes that one.'

My good humour starts to restore itself as I manage to shove cheese and wine simultaneously into my mouth.

'Now what is this story?' asks my father. 'You were all gone so long I was about to call the police.' This is a standard line of my father's and he has no idea of the irony.

We all look from one to the other. There is not a chance of me telling the story because I can barely open my mouth for all the cheese in it.

'I'll tell it,' says Barney gloomily. 'Well, I saw this man and I have to stress very strongly at this point that he really looked as though he was having some sort of fit . . . '

2

My parents' house is located just on the village outskirts. It's a traditionally Cornish building, the walls are covered with slate tiles and a creeper covers the whole of one side of the house. The grand old lady sits in state on top of a hill with a driveway in front and surrounded by an overgrown garden. Inspired by Alan Titchmarsh, my father periodically dons his gardening beanie hat (unbeknown to him they have become very trendy and he can't understand why Barney keeps borrowing it) and makes a pilgrimage into the undergrowth, determined to transform it into a paradise worthy of The Chelsea Flower Show. My mother makes sandwiches and a flask of coffee for us while we watch him from one of the upstairs windows as he gets into fights with various plants and swears at bits of machinery until, utterly defeated, he rolls back in at the end of the day declaring his absolute hatred of all things green.

Inside is fairly chaotic and most of the action seems to take place in the big old kitchen at the back of the house. I really don't know why because very little cooking seems to take place there but Barney did set light to a Pop Tart in the toaster last week and had to douse it with the fire extinguisher.

A big dresser dominates one wall of the kitchen, and it is draped with dog leads, party invites, a rope of garlic from our recent French trip, photos and postcards, dodgy props that my mother collects from each play run and all manner of other trivia. A large sofa sits across another wall — the material is worn from countless bottoms and the back of the sofa is piled high with colourful cushions.

The rest of the house is decorated in my mother's usual distinctive style. A sort of Cath Kidson crossed with Liberace. Yes, quite scary.

Our family are a gregarious bunch who have never really identified with the concept of being alone. Probably due to the fact that in a family of seven it's never been possible to be alone. You can't even sit on the loo without someone shouting at you through the door. But it does mean that someone is always around for a friendly card game such as Slam! (until Barney renamed it Slap! with the obvious accompanying permutations) or a trip down to the pub.

I have just got changed from work and am wandering back down to the kitchen. The phone has been ringing since I came out of my room and I pick it up in the hallway downstairs. I really hope it's not my mother's agent because he is really scary and tends to shout at everyone (except my mother and father because they are both inclined to wander off and leave him to it whereas the rest of us stand, shaking in our boots).

'Hello?' I say tentatively.

'Clemmie!' exclaims my sister. 'It's me!'

'Holly!' I say in sheer relief. 'I thought it might have been Gordon.'

'Well, I can shout at you if you want me to.'

'No, no. Mr Trevesky has been shouting at me all day as it is.'

'What for?'

'Oooh, nothing.'

'Come on, Clemmie. What did you do?'

'Okay. I went the wrong way through the kitchen doors and managed to punch Wayne in the face with a tray.'

'Well, I'm sure it was an accident.'

'For the third time this week.'

'Oh. Well you probably needed a bit of a shouting at then.'

'Yes, but there are limits. And Wayne's nose has always been wonky. In fact, I might have straightened it up for him. Anyway, when are we seeing you next?'

'Well, that's why I'm calling. James is working this weekend so I thought I might pop down and see you all.' Holly is my younger sister and we're really close but I haven't seen her much since I got back from my trip. I have yet to meet James, her rather exciting-sounding boyfriend who she got together with while I was abroad and the story of which my mother told me in snippets during the three-minute conversations whenever I called home.

'That would be lovely!' I say with genuine pleasure. 'I'll ask Mr Trevesky for a day off.'

'Why don't you ask him for a couple of days and come back with me to Bristol? I could take the afternoon off and we could go shopping or something?'

'That would be nice but I really ought to use

my holiday to look for a proper job.' I try to sound more responsible than I'm feeling.

'Why don't you have a look in Bristol? It's a fantastic place!' Holly lives in Bristol so she is somewhat biased.

'I haven't really decided where I want to settle yet.' My last job was in Exeter and believe me when I say that I simply cannot return there. Ever.

'Well, I would love to have you here and there are some really great people. Why don't you come up and see how you like it? It could be a fact-finding mission.'

'Okay, that would be really good actually,' I say, my conscience slightly mollified. 'I'll ask Mr Trevesky tomorrow.'

'Besides, it's really exciting at the paper at the moment!' She lowers her voice. 'Emma has resigned!'

'Emma? Does the social diary thing?'

'She not only covers our illustrious society pages but does a bit of PR work as well. She knows everyone there is to know in Bristol.'

'Daddy is the QC?' I remember her well. Really snotty. One of those I-don't-need-to-work-I-just-bash-the-keyboard-for-a-lark people. Most of the people at Holly's paper are familiar to me as I have been to a couple of their work parties.

'No eyebrows,' adds Holly as a further aide mémoire.

I nod understandingly. 'I remember, difficult to trust someone with no eyebrows.'

'Exactly my opinion! James says I'm being

stupid. Anyway, she's just handed in her notice.'

'Why? Did she find another job?'

'Well, that's what's so strange. No one knows. She didn't mention to anyone that she was thinking of leaving. She just didn't turn up for work one morning and the next thing we know she sends in a letter of resignation by fax. But she's left all her stuff here. Even her lunchtime shopping, a lovely little Whistles top from the sale . . . ' Holly sounds incredulous about this as she rightly should. There is no way I would leave any of my sale purchases lying about. 'She's just gone.'

'Well, what does Joe say?' Joe is the editor of the paper.

'He says to mind our own business. Ha! Fancy saying that to a bunch of reporters!'

'Oooh. Something might have happened to her,' I say, intrigued. 'What does James think?' James is a detective in the police force so surely this would be just his tipple.

'James says to mind my own business too.'

'Oh.'

'At least it makes work more interesting.'

'How's it going at the moment?'

'I need a story,' says Holly gloomily. Holly wrote an incredibly successful diary for the paper while I was away about shadowing a detective from the police force. James was said detective and that's how they got together. The paper wanted her to do another diary but she opted for a senior place on the features team instead so she could stay in Bristol with James. 'Anyway, how's everyone? Mother okay?'

'They've just started the main rehearsals for *Calamity Jane*. Dad is hoping they'll all shoot each other.' Only a few weeks into her annual summer holiday my mother got bored and became involved with the amateur dramatics society.

'Oh God, that sounds a nightmare.'

'It is a bit. Barney and I sometimes pop down to see the rehearsals. Sally is really good.'

'What is Catherine like?' Catherine Fothersby is one of the leads in the play too and let's just say our two families have never seen eye to eye. Mostly because the Fothersbys wouldn't even dare look at any of us properly in case we curse them or something. They're a bit godly and seem to think we're the spawn of the devil. Goodness knows where they have got that idea. It can't have anything to do with my mother dressing up as a she-devil on Hallowe'en and then rattling chains outside our local, reputedly haunted pub at two in the morning. The vicar thought that was hilarious.

'Very good as Katie, actually, which will pain the Fothersbys to think their daughter has some acting talent.'

'She doesn't have as much as the other one,' says Holly darkly.

'You mean Teresa?' Teresa lives in Bristol. I haven't heard the entire story but I think Holly and she have recently crossed swords.

'I'll tell you about it when I see you. How are Barney and Sam? Recovered from France?'

I told Holly about the arrest the night we got back from France. 'Barney's still a bit sheepish

17

about it. We've got Charlotte here *again* on Friday.'

Charlotte is Sam's new girlfriend. Her parents have a weekend house in the village, although I'm not convinced it actually exists as she spends most of her time here eating supper with Sam. I'm being a bit mean as there is nothing wrong with the girl at all; in fact, she's fritefully, fritefully nice.

'I quite like her.'

'Ra-ra Charlotte? You like ra-ra Charlotte?'

'Why don't you like her?'

'For starters she sends our mother into melodramatic overdrive. I think it must be her accent because mother starts speaking the same way and behaving as though we're all in a Noël Coward play. She says things like, 'Isn't the honeysuckle just too, too sublime at this time of year?''

'She wouldn't know honeysuckle if it throttled her. She hasn't set foot in the garden for years.' My mother's complete aversion to flora and fauna is bizarre considering she has named one daughter after a fruit and the other after a bush.

'And she called me Daphne the other night.'

'God, Noël Coward crossed with *Calamity Jane*. It must be terrifying.'

I giggle and think how much I miss having Holly at home. 'When are you coming back?'

After we have said our goodbyes, I wander through to the kitchen. It's early evening which means that most of the family will have congregated here with their grasp firmly on a large drink. This tends to include Barney and

18

only marginally less often, Sam. Which is ironic because neither of them actually live here.

Barney lives in the village with three other boys from the surf shop up at Watergate Bay where he works. Their house is a pit. Believe me when I say this, because I'm not renowned for my purist hygiene attitude. I have been known to pick bits of toast off the floor and eat them, or indeed to eat a yoghurt past its sell-by date on the grounds that the manufacturers are being hysterically pedantic and it's probably fine. Whenever I nip down to visit Barney, I always dread going into the kitchen. He really ought to supply those little plastic shoe covers that I could pop over my flip-flops because it is truly disgusting. My mother absolutely refuses to go into the house and insists that Barney talks to her through one of the windows. But what else would you expect of four boys living together?

Barney is a bit of a surf dude. His blond hair is fashionably long and he wears lots of T-shirts over one another. He absolutely loves surfing and thus his job in the little café and surf shop in Watergate Bay is perfect for him. When we arrived in Cornwall in our teens, we quickly picked up that surfing was compulsory. After school, everyone would pack up and rush down to the beach where we would all don wetsuits and leap into the water, paddling out to reach the waves. But those boards were bloody heavy and I needed at least a ten-minute rest on mine after all that paddling before I could get down to any actual surfing so I have tailed off to the occasional boogie board session.

Barney is usually lovely to be around. I have to say he is pretty irresponsible and I normally end up doing stupid things when I am with him but this is all part of his charm. But the last few weeks he has been a bit moody, and not just as a result of his escapade in France. From what I can gather there is a girl involved, who he quite likes but, word has it on the family grapevine, she is not all that enamoured of him. Which is absolutely unheard of. Maybe this is the reason he is taking it quite hard — he probably doesn't know what to do. I mean, it's never happened to him before.

This evening it's just Barney and my parents who are present if incorrect in the kitchen. Barney is sitting on the Aga (it is turned off, we're just coming into September) drinking a beer from the bottle, my mother has a gin and tonic clasped tightly to one bosom and a cigarette to the other and my father is drinking his beer from a glass. They are discussing a posh dinner party my parents attended last weekend. Apparently my mother showed herself up appallingly as she was sat between two triathletes and kept asking them when they played the table tennis bit.

' . . . but Mum, you must have known who they were. They're quite famous, you know.'

'Darling, I simply hadn't a clue. I haven't the slightest interest in all this running around.'

'They're triathletes so they also cycle and swim. It's a tough competition.'

'Yes, I know what triathletes do but when do they play the ping pong? Surely it wouldn't be after the swimming otherwise the bat would get all wet.'

'No, you're right. It's not after the swimming.' There's a distinct note of resignation in Barney's voice. They obviously have been talking about this for quite some time.

'Can I get you a drink, Clemmie? Was that Holly on the phone?' asks my father.

'Em, yes please, and yes it was Holly on the phone.' I sink into the leather armchair next to the Aga.

'Darling, darling, darling. Darling. What on earth are you wearing?' says my mother, looking me up and down.

I look down at my admittedly eclectic mix of clothing. A pair of cut-offs from my round-the-world trip combined with several jumpers, none of them mine, and a large pair of woolly socks. Nice.

'Whose fault is this?' I say and glare at her. My mother took it into her head while I was away to completely turn out my wardrobe and give whatever items she didn't like to the local charity shop. Which is extremely aggravating, especially when you glimpse various neighbours wearing your old cast-offs.

My taste in clothes is precarious at the best of times but my casual wardrobe seems to have been the main casualty of this little onslaught and has left me with precious little. Don't get me wrong, I absolutely love clothes, but they always seem to look different on me to how they look on the hanger. Holly looks fabulous in something and then I'll put it on and look as

21

though I work for a very bad hairdresser. I think I must just be an awkward height or something.

'How is Holly?' asks my mother, blowing smoke rings and watching them float away.

'Needs a story. She's coming down for the weekend.'

'How lovely! I must remember to buy some of that muesli she likes.'

'Which muesli?'

'You know, the crunchy one.'

'That's me.'

'Hmm?'

'I'm the one who likes muesli. Holly hates it.'

'Are you sure?' My mother frowns.

'Quite sure. Anyway, she wants me to go back to Bristol with her and stay a few days.'

'That would be nice and you'd get to meet James too. He is simply divine. Would dear Mr Trevesky give you some time off?'

'I'll ask tomorrow. Have you got a rehearsal this evening?'

'Are you coming?' she asks as my father hands me a large glass of white wine.

Barney and I often wander down to the village hall to watch the am dram society in action, not simply for pure entertainment value, although it is worth it just for that, but because a friend of mine, Sally, is in the troupe. I don't know if troupe is the collective noun for a bunch of actors: I once asked my father what a group of actors was called and he said, 'A pain in the arse'.

I look over to Barney, who grins and nods slightly. Maybe his new amour is in it. Actually, she probably isn't. It's pretty slim pickings down there apart from Sally. There's the vicar, who is playing the lieutenant, Catherine Fothersby, who is playing Katie, and a woman called Mavis who plays a lot of the walk-on parts and is so absolutely thrilled to be on stage that she grins inanely throughout all her lines. She delivers the news of drownings and maimings with a broad smile on her face but my mother hasn't the heart to replace her. Sally is actually Calamity Jane. Which is great because she's great.

After supper our father tells us he'd rather slit his wrists than have to sit through another rendition of 'A Windy City' so just Barney, Morgan, my mother and I walk down to the village hall. The village doesn't have any street lamps so we have brought a torch. Barney has had to confiscate it off my mother though as she keeps wanting to look at stuff in the trees and won't keep the beam on the ground.

'Are you coming over on Friday night, Barney?' she asks. 'I've invited Sam and Charlotte.'

'Aren't you going clubbing in Torquay?' I ask Barney with a frown. Actually it's amazing that Sam and Barney are still such good friends. Sam is an old fuddy-duddy solicitor who works too hard and suppers with my parents on a Friday night while Barney whoops it up at the nearest watering hole.

'We're going Saturday now instead. What are you planning to give them to eat?' A very wise and astute question. You see? He's not really stupid. My mother is very hit and miss on the cooking front. Guests never know whether to have a KitKat in the car on the way over here.

'Your father was going to cook a curry.'

'Well, I'm around then.'

'Clemmie? You too?'

Hmmm. An evening with Sam and ra-ra Charlotte or a few drinks with Sally. Oooh. That's a tough one.

'Thanks but Sally and I are going out.'

'Would Sally like to come and have some supper first?' Sally would probably love to come and have some supper first but I hesitate for a second. After being away for a year, it has been embarrassingly difficult to come back and re-occupy my old bedroom at home, even with a family as laid back as my own. Charlotte must wonder what I am still doing here at the grand old age of twenty-six. 'Did you have to invite Charlotte?' I ask sulkily.

'She's nice!' protests my mother.

'Why can't they have supper at Charlotte's house? Which one is it anyway?' I demand.

'I've told you. It's the one with the red, you know, whatsit.' My mother hasn't got a clue which house in the village Charlotte's parents own. She never listens when people tell her details like this, she just glazes over and starts sliding down in her chair.

'It's the thatched one, next to Mrs Fothersby,' says Barney calmly.

'They wouldn't have any food in, they're only weekenders. Besides, you know that Sam is almost family. We always try to support him.'

'Humph.'

24

Sam was brought up by an aunt after his parents died when he was quite young. The aunt has since died too and now Sam lives in the house he inherited from her in the village. But of course he doesn't actually live there because as far as I can see he lives in our house, littering the place with empty rhubarb yoghurt cartons.

Our conversation is brought to an abrupt conclusion by our arrival at the village hall. My mother leads us blinking into the glaring electric light. Barney and I meekly go to the back and sit down as we have been taught to do since the age of zero whilst Morgan gets to accompany my mother up on to the stage. We are normally in more salubrious surroundings than the breeze blocks and plastic chairs of our village hall. Luckily there is only a small main cast to manage in *Calamity Jane*, but it does require a large number of extras which wouldn't normally leave a huge number of people in the audience in a small village like ours. However, such is the pull of my mother's name that people literally come for miles and miles to see her productions so she is risking it on this occasion.

The main cast are here tonight. Sally gives me an enthusiastic wave over the top of everyone's heads and I grin and wave back. Matt, the vicar, (who we all secretly rather fancy), waves to us too. Catherine Fothersby completely ignores us. Catherine permanently wears a very pained sort of wet mackerel look. Her dark, shiny hair is cut into a bob and very neatly pushed back behind her ears. It just makes me want to rush over and give her hair a good ruffle. She occasionally

25

wears an Alice band too. Yes. Exactly.

Both Catherine and her sister Teresa are actually quite good-looking in an annoyingly perfect kind of way, but they ruin the whole thing by standing in ballet poses and clasping their hands together and looking as though they're about to burst into song. Holly and I look like a pair of baby elephants charging about next to them. And they are always dressed beautifully. They never seem to make any shopping boobs. Their jumpers always sit perfectly on them, none of their clothes are ever creased (maybe because they wouldn't dare to) and their tights never ladder. And they both always wear a little gold crucifix which sits perfectly in the hollow of their throat. I can't see Catherine only remembering to shave one armpit before going to aqua aerobics as I did last week. The instructor kept insisting we clap our hands over our head and in the end I had to make out I had a dodgy arm.

I have no idea why Catherine is involved in this production because, as I have mentioned, her family are a bit godly and have always regarded my family and in particular my mother as part of some sort of un-Christian sect. But Sally thinks Catherine has a crush on the vicar and that's the only reason she auditioned. But if this is the case then she is completely barking up the wrong tree. Matt has, by his own admission, an appalling nicotine and booze habit (always to be found either in the pub or skulking in the graveyard with a fag), laughs raucously and generally has an infectious joie de vivre. And he absolutely adores my agnostic mother (which

26

normally would be the kiss of death where the Fothersby family are concerned) who he cheerfully tries to convert from time to time.

Bradley charges in at the last minute shouting, 'Sorry I'm late darlings! The A39 was backed up all the way to Launceston. Some silly cow had thrown all her husband's clothes out of the car window and a pair of boxers landed on someone's window screen and caused a five-car pile up. Bloody tourists. All before the Wadebridge exit too.' Now this may be true and it may not. He shrugs his cashmere-mix coat off his shoulders and unwinds his scarf. 'Did you start without me?' he says, clapping his hands together. Bradley plays Wild Bill Hickok but the only thing they have in common is that their names start with the letter B.

Barney and I grin at each other. We don't come to watch the rehearsals at all, we come to watch the actors, Bradley in particular. He is now insisting on leaning on the back of one of the chairs and gossiping madly with Sally and the vicar. Catherine has already arranged five plastic chairs on the stage where they'll do their read-through and is sitting primly with her script open. She looks rather martyred. My mother finally manages to get them all sitting around in a circle and the read-through begins.

This is the boring bit for me and Barney and I'm anxious to find out about this girl my father has mentioned.

'So,' I begin and raise my eyebrows hopefully. 'How's tricks for you?'

'Fine. How is Holly?'

'She's good. Needs a story. One of the girls at her office has gone missing though so maybe she should write about that.'

'Which one?' Besides being part of a family of voracious gossips, Barney has visited Holly's office a couple of times and let's just say the girls started appearing through cracks in the woodwork so he has pretty much met them all.

'Do you remember Emma? Daughter of the QC?'

'Stuck up?'

'That's the one. She seems to have disappeared.'

'Really? Blimey . . . '

I frown to myself. How have I managed to be so neatly distracted? I don't want to talk about Emma.

'So,' I say again. 'Are you seeing anyone at the moment?'

'Er, no. No one at all.'

'Would you like to be seeing anyone at all?' Subtle, Clemmie. Very subtle. He didn't see that coming.

He looks across at me and frowns. 'Who have you been talking to?'

'Do I have to be talking to someone to be interested in my brother?' I give a forced little laugh and then cave in dramatically. 'All right, it was Dad. I was talking to Dad. He said you liked someone.' God, I'm not sure if I would ever hold out under torture. They would only have to politely ask me if I wanted tea or coffee and I'd spill my guts. 'Who is it?'

'I'm not telling you that!'

'Why not?'

He shifts position in his seat and looks uncomfortable. 'Well, I'm not terribly sure she likes me.'

I look at him in shock. I mean, I know that I'd heard this on the grapevine but it is still a surprise to hear it from the lips of my brother.

'Doesn't like you? Are you sure?'

'Absolutely sure. She won't even look at me like that.'

'But why, Barney? Why?'

'Bloody hell, Clemmie. I don't know. I've never really had to think about it before.' He looks at me in genuine bafflement. Far from being vain about his looks, Barney seems to accept them as though they are like a wonky set of teeth or something — they set him apart from everyone else but are otherwise completely meaningless.

'Well, can't you just simply move along? Put it down to experience? Your first one, admittedly.'

'The problem is that I kind of like her. In fact, she's probably the first one I've really liked.'

Ah. I relax slightly in my chair. I do not have a similar track record to Barney in that I have had my fair share of knocks on the love front, but I am willing to share my hard-earned knowledge with my beloved brother. 'That could be the problem, Barney,' I say sagely. 'When they know you're keen, it tends to take the edge off slightly.'

'But she doesn't know.'

'Oh.'

'She won't even give me the time of day, let alone let me confess undying love.'

'Ah.'

'I don't really know what to do.'

'Hmm.' I'm not really being a lot of help.

'Except . . . '

'Except what?'

'Well, I know she likes men who make their own way in the world. You know, like Sam. He has his own law firm, done really well for himself and he's only twenty-seven.' Yes, I can see his point. Barney and I must look like the anti-Sam. 'I just wonder if she would look at me differently if I didn't spend my life surfing and working in a café.'

'But that's you, Barney! You love your surfing and your way of life. No responsibilities, no worries, that's always been you.'

'I can't stay that way for ever and just lately it feels . . . I don't know, it feels like it hasn't been enough. Like there could be more to life.'

'What does Sam say?'

'I haven't told him. I haven't told anyone. Dad saw me with this girl the other day and guessed.'

'He's pretty astute,' I murmur. 'So who is she?'

'Oh no, Clem. I'm not telling you that. Mum will only have to ask you to pass the sugar and you'll blurt it out. But promise you won't mention any of this?'

'If I haven't got a name then I have nothing to tell, have I? Anyway, what are you going to do?'

'Well, I'm not going to get on the nearest plane to Singapore.' He looks across and smiles at me.

'No, I know just I do that.'

'I'm going to join the cricket team,' he announces as though he has just found the solution to Third World poverty.

'That's your plan? Join the cricket team? Oh yes, Barney, that's a punch and a half. That's sure to bring her round.'

'It's a start. I want to become more . . . respectable. An upstanding member of the community. I'm going to think about a proper job too. Show her that I can make my way in the world.'

'Come on, Barney! Are you sure you want to do all that? Is she really worth it?'

'I think so. Will you help me?'

'As opposed to Sam? You're not going to tell him?'

'It's not really a boy thing, Clemmie.'

'Can I tell Holly?'

'Only if she's going to be of some help. But no one else.'

'I have to say I'm not really convinced it will work.'

He sighs. 'Well, there are some complications so I have a joker to play.'

'Complications? What complications?' I ask curiously.

'I think you might find out by yourself, Clemmie.'

I try to question him further but he won't be drawn and then my mother shouts at us to shut up because Catherine says she can't concentrate.

God, let's just hope it's not her.

3

The next morning, I walk down to breakfast to find my mother ensconced in the kitchen feeding Norman the seagull pilchards from a jar. Norman is a recent addition to our family and just another small example of what happens when my mother has more time than strictly necessary on her hands. She found Norman flailing about with a broken wing when she went to visit Barney at his café at Watergate Bay. She took him to the vet and since then he has become a house guest chez Colshannon and will be until his wing has completely mended. God knows when this will be because Norman certainly seems to have made himself at home and I can't really see him embracing his freedom with any great enthusiasm when it comes around. I'm not so bothered but, you know, seagulls are whacking great things and he can give you some really nasty looks sometimes. My father and Morgan, however, are counting the days.

'Can't you feed him outside?' I moan. The very smell of pilchards makes me feel sick, especially this early in the morning.

'Darling, it's a bit nippy out there for him.'

'Well, it's a bit whiffy in here for me.'

'SORREL!' exclaims my father as he comes into the kitchen carrying the morning paper. 'If we must keep that god-forsaken bird at all then

32

please feed him outside. I simply cannot face him watching me while I read the paper.' My father thinks that seagulls are the very scourge of the planet. There's certainly rather a lot of them in Cornwall.

My mother takes Norman outside but the persistent smell of pilchards still lingers. I try not to think about it too much and manage to shovel some Frosties down my throat. I collect my bag and grab my waitress apron from the coat rack. My mother comes back in holding the empty jar just as I grab my keys and make my exit through the back door. I hear my father roar, 'Those are my pilchards in Mediterranean olive oil from bloody Fortnums!'

I smile to myself and make my way out to my car. My car is the only thing I have to show from my term of gainful employment. Apart from a fast ticket to nowhere on the career train. I'm not quite sure how something so wonderfully promising could have turned so sour so quickly. In fact things changed so dramatically that within a week I had bought my plane ticket and was packing my rucksack.

You see, I had just come out of a one-sided relationship. Heavy on my side and feather-light on his. Well, I didn't know it was feather-light at the time yet it turned out to be practically airborne. While I was planning our future, mentally picking out new duvet covers, he was treading water. I think he simply became more and more addicted to his increasingly glamorous lifestyle, for glamorous was what it had become, and when the crux came and he had to choose between me and his career, it was time for me to go. You see, Seth valued art for an insurance company and his specialty was the Renaissance period, so he flew all over Europe for the company.

I met him when I was doing some work experience at the aforementioned art valuation and insurance house in Exeter just after leaving university. Seth was a graduate trainee and a couple of years older. It was my first day on the job and I was feeling incredibly gauche and awkward in my hand-me-down suit from Holly. My new shoes were pinching and I had nothing to put in my brand spanking new leather attaché case which had been a present from my parents.

I was waiting in reception for someone to come and collect me. Seth marched in and it seemed as though the sun came out. I can still remember him now seeming so effortlessly at home, handing out friendly instructions to the receptionist, looking so urbane and comfortable in his smart suit. He immediately whisked me out on a job to value a painting in Plymouth as he thought I wouldn't want to spend my first day learning names in the office. He was absolutely gorgeous and I was smitten. If I had looked for the signs then perhaps he would have seemed a wee bit arrogant and maybe slightly full of himself but I just saw him as incredibly worldly-wise and accomplished. His hair brushed back from his forehead, one arm casually resting on the steering wheel, the other on the gear stick. He was always obsessed with the 'right' things. The right watch, the right pen, the right clothes. The right girlfriend. Blonde, of course.

Art valuation and insurance houses are a bit thin on the ground so when his firm offered me a position, I gladly accepted. Seth was on an eighteen-month placement in the London office but no matter. What was a mere few hundred miles where love was concerned? Besides, after the eighteen months was up, he would be back and we would be together. So with my new art history degree in one hand and my fresh-faced naivety in the other, I skipped into the offices of Wainwright and Wainwright ready to surprise the new love of my life with the wonderful news that we would actually be working together.

Surprise him? He damn near had a coronary on the spot. The fact that he never wanted a single person at work to guess that we were seeing each other hadn't really worried me at all. I just thought that not only was he being incredibly professional, he was being downright noble to protect me. He didn't want to jeopardise my career at Wainwright and Wainwright because Mr Wainwright didn't like any personal relationships between his staff. The fact that another employee and Marjorie from accounts had been seeing each other for four years completely passed me by but our weekends together were always wonderful and he met my family several times so I had no reason to feel insecure.

Our eighteen months apart passed quickly. By then Seth had moved out of graduate status and was starting to value his paintings solo, and as such had to start travelling further and further afield. I was still training, but I loved my work, it was interesting and challenging by turns. I loved looking at new pieces of art and the occasional puzzle that came with the valuation.

At the end of his eighteen-month placement, Seth decided to stay in London. He told me that the scope for work was wider and he would be given more exciting projects than in Exeter. He also said that we had managed to make it work thus far so surely we could carry on. Of course with the extra travelling and the networking dinners and parties he had to attend, we did see less of each other. More often than not, I would turn up on my parents' step solo. If his absence was noted then no comments were made.

And I started to think it a little strange that no one in the company knew about our relationship. I tentatively suggested to Seth that we should start letting people know but he convinced me that both our careers would suffer and I believed that he knew best.

Then one day Seth called me and asked me to double-check a valuation by looking up the date of a painting in our library. The Exeter office had a far more extensive library than in London because space was at much less of a premium. So off I trotted, returning within half an hour with the information he wanted.

A few weeks passed and I thought nothing of it until I was summoned to the office of Mr Wainwright himself. Such was the rarity of these decrees that it was with some trepidation that I went to his office on the top floor of our building. As I knocked and entered, I knew something was seriously up because not only was Mr Wainwright there but also his private secretary and Seth, refusing to make eye contact and just staring at the carpet.

Apparently a mistake had been made in that valuation. My mistake. Seth had told them that I had given him the wrong information and as such he had misvalued the painting. I knew damn well what I had given him and unfortunately it wasn't a quick biff in the mouth. The quote was for a long-standing client, it was an embarrassment and, as Mr Wainwright said, made us look as though we don't know our arses from our elbows. Well, he didn't quite put it like that but you get the gist. Of course, Seth was seriously berated for not double-checking my work as he was the senior member of staff and I was told that although I wouldn't be losing my job, this would be marked against me.

I'm afraid I saw red. Deep, crimson red. About the colour of Seth's blood. I started to tell them how Seth had cocked up the valuation and they looked confused. I went on to inform them of his insect-like nature, where he could stuff our relationship and they looked wary. Seth told them I was obsessed with him, practically stalked him, and they looked scared. Eventually I tipped a cup of coffee into Seth's lap and walked out.

I don't think matters were helped by the fact that Mr Wainwright had just had a new carpet fitted in his office and later that day I was dismissed and escorted from the office.

For a while I was furious. I came home to my

family and the rage really set in. I ranted on about court cases and suing them. I imagined my revenge on Seth and his well deserved comeuppance. But slowly, as I calmed down, I realised that not one person could verify my story. Nobody could verify that Seth had messed up the valuation and not one person at the office had known that Seth and I had been going out together. Seth had been there much longer than me and was much more senior and so naturally they believed him. And anyway, I really couldn't go back to work there after what Seth had done to me. I simply couldn't. He even had the nerve to call me, not to apologise but to try and gloss over the whole affair by saying that he thought it was better for me to have this marked against me rather than him have a blot on his copybook career. I shouldn't have over-reacted so much but I'd get another job and couldn't we let bygones be bygones?

No, we bloody couldn't.

But after a few days the grief really took hold. I couldn't quite believe this man I thought I knew, slept with on a regular basis, shared countless things with, even thought I might marry one day, was not the man I thought he was at all. At what point in our relationship had he changed so much? And why hadn't I seen it? It was all just too big for me to handle. So I did the only thing a young woman in my position could do. I ran away.

Of course, I didn't call it that at the time. Getting away, I think I said it was. Time to think, to reflect on my next move. I had a marvellous fantasy of how Seth, desperate to track me down, would come to my parents' house, beg and plead to see me, only to be told that I had gone abroad and couldn't be got hold of. It was such a brilliant idea that one week later I found myself on a plane to Singapore. Of course, for the next few weeks when I realised Seth wasn't coming anywhere near me, I wept down the phone to my mother from far-flung places, but eventually I started to be able to reconcile myself to the facts. Thankfully the anger seems to have worked its way out and now I am left with simple resignation at my fate. That's not to say I wouldn't take a swing at Seth if I had the misfortune to come across him but I have generally gotten over the fact that I am going to have to start over from scratch as far as my career is concerned. Anyway, I worked for a while in Australia, celebrated two birthdays in Thailand and Hawaii respectively and then, after having been away for just over thirteen months, returned home a few weeks ago with a severely depressed Visa card in need of hospitalisation. Hence my hasty job at Mr Trevesky's café in Tintagel.

I pootle off down the country lanes to Tintagel. Although there is a distinct chill in the air, the sky is a clear blue so I wind down my window and breathe in the smell of the damp hedgerows. Dinky little signposts mark the routes to various villages: Trebarwith, Polzeath, Pendogget. 'By Tre, Pol and Pen, you will know the Cornish men.' The little rhyme repeats itself in my head as I get tantalising glimpses of the sea through the farmers' gateways. The pace of life is so much slower down here in Cornwall, which is probably a good thing as most of the time you're sitting behind a tractor while the farmer decides to chat to the cows for half an hour.

As I am sitting behind one of the aforementioned tractors, I start to think that I really ought to start to consider what I am going to do next. Although waitressing at the café is an extremely worthy vocation, it's definitely not something I want to do for the rest of my life. I've already been through one pair of flip-flops for one thing. And as much as I love my family, I really would like a place of my own, free from pilchard-eating seagulls and suchlike. The vague thought of another man some time in the future has also flitted through the inner recesses of my mind, but only flitted. I have been left with a deep distrust of men, but worse than that I have been left with an even deeper distrust of my own judgement.

One look at my watch tells me that Mr Trevesky probably hasn't got to grips with the whole slower pace of life theory yet and so I overtake the tractor by accelerating to G-force on a small inlet and arrive in Tintagel in about ten minutes. As it's still relatively early, the small town hasn't quite woken up yet and I park easily in one of the hill-top car parks, normally so overcrowded that you can't move. I spend a couple of seconds gazing at King Arthur's castle, thinking, as always, how marvellously romantic it looks, quickly followed by how unsatisfactory their lavatorial arrangements must have been. I sigh to myself, grab my bag off the back seat and then make my way down towards the café.

By the end of the day I have only mixed up three of the side orders. A new record, I think, for me. One mashed potato, a salad and a chips (or French fries as Mr Trevesky likes to call them, because Clemmie we are not *that* sort of café. Rick Stein has an awful lot to answer for) and I have managed not to go the wrong way through the kitchen doors. Wayne has been playing up to Mr Trevesky and giving me a deliberately wide berth while protectively clutching his nose, which just makes me want to bash him on it with my tray.

The day has been quiet and I suddenly realise it's Friday which is changeover day for the tourists. And Friday means Sam and Charlotte are coming to supper tonight. Damn.

Sally accepted my mother's invitation to the same supper with great alacrity at the rehearsal the other night so there is no way I can get out of it. At least Barney will be there too.

As soon as I reach home, I run upstairs to have a bath and wash my hair. For some reason I always seem to get food in it. The last time Sam was here he kept picking out bits of carrot, sparking much hilarity for everyone except me.

I feel better after a splash about. I make a vague attempt to dry my hair but it's so thick that it takes me about half an hour and I tend to lose interest halfway through. It's quite long and sits just below my shoulders and adamantly refuses to do anything I ask of it. It has a rather wild, untamed look and my mother likes to refer

41

to it as a mop. I'm dark blonde but add streaks of light blonde now and then. Of course, since I've returned from my trip abroad I haven't had to do anything because the sun had taken care of it. I just wish the freckles would go.

I wander downstairs with still-wet hair to see if I can help my father in the kitchen. It is supremely comforting to watch my father at work. My mother tends to make huge dramas out of making baked beans on toast. There are fire extinguishers everywhere in our house because something inevitably catches light and my mother runs around shrieking 'Shit McGregor!' at the top of her voice, which is her very annoying catchphrase and has something to do with a Scotsman, a loch and a boat. But please don't ask her about it. She then has to partake of a couple of slugs of the cooking sherry and have a long lie down on the sofa.

My father is calmly pounding spices with a pestle and mortar at the kitchen table, a glass of white wine by his side. No curry sauces from Sainsbury's for him. I take over the pestle and mortar and the white wine. 'Where's my mother?' I ask.

'It would be too much to hope that she's handing Norman back to the arms of Mother Nature, although Mother Nature would almost certainly refuse him, so I think she's gone down to the off licence.'

'Bloody Sam. She always spoils him,' I grumble.

'Now, think of Sam as Norman the seagull.'

I stare at him doubtfully. My father likes Sam so I can't quite see where he's going with this.

'Large and smelly?'

'No. He is in need of a home.'

'And my mother likes him more than the rest of us?'

'Er, no. Just that he is in need of a home.'

'But Sam doesn't like pilchards.'

'No, I didn't say he did.'

'Can we release him back into the wild?'

'Clemmie, I think we've gone as far as we can go with the Norman metaphor.'

'I'm going to tell Sam that you said he smelled like Norman.'

My father opens his mouth to say something else and then smiles when he realises I'm joking. 'God, I hate that bloody seagull,' he says and takes a huge slug of my wine.

Sam arrives first, bearing two bottles of wine, and lets himself in through the back door. By this time I am sat on the table with my second glass of wine, talking to my father about the joys of French fries. We can talk for hours about the stupidest things.

My father gives Sam's shoulder a friendly squeeze. I wave at him; we find it quite difficult to know how to greet each other. If you have known someone since the age of fourteen, when both sexes are extremely jumpy about this physical contact malarkey, you're sort of left with the residues.

Sam helps himself to a bottle of beer from the fridge and comes to sit next to me on the table. He's changed out of his usual suit and is wearing faded jeans and a thin jumper pushed up at the sleeves.

'So, my young whippersnapper, how has your day been?'

'Well, I only mixed up three side orders but Friday's a slow day.'

'How's Wayne's nose?'

'Broken, I hope.'

'They are pretty confusing, those kitchen doors.' He nods thoughtfully and then takes a swig of beer. I am about to agree wholeheartedly with him but he hasn't quite finished. 'Imagine, two different sets with IN and OUT written on them. I can see how you could get them mixed up.'

My father guffaws into his wine while I purse my lips and glare at a grinning Sam. 'Sorry,' he says. 'But you must admit that it's quite funny.'

Er, no. Not from where I'm sitting because he clearly hasn't had a half hour lecture from Mr Trevesky on the subject. This is the trouble with Sam and me. We start off okay but quickly degenerate into some sort of row.

'It's not as easy as you think it is,' I bristle.

'I used to wait tables too. Do you remember? That summer up at Fistral Beach.'

Bugger. Yes, he did. 'But you and Barney just pissed about all day. Waiting tables has moved on a bit since about a decade ago.'

'Technological advances?'

'I bet you didn't have doors with IN and OUT on them.'

'No, you're right. Barney wouldn't have lasted very long if we had. But it didn't help that you and Holly used to spend your time putting in orders for fruit salad without any apple.'

44

'You used to pretend you didn't know us!'

'I think we quite wished we didn't.'

Sam and I grin at each other, united in our shared memories for a second.

'Your mother and I are so proud,' sighs my father. 'Two of our children waiting tables.' He smacks his lips together, looks misty-eyed and we all laugh. This is done in his very charming, twinkly fashion and I know he is just kidding. I also know that if Sam had said the same thing I probably would have lamped him one.

'Barney said that Holly might be coming back for the weekend?'

'She's arriving tomorrow morning,' I confirm and Sam looks delighted at this piece of news.

'How are she and James?'

'Good, I think. I spoke to her the other night. She needs a story.'

'Oh, she'll find one. Holly always lands on her feet, it's one of the things I love her for.'

'I love her for it too.' While at the same time feeling slightly grumpy about it. If Holly is the sister who falls on her feet then I am undoubtedly the sister who falls on her arse.

'How long is she down for?'

'A couple of days, then I'm going to go back to Bristol with her.'

'For how long?'

'Oh, just until the end of the week.'

'I bet Mr Trevesky is glad to see the back of you.'

Talking of backsides. 'Where's Charlotte?' I ask.

'Still stuck on the A39.'

'With her parents?'

'No, just her this weekend.'

'Getting pretty serious, Sam?' my father twinkles from over by the work counter. In fact he looks like he's crying. Would he be that upset at Sam leaving the fold? As I said, he is almost like a son to him. I peer a little closer. Oh. He's peeling onions.

'Serious enough, Patrick,' Sam smiles back.

My mother bursts through the back door in a pretty twirly dress (which would look awful on me), carrying what looks like the entire off licence with Morgan trotting behind her. Sam immediately leaps up and rescues her from all the carrier bags. When freed from her load, she gives him a huge hug and a kiss. 'Sam, so lovely to see you! God, I need a fag. Where's Charlotte?'

'On the A39,' we all chorus.

'Oh, that's too bad. Clemmie, darling, do you want to borrow a dress?'

'No, thanks. I'm fine as I am.'

My mother gives me the sort of look that tells me that she begs to differ but she wisely moves on. 'I nearly ran over Barney coming up the hill.'

Just on cue, Barney comes panting through the door. 'Thanks, Mum. You didn't think to give me a lift?'

'But darling, you were doing so well. I didn't want to interrupt your stride. Besides, I never stop on hills because I don't really know where the handbrake is.' The last time she stopped on a hill she had to abandon the car and walk the rest of the way.

Sam and Barney do a manly slapping and handshake jobby. 'Where's Charlotte?' Barney asks.

'On the A39,' I say again. Probably teaching it to say its vowels, I nearly add but manage to stop myself at the last minute.

'Barney, I'm just going to go to the fridge to get another beer,' says Sam. 'Please don't hit me with a chair.'

'Ha ha.' This is Sam's favourite new joke — to check everything with Barney in case he decides to hit him with a chair. We think it's very funny.

Sam helps himself to a beer from the fridge, passes another to Barney and then Barney settles in his normal place on the Aga. I hustle Sam off the table, seconds after he has just sat back down on it, and start to throw some placemats and cutlery around. Sam takes the bunch of cutlery off me as I pick it out of the drawer. 'Clemmie, I'll do that.'

I smile gratefully at him and join Barney at the Aga while Sam lays the table, arranging the knives and forks pedantically. I was just going to throw the pile into the middle and let people help themselves, but anyway.

The doorbell rings and my mother goes through to open it. It must be Charlotte rather than Sally because we can hear my mother going into overdrive with noisy greetings. The door to the kitchen is thrust open as though we're in Act I and a figure is bundled in.

'Darlings! *Look* who it is!' says my mother, who seems to have launched into her frightening Noël Coward mode which involves lots of

47

eye-rolling and random emphasis on words. Honestly, it's like having the entire Royal Shakespeare Company on drugs and in your kitchen.

Charlotte is wearing a navy blue linen skirt with opaque blue tights and flat Gucci loafers. Her mousy brown hair is scraped off her face into a tight bun at the nape of her neck. She doesn't wear any make-up whatsoever and she could really do with her eyebrows being done. I can't fathom what Sam sees in her.

Sam had been leaning languidly against one of the units as she entered the room but has now sauntered over to kiss her. Barney has slipped off the Aga and my father has washed his hands and they are both waiting to greet their guest with a double London kiss. We normally do just one down here.

Charlotte hands over her gifts of wine and flowers to my mother.

'Charlotte, you *really*, really shouldn't have.' Yes, Charlotte, I wish you hadn't too because my mother will then bury her head into the bouquet to smell the flowers as I have seen her do many, many times on stage. I hope she calms down soon.

I move forward to kiss Charlotte dutifully. 'How was your journey?' I enquire politely.

'Awful. Rally, rally awful. I don't know why they simply can't build a motorway.'

Because we're trying to stop dreadful week-enders like yourselves buying up half the county, I think to myself, but I am spared from having to make a response by a knock at the back door and the appearance of Sally.

Charlotte sits down at the table and looks nervously around her. She isn't terribly fond of my mother's menagerie of animals (Morgan always makes a delighted beeline for her). Sam goes about getting her a gin and tonic and Sally kisses all of the family hello.

'Is curry okay with you, Charlotte?' asks my father politely. 'I'm afraid it's all I do.'

'Super, Mr Colshannon. I simply love curry.'

'Please call me Patrick.'

'Patrick, then,' she gravely acquiesces.

'Sally?' he asks. 'Okay for you too?'

Sally doesn't reply because her mouth is full of the Kettle Chips my mother has just opened but she makes suitable tummy rubbing-motions.

'Charlotte, tell us *all* about your week,' says my mother.

Did she have to ask? Couldn't we have ignored basic good manners, just for once? Charlotte works in the actuarial department of a large insurance company which, in my mind, counts as another very large mark against her for being mind-bendingly dull. I don't really understand what she does although she's already explained it to me in an actuarial-work-for-idiots tone of voice. I make a face at Sally. God, here we go.

'Well, it's actually been rally rather interesting . . . ' I must have visibly slumped at this point because my father gives me a good kick on the shins which perks me up no end.

'Did I tell you that Clemmie used to work for an insurance company?' says Sam at the end of her Weekly Actuarial Bulletin.

'Clemmie? Rally?'

All eyes turn on me. 'I did not work for an insurance company!' I say indignantly.

'Didn't you? My mistake,' says Sam calmly. 'What exactly was it you did then?'

'I valued art.'

'For an insurance company?'

'Well, yes.'

'Oh, you're quite right. That's not working for an insurance company at all,' he says dryly.

'But you work in a café now, don't you, Clemmie?' This is clearly baffling Charlotte as she looks in confusion from Sam to me.

'Yes, I do,' I say with as much dignity as I can muster. 'I'm just paying off a few debts from my trip while I look for another job.'

'Well, from the state of you when you got back from your trip at least we know you had a good time,' remarks Sam wryly.

'I've told you before. I caught a virus,' I say through clenched teeth.

'Do all viruses have Jack Daniels printed on them?'

'Darling, we nearly didn't recognise you when the British Airways steward pushed you out in that wheelchair.'

'I was ill.'

The actual truth is that I spent the last night of my trip having a few drinks with some friends, fell asleep in someone's room and then woke up to find I only had an hour before my plane left. I had to pack in the taxi on the way to the airport and then arrived to find a five-hour delay as well as a long lecture from the check-in staff. I turned up in England twenty-four hours later, after having caught some sort of virus en route and losing one of my shoes. Things haven't been going any better since. I choose not to enlarge on the disaster that is my life thus far and luckily Charlotte doesn't ask any more questions because my father leaps in hastily with a few of his own.

'So what plans have you and Sam got for the weekend, Charlotte?'

'Well, I rally want to see the Eden Project so Sam has promised to take me.'

'Just as long as Charlotte agrees to come surfing with me on Sunday,' interjects Sam.

'Have you been surfing before, Charlotte?' asks Sally sweetly.

'No, but I ski an awful lot so it can't be very different from that, can it?'

'Oh no. You'll be standing within the hour, riding the tubes with the rest of them,' I say cheerfully. Charlotte may well drown herself within the hour, let alone still be united with her surfboard. 'You just need to remember to paddle out really far and wait for the big ones.'

Barney shoots me a warning look. 'Come up to Watergate Bay, I'm not working in the morning so I'll come surfing with you.'

Damn it. Barney, being a bit of a whiz on the old board and having a life-saving qualification to boot, isn't going to let her drown. God, the arrogance of the upper classes never ceases to amaze me. No I'm-worried-I'll-make-a-tit-of-myself troubles for our Charlotte. They're sent forth from the nursery with an unshakeable confidence in their own inner perfection.

My father starts to lay dishes on the heatproof mats on the table and Sally and I get up to help him. A delicious-looking korma sprinkled with fresh coriander, a fresh salsa of tomatoes and bananas, pilaf rice with cloves and cardamom, okra in a tomato sauce and rich spicy Bombay potatoes appear. My mouth waters greedily. My father knows how to make a mean curry.

'How is *Calamity Jane* coming along, Sally? Sorrel?' asks Sam as the plates are handed out and my father makes my mother put her cigarette out. Barney and I have no pretensions towards visitors and start digging in first.

'Fine, we're just trying to work out how to manage the stagecoach scene, aren't we, Sally?'

'You know the one, where Calamity Jane is being chased by Indians across the plains?' asks Sally. Sam has had to sit through the video almost as many times as we have so this is a safe bet.

'Are you going to use a real stagecoach?'

'That's the idea,' my mother replies.

My father frowns at her. 'Darling, is that wise? Do you remember that play you were doing when we met?'

'The amateur one?'

'That's the one. They had you swinging out over the audience in a model aeroplane? You kept having to be retrieved from the rafters.'

'Oh yes, I do remember! They swung me out into the dress circle. Once it took them over two hours to cut me down.'

'Gordon was up there practically cutting the wires himself, as I remember.'

'I'd just met him, bless him, and he'd asked to represent me. He'd probably leave me up there now. Anyway, don't worry about the stagecoach, darling, because I've asked the set designer from the National for a few ideas.'

There is a few minutes' silence as everyone appreciates the food. Charlotte says, 'Patrick, this is simply super.'

'Thank you. Not too hot for you, Clemmie?' My pathetic curry threshold is well known in the family.

'Rally good.' Bloody hell, I'm starting to talk like her now. Her accent must be contagious. Sam must think I'm blatantly taking the piss because he shoots me a nasty look.

Thankfully Sally and I can excuse ourselves as soon as the meal is over. I interrupt Sally's jolly gossip with Barney as soon as the last mouthful has been taken and we go out together into the chilly evening air.

'God, she's awful!' I exclaim as soon as we're out of hearing.

'Clemmie, she's not that bad. Just a bit thick-skinned, that's all.'

'What on earth does Sam see in her?'

'Well, she is rather pretty.'

'Is she?'

'Her work does sound a bit boring though.'

'A bit? Bloody hell, he probably has to shag her to shut her up. Actually, maybe that's how he started going out with her.'

'Just a difficult pause in conversation?' Sally giggles.

'Exactly,' I say vehemently and we start to stride down the hill towards the pub.

4

Holly and I are sat on a sofa, sipping our hot chocolates and looking at Watergate Bay. She arrived just this morning and we have come down here in the hope of a chat with Barney. Holly tried to persuade me to take a walk on the beach but we only got about a hundred metres and then I got too cold because I am only wearing three-quarter length linen trousers, which sit just below my hip bones, and a little T-shirt which I either last wore when I was twelve or has shrunk in the wash. So we retired to the café for a hot chocolate. The waitress is very offhand with us until we tell her that we're actually Barney's sisters and then she becomes very chatty. After she has served our hot chocolates, she bustles off to find him. He is supposed to be here, waiting tables, but it does not surprise me at all that he is somewhere else.

'These are very fattening, you know,' says Holly, delightedly sipping from her mug.

'Hmm, I know,' I say, practically face down in the stuff. Barney's café makes the best hot chocolates ever. Lots of cream, mini marshmallows and little chocolate drops. Neither of us is very good at dieting; we both tried a detox diet a few years ago and managed to convince ourselves that carrot cake was the only way to consume the obligatory carrot each day. We didn't lose any weight.

The café is built on stilts (the surf shop is housed down below) and has huge, comfy sofas which face out over the bay. The beach stretches for about a mile in each direction before dramatic cliffs cut it off and this stretch of sand is famous for its water sports. Kite surfing, waveski, and kite buggying — and Barney can do them all.

'It's so nice to see you!' Holly says.

'You too.' It is actually lovely to see her. 'Especially by ourselves,' I add on. The last time we saw each other was the last night of my mother's latest play. The whole family turned up and so the dressing room was a tad overcrowded, which somehow caused my mother's dresser, Mildred, to swallow a needle she was using to make repairs with. Everyone was most distressed, particularly my mother as Mildred had also swallowed some beading from her final costume that was on the end of the needle. Funnily enough Holly and I didn't get much chance to chat.

'Anyway, tell me what's been happening here. How's everyone?' Holly leans back into the snuggly recesses of the sofa.

'Fine, we're all fine. Sam and Charlotte came to dinner last night.'

'Did you have a fritefully nice time?'

I grin at Holly. 'Fritefully. I honestly do not know what Sam sees in her.'

'Oh, she's not such a bad old stick.'

'Now you're talking like her,' I say, still cradling my mug and taking surreptitious licks from the rim.

Holly grins. 'But she's not!' she protests. Holly and the rest of the family have an annoying habit of remaining adamantly faithful to Sam but he and I have always had a much more, I don't know, tense relationship, I suppose. We are not perfectly at ease with each other, whereas he slots in beautifully with the rest of the family. If I am being honest, this slightly irritates me.

'How long have they been going out again?' I ask idly. Sam and Charlotte got together while I was abroad so I have not been party to the usual insider knowledge.

Holly shrugs, 'A couple of months or so. I think she's pretty.'

'Pretty boring. Holly, she's an actuary!' I stare at her, willing the awfulness of this to sink in.

'Clemmie, do you know what an actuary is?'

'Well, no. I don't. But it sounds incredibly tedious whatever it is. What is it, anyway?'

'Actually I don't know either. But I'm sure it's not as bad as it sounds. Charlotte is really nice when you get to know her.'

'I told her that Morgan would pee on her if she stood still too long.'

'Clemmie! That's really horrible!' says Holly, grinning slightly. 'Is that why she is so fidgety around him?'

'She was annoying me and I wish she would stop putting on that accent.'

'But Charlotte really speaks like that. She's not putting it on.'

'Truly? God, can you imagine if she marries Sam. I might actually have to kill my own mother.'

'Do you think Sam and Charlotte are serious then?'

'I don't know but she certainly seems to eat a lot of supper with us.'

'I wonder if he will go back to London with her.' Sam actually worked in London for a while and we thought he would settle there, but he surprised us all by just suddenly returning to Cornwall and putting down roots. He never told any of us what happened or why he returned which is absolutely infuriating because it's bound to be something completely pathetic like he found the water too hard or some such.

'Maybe. I think his work takes him there occasionally.'

'Hello, you!'

We swivel round to see Barney grinning at us with his customary just-got-out-of-bed look. But then he probably has.

Holly leaps up and they hug tightly. 'How are you?' she beams at him when they break apart.

'He has girl trouble,' I put in.

'Thank you, gobmouth. I was wondering how long it would take you.'

'At least I waited until you got here.'

'Girl trouble? What sort of girl trouble?' asks Holly.

'He *likes* one.'

'Likes one?' She turns back to Barney with raised eyebrows. 'Bloody hell, girl trouble usually means they won't leave you alone. Who on earth can this goddess be?'

Barney opens his mouth to reply but I get in before him. 'Well, he won't say. She doesn't like him back though.'

'Good grief! What is the world coming to! Probably be good for him.'

'Hello?' says Barney.

'He's determined to change his ways.'

'How on earth is that going to help?'

'I'm still here,' says Barney.

'He thinks she won't even give him the time of day because he's a bit of a wastrel. So he thinks that if he gets a proper job and stuff, he might stand a better chance.'

'Clemmie! Do you mind if I tell Holly?'

'Sorry.'

'Well?' demands Holly.

'Actually Clemmie has summed it up pretty well.'

'Apart from who she is?'

'Holly, if there is anyone more gobby than Clemmie, it's you. So if I haven't told Clemmie then I am hardly likely to tell you.'

Holly looks wounded by this but makes a good recovery. 'So what's your plan?' she asks doubtfully.

'I just thought she might take a bit more notice of me if I became responsible. It's not exactly going to do me any harm, is it? She might start to take me more seriously.'

'Are you going to pull out of the worm-charming competition at Blackawton?'

This is a contest where everyone is given a patch of ground in which to bring out as many worms as possible in an allotted time, usually by thumping the ground as though it is raining (although there are other more dubious methods). Barney and I look at Holly in horror. The family love this event. Mother makes a picnic and everything. Besides, Barney is really good at it.

'Do I have to?' he asks.

'Well, let's face it, it's not something a responsible person would do.'

'Maybe you could do it and not dress up as a rain cloud this year?' I suggest helpfully. 'That smacks of responsibility.'

'Maybe,' says Barney gloomily.

'Is she really worth it, Barney?' asks Holly.

'She's special,' he says simply.

'Special, loony special?'

'No, just special special. Will you help me?'

'That's quite difficult if we don't know who she is,' says Holly, but seeing the forlorn look on Barney's face adds on quickly, 'but we'll help you, won't we, Clem?'

'Of course!'

'You're not to tell anyone by the way. No one else knows.'

'Not even Sam?'

'Not even Sam.'

Barney is getting dirty looks from the owner of the café so he says he'd better go and look as though he's doing some work and disappears.

There's a small silence as we both finish off the dregs of hot chocolate.

'And how are you feeling about stuff?' Holly asks. By stuff she means Seth.

'Fine.'

'Fine?' she queries. Ah, my sister knows me well.

'Well, still disappointed. In men generally, I

59

think, though.' I try a little grin for size. This disappointment still feels relatively fresh because, such was my haste at leaving the country over thirteen months ago, I didn't have time to perform the one vital thing that all relationship divorcees should do without delay. The exorcism. It wasn't until a couple of weeks ago that I managed to unpack some of the boxes from my hasty retreat from my flat in Exeter. Of course, I meant to throw anything vaguely associated with Seth straight in the bin. But this proved harder than I'd thought. I had saved all the cards and presents Seth had given me over the course of our relationship. Not that there were many of those but it wasn't always easy for Seth to get down to the shops. A less charitable person, namely Barney who is generally regarded as one of the least thoughtful people in the household, suggested rather mean-spiritedly that he could have had something delivered. At the time I dismissed this cynical suggestion out of hand but now I secretly think Barney might have had a point. Barney had had to frogmarch me down to the dustbin to throw it all away but still the feelings of sadness lingered.

'Men aren't really on my agenda,' I say with a wry smile. 'Maybe when I return from the convent in twenty years' time.'

'Come on, Clemmie! That was just bad luck with Seth.'

'Bad luck? I lost my job because of him! How can one person have such bad judgement?'

'Well, that was awful. But he was becoming a bit pompous. Barney nearly decked him when he saw him.'

I frown. 'When did Barney see him? He didn't tell me.'

'Hmm?' Holly looks sort of startled. 'Oh, he bumped into him in Exeter.'

I narrow my eyes at her. 'Barney bumped into Seth in Exeter?'

'Er, yes.'

'Does Barney know where Exeter is?'

'Of course Barney knows where Exeter is! Anyway, are you looking for a job?' she asks, neatly side-stepping me.

'I can't really find anything down here.'

'Have you looked?'

'Of course! Funnily enough, jobs valuing art are a little thin on the ground in north Cornwall, and anyway, I don't really know if I fancy going back to it.'

'What would you like to do?'

I sigh. 'I don't know. Something to do with art, I suppose. I do miss that bit.'

'You could come down to the paper with me when we're back in Bristol and talk to the people in the job section. They'd have an idea of what's about at the moment.' I've managed to book some holiday with Mr Trevesky and I'm going to go back to Bristol with Holly. I think he was quite pleased to see the back of me for a few days after the Wayne/nose debacle.

'Ooh, good idea. Thanks, Holly. By the way, have you found a story yet?'

'God, I really need one. Even Joe is starting to

mumble about one-hit wonders.'

'One will just turn up out of the blue.'

'Will it? I'm starting to wonder.'

'Talking about turning up, has Emma?' I ask.

'Not a dicky bird. Nobody has heard a word from her since her resignation. Poor Rachel had to cover the social diaries and she really hasn't got a clue.'

'Maybe Emma has got another job.'

'Maybe, but you'd think she'd clear out her desk before she left, wouldn't you?'

'She left all her stuff?'

'Yes, it's like she went home from work one day and then just decided not to bother coming back. But then her father is so rich she could afford to do that if she wanted to. Jenny in HR got a phone call from her father asking us to post it all to him. When she asked him why Emma had left he got very irate and told her not to ask so many questions.'

'What's her father's name again?'

'Sir Christopher McKellan.'

'McKellan?' I query with a frown. 'I think I've heard of him.'

'You might have done. He's a QC in Bristol. Won a famous case a few years ago. Anyway, Jenny wants me to drop off Emma's things at her father's house and see if I can speak to her to make sure she's okay. He's got a second home down here.'

'Whereabouts?'

'Rock.'

'And Emma is there?'

Holly looks momentarily surprised. 'Well, I

presume so. That's the address he gave to Jenny.'

'I wonder why she resigned so suddenly.'

Holly shrugs. 'Probably wanted to go to Bermuda or something and didn't have enough holiday.'

'Yes, but it can't have been anything planned because she would have taken her things with her. Did she say anything to anyone at work?'

'Oh come on, Clemmie. You've met Emma. She's hardly going to win Personality of the Year. She wouldn't deign to speak to anyone at work.'

'Maybe something has happened to her.'

'If anything was up with the daughter of Sir Christopher McKellan, believe me, everyone would know about it. Come on, we'll go home via Rock and get rid of her things.'

★　★　★

Since Rock is all the way around the other side of the estuary, we decide it will be quicker to park in Padstow and catch the little ferry over to Rock. Of course, we forget to work in the extra twenty minutes added to the journey by a holidaying granny who didn't realise her wheelchair would get stuck on the beach at the other side.

Holly is watching the unfolding drama with delight, her hand shading her face from the sun, while my attention is caught by a rather good-looking man on the other side of the queue.

'Ooh, look Clemmie! The ferry man is having to lift her out of her wheelchair now! God, I think she's taking a swipe at him with her handbag.'

I only notice the man because he looks rather lost. He doesn't seem like a tourist and yet doesn't belong here either. But he's rather nice-looking. Chestnut coloured hair, short at the sides and long on top. Straight, even features, and wearing a tweed jacket and cords. He's by himself and I wonder what he's doing here.

Once we all disembark at Rock, the young man walks ahead of us for a little while and then stops to consult a piece of paper. Holly and I get distracted by the RNLI gift shop and when I look again, he's gone. After we have purchased some shells from the shop (someone stop me, please, why can't I resist them? I have an EU mountain of shells at home), we wander up the main street along the shore, looking for Sir Christopher McKellan's house.

His second home makes me quite want to see his first. It is a corner house and sits directly on the sea front. Its freshly whitewashed stone walls and neat little garden all shout money. Storm lanterns stand on the windowsills and cream curtains are tied back with rough, thick rope. I can tell that inside will be decorated in soft pastels and squishy sofas. I desperately need to pee and wonder if I could partake of their facilities and at the same time have a good nose about inside, but Holly tells me Sir Christopher McKellan is none too friendly with strangers and I'm better off going to the pub. So I leave Holly to it and walk over to The Mariners to use the loo there.

Holly is waiting for me when I emerge and we are just about to wend our way back to Padstow when I see that the young man from the ferry queue is walking intently towards us as though he wants to speak with us. Even Holly is looking decidedly perkier.

'Hello,' he says when he reaches us.

'Hello,' we both reply. I don't know about Holly because she is practically engaged to James, but I don't open my mouth too wide in case I start to drool. Eye to eye he is even better looking.

'I hope you don't mind but I've just noticed you coming out of Sir Christopher McKellan's house and I wonder if you can help me.' His voice is pleasant with a trace of a Northern accent. 'I've come all the way from Cambridge. I'm looking for Emma.'

'Well, that's her father's house but I asked the housekeeper if Emma was there and she said no.'

'I know. I've just asked her too. Do you know Emma?'

'Well, I used to work with her but she resigned last week. I was in the area and so dropped off her things. You could try her address in Bristol? That's where she lives.'

'I already have. I was hoping someone here could help me.'

'Are you a friend of hers?'

'I'm Charlie,' he says simply, by way of explanation.

We must both look a little bemused because he goes on to say, 'Didn't she tell you? I'm Emma's fiancé. We're engaged to be married.'

65

5

Fiancé? Emma? I glance quickly at Holly because surely she would have mentioned the fact that Emma has a fiancé? That's the sort of news that would make either of us immediately reach for the phone. Holly gives a small shake of her head to indicate that she is as baffled as I am.

So where is Emma? Because if I had a fiancé, especially one who looked like this, I wouldn't be very far behind him. I have an anxious look around and even a quick peek behind me. Surely she should be superglued to his very broad, tweed back and not letting him wander around Cornwall unchaperoned?

'Emma? Emma McKellan?' Holly repeats, just to make sure we haven't got our Emmas mixed up.

'Yes, Emma McKellan.' He looks to each of us anxiously. 'You did say you knew her?'

'Of course we do,' replies Holly. 'Wrote the social pages on the paper. Nice girl.' Now she definitely is getting her Emmas mixed up. I do not remember Emma being a nice girl. Holly glances round suddenly as though she's trying to remember where she is. Her eyes alight on the pub.

'Charlie, did you say your name was? Why don't we all go get a drink and we'll see if we can help you.' Holly must be curious to say the least;

66

she isn't normally so accommodating to strangers around lunchtime. 'Come on.' She tugs slightly on Charlie's arm and leads him towards the door of the Mariners.

Once inside, she pulls out a chair and sits Charlie down, and he appears to crumple slightly. He slouches forward and puts his head in his hands.

I look over to Holly and make a drink gesture with my hand. It might help to loosen poor Charlie up a bit. She disappears off.

I try to think of something innocuous to say while we wait. He still has his hands over his face. The weather seems a bit amateurish; perhaps I could comment on the ferry queues, or maybe he might like to see my new anklet, recently purchased? Luckily Holly returns pretty smartish with three glasses and a bottle of whisky. She obviously knows the barman as he is still reading the paper.

'I'm Holly, by the way. Holly Colshannon. And this is my sister, Clemmie. I work on features at the paper.'

'Charlie Davidson.' He looks up and smiles a half smile at us which doesn't quite reach his eyes.

'So,' Holly says in a very efficient fashion as she unscrews the lid and pours the amber liquid. 'Wow! Emma is getting married! She hasn't told us! She is a dark horse. Is that the reason she resigned from work? Wants more time to concentrate on the wedding?'

'I don't think so.'

Holly ploughs on. 'When is the happy event?'

'A week today.'

Holly stares at him open-mouthed and I have to wrestle the still-glugging bottle out of her hand before it spills all over the table.

'A week today?' she repeats. 'You mean that you and Emma are getting married next Saturday?'

He runs his hand through his hair in the very clenched, tight fashion of someone truly stressed. 'Only if I can find her.'

'You can't find her?'

Is Holly just going to repeat everything he says? I try to ignore her and say to Charlie, 'Is she missing?'

'Well, I think her father knows where she is. I certainly don't.'

'But she hasn't said a word to anyone in Bristol about getting married.'

'I shouldn't think she has. It was supposed to be in secret. So her father didn't find out.'

'But why would she disappear on you less than two weeks before her own wedding?' asks Holly urgently.

'I think that's why Charlie is here,' I say. 'To find out.'

'I would settle for just finding *her* at the moment,' he mutters.

'You said you've tried her flat in Bristol?' asks Holly in a more businesslike fashion.

Charlie slumps back down in his chair. 'Yes, but her flat-mate is always out. Their neighbour says she hasn't seen Emma for about five days.'

'And then you came here?'

'No, after that I went to her father's house in

Bristol. Then I visited your paper, where they told me she no longer worked. Then I came down to Cornwall. Emma told me about their holiday home and I was hoping she would be here.'

'But Sir Christopher didn't know you were getting married?' Holly gives me a look as she finally hands me my glass of whisky. I hate whisky.

'He didn't approve, but Emma got cold feet at the last minute and went to see him for his blessing, although I didn't agree with her going because I knew he would never consent. That was the last I heard from her.'

'So what did he say when you went to see him?'

'That Emma doesn't want to see me. Ever again.'

Oh. Right. That seems fair enough. Well, it seems to be an open and shut case to me, Detective Colshannon. I slump back into my seat and take a tentative sip of my whisky. Nope, it's no good. I still hate it.

Emma is not kidnapped or a missing person. Not stuck in a loo somewhere yet to be discovered. Just had a row with her fiancé and fancied a few days off. I do think she could have called in though and saved everyone a lot of trouble.

'Why would Sir Christopher not approve?' asks Holly sympathetically.

'We don't quite see eye to eye. In fact, he positively despises me.'

'Why? Have you done something dreadful?'

Yes, good question, Holly. I lean forward and look at him curiously. What did he do that was so heinous? Did he make a pass at her mother? The chambermaid? The cat? Or are we sitting here supping whisky with a mass murderer? All jolly thoughts. I make another attempt with the whisky to calm my nerves.

'You've never met Sir Christopher?'

Holly and I both shake our heads. 'I have met him but we haven't been formally introduced,' puts in Holly.

'In simple terms, he thinks that I'm not good enough to marry his daughter.'

'Why not? You don't look like too much of a reprobate to me,' says Holly.

'I didn't go to the right school. I just went to the local grammar but he wants someone who went to Eton or Rugby for Emma. I don't shoot or ride or do anything that he would consider worthwhile. He asked me about my friends but I don't move in the right circles. And I don't have a good enough job or earn enough money to keep Emma in the manner to which she is accustomed. That's a reprobate in Sir Christopher's eyes.'

'What do you do?' I ask curiously.

'I'm a teacher.'

I frown and shoot a quick look at Holly because, after all, I have met Emma a couple of times and from the extra stuff I know about her through Holly, a teacher simply wouldn't cut it for her.

'How did you meet?' I ask, curious to know how this odd romance came about.

70

'She'd come up to visit a friend in London and I met her at a party there. I'll never forget the first time I saw her. She was wearing a black velvet dress . . . ' He starts to go a bit misty-eyed on us at this point and I quietly boggle into my whisky glass. Never forget the first time he saw her? Has she had a major personality transplant since I last met her? Or did he take that aloof manner of looking down her nose at you as simply endearing? 'We didn't really get a chance to talk to each other until later that night — '

'When you moved in for the kill?' I ask keenly. God, it's demon stuff, this whisky. A few sips and I'm talking like Jenny Eclair.

He gives a nervous little laugh and looks at me slightly censoriously. 'Well, it wasn't quite like that.' No, of course not Clemmie. Don't be so crass. Emma wouldn't have covered that at finishing school. 'We bumped into each other in the kitchen and I made some inane remark about parties or something and then we just started talking. I asked her out for lunch the next day and things just went from there. We started seeing each other. But she would always come up to Cambridge at the weekends, I would never go to Bristol. Eventually we got to know each other well enough that I started to ask about her family, and then she told me about her father. I think she has always been a little afraid of him . . . '

'Afraid?' puts in Holly. 'God, I've always been bloody petrified. I've come across him a few times professionally.'

'Anyway, things got serious but I sensed that

71

her father always sort of hung between us and until we had sorted him out we couldn't go any further. I got the impression that I was not the normal sort of man she dated. So I persuaded her, against her will I might add, that her father and I should meet.'

'And?' I demand. This is just getting interesting. In my new-found enthusiasm I take a gulp of my drink and damn near blow my head off. I have to interrupt his story for a few minutes while I choke and have to be slapped on the back by Holly. I eye her warily. She does like to try out the Heimlich manoeuvre now and then. As soon as my eyes cease to water, Charlie continues.

'Well, of course it was an absolute disaster. For some peculiar reason I thought that Emma had somehow been exaggerating madly but he hated me on first sight. Kept asking me about my job prospects and who I was friends with. We went back to Cambridge that night and Emma said that she hadn't really expected anything else.'

'So what happened then?' Holly asks.

'Nothing for a while but, when I realised I wanted to marry Emma — '

'Aaah, that sounds nice,' I say. Both Holly and Charlie give me a look and I make magnanimous carry-on gestures.

'Well, I knew that I at least needed his blessing. I actually thought Emma's happiness would be more important to him than me having the right connections.' He shakes his head.

I wonder about my own father in all of this. What he would do? I think he would leap up from his armchair, his newspaper trampled underfoot in delight, grasp the lucky man firmly by the hand, give him a few pints of whisky and then turf him out of the house before he had a chance to change his mind. Bugger the right connections.

After a few seconds, Charlie rakes back his hair with one hand. He really is very attractive; no wonder Emma obviously thought bugger the right connections too. Charlie continues, 'So I went back to ask for his permission to marry Emma. He refused and then told me all those things I've just told you.'

'What? He sat you down and told you that you didn't have a good enough job and didn't go to the right school?'

'And then had the arrogance to pat me on the shoulder, said he hoped there weren't any hard feelings but I would see it was for the best in the long run. But on the way home I decided to ask Emma anyway. I explained the situation with her father but she said that she didn't care and she would marry me.' That sounds nice; I brave a smile and celebratory sip of my whisky. 'That was about four months ago.'

'And has she seen her father since then?'

'Well, no, they've always had quite a difficult relationship. Not exactly warm. Her mother died when she was young and I don't think there was a lot of love at home.' I think of my warm, friendly childhood. Lots of chocolate and telly. Mind you, it's pretty easy to nick some Dairy Milk from the larder and slip through to the sitting room while your mother is yelling at three six-foot boys.

'I live in Cambridge and we've been making arrangements for her to move up to live with me.' Charlie reaches into his inside pocket and pulls out some papers. 'Look, these are all the job applications she's made.' He dumps the wad on the table and slumps back in his chair. Holly pours him another finger of whisky while I have a cursory look at the papers. All letters from newspapers. Most of them refusing her application but a couple offering an interview. I note the dates on them — all of them about two weeks ago.

'We started making arrangements for the wedding. Booked the church, that sort of thing, and, coupled with the fact that she was moving up to Cambridge to be with me, she started to talk about making peace with her father. I think it's been really worrying her lately.'

'And?' prompts Holly.

'And then she called me to tell me that she was going to visit her father, just to see if he would give us his blessing. I think she was even hopeful of persuading him to come to the church. It would have meant so much to Emma. I asked if I could do anything and she said no. I then told her to call me as soon as she got back. That was five days ago. I haven't heard a word from her since.'

'Not even a message?' I ask, leaning forward in my seat, empty whisky glass in hand. You know, that whisky stuff can grow on you. You just need to get those first few nasty gulps down and then it's not so bad. I remember I developed a similar addiction to some cough syrup when I was ten. Unfortunately my mother could tell a fake cough from a real one about a mile away.

I hold my glass out to Holly for another drop. Charlie doesn't seem to have made much headway with his and has now started to shred one of the letters in front of him. Should I make sure it's one of the rejection ones rather than an interview offer? I decide to leave the shredding fingers be.

'Nothing. I've been going out of my mind with worry. I've called everyone I can think of. I've even called her father but he refused to speak to me. In the end, I took a few days' leave and came down to find her.'

Golly, he must really care about her. Once Sally and I got cut off at high tide on Trebarwith beach and had to spend the best part of four hours on a rock. I kept expecting to hear the buzz of the search helicopter overhead but when we finally returned home my parents just thought I had been out drinking and hadn't even bothered to look under the bed for me.

'So where do you think she is?' I ask.

'She must be with her father. He must have somehow persuaded her not to come back to me. God knows what stuff he could be feeding her with.'

Stuff? Goodness, is he a drug dealer as well as a tyrant father? Has he got her doped up to the eyeballs? I must look somewhat alarmed because Holly says impatiently, 'Lies, Clemmie. What lies he could be feeding her with.'

Ah.

I see now.

My mistake.

Holly continues, 'Well, that's all well and good if he's persuaded her to call off the wedding, but it seems a bit extreme for her not to return to her flat or her work. And not to explain to you.'

'Maybe he knows that if we managed to speak to each other we'd sort everything out between us.'

'But he can't keep her there against her will!'

Charlie gives a hollow little laugh, 'Oh, can't he? You don't know Sir Christopher McKellan. He's absolutely convinced that Emma would be making a big mistake in marrying me, regardless of how she feels about it, and he only needs to keep her there until next Saturday. He'll persuade her that I don't love her or something. That I just want her for her money, and hope that I'll give up looking for her. Well, I won't. I want to marry her.'

'Do you think she's at his house?' I ask.

'That's the problem. I don't think so. I've sat outside the house in Bristol day and night, hoping I might just catch a glimpse of her, something to reassure me that she's okay, but I've seen nothing. I don't think she can be there.'

'Where else could she be?'

'I don't know. I've racked my brains. That's why I've come here. I just want to talk to her. Convince her that I love her for her alone, and make sure that her father hasn't told her otherwise. If she still wants to call off the wedding then that's fine. I mean, of course I'll be upset, but I want to hear it from her own lips.'

He bows his head and I look towards Holly.

'What about her friends? I mean, you must know some of them? Could one of them speak to Emma for you?' Holly asks.

'Well, she did tend to keep that side of her life sort of separate, and she always came to Cambridge so I have never had much occasion to meet them. I think they might have been a bit snobby too, old friends of the family, that sort of thing, and she was always worried they would sneak to her father about us.'

'They don't sound like very good friends to me,' I murmur.

'Of course, we do have the friend whose party we met at in common but she's away on holiday for two weeks. Do you know if she was particular friends with anyone at the paper?'

'There are a couple of girls she works with but I don't know how friendly they all were. I could give them a call and ask around for you.'

With this Charlie seems to pull himself together slightly. 'Look, I'm sorry to dump all of this on you two. To be honest, it's a relief just to tell someone who knows her. Will you tell them that all I want to do is talk to her? Let me write down my mobile number for you.' He takes a minute to find a pen in his pocket and I tear off a bit of paper bag from my shell purchase for him to write on. He hands it over to Holly.

'I'll call you,' she says, studying the paper for a second.

After a moment, Charlie hauls himself from his seat and gathers up what's left of his letters and stuffs them back into his inside pocket. He runs his fingers through his hair again and I suddenly feel terribly sorry for him. He looks like a little boy lost.

He looks at us both in turn. 'Thank you,' he says. 'Thank you for letting me talk to you. And if you find anything out, Holly, I'd be very grateful.'

He ambles out of the pub and Holly and I watch him go in silence. When the door has shut on him, I lean back in my chair and determinedly sip at my whisky.

'Bloody hell, so that's what's happened to Emma,' says Holly.

'What on earth is she doing disappearing on that gorgeous chap a week before her wedding? She must be absolutely mad.'

'I can't believe she hasn't told any of us.'

'Well, she might have done. They could be very good at keeping secrets.'

Holly looks at me pityingly. 'Nobody who works at the paper is very good at keeping secrets. But she should have been gloating all over the place with that hunk in tow. Why on earth did he pick Emma? I mean, he must have actually got to know her by now?'

'Perhaps he's never put greasy fingers on her Gucci handbag.'

'No, she wasn't very happy about that.'

'Maybe she has some hidden assets.'

Holly snorts. 'Well, they must be bloody well hidden because I've never glimpsed any of them.'

'And then not only does Emma hook this gorgeous guy but it looks suspiciously to me as though she's thrown him over too.'

'Unless Sir Christopher McKellan really is keeping her prisoner. Hmmm,' Holly says thoughtfully, 'I think I might have an ask around for Charlie. I'll give the girls she works with a call at the paper. Just in case her father really is keeping her at home or something.'

'But maybe she really doesn't want to see him. It's not any of our business, is it?'

'No, but a phone call wouldn't hurt, would it? Then at least Charlie can hear it first-hand from Emma.'

'I suppose.'

'Besides, I think there is more to this than meets the eye. It seems a bit overdramatic to finish with your fiancé by disappearing off the face of the earth. It's not like he even lives in Bristol! And yet she doesn't come into work or go back home. It just seems strange, that's all.'

'Maybe she knew that he would try to find her and talk her out of it.'

'But she didn't plan it, did she? She hasn't booked any time off work or even called in sick. Emma just goes to visit her father one night to get his blessing for her impending marriage and doesn't come back.'

Now when Holly puts it like that, it does sound kind of sinister. 'What is this Sir Christopher McKellan like?'

'He hasn't made many friends in Bristol. He is extremely hard. He prosecuted a notorious drugs case a few years ago where the general opinion was that the person being tried should get off. But he pushed for a maximum sentence and got it. Thank God the death penalty isn't around otherwise he would have pushed for that and probably got it too. All sorts of ugly stuff came out afterwards about jury interference and stuff. The defending counsel tried for a mistrial but it was thrown out. And no one has quite forgotten about it.'

'God, I wouldn't like to be in Emma's shoes,' I mutter.

'Don't really fancy Charlie's either.'

'If I was Charlie, I wouldn't fancy Emma.'

'Too bloody right. I'd be making for the hills shouting, 'Sorry, love, the wedding's off!' over my shoulder.'

'Seems strange that she didn't mention her engagement at work.'

'Well, you know what a snob she is! She's probably ashamed he's not titled or something and worried that it would get back to her father somehow. I'll see what I can find out. Now! What are we doing tonight?'

I stand up and loop my bag over my shoulder. Holly picks up her bag and links arms with me as we walk towards the door. 'I don't know what Mum has planned. Cocktails and a takeaway perhaps?'

'Maybe a chocolate orange too?'

Clever girl. I smile and nod while Holly opens the door for me.

6

The next morning, I wake up early even though it's a Sunday and tut to myself in irritation. I try to have a little pretend slumber to lull my body back to sleep but after about ten minutes I give up altogether as I can hear squawking, barking and swearing from downstairs and that's just my mother. I get up, throw on a towelling robe and pad down to the kitchen.

Everyone seems to be outside or not around so I take advantage of a few precious minutes of solitude to make a pot of tea and then sit at the kitchen table picking my nails. I am still thinking about Charlie. It does seem bizarre that Emma didn't tell anyone at the office about her engagement, but maybe she was petrified of what her father might do. I can't imagine anyone being that scared of their own parent though. Embarrassed, yes. Scared, no.

I try to fit what he told us into my mental picture of Emma. I have met Emma on a couple of occasions in the past and a few years at charm school really wouldn't go amiss. The first time was at an office bowling trip and I happened to be staying with Holly at the time so naturally I tagged along. I remember Emma specifically because while everyone gamely put on those horrible little bowling shoes which, I don't care what anyone says to the contrary, really don't go with anything, Emma made a huge fuss. Firstly

81

she said she would wear her own shoes, thank you, and then when the staff said that she couldn't, she insisted they douse the shoes in that antiseptic spray (which I strongly suspect is furniture polish anyway). I think everyone has an innate fear of catching something nasty from bowling shoes but to be honest, after living with Morgan the Pekinese I'm just heartily glad that they haven't been peed on. Emma then insisted that they put her shoes in the manager's office because they were from Prada (and at this point she said it loud enough for everyone to hear, which seemed slightly strange if she didn't want them to get nicked). She then spent the entire evening in a massive sulk and acting very much as though it was putting her out greatly just to be there.

When Holly introduced us at one point in the evening she looked at me as though I had just crawled out of one of those bowling shoes and also needed a good douse of antiseptic spray. Although she isn't exactly an oil painting Emma does dress extremely well, which just makes me feel even more second-rate standing next to her, particularly when she looks me up and down in disdain. So she seems a strange choice for Charlie but maybe he finds something distinctly appealing in her off-hand manner. And I really did feel sorry for Charlie. Nothing he told us boded well on the happy-ever-after front. Not that Emma would be my natural choice for happy-ever-after but a disappearing bride-to-be doesn't sound too good. But she might just be having a major strop about the flowers or something.

My mother launches herself through the back door with Norman tucked under her arm and carrying a glass casserole dish.

'What's that for?' I ask, indicating the dish.

'Hmm? Oh, food for the badgers. I started putting some scraps out on the lawn at night for them a couple of weeks ago which was simply a huge mistake. Now if I forget they come and knock on the window. Is your father around?' she asks.

'Haven't seen him. Why?'

'He has banned Norman from the house.' Morgan will be thrilled to hear this, the two of them have been battling for supremacy.

'Why?'

'A small misunderstanding about some white-bait. And your father has very cruelly suggested that Norman might be malingering.' She looks wounded by this allegation.

'Hmmm.'

'Do you think it's too early for a cigarette?'

'Far too early. Have you got rehearsals today?'

'One at lunchtime,' she says, bustling over to the fridge with Norman smiling smugly at Morgan from his eyrie. If he could have flicked up a webbed foot in a two-fingered gesture then he would be. 'Matt is fitting it in between his services. What are you doing today?'

'Don't know yet. I'll see what everyone is up to. Barney might be working, I suppose.'

'No, I don't think so. Your father was going to help him write his CV. I really don't know what's come over him lately.'

I clear my throat and change the subject. 'You have remembered that I'm going back to Bristol to stay with Holly for a few days?'

'Are you? That's nice, dear.' This is the fifth time I've told her and I know it will still be a complete surprise to her to find I'm not at dinner on Monday night. 'So you won't be around on Wednesday. That's a pity because Gordon is coming down.' She frowns to herself. 'I must remember not to let Norman in that day. Gordon is allergic to feathers.' I hope she doesn't remember. Gordon versus Norman in some sort of stand-off would be almost worth sticking around for. I really don't know who the smart money would be on.

I'm just about to make some sort of neutral comment when my father comes in and gives my mother a very stern look. 'I sincerely hope that isn't a seagull under your arm, Sorrel.'

I smile to myself and slip away to get dressed.

★ ★ ★

By the time I've got back downstairs, admittedly with a slight detour to the sitting room with a magazine, I discover that it's past twelve o'clock and Holly has departed for the day, leaving me a cryptic note saying that she's got some work to do but she'll meet me in the village pub at one. I've got some time on my hands so I decide to set off early for the walk down to the village. I manage to make it stretch to twenty minutes and I must really have been dawdling some because I was overtaken by an octogenarian and a two-year-old.

I'm already thinking about what I might fancy to eat as I push on the latch of the ancient oak door of the pub. To my surprise Holly is already there, sitting perkily at a table about ten feet in front of me with a bottle of wine and three glasses to hand.

'Hello!' I greet her. 'I was expecting you to turn up harassed and late.'

'Well, here I am early and calm. Glass of wine?'

'Ooh, yes please.'

'You do realise those Timberland boots are too big for you?'

I frown and look down at my feet. I was hoping to have got away with it as they are buried under my jeans. 'I know. They must be Barney's. Unless my feet have shrunk, of course.'

'I think they must be Barney's. I would remember you having clown feet. Sam is joining us, by the way. I just bumped into him. You'll never guess what? I've found a story! I've been working on it all morning!'

'Is that what you've been up to? What's it about?'

'*Tyrant Solicitor Holds Daughter Hostage From Her Wedding.*' Holly sketches out the headline with her hand. 'Ring any bells?'

'You're going to write about Emma McKellan?'

'I just started thinking about it during the night. What if Charlie is right? What if Sir Christopher really is keeping Emma from marrying him? I mean, one day she's in work and the next she has disappeared off the face of the earth. It's a great story! Thank God it has come along when it has, you said my luck might change overnight! And what a scoop! The whole of Bristol has been waiting for Sir C to have a fall. I'll be some sort of folk hero!' For some reason a picture of lederhosen flashes into my head. I'm not sure that's what Holly means. 'I can see the headline now! I've just been doing some research this morning and I called Joe at home.'

'What did he say?'

'Well, he was understandably a little cautious. Just told me to do some research first. I don't think he's very keen on being sued by Sir Christopher.'

'I can see his point. So where are you going to start?'

'Joe wants to hear my ideas this afternoon so I thought we should find Emma first.'

'Find Emma?'

'Yes, we find Emma.'

'We?'

'You're not doing anything better, are you?'

'I suppose not,' I say doubtfully. 'What do you want me to do?'

'Well, I've been back to Rock this morning to see what I could find out from the neighbours. Apparently Sir Christopher is in residence at the moment but no one has seen Emma, which is not to say that she's not there but it seems unlikely. Anyway, I thought you could pay Sir Christopher a little visit.'

I stare at her in horror. I was thinking more along the lines of some gentle library research or something. I can already feel my fringe starting to curl. 'You have to be kidding.'

'He knows who I am. I've come across him a couple of times. He doesn't know you,' she says pleadingly.

My own mother won't know me by the time he's cut me up into little pieces and floated me down the River Camel. Holly must take my absolute horrified silence as some sort of tacit agreement because she suddenly starts warming to her theme.

'When I think about poor Charlie and the reasons that Sir Christopher doesn't want his daughter to marry him, it just makes my blood boil. It's not fair that he can just lock up his daughter and stop her from marrying the man she loves! It will be a blow for the sisterhood! And what better way than two sisters working together! We can be like . . . partners!'

Yes, but there's always one numbskull in the partnership, isn't there? Always one poor sod who does all the dirty work while the other leans back and takes the glory. Sherlock Holmes and Dr Watson. Scooby Doo and Shaggy. History is littered with their corpses.

I feel very sorry for Emma. Really I do. Just not sorry enough to do anything about it. And I really do think that Sir Christopher sounds a bit of a bastard and deserves anything he may have coming to him. I'm just not liberating heroine sort of material. I prefer to sit on the pavement and clap as they go by.

Just at this moment Dave the barman appears at the table and asks if we would like to order because it's getting near two o'clock and the chef is getting pissy. I don't suppose Dave fancies a little moonlighting, does he? He's always been helpful enough. I'm just about to open my mouth and say no starter for me but would you mind popping down to visit Sir Christopher once you've finished here when Holly explains we're waiting for Sam. Damn.

Holly at last begins to understand that I'm not so keen on her idea. My trembling bottom lip may have something to do with that.

'Would you do it for me, Clemmie? I really do need a story right now. I really, really do.' Her voice has a pleading sort of appeal to it. Trust Holly to sniff out my one weakness. The fact that she's my sister and needs my rather green help right now. She turns her big blue eyes on me. I try to focus on something else. The menu, the bar, the rather over-large blackboard of specials, but it's no good, I can feel them boring into me. I foolishly look at her. Damn.

'Well, what would you want me to do?' I ask cautiously.

Holly takes this as an out and out carte blanche that I'll do anything she wants and lets rip a little squeal of joy. 'I knew you'd come through for me, Clemmie!'

Why? Because I'm stupid? Or just incredibly naive? Need a mad axe-man of a father taken care of? Well, look no further than Clemmie Colshannon. Gullibility is my calling card.

Holly rushes on, 'I thought you could just say

that you work with Emma, heard about her giving in her notice and wondered if everything was all right.'

I spot a fatal flaw in her plan and my spirits rise a little. 'Why am I in Cornwall? Ha! Shouldn't I be in Bristol?'

Holly looks at me pityingly. 'Your parents live in Cornwall. In fact, say that Jenny from HR asked you to drop off Emma's things as you were down for the weekend but no one was in yesterday except for the housekeeper. That's true enough. And you wanted to make sure Emma was okay.'

'What good is that going to do? He'll just say everything is fine and then chuck me out.'

'Hmmm, maybe you're right. I'll have to think of something . . . '

Hopefully this means I have managed to talk her out of it. Sam suddenly appears at my elbow and I nearly jump out of my skin.

'Hello, you two. God, sorry I've been so long. I had to see Charlotte off and then I bumped into Trevor.' No further explanation is needed. Trevor is our ancient organist and even the simplest how are you? takes about ten minutes because Trevor is stone deaf and you have to repeat everything at about twenty million decibels. Sam leans over and plants a kiss on Holly's cheek. He gives my shoulder a friendly squeeze and sits down at the table. Holly pours him a glass of wine.

'So what's going on? You two look like you're having a very exciting, tense discussion.'

'Holly's trying to persuade me to go and visit

a mad, blood-thirsty barrister for a story of hers. You wouldn't go, would you, Sam?'

'For you, Clemmie?'

I smile hopefully at him.

'Not in a million years. What's the story?'

'Well, a girl I work with has disappeared. Shortly after handing in her resignation by fax,' starts Holly.

'This would be Emma?' interrupts Sam. 'I remember Clemmie telling us about her.'

'Her fiancé, who none of us knew she had by the way, turned up yesterday while we were dropping Emma's things off in Rock and told us that Sir Christopher McKellan, Emma's father, is practically keeping her prisoner because he doesn't want her to marry aforementioned fiancé.'

'Sir Christopher McKellan, did you say? But Clemmie didn't mention that her father was Sir Christopher McKellan.'

Oh God. Even Sam has heard of him.

'This is not the same bloodthirsty barrister that Holly wants you to visit, is it?'

'Yes, it bloody well is!' I say emphatically.

'Make sure your insurance is up to date before you go,' he murmurs. 'Did you say he's keeping his daughter prisoner?'

'We found out from her fiancé.'

Sam frowns. 'Why on earth is he doing that?'

'He doesn't like the fiancé. They were getting married in secret and then he found out and is keeping Emma away from her own wedding. It's next Saturday.'

'Are you sure it's wise, Holly, taking on

McKellan? He would be a fairly formidable opponent.'

'I'm not scared of him.' I stare at her in utter disbelief. I wouldn't bloody well be scared of him either if I had a big sister to hide behind. 'The point is that he shouldn't be allowed to take away people's free choice. You'd think we're still living in the iron age with a father dictating who his daughter marries. The man has some sort of God complex and it's about time someone took him on.'

'All right, all right, don't get all feisty and women's lib on me. I'm just saying be careful. That man wouldn't think twice about squashing your career like a fly.' Sod Holly's career. What about people's heads? Does he think twice about squashing them? Would it look self-seeking to ask?

My lips are poised with all these questions and many more besides when Sam looks over at me. 'Look, you're scaring Clemmie. Let's talk about something else.'

Holly wisely sees that her stooge is rapidly losing the will to live and adds on quickly, 'Yes, let's talk about something else. Let's order! I'm ravenous.'

I, funnily enough, have had the edge taken off my appetite. I half-heartedly peruse the menu and choose some sort of baguette thing while the other two go the whole hog with chicken and lamb. Dave takes the order and goes off kitchenwards without a care in the world.

Holly folds her arms and leans on to the table.

'So what's been going on here? How's Charlotte?'

Sam throws a quick look at me as he probably knows Charlotte isn't my favourite subject in the world. I'm busy gulping back some wine, and anyway, if Charlotte stops us talking about Sir Christopher for any period of time then I definitely want to hear about her. 'Yes, how is Charlotte?' I ask. 'Dear Charlotte. Is she well?'

'Em, yes, she's fine.'

'How was the surfing?'

'I don't think it was as close to skiing as she would have liked. But Barney was really good with her.' Both Holly and I beam at the mention of our beloved brother. 'Pulled her out from underneath a couple of waves.'

'Was the surf up?' I ask, temporarily lulled by a wonderful picture of Charlotte drowning under two-foot paddling waves.

'It was big. Not ideal learning conditions.'

'We were up at Watergate Bay yesterday morning and saw Barney briefly.'

'Yeah, he knocked off after lunch.'

'I forgot to ask him if he was seeing anyone?' Holly asks innocently and shoots a little look at me.

'Nope. No one on the horizon since the last one. What was her name? Had a nose stud.'

'I remember. Our mother kept thinking it was a rather large bogey and offering her a tissue.'

'That's the one!'

'I think her name was Lucy.'

'Aaahh. Juicy Lucy. I wonder what's she's doing now.'

Sam and Holly carry on with their Lucy reminiscences and I smile to myself and watch them together. They fall into this effortless camaraderie full of shared memories and past history which I sometimes wish I could replicate with Sam. But our relationship has a more edgy feel to it, like two prize fighters circling each other. One minute I think I know where I am with him and then he seems to change all the rules. It has been like that ever since I came back from school one day and found him lolling about with Barney in the sitting room. My parents have always adored Sam and when they found out that his aunt in the village often couldn't get home from work in time for supper, they started to feed him every day after school. He soon settled into an easy relationship with all the family, letting himself in the back door with his key.

I used to have a pet hamster called Rollo and one day my mother and I came home from the supermarket and found Sam, Barney and my father all standing in front of his cage trying to look completely innocent. Apparently his wheel had been annoyingly squeaky and they'd decided to oil it with a cooking oil spray but they'd completely overdone it and poor Rollo had turned into some sort of otter and had to slither everywhere with his hair poking up at peculiar angles. I remember thinking then, as they laughed guiltily, how much I would have liked to be in that little clique.

Holly brings me out of my reverie by pointing out that my mother's rehearsal must have finished because the whole cast has just trooped in.

'Either that or they've got so pissed off with my mother that they've left her trussed up on the stage.' Unfortunately that tantalising little thought has to remain just that as she drifts in behind them all wearing some sort of kaftan and a chain belt.

'Darlings!' she says as she spots us and wanders over.

'Sorrel, you look very Arabesque,' says Sam diplomatically.

'I do, don't I? We have just had the most exhilarating rehearsal! I feel quite, quite exhausted!'

Matt comes over. 'I suppose it's no surprise to find you lot in here, do you want a drink?'

'Matthew, darling, I simply have to tell you that you were fabulous today!'

'No, Sorrel. *You* were fabulous.' This is their little witty repartee thing; it usually goes back and forth until my mother finally agrees that she is fabulous and I don't think she's joking.

'Oh, Lord,' says Matt. 'There's Trevor, I'd better go and say hello. I think he's getting even more deaf, if that's possible. He kept missing the start of the hymns at this morning's service. One minute I was murmuring peacefully about gentle pastures and the next I was yelling 'TAKE IT AWAY TREVOR' up the aisle. Poor Mrs Gill looked as though she was going to have a heart attack every time I did it. And he's not exactly zippy in his delivery so we were finishing about three minutes before he did.'

Matt moves away just as Catherine Fothersby arrives. She is wearing a neatly pressed blouse and skirt but has tied a peasant scarf (also neatly pressed) over her perfectly shiny hair in a moment of recklessness. The effect is terribly twee, down to her petite gold watch.

'Hello, Catherine,' we all say dutifully. Sam even takes it one step further and asks her how she is.

'Quite well, thank you,' she rejoins politely while her eyes follow Matt over to Trevor.

'How are the rehearsals coming along?' he recklessly asks, risking life and limb.

'Well, Mummy is very glad that Matthew has a part.'

'Because he can prevent the whole thing deteriorating into debauchery and wantonness?'

She looks vaguely shocked at this and I smother a grin. 'No, because I don't have to miss any church activities.'

Sam is vaguely nonplussed and takes a gulp of his pint. 'That's what I thought,' he murmurs.

'In fact, it's the only reason I was allowed to do it.'

'*Allowed* to do it?' I query before I can stop myself.

'Well, Mummy didn't want me running around with a group of . . . actors.' She does have the grace to look vaguely embarrassed about the implications of this as two of us are daughters of the biggest thespian around. My eyes wander over to my mother, who is leaning against the bar with two drinks lined up in front of her telling Dave some story which involves enormous gesticulations and a fag hanging out of her mouth.

I can see Mrs Fothersby's point.

7

After lunch, Sam says he has some work to do.

'Well, I simply must get going too, tonnes of things to do! Lovely to see you, Sam. See you later, Holly!' I burble before the subject of visiting barristers can rear its ugly head again. I get up to go but Holly grabs hold of my arm. Damn. I hoped she might have forgotten all about it.

I turn back and raise my eyebrows in an and-was-there-something-else? enquiry.

Sam chuckles, kisses Holly roughly on the cheek, squeezes my arm and then heads home. Lucky sod.

'What's all this kissy-kissy stuff with you and Sam?' I demand.

'What do you mean?'

'Well, he always kisses you and never me.'

'Don't be ridiculous, Clemmie. Of course he kisses you.'

'He does not!'

'Clemmie, this is obviously some sort of elaborate smoke-screen to get you out of visiting McKellan.'

'It isn't,' I say sulkily.

'You promised.' Did I promise? I can't remember. 'You simply have to go. We need to find out where Emma is.'

'What about all this stuff we've just been saying about what a monster he is?'

'Only to his daughter, Clemmie,' says Holly impatiently.

'That's the bit that worries me,' I explain slowly. 'If that's what he does to the daughter he adores, imagine what he'll do to a complete stranger.'

'Don't be ridiculous, Clemmie. He's a QC. He has put away some of the nastiest criminals around.'

'Oh, great. So he'll know exactly where to hide my body. That makes me feel so much better. Just tell me what the point of all this is? I'll say, 'Hello, Sir Chris. How you doing? Can you tell me where Emma is?', at which point he'll say 'no' and that will be that. Where is that going to get us? Charlie said he didn't think she was at the house anyway.'

'You might gain some valuable clues. Try to get yourself invited in — '

'IN?' I shout. 'IN? Bloody hell, Holly, I didn't realise I'd be going in the house.'

'What on earth did you think then?'

'I thought the aforementioned piece of dialogue would all take place on the doorstep in broad daylight. Hopefully in view of a couple of passers-by.'

'Of course you have to go in, Clemmie. What would be the point otherwise? As I was saying, you get yourself invited in. Say you're from Emma's work or something and then keep your eyes open. Look for clues. Try to prolong the conversation.'

'I think we should just go back and see Charlie.'

'But we haven't discovered anything. Besides, it will be a better story for me if I can reunite the happy couple myself. Maybe they'll even let us have a photographer at the wedding!'

Now she really is going mad.

★　★　★

Back at home, Holly chivvies me to get changed because apparently I can't possibly go and meet Sir Christopher dressed as I am. Perhaps I should wear something dark that won't show up the blood.

'What sort of thing did you have in mind?'

'Something casual but smart. After all, you are a young professional staying with her parents for the weekend. I might have to lend you something.'

'What's wrong with my clothes?'

'Clemmie. Please.'

'Clemmie please what?'

'I'm surprised you have to ask.' Well, actually I do. What is she talking about?

'Maybe we should go tomorrow instead,' I offer.

'And have you disappear on me? No way. We're going now before your courage fails you altogether. Come and choose something from my suitcase.'

'Maybe we should wait until Dad gets home,' I try eagerly. I'm pretty sure he would have something to say about Holly forcing her poor elder sister to do such a thing.

'Why would we do that? So you can sneak to

him. Absolutely not.'

Poo.

She bundles me through to the bedroom and I sit on the bed while she rummages through her suitcase. I wonder if I should call Mum on her mobile and tell on Holly. But she would probably tell me not to be so spineless and that it all sounds fabulous fun.

Holly eventually selects a coral patterned skirt with a sort of thin black jumper thing and a trendy pair of flip-flops, all of which I quickly change into and then, despite my requests for a last meal of ice cream and cookies, she hustles me downstairs and into her car. She has an MG Midget whose name (which incidentally is Tristan) should have been on the scrap yard list quite a while ago. God, I'd forgotten what it's like to get into this little car. Since I can't seem to part my legs more than a few centimetres due to the tight skirt I'm wearing, I have to go for the head first technique (favoured by Barney and Sam) and almost lose one of my flip-flops in the process.

We set off with feelings of trepidation on my part, not only due to my impending visit but also because Holly seems to drive as though we're in some sort of cross-country rally.

'Remind me again what I'm saying.' I shout from my 45-degree angle over the noise of the engine.

'You work with Emma and heard that she had given in her notice and wondered if all was well. Jenny asked you to drop off her things since your parents live in the area.'

'Who am I supposed to be?'

'I've just said, someone who works — '

'No, I mean my name. What do I call myself?'

'I don't know, just don't use Colshannon because he knows me.'

'I'll use Trevesky. What if Emma is there and he calls her down?'

'Emma isn't there,' yells Holly confidently. 'Charlie said she wasn't.' It's all very well to be confident from the getaway car, isn't it? 'Try to start a conversation and get yourself invited in.'

'Now, it won't be my fault if he takes one look at me and then just chucks me out,' I warn Holly.

'I know, but do try. Otherwise I don't know what we're going to do next, Clemmie. And just think, that poor girl's wedding is in less than a week's time.'

Yes, I must remember why we are doing this. Not for the sheer entertainment value of taking on a mad barrister who puts away unfortunate youths just for the hell of it. But for Emma, who I'm not very fond of, but nevertheless deserves to be present at her own wedding.

I look over to Holly, who is anxiously leaning over the steering wheel, and we travel in silence for the rest of the journey to Rock. Once in the village she pulls wordlessly into the kerb about fifty yards from the house.

'Now, don't be nervous,' she advises nervously after she has applied the handbrake. 'I'll be waiting here.'

I nod dumbly. I can't quite believe I'm doing this. Am I mad or stupid or a unique combination of both? I scramble out of the car and, as I start walking uncertainly towards the house, I realise that I'm bloody petrified. 'I'm Clemmie Trevesky,' I whisper to myself just to make sure my voice is still working. 'I'm Clemmie Trevesky, how do you do.' What is the worst that can happen? My mind quickly scrolls through the huge number of possibilities and I realise that this isn't doing my self-confidence any good at all. I knock as quietly as I can on the small, pale blue door. After about two seconds I decide that no one is in and I am about to leg it when the door opens on a chain. A decidedly short female peers out. Her bowed eyes and floral apron tells me that this isn't Sir Christopher's girlfriend. This must be the mad but insanely loyal housekeeper who will help him hide the body.

'Em, hello. Is Sir Christopher McKellan around? Or Emma . . . ' I nearly slip up and call her Trevesky. But that's me. ' . . . McKellan?'

The woman peers more closely at me and then, after a second or two of appraisal, says, 'Can you wait a moment while I fetch Sir Christopher?'

I nod. Absolutely. I could wait a lifetime if she wanted. No rush. No rush at all. I turn my back to the door and look out over the small bay. Small yachts bob gently up and down on the water and I heartily wish that I could be on one of them.

A whoosh of air suddenly assaults the back of my head and tells me the front door has been opened with some force. I spin around to be faced with the infamous Sir Christopher McKellan.

All I can say is that Holly has not exaggerated in her description of him. The man has to duck slightly below the door frame but still towers over me. He is dressed in navy cords with a checked shirt and this blatant attempt to soften his look doesn't fool me in the slightest. His black eyes bore into me and he is wearing the sort of expression that must make his adversaries throw up their briefs and run for the hills.

'YES?' he snaps, making me jump.

'He . . . hello,' I manage to stammer. 'I'm looking for Clemmie Trevesky. I mean, I am Clemmie Trevesky and I'm looking for Emma.'

'And WHY would you be doing that?'

My voice jumps an octave with nerves. 'I work with her, or rather used to work with her. Jenny asked me to drop her things off with you and I was just worried that she left work so quickly, that everything was all right.'

He stares at me for a second and then says in a quieter voice, 'You'd better come in.'

My first insane reaction of triumph is quickly replaced by complete fear. 'In?' I repeat. 'You want me to come in?' I had still been wildly clinging to the hope that he would just shut the door in my face.

'Yes, in the house.'

'Of course! In the house. Where else? Ha, ha!'

God, Clemmie. Did you have to add on that psychotic little ha-ha on the end? I follow the soft tap of his leather shoes across a stone-flagged floor and into a large, low-ceilinged sitting room where a wood fire is already softly crackling in the grate.

As I predicted, the room has two huge pale blue sofas which look as though they might swallow you up whole, and the interior designer has clearly been briefed with a Kensington-by-the-sea look. The bowl in the centre of the old teak coffee table is a huge fossil shell, the wall lights are decorated with shells and the heavy, expensive curtains are tied back with pieces of old rope.

Sir C will probably never feature on my invitation list but he apparently features with many others' if the line of stiff white cards on the mantelpiece is anything to go by. A huge desk sits grandly under a bay window, spread with papers and files, and a half-drunk tumbler of whisky sits to one side of it.

Now Holly said to look for clues. Again, a little more questioning on that front would, at this current moment of time, have gone down a treat. Should I be actually looking for Emma? Under the sofa? Behind the door? What sort of clues should I be searching for?

Sir Christopher leans against the mantelpiece and runs a hand through his black hair. He makes no suggestion that I sit down and nor do I. There's a better getaway to be had from the standing position, thank you.

'Who told you that she had left work?'

'Em, Joe told us. Our editor, Joe.' In my current nervous state I've not a clue what Joe's surname might be and pray that he won't ask. He might try and turn this into a quick fire

103

round of twenty questions on the *Bristol Gazette*. Maybe I should have questioned Holly a little closer, learned a bit more about the newspaper and Emma. Holly has an infectious sang-froid attitude to life which means that preparations for any event are rather thin on the ground.

He seems to relax slightly which is strange. 'Nice to get away from the city, isn't it? Breathe some fresh sea air.'

'Absolutely!' I agree eagerly, but then I would pretty much agree to anything he says at the moment. 'All that smog!'

'Can I offer you some tea?'

'No, thank you. I can't stay very long.'

'Have you lived in Bristol long, Miss . . . ?'

'Trevesky. Clemmie Trevesky. Em, no, not long.' So, please don't ask me anything about the city because I know bugger all.

'Whereabouts do you live?'

'In Clifton,' I answer confidently. Holly lives there so this I know.

'Me too. Up by the suspension bridge.'

'Really?' I'm racking my brains to remember the name of Holly's road. Damn her. Here it comes.

'What about you?'

'Oh. You know. By the, er, square.' Holly and I drink wine on that patch of grass in the summer. 'By the Albion pub!' I add triumphantly. I may not know my street names but by God I can remember the pubs.

He looks satisfied at this. 'Well, I mustn't keep you. Emma isn't here, I'm afraid,' he says quietly.

104

I resist the temptation to clap my hands together and skip out of the room. 'Well, we were just a bit worried about her,' I warble. 'She left so suddenly. Should I have dropped her things off in Bristol? She might want some of the clothes she'd bought in the sale,' I improvise wildly, remembering the Whistles top Holly had mentioned. I wonder what colour it is and whether it would have suited moi.

'I'll make sure she gets them, but as I mentioned she's not here.'

'Right. Good.'

There really doesn't seem very much to add and I'm about to make my excuses and leave when he suddenly asks, 'If I can't offer you tea then would you like an early drink?'

Would I like a drink? I can't think of anything else, apart from not being here, I would like more in the world. And he seems to be satisfied with all my answers and is relaxing his guard a little. Any minute now he could tell me where Emma is.

'Yes, please,' I say rather quickly.

'Whisky?' he asks.

I nod hastily, I have no wish to offend a whisky drinker. 'Love the stuff.'

He goes over to a silver tray lined with tumblers and a decanter. I take another look around the room and edge over to a half moon table sporting a couple of photographs. One of them is of a young-looking Emma sitting on the lap of a woman I can only presume is her mother from the resemblance. Then there's another of Emma standing between two men, one of whom

105

is her father. I stare at the other man. He looks vaguely familiar but I simply cannot place where I might have seen him before . . .

'Here,' an arm slightly nudges me. I claim the proffered glass and thank him. 'Won't you sit down?'

We move back towards the sofas by the fire and I perch timidly on the edge of one. I even manage to take a sip of the whisky without my eyes watering. Sir Christopher plonks himself on the opposite sofa and has a bash at looking a little less scary. Close, but no cigar.

'So you know Emma?' he rejoins jollily.

'Yes, yes. We worked together. In PR.' I take another nervous sip. 'At the paper.' Of course at the paper, Clemmie, where else? 'So everything is all right with Emma?' I venture.

'Of course. Why shouldn't it be?'

'Absolutely. Why shouldn't it be?'

'So tell me, Miss . . . '

'Trevesky,' I helpfully fill in for him again. Goodness, he has a problem with names. Maybe he isn't the bloodthirsty barrister we thought he was. This little glimpse of humanity makes me relax for a second. But only for a second because the wily old goat's next question comes soaring through the air and knocks me off balance.

'Why didn't you telephone?'

'S . . . sorry?'

'You dropped her things off yesterday. You didn't need to return. So why didn't you telephone? I presume you can use one; in fact, I get the impression that they are positively de rigueur in the modern home.'

'Well, my parents live down here and I thought I would just pop in.' In my nervousness I chuck the drink down my throat and manage to spill most of it over my front. I start to brush myself down but he doesn't take his dark eyes from my face.

'Where is home, Miss Trevesky?' His voice is steely. I don't like the turn this conversation is taking. 'Because if it's not Daymer Bay or Polzeath, and I'm betting that it's not, then Rock isn't really on your way anywhere.'

'I thought I would just pop in,' I warble. 'Check on Emma.'

'You know, Miss Trevesky, I don't remember Emma ever mentioning your name, which is strange considering she only has two other colleagues in her department at work, both of whom I have met.' This is why he was pretending to stutter over my name.

'I'm new,' I squeak.

'Then you wouldn't know Emma well enough to be worried about her, would you?'

I stand up now and, trembling slightly, place my empty tumbler on a spindly side table. I can hear myself say in a voice that doesn't quite sound as though it's coming from me, 'Well, thanks for the drink, I really must be going now.'

He stands up too. 'Do you want to know what I think?'

Er, no. Not really.

'I don't think you know my daughter at all. I think you have tricked your way into my house under false pretences.' His voice starts to gain some momentum. 'I think you are a fraudster and a liar!' he booms. Christ, that's a bit strong, isn't it? 'What have you got to say for yourself?' he yells at practically ten million decibels.

'I say, I . . . I say . . . ,' I stutter as though I'm about to tell him some fabulously funny joke except this isn't funny at all.

'I think you have been sent here,' he says in a dangerously quiet voice. He starts to walk towards me and although I don't feel as though my legs will even take the weight, I start to do a trembling knock-knee chicken combined with the one-step tango towards the door. 'I think a certain young man from Cambridge has sent you to do his dirty work.'

'No!' I pipe up in a shrill voice, 'that's not true at all!' Actually it's a certain young lady from Cornwall who has sent me to do her dirty work but he may not want to split hairs. This must be how he performs in court. I really wouldn't fancy being in the box if Sir Christopher is prosecuting but at least you get someone to defend you, don't you? Whereas now it's just little old me and my sister waiting outside in a car which probably won't even start. No wonder Emma has turned out the way she has; in fact, I'm starting to have a certain amount of sympathy for her.

We've reached the hall and with one quick movement I scuttle towards the front door.

'I want you GONE from my house and I don't want you to come back.'

We share this one common goal because, by God, I wanted me gone too. Trembling madly, I start the mammoth task of unlocking the front door. At last I have it open, but as I make my bid for freedom Sir Christopher's hand catches hold of the wood.

'You can tell him from me that my daughter will never marry him. In fact, she will never set eyes on him again. You take that message.'

I nod frantically, my fringe well and truly frizzled up by now, and at last he lets the door go. With a wild yelp, I hurl myself out on to the pavement.

Holly must have been somewhat alarmed to see her older sister, skirt hitched up around her knickers to aid a better running motion and with a new frizzy hairstyle, pelting it along the pavement yelling, 'START THE CAR! START THE CAR!'

8

When we reach home, Holly wraps me in a nice warm blanket, parks me on the sofa and forces a whopping great G&T into my trembling hands. She had managed to compel most of the story out of me on the way home, despite me being absolutely incoherent for most of it.

I take a shaky slug of my gin and snuggle into the blanket. Bloody hell, that wasn't funny. Not funny at all. Charlie must be absolutely mad to take that man on.

Holly sits opposite me, cradling a glass of gin herself, deep in thought. I occasionally peep out at her but mostly keep my head down and the gin flowing. I prefer Holly when she is deep in thought anyway, it keeps her out of causing trouble elsewhere.

Eventually she speaks. 'So he actually said that Emma would never be seeing Charlie again.'

I nod from beneath my blanket.

'The man must be almost holding her prisoner. How awful for poor Emma.'

Sod poor Emma. I'm more concerned about me at the moment and my own very stressed nervous system. It can't be good for you to have this amount of adrenalin whooshing around.

'But where on earth do you think she is?'

'Haven't got a clue,' I mumble. 'He said several times that she wasn't in the house.'

'Maybe he was just saying that to throw you off the scent.'

'I got the impression it was more of a message. More of a she's-not-here-and-you'll-never-find-her jobby.'

'And you didn't glean any clues?'

'Nothing.' I shake my head and have another shiver to myself.

'You're still coming back to Bristol with me?' Holly and I had planned to set off this evening and, considering my idea of happiness at the moment is a few hundred miles between me and Sir Christopher McKellan, then to Bristol I am going. I nod to Holly.

'How on earth are we going to find her, Clemmie?'

This time I manage to pop my head out from underneath my protective layers. 'What do you mean 'we'? I think I have done more than my duty for the Emma/Charlie cause and I'm not bloody doing any more.'

'No, no, I don't want you to do anything like that again.'

'You wouldn't get me doing anything like that again,' I say betwixt gritted teeth.

'I was thinking more along the lines of some library research with me.'

'Why do you need me along? Can't I just stay at your flat and watch TV?'

'But it's been so much more fun working together and two heads are better than one. Besides, don't you want to see how it turns out?'

'No.'

'Come on, Clemmie. I'm only talking about

some gentle research. No more Sir Christopher McKellan characters.'

I again shiver at the mention of his name. 'Tell me what you mean by gentle research,' I say suspiciously. Knowing Holly this could mean a spot of gentle lion-taming or something equally heinous.

'Well, I thought perhaps we could go to the paper tomorrow and have a look through some old stories on Sir Christopher. See if we can find something that might tell us where he's hiding Emma. Of course, Joe is going to want me to verify my sources first.'

'And then what?' I ask warily. Would she want me to swing through an open window with a knife in my mouth? Would she lower me through a hatch in a *Mission Impossible*-style harness?

'And then we'll reunite the happy couple! More gin?'

Holly skips off happily to the kitchen while I hunch huffily into the sofa. I've always considered Holly's blissfully blasé attitude to life as one of her many assets but now I'm starting to think it's a downright menace. Lucky for her she returns with the bottle.

'As long as I'm not involved in the reuniting,' I stipulate.

'But you'll help otherwise? The wedding is only a week away and I really do need this story,' says Holly pleadingly.

'Okay,' I say sulkily.

'What are you two doing in here?' asks Barney as he comes in. 'Everyone's in the kitchen.'

'I know. That's why we're in here,' I say

grumpily through my blanket.

'Holly, what have you done to Clemmie?'

'Nothing at all! She's over-reacting terribly. She just had to go and see someone for me for work. That's all.'

I view her from my huddled position. As soon as I can drag myself off this sofa I'm going to lamp her.

'Come on through. We need the gin back.'

With the blanket still draped around me, I shuffle through to the kitchen after them and park myself in front of the Aga on Norman's beanbag. I hope he hasn't been doing anything nasty on it. My father is busy preparing some food and my mother is lying with her legs dangling across a chair wearing an eye mask and with a cigarette in her mouth. Sam is sitting at the kitchen table calmly eating pistachio nuts while talking on his mobile.

'Holly made Clemmie go and see someone for a new story,' announces Barney.

'Really? How did it go?' asks my father.

'Not well.'

My mother is starting to stir now. She can smell a little bit of gossip a mile away.

'Holly made me pretend to be someone else and go and see this mad barrister who has kidnapped his own daughter.' My father looks in horror at Holly, who is making an I'm-going-to-kill-you face at me. I stick out my tongue at her.

My father turns back to me. 'What happened?'

'He threw me out.'

My mother lifts a corner of her eye mask and

sits up. 'Darling, it sounds fabulous! Then what happened?'

'He threatened me!'

My father frowns at Holly. She makes another by-the-time-I've-finished-with-you-McKellan-will-be-a-walk-in-the-park face at me. I decide to shut up.

'Well, I hope you shit McGregor-ed him,' my mother says indignantly. I forgot to mention that this very annoying expression can sometimes be used as a verb. Roughly translated it means, in lieu of conversation, give a good kick on the shins and run. Again to do with the Scotsman, the loch and the rowing boat. Again don't ask.

'I wish I had. But I just concentrated on the running bit instead.'

'Darling, are they your clothes? You really look quite nice.'

Holly is very keen to change the subject so since Sam has come off the phone she asks hastily, 'How's Charlotte?'

I glare at her. I'm very happy talking about me and have no wish to hear about ruddy Charlotte.

'She's good. She's just off to an actuarial dinner.' That'll be a laugh a minute. 'Anyway, you've been to see McKellan? Did you find out anything about Emma?'

'Only that she wasn't there. Which we knew already. Holly always gets me involved in these things and she never thinks them through properly.' I look daggers at my sister.

'Clemmie, pot, kettle. Have you all met?' Sam steadily deshells another pistachio.

'That's unfair! I think things through!'

114

'So you had thought things through when you got on a plane to Singapore?'

'Of course!' I had actually thought about getting on the plane, I just hadn't really addressed the issue of getting off it.

'How about the plane after that to Australia?'

I hesitate. God, what is it with Sam and my trip abroad? He has been on my case about it ever since I got back. It's as though he really begrudges me going. I'm about to think up an enormously stinging reply like 'Ho!' when he saves me the trouble by moving on and saying, 'Anyway, I don't think you should be messing with McKellan. He has a really bad reputation.'

'Well, McKellan shouldn't think he can stop two consenting adults from getting married. This is a free country, last time I looked.'

'How do you know that this Emma wants to be found? Maybe she's decided she simply doesn't want to marry him.'

'Then surely she would tell him? She wouldn't just not turn up for work the next day. She wouldn't go to visit her father and not come back.' I look as haughty as I can from the indignity of my beanbag. I really hope Norman hasn't pooped on it.

Sam shrugs in an infuriating manner. 'Maybe. I'm just saying that you and Holly seem to charge around tackling things head on without even considering the other options.'

'I do not charge around tackling things head on.'

'I'm sure Wayne and his bent nose would beg to disagree.'

Boy, if only I had a tray and a double-hinged door now.

'When is Mr Trevesky expecting you back at work?' asks my father, trying to abate the row.

'I'll be back from Bristol by the end of the week.'

And by then we'll have found Emma, reunited her with Charlie and I'll be expecting a big fat apology from Sam.

★ ★ ★

In Bristol the next morning I am woken by Holly and, more importantly, a cup of tea. I stretch out blissfully and wriggle my toes. No French fries, mashed potatoes or mixed vegetables to think about for the next few days. No smelly seagulls eating bits of fish. Just Holly and me and perhaps a spot of shopping. Bliss-ikins. I could certainly do with a spot of relaxation because the journey last night to Bristol was far from fun. The roads in and out of Cornwall aren't particularly renowned for their brevity but the harrowing bit started when we reached Bristol. Tristan then, for some personal and private reason of his own, decided to give up the ghost at one of the main roundabouts and we had to get out and push. Luckily we were on a hill, so Holly managed to bump-start him again to a rather unnecessary volley of hooting and shouting.

Holly lives in a small two-bedroom flat in the Clifton area of Bristol. It's on the first floor of a large Regency house and has those huge high ceilings and sash windows. She has always lived by herself, a fancy I think all members of our family share with her since we grew up in an extremely noisy household. Besides Barney we have two other brothers, so seven of us under one roof, not to mention a small menagerie of animals, has certainly given rise to a few living-alone-on-a-desert-island fantasies. Holly says she still waits outside her own bathroom if the door is closed until she remembers she actually lives alone.

Holly sits on the end of my bed in her towelling robe and hugs her knees into her chest. 'I thought you might want to come in to the paper later this morning and talk to the people in the jobs section. I need to speak to Joe this morning about the McKellan story.'

'Great. I'll have a wander down Park Street and then come on to the paper.' I take little sips of tea and grin at my sister who is looking suitably envious. 'Are we meeting James at some point?'

'Tonight probably. Do you want to walk down or come with me and Tristan now?'

'I'll walk. Thanks all the same.'

I love Holly but I draw the line at Tristan.

★   ★   ★

I have been looking forward to shopping in cosmopolitan Bristol. The local shops in Cornwall seem to carry an alarming range of bicycle parts and fish bait. The last time I went shopping in Plymouth, when I was more gainfully employed, I was absolutely convinced that a pot of anti-ageing cream from Elizabeth Arden would change my life. I excitedly approached the beauty counter of the local department store only to be told that they thought Liz might work on the leather goods counter and maybe I should try there. So the thought of shopping in Bristol is my idea of Mecca.

There are, however, other considerations to take into account and it soon becomes apparent to me that although waitressing in Cornwall might pay a small mortgage plus fish and chips every week, it doesn't stretch quite as far in Bristol. Mr Trevesky would be absolutely appalled as even a cup of coffee is pushing it. It also raises the very ugly and unwelcome question of where I am actually going with my life. Will I ever need a crystal-covered little black cocktail dress? When would I wear some fabulous knee-high, leather boots if I haven't the job to match them? More importantly, will I ever know what to wear with them? And that's just the tip of the iceberg where clothes and me are concerned. I can see something breathtaking in a magazine or on a model, put the exact same thing on me and look dreadful. I have the wrong sort of frame and just seem to be all limbs. I don't mean that in a fabulous leggy sort of way, just in a gangly, scarecrow fashion. Wherever I seem to look there is always one of my limbs in the picture so I end up wearing a peculiar mismatch of clothes. I wish I had Holly's sense of style. I remember Seth always trying to get me to wear flash designer dresses, only to find that I actually looked better in a pair of jeans and one of Barney's jumpers. I think that was one of the reasons he always used to go by himself to the gallery openings — I never looked quite good enough on his arm.

So while I have an enjoyable few hours wandering about and indeed manage to purchase a bikini from the bargain bin without an accompanying coronary, I am glad when late morning approaches and it is time for me to make my way down to the national headquarters of the *Bristol Gazette*.

Holly works in a large, impersonal office block manned by security guards and several triffid-like plants, both of whom you have to wrestle with in order to gain access to the floor where the editorial part of the paper is based. After being questioned, my bag searched and new bikini admired, I am eventually allowed to sally forth. At the third floor, I tentatively step out of the lift and have a good look around. The massive insignia of the *Bristol Gazette* hangs over the reception desk. Sophie, a nice but vacant-looking girl who I have met a couple of times but who totally fails to recognise me, looks up from her magazine and then points me in the direction of the features desk. The office is completely open plan and I weave my way through desks littered with phones and computers.

As I approach the features corner, I am relieved to see Holly. She's on the phone but waves at me to sit in the chair opposite her, which is one of those exciting big leather swivel ones, and I have a happy time while she finishes her call.

'Good shop?' she asks as she replaces the receiver.

'Bikini,' I answer.

'Ooh, let's see.'

I duly produce it and Holly duly admires. I'm just about to ask if she would mind accompanying me on a future shopping trip when a voice snaps behind me: 'Holly! When you have quite finished looking at your sister's pants. Hello, Clemmie, how are you?'

I open my mouth to answer and then realise it's not really a question at all. This is Joe, Holly's esteemed editor. Who is also, quite frankly, bloody frightening. He always wears rather startling clothing; today it's a bright yellow shirt and a lime green tie which is so vibrantly patterned that for a moment I think I'm going cross-eyed. I like it.

'Look, Holly. I don't like to make a mountain out of a sandhill but quite frankly you're up shit creek without a canoe.' Joe likes to talk in metaphors. Unfortunately he mixes them all up which makes him not only bloody frightening but bloody confusing too. 'You need a story. And looking at your sister's pants isn't going to get you one.' I frown to myself. Is that just another mixed up metaphor or is he really talking about me? And would the fact that they're bikini bottoms make it any better? 'Now, I like the sound of this McKellan story. Come and talk to me about it in my office in twenty minutes.'

I'm about to snuggle down into Holly's chair and indulge in a serious session of Solitaire on her computer when Holly says, 'I think Clemmie should come too as she might be able to help.' I look at Joe anxiously. Please say something like, we never involve civilians in our work, go home immediately, Clemmie, and watch *Home and Away*.

Unfortunately he does no such thing. 'Very well, as you're already involved.'

Joe as well as Sir Christopher? Some bloody holiday this is turning out to be.

★ ★ ★

While we're waiting, Holly decides that this would be a good opportunity for me to go down to the job section and talk to Ruth about finding a job in the art world. Ruth is an efficient girl with very short hair and a paperwork system that apparently works like traffic lights (red, orange, green and er, dark pink), but despite being so staggeringly capable she really doesn't have any good news for me on the job front. Any small hope that there might be a plethora of employers waiting for me quickly evaporates. Ruth narrows the search until we're down to a museum tour guide. Which is fine but I actually get paid more at Mr Trevesky's café. And if this is what it's like in Bristol then God help me if I want to stay in Cornwall. When Holly returns to collect me for our meeting with Joe, she finds me slumped at Ruth's desk with my head buried in my arms. If I happen to meet Seth ever again then, God help me, I swear I will throttle him.

A couple of minutes later Holly forthrightly knocks on Joe's door, just below the EDITOR sign.

'COME!' he yells from inside and we tentatively enter. Joe blows out a lungful of smoke and narrows his eyes at us. 'Ahhh. Double the trouble. Sit down, sit down.' He waves us impatiently towards two chairs. There's about ten tonnes of paperwork on mine and I hover uncertainly, wondering whether to remove it or perch awkwardly on top of it. Joe might get pissy if I crease it so I remove it.

'Now I've been thinking about this McKellan case, Holly. And the more I think about it, the more I like it. I need you to take the bull by the nails on this one. An awful lot of people would like to see him brought down so a story like this will be worth its weight in salt. We, of course, will be doing it for the sake of Emma, because after all she used to be one of our employees and I think we should do our best by her.' He pauses and looks over at Holly. 'Besides which, I really would like her to come back to work; I can't find anyone to write these bloody social pages of hers. She was so bitchy about everyone; 'High Society' has never looked so bleak. We're pushed to write about lunchtime at McDonald's at the moment. You don't know anyone who could write it, do you?' He looks hopefully from one to the other of us and I shake my head vehemently.

'Anyway . . . ' He addresses himself again to Holly. 'That should be your angle. We're concerned about Emma. Local paper looks after

122

its own feel to it. Now, no putting the horse before the cart. We can't afford any cock-ups on this. Verify your facts.' He looks carefully from one sister to the other. Why's he looking at me? Why? 'Ver-i-fy your facts. This paper cannot afford to be sued by Sir Christopher McKellan which, I needn't remind you, would certainly be the end of your career and probably mine too. You know where to find this Charlie character?'

'I've got his mobile number. But obviously we need to make sure he's not some sort of nutcase. We need to check that Emma really is engaged to be married to him.'

'So how are you going to do that?'

'She must have *one* girlfriend she's told.' Holly looks over at me at this point for some sort of female collaboration. I start nodding. No. Stop nodding, Clemmie. Stop it immediately. Do not get involved.

'You'll need more than one girlfriend,' remarks Joe.

'Also,' continues Holly, 'I think Charlie mentioned something about the church being booked. So we can find his local church in Cambridge and see if it really has been.'

Joe lets out another stream of thoughtful smoke. 'Yep, that's worth a try.'

'Then after we have found Emma . . . ' I love the way she says that, as though we can just pop down to Sainsbury's and find her sitting on the Emma shelf, ' . . . we will reunite the happy couple, along with an exclusive piece on how Sir Christopher McKellan, supposed defender of all that is good and right, prevented her from marrying the man she loved!'

'You believe this Charlie character then?'

'He seems very genuine. And McKellan definitely didn't want Emma seeing him when Clemmie did her bit of research.' Again she looks across at me while I take a deep interest in Joe's shoes. Hand stitched. Such workmanship. Absolutely fascinating.

'Emma might even have told someone here at work about the engagement. I can't think why she would keep it to herself,' says Joe.

'You know how snobby she is in that diary of hers. Probably couldn't bear to turn the spotlight on to herself. Charlie is gorgeous and she might have been worried that people would say he's marrying her for her money or something.'

'Probably didn't tell you because you're all such motor-mouths.'

'I think she was nervous about her father finding out. Wanted to keep it a secret.'

'Don't blame her on that one. If Sir Christopher McKellan was my father I would feel the same way. God, when I think about that lad he put away. What was his name?'

'Martin Connelly.'

'That's right, Martin Connelly. Anyway, I don't need to tell you, Holly, that you really need this story.'

'I know.'

He looks at us both in turn which seems to conclude our interview and we both get up. I reach the door first and am out in the corridor before Holly can throw her bag over her shoulder.

We start walking together towards Holly's desk. 'That wasn't so bad, was it?' she comments lightly. 'God, he's really keen on the story now. I hope Charlie doesn't turn out to be some sort of nutter.'

I actually really, really hope Charlie turns out to be a raving bloody lunatic and we can just drop the whole thing. 'So what do we do now?' I ask.

Holly beams at me. She must truly love her job, it's as though a light has been turned on inside her. 'I think she has a flatmate so let's get her address from human resources and go down there.'

I look at my watch. 'It's still early though. If the flatmate works then she won't be home yet.'

Holly frowns. 'Good point. Well, let's try and find this church they must be registered at. What was Charlie's surname again?'

'Davidson,' I answer automatically.

She flings herself down into her chair while I take a more tentative seat in the one opposite. 'Let's call directory enquiries for his address and, failing that, try every church in Cambridge.'

Holly starts tapping away on her computer keyboard. 'Where's your laptop?' I ask suddenly, out of curiosity. Normally it's like a third arm to her but knowing Holly she has probably left it somewhere.

'In with the IT department.' She gestures with her head over the top of a partition to the right. 'We had a thunderstorm last week and lightning came down the modem line and fried it.'

'That was unlucky.'

'Christ, you would think so, but the way the IT department are going on you'd think I'd planted it in a field with a large metal coat hanger attached to it.'

'What are you doing?' I ask, gesturing at her still-tapping fingers.

'Trying to bring up details of all the churches in Cambridge. Church of England, do you think?'

'I should think so. Can't we just ask Charlie?'

'God, no! I want him to think we're his new best friends! He could take this to a rival paper. We can if we get desperate but I don't want him to think we're doubting him at this stage. There!' she says triumphantly after a few more minutes, then gets up and disappears. She reappears a few seconds later waving a piece of paper fresh from the printer.

'Do you want to make a start on these?'

'I suppose. What am I saying to them?'

'That you used to know one of the happy couple, heard they were getting married at this church on Saturday and wanted to make sure when it is so you can send them a card.'

'And what if it's not that church?'

'Just say you made a mistake and ring off,' says Holly impatiently. 'Honestly, Clemmie! You have no head for subterfuge!'

'What are you going to do?'

'Try and find his address. Davidson isn't exactly unusual though.'

Ten minutes later Holly has drawn a complete blank and I have called one rector who was out, one who thought I was asking about Jim

Davidson the comedian and kept telling me he's already married even though I was screaming CHARLIE DAVIDSON down the phone at twenty million decibels, and then one ancient-sounding vicar who went off to check his records and never came back. The number still comes up as an engaged tone so the old dodderer must have just forgotten all about me.

Holly tears off the bottom half of the list and starts calling as well. Bloody hell, how many churches does a place need? Cambridge must be full of religious megalomaniacs. I make a mental note never to visit and carry on calling.

Half an hour later I have finished my list and am leaning back in my chair waiting for Holly to finish hers. She replaces the receiver on her last call.

'Anything?' I ask.

'Nothing.' She looks despondent.

'Well, we've still got Catholic and other churches to go and three of my vicars were out. They wouldn't get married anywhere else, would they? I don't know, in a synagogue or registry office for instance?'

'Charlie definitely said a church.'

We sit in silence for a few minutes. 'Why don't we see if Emma's flatmate is home? We can take the list with us and re-try the ones that were out later. I left my mobile number with them too, so maybe they'll call back.'

Holly nods and smiles and we gather up our stuff. After a brief stop with human resources for Emma's address, we wend our way back to Tristan. Holly just bundles herself inside without any regard for life or limbs while I hesitate briefly outside the passenger door again. Do I go in head first or legs first? I opt for the former but spend an uncomfortable few minutes with my head down around Holly's knee region while I grapple with my legs.

'There!' I say, finally upright with all appendages present and correct. Holly stifles a giggle, puts Tristan into first gear and we set off. Holly hands Emma's address over to me and I look at the road name. 'Redland Road,' I say. 'Where's that?'

'In Redland. Another area of Bristol.'

'Do you know where that is?' I ask nervously. Between us Holly and I have absolutely zero navigational skills. Holly doesn't know the difference between her left and right and I can only hazard a guess. I think it must be something to do with our mother shouting STAGE LEFT!, STAGE RIGHT! at us when we were young, which obviously depended on her interpretation of where the audience was and had nothing to do with the actuality of left and right.

'Yep, don't worry.'

We set off at breakneck speed and, since I can't appreciate the sights of Bristol as they are just a blur, conversation is nigh on impossible. I'm beginning to think that this is at least a lot more interesting than lying on the sofa reading magazines.

We arrive in Redland Road and spend a few minutes looking around for the appropriate number. We find a large old Victorian house with the matching digits, Holly parks up and we both scramble out of Tristan. Holly sort of falls out on to the pavement while I edge my way out on my hands as though I'm in a wheelbarrow race. Not the most delicate pair of sisters; it's no wonder that Catherine and Teresa Fothersby look so blooming marvellous next to us.

'Do you know what this girl's name is?' I ask, brushing the gravel off my hands as we walk towards the house.

'One of Emma's colleagues said she thought she was called Tasha.'

'This is quite nice, isn't it?'

'Redland is predominantly a student area, so yes it is quite nice. But then I wouldn't expect Emma McKellan to live anywhere too shoddy, would you?'

We are standing on the doorstep of the house, studying the array of buzzers before us, when the door suddenly opens and out spills a dark-haired girl with a head full of spiral curls. She grins infectiously at us. 'Who are you looking for?' she asks sociably as she steps out, coat and bag slung over her arm.

'We're looking for someone called Tasha? She lives with Emma McKellan in flat three.'

'That's me!' she beams at us. 'But I'm afraid if you're looking for Emma you're out of luck. I think she might have gone to stay with family somewhere.'

'Yes, we know,' says Holly. 'Actually we wanted to speak to you. You don't have five minutes to spare, do you?' Holly puts on her marvellous Labrador-esque pleading look that she uses with me when she wants the last bit of chocolate.

129

It seems to do the trick. Tasha hesitates for a second and then her face relaxes. 'Well, I was only off to the supermarket so I've got a bit of time.' She opens the door again and we follow her into the hall. She uses her key to open another door and we follow her into the flat.

'We weren't expecting to find you in,' says Holly.

'I work as a physiotherapist at the hospital. Shift work, so you were lucky to catch me at all!' explains Tasha with a smile. She leads the way into a large sitting room and dumps her coat and bag on the sofa. 'Would you like some tea or coffee?'

'Tea for me, please!' I rejoin enthusiastically. Holly agrees with the request and we follow her to the doorway of the kitchen.

'So do you know Emma?' asks Tasha cautiously.

'I worked with her at the paper. This is my sister, Clemmie, who's staying with me at the moment,' says Holly. Tasha looks from one to the other of us, notes the resemblance and looks suitably relieved that we're not from the tax office or anything else heinous. 'You know that she's gone to stay with family and obviously she hasn't been into work,' continues Holly. 'But I ran into her fiancé Charlie the other evening.' I look at Tasha carefully to note her reaction. She doesn't seem unduly shocked or surprised. 'He wanted to know where he could find Emma and, since we didn't know that she had a fiancé, we didn't want to give him any more information without checking with someone first.' Very good,

Holly. Very convincing. The fact that we don't have any information whatsoever to give Charlie is completely immaterial. I just hope the questions don't get that far. 'Did you know about Charlie, Emma's fiancé?' asks Holly carefully.

The kettle switches itself off with a loud POP and Tasha turns towards the countertop. She doesn't say anything for a few minutes while she gets out mugs and teabags. Holly throws me a puzzled look. Tasha finally turns back towards us and looks Holly squarely in the eye.

'Yes, I knew about Charlie,' she says quietly. So he's not a nutter after all. 'But it was a big secret. Might still be for all I know. Why was Charlie looking for her? I actually thought she might be with him.'

Tasha squeezes the teabags out and plops them in the bin. After she has added the milk, she hands one mug over to me and one to Holly. She leads the way back into the sitting room and we all sit down. It's actually quite a beautiful room: large bay windows, a polished wooden floor and stylish furniture.

'Charlie says she just disappeared. Apparently she went over to ask for her father's blessing for the marriage.' Holly looks carefully at Tasha for her reaction. 'And she never came back.'

Tasha frowns to herself. 'No, she didn't come back that night but I didn't think anything of it. I called her father the next day to see when she would be back, we'd said we would go to a new bar that evening for her social diary, and he said she had decided to have a break for a little while.' Tasha shrugs her shoulders at us. 'I thought it was a bit strange but it wasn't as though she was a missing person or anything. Her father absolutely adores her; he would be the first to kick up a fuss if anything happened to her.'

'But she told you about Charlie?' persists Holly.

'Oh yes. I don't know who else she told, we're not exactly best friends. Emma can sometimes be a bit difficult to get along with but I think she simply couldn't keep it from me, especially living together and everything. She certainly became easier to be with after she met Charlie — she was absolutely smitten with him! I've never seen someone so much in love!'

Holly glances over at me triumphantly. 'And they were planning to get married?'

'Yes, in Cambridge on Saturday. I'm not going, I don't think she has really invited anyone. Of course her father knew absolutely none of this. I think he's always wanted her to marry some bigwig with connections and Charlie simply didn't fit the bill. He's a teacher and from the North somewhere. Not like Emma to even give someone like that the time of day but I have to admit that he looks absolutely gorgeous from the pictures she's shown me. But as the wedding arrangements got underway, Emma became more and more worried about her father. She does care about him and she didn't want to get married without him knowing. I suppose that is what she went over to see him about. It's difficult to have long conversations with her because of my shift pattern. So Charlie is looking for her?'

'Yes, she hasn't been in contact with him since that evening. Did she seem to have any doubts about the wedding?'

'God, no! She absolutely couldn't wait!'

'Do you think you could check her room?' asks Holly. 'See if she has picked up any of her stuff?'

We all get up and follow Tasha down a short corridor and into a room. A brass double bed fills one corner while another wall holds a large dressing table dotted with lotions and potions. I wander towards it and pick up a small framed photo of Charlie. Tasha opens the door of a mahogany wardrobe. 'I think all of her clothes are here; it's very hard to tell, there's so many of them.'

I peep round another door on the far side of the room to find a small en-suite bathroom. Tasha and Holly follow me over.

'She's left her toothbrush and all her toiletries!' Tasha says. 'I don't think she can have come back to pick up anything.'

Just then my mobile rings. I leave Holly and Tasha in the bedroom while I wander out to the corridor to take the call.

'Is that Miss Colshannon?' asks a gentle voice.

'Yes, it is.'

'This is the vicar of St John's in Cambridge. I understand that you wish to talk to me?' Here we go, another vicar. It seems you can't swing a cat without hitting a vicar in Cambridge.

'Yes . . . ' And off I launch into my tale, but as soon as I utter the name Charlie Davidson the vicar interrupts me.

'Yes, I know Charlie and Emma and yes, they are getting married here on Saturday. Is there anything else I can help you with, Miss Colshannon?'

9

Holly can hardly contain her excitement as she scoots towards Tristan.

'This is marvellous, isn't it, Clemmie?' she calls over her shoulder.

I have to say things are certainly hotting up. 'Terrific!' I rejoin enthusiastically. 'The old horror must definitely be keeping poor Emma prisoner!'

'Imagine popping over to your folks for a spot of supper and won't-you-please-come-to-my-wedding-ing and then not being allowed to come home just because your father doesn't fancy your choice of groom.'

'He must be some kind of monster.'

'Oh, he is.'

'But how long can he keep her locked up for?'

'Probably until Saturday. That way the wedding is postponed. We simply must find her, Clemmie. That poor girl.'

'I know. She must have missed a few dress fittings as well.'

'But how on earth are we going to find her?'

'I don't know. Maybe tomorrow we should have a good look through the archives. See if any past stories about Sir Christopher highlight anything.'

We muse in silence on this for a moment. 'Are we seeing James tonight?' I ask after a minute.

'Yes! He's got loads of work on at the moment

and he's just put his flat on the market so he said he might be late.'

'He's selling his flat? So is he — '

'Moving in! I'm so excited, I'd have moved into his place but he used to live there with his ex so he thought it would be better for us if he moved in with me.'

'Bloody hell! Why didn't you tell me?'

'You're hardly renowned for your secret-keeping skills, Clemmie. I didn't tell you because I don't want our mother to know just yet. She'll start picking out a hat.'

'Actually, I think she's already done that.'

'Oh God,' groans Holly. 'I'll have to keep James away from her, she'll start making inappropriate comments.' As you might have guessed, our mother is not a creature of subtlety. She abhors subtlety. She says it's exhausting trying to figure out what anyone is trying to say. 'By the way, you can't mention anything about this case to James.'

'Why not?'

'He and I have a golden rule that we never talk about work.'

'Why not?'

'So neither he nor I can be accused of professional misconduct. Giving each other the inside track on something. It just wouldn't be right.'

★ ★ ★

We've only been back long enough to get ourselves some wine and park ourselves on the

136

sofa when there's the sudden noise of a key in the lock and we both instinctively turn our heads towards the door. James must be home.

Holly gets up just as he enters the room and for once my mother's description is not wrong. James is tall and broad with sandy blond hair and a beautiful pair of green eyes. He is gorgeous, there is no doubt about it, and certainly the nicest police officer I have ever had the misfortune to set eyes upon.

He dumps the box he's carrying by the door and then turns to me and smiles while extending a hand.

'God, Clemmie, it's so nice to meet you at last. Holly talks about you all the time.'

'Anything good?'

'No, nothing at all.' He grins at me while we shake hands and he then goes forward and kisses Holly. I like the way he clasps her to him and really kisses her. Not just a meagre peck on the cheek. It makes me think how much I would like someone to come home and kiss me like that. Seth was always in such a rush to change and go out again that he barely managed to say hello a lot of the time.

Holly pours him a glass of wine. 'I've got a story!' she says.

'Great! Is it a goody?'

'It will knock your socks off!'

'I'll look forward to it. Is there something amazing for supper?' he asks her.

Holly frowns. 'Actually, I haven't really thought about it.'

'I didn't think you would have so I thought I'd

take you both out to dinner.' I think I'm going to like James. He leans back into the sofa, pours us all another glass of wine and then asks me how Norman the seagull is getting on. A subject close to everyone's heart.

★   ★   ★

The next day Holly pulls me out of bed at the crack of dawn without any apologies as she is excited about her story. I really hope that one day I could get this much pleasure from a job. She presses a cup of tea into my hand and pleads with me to get dressed quickly. I haul on the obligatory clothes but find that the only footwear I have brought with me are a pair of cowboy boots that I was wearing under my jeans yesterday so I am forced to wear them with a skirt. I barely get a chance to clean my teeth before she drags me out of the flat.

'Clemmie, what on earth are you wearing on your feet?'

'Cowboy boots. I would have thought that was obvious.'

Holly looks absolutely appalled.

'They are all the rage in Cornwall. Sienna Miller was visiting last month and she was wearing a pair underneath her dress,' I say with as much dignity as I can muster, and all I can say about Sienna is that she might have done.

I've obviously managed to spin this story with a firm degree of conviction as Holly actually looks quite impressed. At least she doesn't make me take them off and wear a pair of her shoes.

When we get to the paper, we make our way down to the research library at the *Bristol Gazette*, which is basically a desk, a computer and a couple of microfiche readers. Holly pulls over another chair from a neighbouring desk and together we sit down.

I munch on the conciliatory bacon sandwich that she bought me en route. I couldn't eat it in the car because I was concentrating too much on bending in to the corners as Holly hurtled through the streets. 'So what are we looking for again?' I finish my bacon sarnie, professionally lick my fingers and then focus on the microfiche reader.

'Well, I'm going to search for information about Sir Christopher on the internet and I thought you could go through all the past stories that the paper has written about him.'

'That sounds very long-winded. Is there no super whizzy high techno thing we can use?'

'No, Clemmie,' says Holly patiently. 'There is no super whizzy high techno thing we can use apart from your brain. If we can call that super whizzy and high techno. Now, I'll just get you the reference microfiche pages from the computer and then you have to get the relevant page up on the reader, like this.' She demonstrates how to use the reader and then I get to work.

An hour and a half later, I have found absolutely zilch. Lots of stories about Sir Christopher McKellan's dazzling legal career but nothing that could be useful to us when we're trying to find his daughter. Of course, it would help no end to know what I am actually looking for.

'Holly.'

'Clemmie.'

'I have read an awful lot about Sir Christopher McKellan's numerous court appearances, his closing briefs and his statements to the press. So, just remind me. What are we actually looking for?'

Holly looks up briefly from the screen and leans back thoughtfully in her chair. 'Anything that might lead us to Emma.'

'And what would that be exactly?'

'Well, if you're right then Emma isn't with her father. So who would Sir Christopher trust enough to put her with?'

'Maybe she's just staying in a hotel somewhere.'

'With no one to guard her? Don't be silly, Clemmie!'

'Holly, all I have read about for the last hour and a half is his bloody court appearances and various cases. I can't see anything that might give us a clue as to Emma's whereabouts. Unless he's put her with one of the many people he's put away. Which seems kind of doubtful. Does he have any family? Sisters, cousins?'

'I'm looking for any relatives. His father was a high court judge so I've looked him up in *Who's Who* and Sir Christopher is an only child.'

'Aunts and uncles?'

'All dead as far as I can see. I can't find out if he's got any cousins.'

'But you'd have to be pretty close to them to

ask them to hold your only daughter hostage, wouldn't you? I mean, we don't know our cousins that well, do we?'

'Exactly. So while I haven't ruled that option out, I'm now looking for old friends, which isn't as easy because obviously they're not so well documented.'

With renewed enthusiasm I start my search again. The microfiche is starting to make my eyes hurt so I have to read each story about three times before I can make any sense out of them.

'Holly?'

'Hmmm?'

'Do you think people he was at university with might count as old friends?'

'Have you found someone?'

'Well, this article doesn't say they were friends but it mentions that Sir Christopher McKellan was at Cambridge with the now MP for Bristol, John Montague. I suppose they thought it was a little bit of throwaway trivia.'

'Hmm. They might never have even met each other, let alone be bosom buddies. It's hardly a strong lead.'

Something starts to stir slightly in my head. Something I can't quite put my finger on.

'Holly,' I say suddenly. 'Could you find me a picture of this John Montague?'

She shrugs. 'I suppose.'

I get up and walk around to her computer while she taps away. A couple of minutes later she pulls up a piece on John Montague complete with a picture.

'That's him!' I say in high excitement,

pointing at the screen.

'Yes, I know. It says so underneath. John Montague, MP for — '

'No, I mean I saw him. At Sir Christopher's house.'

'What? He was there?'

'Sort of,' I say, still transfixed by the very serious-looking older man before me. Attractive looking in a wrinkly kind of way. 'I saw some photos while I was there. In one of them Emma was standing between two men — her father and this man.'

'Are you sure?'

'Completely. I thought he looked familiar at the time. Must have seen him on the news or something.'

'So they are friends.'

'Of course, why else would there be a photo of him in the house?'

'God, that's been kept quiet. I can't believe it.'

'Well, I suppose it's like you and James. It would look awfully unprofessional if they were seen to know each other. People might suppose they're scratching each other's back.'

'James and I are hardly in the same league as the MP for Bristol and one of the top barristers in the country.'

'So no wonder they can't be seen to have a link. Do you think he would have put Emma with him?'

Holly leans back in her chair. 'I don't know but it's our strongest lead so far.'

'He would be the perfect choice simply because

no one knows they even know each other.'

'I suppose it would keep Emma close to her father in Bristol too, so he could keep an eye on her.' Holly starts to look more excited.

'So what do we do now?'

'We could go and have a scout around his house, see if we can pick up any clues.'

I look at her suspiciously. This has a slight overtone of the Sir Christopher McKellan debacle to me.

'Now, don't look like that, Clemmie. We'll sit outside his house or something.' It's the 'or something' I don't like.

'What happens if she really is there?'

'Then we'll spring her!'

'Spring her?' I ask doubtfully, wishing Holly wouldn't lapse into TV crime speak because I have no idea what she is talking about.

'You know, free her!' Holly is already shrugging on her coat and picking up her bag.

'How do you know where this John Montague lives?'

'Clemmie, he's the MP for Bristol. Everyone knows where he lives.'

'What's he like? Do you think he would hide Emma away?'

'He's very reserved and serious. Whenever I've had to interview him he's always been really courteous. But you don't know how close he and Sir Christopher are, they might go back a long way. We need to go and check it out. I'll see if Vince is around.'

'Vince? You're bringing Vince?' I ask disbelievingly.

'He's the best we've got! Wait for me

downstairs!' she shouts over her shoulder as she disappears Vince-wards. Vince is a photographer on the paper and is simply the most flamboyantly gay man I have ever met. There would be absolutely no chance of you walking away from him thinking, 'He's slightly effeminate. I wonder if he's . . . ' because it is emblazoned across his forehead in pink neon lights.

I pick up my stuff and start wandering towards the lifts. Holly is certainly a woman of action. No dithering about the right thing to do for her. Well, as long as I'm not sent in to do the dirty work I don't mind.

Holly joins me, panting slightly, after about ten minutes. 'Vince is just finishing another job so we're meeting him there.'

She leads the way out to Tristan. 'It's quite lucky Vince is meeting us there. We wouldn't have all been able to get into Tristan,' I comment.

'Yes we would! You could have gone in the back.'

Over my dead body.

★ ★ ★

Fifteen minutes later finds us at a very nice address overlooking the Bristol downs. Holly pulls into the kerb on the opposite side of the road and we stare at the beautiful old house and tasteful garden. A large sycamore tree, already wheedling baby helicopter seeds, sits in one corner swaying gently, while numerous shrubs line the old, low brick walls that encompass the house. All very unlike our own wilderness of a garden which has already eaten up several barbecues, shoes and a paddling pool.

'Golly, at least Emma gets to be held hostage in the lap of luxury,' I say. 'So what do we do now? Do we just wait to see if she comes out?'

'She's not going to come out, Clemmie!' says Holly scornfully. 'She's probably locked in or there's a couple of people watching her.'

'Of course, John Montague will be there.'

'I don't think so because I called John Montague's office before we left and asked for him. I was told he was in a meeting about environmental controls for most of the day.'

'That might just mean he's got his feet up watching the football.'

'Clemmie, not everyone has the same mindset as you. MPs do work, you know. So he's not home but he's probably got the housekeeper watching her or something. She's probably locked in one of those bedrooms.' I take a look skyward to one of the distant rooms at the top of the house.

'Poor Emma,' I murmur.

'I thought Vince could take a few photos and we could do a recce.'

She's doing it again. 'A recce?'

'A reconnaissance, Clemmie. God, you should get out more.'

'So should you and stop watching the TV. Well, I might just stay in the car, have a little nap and leave you to it.'

Holly looks at me in horror. 'And miss all the

fun? Without you we would never have found Emma.'

'If she's here,' I murmur, but Holly chooses to ignore me.

'You surely want to share in the glory! They'll probably invite us to the wedding and everything! Emma might even want us to be bridesmaids.'

I look at her with a mixture of fascination and horror. 'Are you sure we're sisters? I'm becoming more and more convinced that they mixed me up at the hospital. I probably belong to some nice, sane family.'

'Come on!' She drags me out of the car, locks the doors and then does a comical zigzag run as though she's dodging bullets over to the cover of the cars on the opposite side of the road about twenty metres from the house.

'What are you doing?' I ask when I reach her ducked behind an old Renault.

'Not being seen,' she whispers.

'Well, you're incredibly conspicuous for someone not being seen.'

'You stay here. I'm going to look through the windows to see how many people are guarding her.'

'Er, okay. You do that.'

I lean against the Renault and have a look up and down the road. It's relatively quiet, just a few cars passing now and then, the drivers of which look on in amazement at the mad-looking blonde (the other one, not me) creeping about. They've probably called the police by now. A lilac Beetle pulls in a few cars away and a broad smile crosses my face. It's Vince. I love this man.

He waves madly out of the window at me, shouting 'Coo-ee!', and then launches himself out of the front seat. He is dressed in black — distressed jeans with a black slashed T-shirt and a woolly hat. 'Ducks, ducks! How are you? It's fabulous to see you! You look well,' he calls as he minces down the pavement, camera in hand.

'I'm fine! No better for my little holiday here, but fine.'

'What has the mad cow got you doing now? Where is she anyway?'

I gesture towards the house. 'Looking through windows. I think James will be here any minute to arrest her.'

'Now he is a gorgeous man. Is he still straight?'

'Yes, I think so,' I grin.

'Hope springs eternal. He might be in denial.'

'No, I think he's definitely straight.'

'And speaking of gorgeous men, how is that divine brother of yours?'

'Which one? Barney?'

'That's him.'

'In a tizzy over some girl.'

'What a waste,' he murmurs.

Holly comes galloping towards us and screeches to a halt. 'She's in there, she's in there! I've just seen her!' she gabbles in high excitement.

'Emma?' I question disbelievingly. 'You've seen Emma?' A little fizzle of excitement starts up inside me. God, I'm starting to see why Holly loves her job so much. 'You mean that she's actually here?'

'Yep, I've just seen her drinking a cup of coffee in the kitchen. Hello Vince. I'm going to call Charlie and tell him where we all are. I'm sure he'll want to free her himself. Boy is she going to be pleased to see us! I want a picture of them as they're reunited!'

She turns her back on us while she dials Charlie's number into her mobile and Vince and I make faces at each other. I certainly hope she knows what she's doing.

'What's she going to do?' I whisper to Vince. 'Barge in there as though we're Starsky and Hutch? We don't know who's home.'

'Would you be the blond one or the gorgeous, dark curly haired one? Ooh, bags be Huggy Bear.'

'Actually, I've always thought I would be the dark one because, you know, I'm convinced that — '

'Clemmie! Vince!' Holly makes us jump. 'What are you two talking about? Really! We have better things to be thinking about. Charlie is coming straight down.'

'How are you going to reunite them if she has ten people guarding her?' I ask. Small points always seem to escape Holly.

'Actually I thought I might just go and ring the bell and say I'm collecting money for charity or something and see if I can get a look at her captors. Perhaps see how many there are. Then I thought we'd be better placed to make some sort of plan. We can always call the police to free her!'

Holly looks absolutely thrilled at the prospect of this.

I look at her doubtfully. 'Just as long as I'm not ringing any more bells.'

'And we must have pictures of their wedding, Vince. It's on Saturday, are you booked out on a job?'

Vince shakes his head.

'Great. God, I can't wait to see her face. I'm going to ring the bell.'

'Who are you going to say you are?'

'I'm going to say that I'm collecting money for charity.'

'But you haven't got a collecting tin,' I point out helpfully. Do you see what I mean about her? The details are always a bit sketchy.

'Well then, I'll say I'm conducting a survey,' Holly waves her notepad at me. She tries to walk off calmly towards the house. Vince and I watch her.

'I can't believe Emma's there,' I murmur.

'God, it's a hell of a story for Holly.'

We watch Holly as she saunters up the front path and rings the bell. A few minutes later the door opens. Vince and I squint towards it. Bloody hell. That looks like . . .

'Emma. That's Emma,' says Vince suddenly and scuttles towards her.

It takes a few seconds for my befuddled brain to catch up, and then a few more for me to catch up with Holly and Vince who are both now staring in wonderment at Emma on the doorstep who, I have to say, looks equally surprised to see them.

They might well be looking with some surprise at her because she looks a shadow of her former self. There are no designer labels in sight, just some tracksuit bottoms and a puffa waistcoat in various shades of taupe and navy blue. Her brown hair is drawn starkly back into a ponytail and she's wearing no make-up. I hope she's got time to change if Holly doesn't keep her gassing on the doorstep.

'I can't believe it, Emma,' Holly is saying. 'You could actually have walked out of here. The door was open all this time. Are you all right? Is there someone watching you?' she asks in a whisper.

'Er, no. I'm here by myself. What on earth are you doing here, Holly? How did you find me?'

'Oohhh, a little bit of sleuthing, Emma. Nothing special,' says Holly with a modest smile. 'Plenty of time to thank me for it later. But now I really think you should put some lippy on.' Holly frowns and looks more closely at Emma. I hope she's going to suggest some foundation too. The girl doesn't look like she's slept in months and she doesn't want to greet the love of her life looking like that. 'Maybe brush your hair too.'

'Why?'

'You have a surprise visitor coming!' announces Holly, grinning from ear to ear.

'Who?'

'Need you ask? Did you really think that your colleagues from the *Gazette* would leave you high and dry! Why, Charlie of course!'

Even I smile at this point. Bless her. Emma looks like she's about to faint, she's that thrilled.

'Charlie?' she whispers. 'He's coming here?'

Holly nods and grins again.

Emma looks at us as though in a trance but the flash of Vince's camera brings her to life. She retreats into the hall and sinks down on to a convenient chair.

'God, Holly. What have you done?' she whispers. Holly frowns. Not quite the reaction we were looking for. A little more gratefulness wouldn't go amiss. Just wait until I tell her what I had to go through with her father. 'You don't know who he is, do you?' she whispers.

'Of course we do! He's your fiancé, the man you're going to marry on Saturday. Charlie Davidson.'

She looks up at us all wide-eyed. I feel quite scared.

'No, Holly, he's not. He is the man I thought I was going to marry but his name isn't Charlie Davidson. It's Martin Connelly.'

Now that name rings a bell. Where have I heard it?

Holly sits down suddenly too on an adjacent chair. 'Martin Connelly?' she queries.

'The man my father put away. Seven years ago.'

10

'Martin Connelly?' repeats Holly, sounding quite weak herself. Of course, this is the case I was reading about this morning. The infamous one that seemed to leave half of Bristol in uproar.

We all stare at each other for a minute. Which is all very nice but I'm not quite sure what all the fainty stuff is about. Of course the fact that her father has imprisoned her fiancé is rather unfortunate but not insurmountable.

'So that's a bit of a coincidence, isn't it?' I eventually say timidly to Emma. 'That you were going to marry the same man your father put away all those years ago?'

This seems to bring Emma back to life. 'Look, I don't know who you are,' she snarls. I take an involuntary step backwards and nearly fall over an umbrella stand. Maybe now is not the appropriate time to remind her that we have actually met on a couple of occasions. 'But you clearly don't understand what's going on.'

Fair enough. I'll give her that.

'It's no *coincidence* that Martin Connelly is marrying me. He did it to get his own back on my father. He's some sort of psychopath.'

Christ, that's a bit strong, isn't it? I wonder if it's worth risking another question. I'm so confused, I think I might have to. I stick my neck out from the comfort of my umbrella stand and ask timidly, 'Er, how do you know that?'

'I would imagine that his name change is a small clue, and the fact that he has lied to me since the day we met.'

Ah.

Emma looks swiftly over to Holly, who is still in shock. 'How long have we got?' she snaps.

'S . . . sorry?'

'When did you call him?'

'About five minutes ago.' Holly looks from me to Vince for confirmation. I haven't got a clue and shrug helplessly. Timings have never really been my thing. 'Look, Emma, I'm so, so sorry. Charlie came to the paper and begged us to help him. He said your father was stopping the marriage, he said — '

'I haven't got long.' She looks furiously from one to other of us. 'Thanks a *lot*, Holly,' she adds vehemently before disappearing up the stairs.

Vince and I make agonised oh-shit faces at each other. This is actually quite bad. Very bad indeed.

'Em, Holly?' I venture to the figure who now has her head in her hands and is busy murmuring 'Oh my God, oh my God . . . ' over and over to herself.

She looks up dazedly. 'What?'

'Did Charlie say he was coming straight down here?' I look nervously over one shoulder.

'Yes, he is.'

'And, er, how long will that take?'

Holly looks over to Vince for some sort of confirmation. I just wish they would hurry up and do those sums. My rather overdramatic imagination keeps picturing Charlie arriving

153

with a manic glint in his eye and an axe in his hand. He has probably learned all sorts of useful stuff in prison, besides the obligatory basket weaving, like the best way to dismember a body. Really useful.

'About fifteen minutes, I think. Probably.'

'Maybe less,' puts in Vince.

I look anxiously at my watch. We probably only have a few minutes. I sincerely hope that Emma isn't bothering to fold anything.

'Do you remember Charlie's hands?' I whisper. 'I remember he had really large hands . . . ' My thoughts are interrupted by Emma joining us back downstairs, dragging an overnight bag. Luckily she seems alive to the possibility of Charlie's imminent arrival.

Holly gets up from her prayer position and looks at her apprehensively.

'Have you a car?' Emma asks sharply. We all nod. 'Then let's go.'

We rush out of the house, slamming the door behind us and, like a little group of ants, scurry across the front lawn.

'Where's your car?' Holly asks Emma. She's certainly a daredevil asking so many questions.

'At the flat. I haven't dared use it in case he spotted it.' Emma shoots her another killer glare as we cross the road but Holly is too busy keeping to her green cross code to notice. She fishes the keys to Tristan out of her pocket as she runs.

'Holly!' yells Vince from the door of his car. 'Call me as soon as you can!'

'Don't tell Joe!' she yells back, making a

throat-cutting gesture, but whether that's meant for Vince or what might happen to Holly I don't know. Vince gives the thumbs-up sign and gets into his Beetle with a certain degree of haste considering Charlie wouldn't have a clue who he is.

And then the musketeers are down to three.

'In the back, Clemmie!' says Holly.

'Eh?'

'GET IN THE BACK!' she roars. Has she ever been in the back? I have trouble getting my handbag in there, let alone my arse and the various bits that come with it. In fact it's actually little more than a ledge. Still, she's under a lot of stress so I do as I am bid and pile myself in and lie across the shelf. Emma and Holly get in after me and we all pray that Tristan will start and not pull one of his prima donna sulks on us. In fact Holly seems to be chanting some sort of mantra.

Tristan starts first time and I swear an eternal pledge of allegiance to him. Holly thrusts him into first gear and we fly out of the parking space, screech around the corner, all without any signals on our part and plenty by other motorists, and start winging towards Clifton as fast as Tristan will go.

We all sit in silence for a few minutes as Holly concentrates on lane-hopping and getting us as far away from Charlie as possible. After a few minutes I risk a look at Emma. She is staring out of the window, anxiously biting a thumbnail and, although I can't quite see her eyes, now and then a hand reaches up as though to brush away tears.

Holly must have clocked the same thing

because she asks timidly, 'Can we take you to your father?'

'No, he'll look for me there. God, Holly,' she snarls suddenly, 'couldn't you have minded your own bloody business for once? You had to come and poke your nose in. Everything is just a story for you, isn't it?'

'No, Emma, it wasn't like that,' Holly protests frantically. 'Well, not quite like that. I really did want you and Charlie, I mean Martin, to get back together. I thought your father was trying to stop you from marrying him.'

There is a heavy silence in the car. I wonder if I should be adding anything to the discussion and then decide against it. They can't actually forget I'm here because every time they address each other they have to look over my knee which is poking through the gap between their seats, but I can still be very, very quiet.

Holly suddenly decides on a destination because, to the furious sound of horns hooting, she makes a huge U-turn near the zoo and starts heading in the opposite direction.

'Emma, we could have stayed if you didn't want to leave,' pipes up Holly, trying, I daresay, to be helpful. 'There were four of us. He wouldn't have dared try anything.' Has she completely lost leave of all of her senses? I'm completely for the running scared scenario. I like the idea of cars being involved.

'I'm not scared of him,' spits out Emma. No? Well, I am. God, it's all about her, isn't it?

'We could have brazened it out. What was he going to do?' Er, kill us all, Holly? And that's

156

probably the best case scenario.

'I COULDN'T SEE HIM BECAUSE I'M PREGNANT, YOU SILLY COW!' bellows Emma.

I'm glad she pitches it thus because it filters through a bit quicker to my befuddled brain. We all look down to her stomach. Well, Holly does but I have to do a pretty amazing neck twist just to get it in sight. It is a little swollen. I personally would have put that down to one too many cream buns but maybe Charlie wouldn't. Oh my God. Could this get any worse?

Another significant silence descends which is just as well because the conversation hasn't been going too great so far. It is actually very welcome for me as I try to make sense of all this. So Emma was due to marry this Charlie character. Right, my brain is fine with it up to here. Then she finds out that he is actually Martin. The same man her father put away in that case I was reading about on the microfiche this morning. Was it this morning? It seems an awfully long time ago. Anyway, the case created quite a bit of controversy here in Bristol because a lot of people believed Martin shouldn't have been sent to prison. There were protests outside the courthouse and Sir Christopher was sent a lot of hate mail over it. Martin was fifteen years old then, very bright and destined for Oxbridge and for great things. He had been taking ecstasy. A girlfriend of his wanted to take some too so he sold her one of his tabs. She died and he was convicted of manslaughter. From what I could gather he was not a supplier of the drug but just happened to sell one of his own supply on. Sir Christopher had gone for the manslaughter charge while others were urging for it to be dropped, and he had got the maximum sentence too. The fact that Martin had actually sold one of his own stash seemed to be the icing on the cake for Sir Christopher because, as he explained, had he not sold it on then Martin would be dead rather than the girlfriend. The fact that she had paid for it rather than been given it seemed peculiarly pertinent too.

The newspapers seemed split on whether Martin should be punished or not. Some said that if he took the drug and sold the drug then he should take the penalty for it. Others said that thousands and thousands of people have done the same thing, Martin was not an official supplier and therefore should not be made a scapegoat. Sir Christopher McKellan believed an example needed to be set. And in front of me sits his daughter who, it would seem, is paying dearly for this example, because Martin Connelly must be one very severely pissed off bunny.

Holly pulls up quietly and soberly in front of a building.

'Where are we?' I ask from my eyrie.

'James's flat. I have a key. It would only be a matter of time before Charlie found us at my flat.'

After I have been levered out, our little group makes its way to James's building. Holly uses a key to let us in the front door, we go up two flights of smart stone stairs and then in a second door to a spacious, airy apartment. There are cardboard boxes everywhere because James is, of course, moving in with Holly, but a huge leather sofa with accompanying TV still sits in the middle of the room and Emma and I make our way over to it and flop down.

'Tea?' Holly asks after a moment.

'Wine?' I'm in need of something slightly stronger.

She nods and then makes her way over to the kitchen, leaving me with Emma's slightly hostile presence.

I wondered briefly whether 'Thought of any names yet?' might be a good opening gambit. I would also enjoy a tsk-men-are-crap chat but decide Emma isn't the girl to have it with because Seth, although extremely crap, would actually come out looking pretty good next to Charlie. I let the silence continue instead and take the opportunity to look at Emma properly. She looks a little shaken but still manages to exude this God-given certainty that she is simply the best thing to have walked on this planet.

Holly returns holding three glasses. She's even managed to find some ice. She gestures her head towards me to take the front glass and then hands one of the others to Emma.

'I've added some water to make a spritzer for you, Emma. You know, because of the . . . '

Her words trail off at the extremely withering look that Emma deigns to give her. Of course, Emma is pregnant. This pregnancy malarkey is already not scoring very high on my fun-for-Clemmie scale. I take full advantage of my baby-free state and start swilling back the booze.

Emma takes her drink and looks determinedly out of the window while Holly sits down on a nearby cardboard box. I sincerely hope that it doesn't collapse on her because I will be forced to laugh and Emma hates me enough already.

'So, Emma,' says Holly hesitantly, probably hoping she's not going to be shouted at again. 'Do you think you could possibly tell us the whole story?'

Yes, this silence, although highly desirable not so long ago, is now starting to play on my nerves.

Emma takes a small sip of her drink and then looks at us both. 'Very well,' she says calmly. 'I met Ch . . . Martin about six months ago at a party . . .'

'In London,' Holly finishes off for her.

'Shhh,' I say, not willing to stop Emma now that she's got started.

'Yes, in London. Did he tell you that?' We both nod. 'Well, he was telling the truth at that point. God knows how he managed to orchestrate it, he must have been monitoring my movements for months. Anyway, we started to chat and then he asked me out the following week. I was completely flattered, I suppose. I mean, you've met him, he's really nice looking and very charming. Perhaps I should have suspected something, but why on earth would I?'

Holly and I shake our heads madly, which seems to be the appropriate response.

'We started to see each other more and more often, always in Cambridge though. He never came down here to Bristol, I suppose for fear of meeting my father again.'

'You didn't know what he looked like?' I ask suddenly. 'I mean from the case?'

'He was a minor at the time so the papers weren't allowed to print pictures of him. Daddy never involved me in his work, he always tried to protect me from it. I was at school anyway and to me it was just another of Daddy's cases, I scarcely paid it any attention. After Charlie and I had been seeing each other for a while, I started to fall in love with him.' Tears well up in her eyes and all at once I feel incredibly sorry for her. 'And he did a very good job of making me think he was in love with me too.'

She pauses for a second and has another sip of her drink. I finished mine ages ago but no matter, the story is engrossing.

'He asked me to marry him which did take me by surprise because it was so early on but he said he simply couldn't wait. Of course, then I wanted him to meet my father. I don't have much family — '

'Yes, we know,' says Holly. 'In fact, that's what made it so easy to . . . ' Her words trail off and she shifts uncomfortably on her box. 'Sorry. Go on, Emma.'

'He said he didn't want to meet my father. Daddy has always been a bit of a snob where my boyfriends are concerned.' Although we try our level best not to, neither Holly nor I can stop our eyebrows raising at this point. I try not to look at Holly and quietly boggle into my glass. Daddy has always been a bit of a snob? Does Emma think she's an amazing free-thinking socialist? She continues, oblivious to our eyebrows, even though she doesn't possess any herself, ' . . . and Charlie, I mean Martin, convinced me that it would be a really bad idea. He said that Daddy would tell me that he wasn't worth marrying and that we should have a private ceremony, just the two of us, and then we could go straight down after the wedding and announce it to him. That way he couldn't do anything about it. Of course, I was so blind with love that I agreed, and it seemed so wonderfully romantic. I can't tell you how exciting it was having this huge, great secret. I would listen to the conversations at work, the girls talking about their love lives, and I would think to myself that I am marrying this gorgeous hunk of a man and wouldn't they all fall off their chairs in shock if they knew.'

A tear falls from her eye and lands on her tracksuit bottoms, where she rubs at it absently with her thumb.

'But you told Tasha, your flatmate?' I say encouragingly.

She takes a deep breath and manages to carry on, albeit in a shaky voice. 'Yes, I told Tasha. I had to share it with someone because I was so excited and I knew that I could trust her. I actually told no one else. I hope she isn't too worried.' I look nervously at Holly. She probably is now that we've put the wind up her. 'I just couldn't face phoning her to tell her the truth. I felt so ashamed.'

'So you were getting married?' Holly prompts gently.

'Yes, and as the wedding got closer I became more and more nervous about doing this behind

Daddy's back. I tried to talk to Charlie about it a couple of times but he just looked at me really reproachfully and said something about how we had made an agreement so I dropped it. But then I found out I was pregnant.'

'But how?' I interrupt. 'I mean, I know how but was it deliberate?' I colour slightly.

'No, I was on the pill but I'd had an ear infection. The doctor gave me antibiotics and told me to take extra precautions but I just didn't believe it would happen to me.' Now, I wonder how many times those words have been uttered. 'Maybe subconsciously I wanted to get pregnant. I don't know. But I was still having periods because I was still on the pill so I simply didn't realise. Then I started to put on weight and felt really tired so I went to the doctor again last week. I suppose I panicked once I knew but I simply didn't know what to do. I didn't tell Charlie, I mean Martin. It all got too big for me and so I went straight round to Daddy and told him everything. It was quite a relief.'

'How did he react?' I ask nervously.

'Of course he was angry at first, but he's not a bad father and finally after all the ranting he said as long as I was happy he was, and did I have a picture of the lucky chap? Daddy knew immediately who he was. I remember he went an almost deathly white and wouldn't speak for a long time.'

'Charlie, I mean Martin, told us that he had asked your father for permission to marry you and your father had refused him.'

Emma gives me a withering look. 'Obviously

my father hasn't set eyes on him since the court case. That didn't stop him from recognising him instantly from the photo though. After all, he did stare at his face for eight hours a day in a courtroom for four months.' I wonder what her father will do if he sets eyes on me again. I dread to think what he must think of me.

'God, what an awful shock for you.'

'I thought it must be coincidence at first. I thought we must simply have met each other at the party and fallen in love and that it was awfully unlucky. Of course, when I started to think about it I could see that he knew exactly who my father was. He had lied about his whole life. He told me he had lived all his life in Cambridge and was a teacher. There's no way a convicted felon can be a teacher. Daddy said he had a really rough time in prison and he regularly received hate mail from him. Martin absolutely despises Daddy, he said in his letters that he ruined his whole life. He missed out on his youth for the sake of one ecstasy tablet which he took alongside thousands of others and yet he seemed to pay for them all. What better way to get back at the man who ruined your life than by ruining the life of his beloved daughter?' More tears run down her face and I hastily fish about for a tissue. I hand over a manky old one that's been buried at the bottom of my handbag. She's about to object but then takes it anyway.

I look over at Holly. I feel unspeakably dreadful.

'So your father hid you away?' Holly asks quietly.

'My father was petrified that Martin was going to do something awful. He wouldn't let me go back to work or to my flat. He called John Montague immediately and I went to stay there. Luckily I hadn't told Martin about John and how close we are to him. My father went to the police but didn't tell them I'm pregnant. The police said they couldn't do anything because Martin hasn't done anything officially wrong, he's just asked a girl to marry him. But you see, if Martin notices I'm pregnant, bearing in mind this is the man I've slept with for the last six months and he knows my body pretty well, then he will never let me go. Do you understand me? He will never leave me in peace if he knows I'm carrying his child. And can you imagine how he would laugh? How I have played into his hands? I mean a divorce would have happened, but a child as well? My God! What a coup for him! An everlasting memory for my father right in front of his eyes.'

'How far gone are you?' Holly asks.

'Fifteen weeks now.'

'You don't look that pregnant,' I say, trying to comfort her. 'I mean, if he did catch sight of you.'

'I simply cannot take that risk. I just can't. Besides, I don't want to see him.' Her voice rises slightly with the emotion. 'I don't want to see his gloating, triumphant face. It would be like some sort of little victory ceremony for him.'

'But he must know that his game is up?' asks Holly in puzzlement. 'He must know that you have somehow found out who he is? Why else is

165

he trying to find you?'

Emma places her glass on the floor and then looks at her hands. 'I don't know,' she says simply. 'Maybe he wants to gloat; after all, we did snatch away his near-perfect revenge just as he was about to pull it off. Maybe he's confused and wants to find out why his carefully laid plans have gone wrong. Or even worse, maybe he has found out that I'm pregnant.'

'But how could he do that?'

'Maybe the doctor's surgery has called about something, maybe he's noticed I now hate the smell of coffee, maybe . . . maybe a lot of things.' She is starting to get anxious; the once still hands are pawing at her knees. 'If he looks back at our last few months together then maybe he can piece something together. I just don't want to be around to see him.'

'But you can't stay hidden for ever.'

'My father wants to move me far away. He knows some people and he's making arrangements.'

'And you've decided to keep the baby?' Holly asks gently.

Emma jerks her head up and looks at us both square in the eye. 'Yes,' she says defiantly. 'I've decided to keep the baby.'

'I'm so sorry, Emma, about letting Charlie know you were at John Montague's house.'

'My father hasn't even let me return to my flat to collect any clothes, so I am stuck wearing these . . . ' She brushes contemptuously at her tracksuit bottoms. 'John's housekeeper had to lend these things to me. Can you imagine? His

166

housekeeper.' Hmm. Sympathy is st-ar-ting to evaporate. 'On top of the fact I am pregnant by someone who just wanted to get back at my father . . . ' Her eyes fill with tears and her voice chokes a little. Okay, sympathy is coming back. 'Besides, if you managed to find me then it was just a matter of time before he did too.'

Holly takes this insult squarely on the chin and makes head motions at me to follow her. We decamp to a corner of the room.

'We have to help her,' whispers Holly.

'I know. I suppose she could stay here. Would James let her?'

'James is going to kill me.'

'Is that a no?'

'But we have to look after her until her father can move her to those people.'

'I know, it is our fault she's lost her little hidey hole.'

'We must not cock up on this,' says Holly firmly.

'The Colshannon girls may cock up a lot of things but I vow that we will not cock up this,' I say firmly.

And with this small promise, we return to Emma and the wine bottle.

11

James is a little bit more than cross. In fact, I don't think I would be exaggerating if I say that James pretty much hits the roof several times and then goes on to hit the roof of the flat above. I stand in the corner of Holly's flat later that day, quite hoping that my part in this won't be over-dramatised or even mentioned at all.

'How can you be so bloody irresponsible?' he roars. 'Whenever you mentioned Emma, I told you to leave it. Couldn't you take a gentle hint?'

'Well, you should have told me what was actually going on,' says Holly defensively.

'Holly, I COULDN'T tell you what was actually going on because, believe it or not, some parts of police work are CONFIDENTIAL. Not to mention the added complication that you actually know Emma McKellan and you're a reporter. I had no idea you were doing a story on the poor girl.'

'Well, maybe the police should have done something about Martin Connelly.'

'What could we do? Arrest him for asking a girl to marry him? We had to wait for him to commit an offence. You should have done your research more thoroughly. Instead you took your information from a convicted felon and Emma's flatmate.'

'Clemmie went to see Sir Christopher McKellan too,' adds Holly sulkily. James looks over in my direction. I'm hoping he might mistake me for a pot plant or something. Does she have to involve me? Does she?

'You sent Clemmie to see Sir Christopher? Oh my God, Holly, you involved your sister in all this?'

Atta boy. That's the attitude.

'I couldn't have gone to see him, he knows who I am.'

'And would probably have explained the situation to you. Why did you automatically assume he was the villain in all this? Didn't it occur to you that Emma had gone to a great deal of trouble not to be found? And that if she really wanted to marry this man then she wouldn't just lie down and let her father lock her away? She had defied him thus far. There are so many questions that simply didn't occur to you.'

'I needed a story,' says Holly sulkily.

'You WHAT? Are you saying you didn't care what the actual facts were? Poor Emma McKellan has been through hell and all you care about is your story?'

I don't think Holly quite meant it that way. She probably meant to say that her need for a story temporarily blinded her to a couple of pertinent facts. I push myself a little harder into my corner while James continues.

'My God! I thought you out of everyone had some semblance of decency but this is the lowest I have ever seen you stoop. And now I've got to explain not only to Sir Christopher but also to my chief how my girlfriend has managed to stir up such trouble.'

Rather him than me. Holly says timidly, and rather hopefully considering the last few words exchanged, 'So the police are getting involved now?'

'NO!' roars James. 'Martin Connelly still hasn't done anything wrong, whereas you have. I'm having to get involved because since your little visit to Sir Christopher McKellan's house this afternoon, he is threatening to charge you with breaking and entering, which I'm not completely sure I want to dissuade him from.' Holly carefully studies her shoes. 'You'd better get back to Emma. I'll discuss with Sir Christopher what we can do to help and then come over later.' He strides from the room and I venture from my corner.

We both sit down heavily on the sofa. I feel like I've been through a mangle, so I shouldn't imagine Holly is feeling too hot either. I remember how furious I was with Seth when he interfered with my job. But while Holly never intended to do anything to harm James's career, Seth was perfectly happy to scupper mine.

'He is pretty mad, huh?' I eventually say.

Holly nods.

'But he will come round, won't he? You just need to explain that you thought you were helping Emma.'

'I'll try,' she says weakly.

'What are we going to do?' I ask, because it suddenly strikes me that despite the intervention of James and Sir Christopher, Emma is still our responsibility. Morally at least. 'Could Emma stay at James's flat for a while?'

'Martin only needs to follow us there one day and we're sunk.'

I shiver involuntarily at this. 'You think he'll be watching us?'

'Well, it won't take much for him to find out where I live. I wonder how long it will take Sir Christopher to make arrangements to get Emma away from here.'

'I suppose we had better get back to her.'

We both get up and while Holly raids her fridge, which was our main reason for coming back here, I peruse the contents of her hall cupboard-cum-cloakroom. I find a very fetching orange bobble hat and a suede jacket with a fringe that Holly must have bought when she was going through a phase. I peer more closely at it. A phase of what I simply do not know.

'You're not honestly wearing that, are you?' says Holly as I return to the kitchen.

'Well, you apparently bought it at some point.'

'It was for a fancy dress party,' says Holly, colouring slightly.

'Oh really. And what did you go as? Someone hopelessly out of fashion?'

'I don't think you can talk. I went as a cowgirl and I didn't wear an orange bobble hat with it.'

'I'm in disguise.'

'He'll spot you a mile off.'

'Nonsense, he's looking for girl-about-town Clemmie.'

'Whereas this is away-with-the-fairies Clemmie?'

'Exactly.'

* ★ ★

I spend the entire journey to James's flat facing
the wrong way in the car, bum in the air, peering
anxiously out of Tristan's back window in case
we're being followed.

'What on earth will we do if I see him
following us?' I say to Holly nervously.

'We just won't go to James's flat. We'll go to
the nearest police station or something.'

'What happens if Tristan breaks down en
route?'

'He won't! He always knows when the chips
are down.'

Funnily enough, I am not reassured by her
words and am very pleased when we reach
James's flat intact and without any nasty
incidents with psychopaths.

'I'm not sure I can do this every day,' I gasp as
we scurry inside. Emma's head peeps around the
doorway of the sitting room.

'We've brought supplies!' Holly says with
probably more cheerfulness than she is feeling.
'I've spoken to James and he's going over to
see your father and they'll decide what we do
next.'

'We wouldn't have to do anything if you had
minded your own business.' Emma looks at us
stonily. Ah. Forgive and forget obviously isn't
very high up on her code of ethics. 'I suppose
someone will let John know?'

'John?' I question.

'John Montague, who I was staying with.' Of
course. The MP.

'Don't worry, James will tell him,' says Holly reassuringly.

'He'll be worried if he finds I'm gone when he gets back. I would have called him but I've left my mobile behind and the phone line is dead.'

'The phone line is dead?' I squeak, my hand involuntarily going to my throat. Has Martin cut them? Is he waiting outside?

'James had them disconnected because he's moving, Clemmie,' says Holly, making eyes at me.

Of course. Mustn't get hysterical. Must be thankful my mother isn't here as well.

Emma gives me a look of sheer contempt and stalks off back to the sofa. She really has the most charming manner. Holly and I busy ourselves in the kitchen making cheese on toast, and have a swift gin and tonic which we drink secretly in order not to make Emma too jealous. We all eat our supper while watching an episode of *Changing Rooms* and then James scares us by letting himself in with his key.

'It's only me,' he calls through to us. We all sit up, anxious for news.

He looks considerably calmer than he did a couple of hours ago. He smiles at Emma. 'Hello Emma. We have met before at one of the paper's bashes. I'm sorry about this business. I've been to see your father and we've decided on the best thing for you to do.'

'What's that?' Emma asks.

'You're going to Cornwall.'

'I can't go there! Martin knows that we have a house in Cornwall.'

'You're not going there, you're going back with Holly and Clemmie.'

'Back with Holly and Clemmie?' Emma makes it sound as though she's being asked to bed up with the Kray twins. I'm not too thrilled about it either.

'But we met Martin Connelly outside Emma's house in Cornwall. He must know we live down there,' I object, purely on practical grounds, you understand.

'Holly said she was just in the area. She didn't say you lived down there. That's right, isn't it, Holly?'

We all look over to Holly, who nods, and James addresses himself to Emma again.

'Besides, they don't live anywhere near Rock. They'll look after you until your father can arrange for you to go to your friends.'

'How long will it take?' I try to make it sound like a polite enquiry but I am concerned as to how long we will have to put up with Emma's company.

'Four or five days, probably.' Oh, okay. Only eternity in Emma-time.

Holly is staring at James. 'But I can't go to Cornwall. I've got to work.'

'Holly, after your telephone message to him this afternoon, where do you think Martin Connelly will look for you now?'

'The paper.'

'And after that?'

'My flat.'

'So you can't return to work or your flat,' I say to Holly, neatly summarising this little exchange.

174

Golly, we are like fugitives.

'We'll all stay here tonight, I'll go and collect your stuff from the flat and Emma's things from John Montague's house and then you can set off tomorrow.'

'You and Emma will have to go in Tristan and I'll go back on the train,' I say, vastly relieved not to be travelling on any motorways in Tristan and at leaving Bristol, the temporary home of psychopaths.

'Is this okay with you, Emma?'

'I'd rather have stayed with John, but I guess it's going to have to be okay, isn't it?' She shoots another nasty look at Holly and me but Holly is too busy looking aghast at James to take it in. Emma picks up our discarded plates and stalks into the kitchen.

'Have you talked to our mother?' I ask.

'I've called her. She says you should all come home immediately. I didn't enlarge too much on the Emma and Martin story because I thought Emma would tell her if she wanted to, but I had to give her a brief outline.'

'So what does she know?'

'Just that you have to look after a young girl who is being pursued by an ex-con after one of Holly's stories went wrong. I didn't tell her exactly where it had gone wrong because I thought Holly might do that herself.'

Holly is anxiously gnawing on a fingernail and doesn't seem to have taken any of this in.

Just on cue, my mobile rings in the depths of my handbag. I know exactly who this will be.

'Hello Mum.'

'Darling! This is just too, too exciting. You must come home immediately. You can't stay in Bristol with that psychologist chasing after you.'

I raise my eyes to heaven. 'Psychopath, Mother. Not psychologist.' James smothers a smile. I wander over to the window and then curse myself for such an amateur mistake. God, that's how they all get caught in the movies. Letting themselves be seen at a lit window.

'I want to hear all the details. Nothing like this ever happens in Cornwall. The nearest we get to drama is Barney falling off his surfboard.'

'It's not terribly pleasant here, you know. You're welcome to come and trade places. We're holed up in James's flat eating cheese on toast.'

She lets out a squeal of excitement at this thumbnail sketch. 'Darling, it sounds absolutely thrilling! I'd be there like a shot. You know how Morgan and Norman love a bit of excitement.' She drops her voice to a whisper and tries to sound concerned. 'Now, who is this poor girl that the psychologist is pursuing? James wouldn't tell me much.'

I glance towards the kitchen where Emma is still smashing plates around. 'Someone Holly used to work with. She disappeared and . . . well, it's a long — '

'You mean the Emma you told us about? The one with the famous QC father?'

'Yes, that's her. But — '

'So Holly found her? Gosh, how clever of her.'

'Well, it's not quite like that — '

'I do hope Emma is suitably grateful.'

'Actually, I don't think she is grateful at — '

176

'Darling, I have to go, your father is pulling appalling faces at me. You will have to tell me all tomorrow. Just do one thing for me and absorb the atmosphere, will you?'

'S . . . sorry?'

'Just in case I have to play a psychologist. I did play *My Cousin Rachel* once at Drury Lane and — '

My father obviously wrestles the phone out of my mother's hands because he comes on the line next.

'Clemmie, it's your father. Now, Sam says he has to drop some papers to a client in Bristol. He was going to send someone else up but he says he'll come and collect you all to save you catching the train.'

For the first time today, I feel vaguely comforted. It will be nice to be in Sam's safe BMW rather than looking over my shoulder on the train and chain-eating flapjacks. 'Say thank you to him. That would be great.'

'He'll be there about ten.'

I duly relay James's address to my father, quite thankful it's him and not my mother who has a tendency not to listen and to write down the first thing that comes into her head.

'Sam has offered to come and collect us. He'll be here about ten.'

'Even better,' says James. 'That'll give you a chance to pop into work first, Holly, and sign yourself off for a week.'

'But what on earth am I going to say to Joe?' wails Holly. 'And I thought you said I couldn't go back to the office?'

'Sneak in early in the morning. You'll think of something,' says James firmly. 'You always do.'

* * *

The following day, when faced with the choice of spending a brooding, sulky hour in the company of Emma or going with Holly down to the paper, I leap at the chance of Holly and a bollocking. At least with Joe you can guarantee the pain will be quick, and if I play my cards right, I could just sit out in reception reading magazines. So I gaily trip up the steps to the *Bristol Gazette* next to a silent Holly. We had quite a difficult night. Holly and I slept together in James's double bed while Emma had the spare room and James took the sofa. I think this was due to the fact that James was still so furiously angry with Holly that he didn't want to sleep with her rather than any consideration for my comfort. This was completely nullified anyway as Holly fretted about James and the paper until the early hours. I tried to ignore her.

As soon as the lift doors open at the third floor, I wave at Sophie and make for the squishy sofa in reception and what looks to be one of the latest gossip magazines. Maybe I could even persuade Sophie to make me a coffee and a small Scooby snack? Holly hovers nervously in front of me.

'I suppose I'd better go and talk to Joe then,' she says miserably.

'Get it over and done with,' I advise, trying to

shoo her towards his office. The magazines are beckoning to me.

'Do you think Sir Christopher has already called him?'

'I think Joe would have been straight on the phone to you if he had.'

Holly looks fixedly at her shoes.

'You haven't turned your mobile on, have you?'

She winces. 'Er, no. Not yet.'

'Hmmm, well maybe the best thing to do is go and find out . . . '

While we have been speaking, the lift doors have been opening on a regular basis as people arrive for work but I am suddenly aware of a figure looming behind Holly.

'Hello Holly, hello Clemmie,' he says in the sort of voice they use on the TV for the really serious nutters.

Holly spins around on her heels.

'Hello Charlie. Er, Martin. Charlie Martin.' Her voice sounds hollow and I realise that she's scared. Which has the effect of making me bloody scared too.

We stare at him for what feels like an eternity but is probably only a few seconds. Unfortunately Holly has already called him Martin so he must know that the game is up.

He has dark patches under his eyes, the sleek chestnut hair of a few days ago is ruffled and uncombed and he looks as though he has slept in his clothes. His eyes are hard and calculating and I wonder how I didn't notice them before.

'Where is she?' he asks in a quiet voice and

takes a small step towards us. We instinctively take one to the side.

'W . . . w . . . where's who?' Ah, good. Holly's playing the stupid card.

'Emma. Where is Emma?' he murmurs with the sort of tight calmness that is truly terrifying.

'I . . . I . . . I don't know,' quivers Holly. I quiver silently over her shoulder.

One step forward. One step to the side.

'You called me yesterday, Holly. You'd found her. Where is she now?'

'I . . . I don't know.'

One step forward. One step to the side.

'When I reached the address you gave me there was no one there.'

Another step forward and another to the side. I bump into something soft and warm and look to see Sophie standing next to me, staring at Martin open-mouthed. Luckily Sophie's desk is now almost between us all. Martin suddenly slams both of his hands down on to the desk, sending post and nail varnish flying.

'You bitch,' he breathes murderously. I am wildly encouraged by the fact that he is still talking in the singular but not very happy at standing so close to Holly.

'Now, Charlie. I mean Martin. Don't be like that. There is no need to be rash.'

A light comes on in Martin's eyes as though it hadn't occurred to him to be rash. Of course, just the thing to elicit a confession. A spot of rashness. He leans over the desk. 'You know where she is, Holly, and you're bloody well going to tell me.'

'But I don't know,' she bleats.

'CUT THE BULLSHIT, HOLLY, AND TELL ME WHERE SHE IS!' he roars.

We all jump out of our skins. 'I left her with her father,' squeals Holly.

The three of us instinctively scurry round to one corner of the desk. We are pinned together as though we were welded that way. I've never really had much to do with Sophie before and I am sure she really doesn't want much to do with me but circumstances have dealt her a bad card and now she is stuck with us. She is quite tall and gangly and there is no way that I am going to let her go. We must look like the creature from the lagoon, a mish-mash of Jigsaw and Top Shop with three heads. One that could do with a few more highlights than the others but we won't go into that now.

At least we have the desk between us. Martin takes a step to one side and we go the opposite way. I look wildly around me, wondering what form our rescuer might take. And the answer would appear to be absolutely none at all. People have noticed our predicament all right, but we have an audience without any participation.

Martin brings his fist down hard on to the desk again. 'DON'T LIE TO ME, YOU BITCH. JUST TELL ME!'

Our rescuer ironically appears in the guise of Joe. His door flies open and he strides out, sending our little pavement crowd scattering. 'What the *hell* is going on?'

A veritable god stands before us with his hands on his hips and wearing a particularly

181

snappy fuchsia pink tie.

'Em, Joe,' ventures Holly politely from our little huddle. 'This is Martin Connelly,' she announces gaily as though she's introducing them at a party.

In one move Joe reaches for the phone on Sophie's desk. 'Right. I'm calling security, Mr Connelly. So you have precisely one minute before they arrive here.'

Actually he probably has a little longer than that by the time they finish their coffee, find their caps and scratch their arses but Martin doesn't know that.

Martin turns pleading eyes on Holly. 'I just want to talk to her.'

Holly doesn't look at him. 'I can't help you,' she says quietly.

Joe puts a hand on Martin's arm. 'You're leaving,' he says firmly.

Martin lets himself be pulled away but when he reaches the lift doors he turns back. 'You haven't heard the end of this, Holly,' he says before being firmly propelled into the lift. We watch as the lift doors take an inordinately long time to shut.

Joe walks back to us. 'All right, everyone. The show is over. Back to work.' He waves his arms and slowly people start to disperse.

The three of us are still standing in a little huddle. 'Holly, Clemmie, perhaps you should come into my office.'

Could we bring Sophie too? I don't want to leave the comforting warmth of her armpit right now. She is certainly going to be added to my

Christmas card list after this. I think Sophie is quite pleased to see the back of us, though, and we slowly follow Joe down the corridor. We positively dawdle outside his door and then unwillingly follow him in.

Joe goes round to his side of the desk, runs his hands through his hair and sits down.

'So that was Martin Connelly, was it? What a charming man, I can see why you believed his every word, Holly.' Ah. Sympathy might be a little short on the ground here. 'Lucky I got there just in the skin of time otherwise murder might have been added to his police record too.' I instinctively put my hand to my neck. He is talking about Holly, isn't he? Surely Martin wouldn't murder me?

'Look, Joe, I'm sorry about — ' starts Holly.

'No, Holly. This really is the thin end of the toast. Sir Christopher has been on the phone to me non-stop since his beloved daughter called him yesterday and told him about your role in this little drama. He's threatening to sue the paper and he's threatening to charge you with breaking and entering.'

'But we didn't break or enter anything!' protests Holly. What's with all this 'we' stuff?

'Well, he's saying you did. And I couldn't really give a stuff if he does charge you because at least it will take the heat off the paper. How on earth did this happen? What did I tell you about doing your research? And be careful how you answer this because you're close to joining the ranks of the unemployed at the moment.'

'We did do our research!' She had better stop

183

using the plural or else she's going to get a good kick on the shins. 'That was the problem! All we were trying to do was ascertain whether Emma was going to marry Martin Connelly and she was! How was I supposed to know that her father put him away! We simply found out that Emma was getting married and then tried to reunite them.' Joe starts to look slightly mollified. 'It would have made a great story. Anyway . . . ' she rushes on hurriedly as she sees Joe's face, 'James wants us to take Emma down to Cornwall for a few days until her father can find somewhere permanent for her and I was wondering if it would be okay — '

'Bloody hell, yes! Go and look after the girl! Do not let her out of your sight! Anything to get Sir Christopher McKellan off my case!'

'Will I still have a job when I get back?' Holly asks in a very small voice.

'That depends on how you do,' he says dryly. 'And since you are partially responsible for the loss of our social diarist, you can bloody well write copy for 'High Society' until I find a replacement. E-mail it to me. You know the drill.' And with a wave of his hand he dismisses us.

★ ★ ★

Sam turns up to collect us at about ten-thirty, which is not a moment too soon for me. I rush downstairs with my bag leaving Holly and Emma to bring up the rear.

Sam is leaning against his BMW as I gallop towards him. 'What on earth have you been

184

doing?' he greets me. 'And what on earth are you wearing?'

I still have on my suede jacket and bobble hat. 'I'm in disguise.'

'You're in delusion. You stick out like a sore thumb. I suppose it's only marginally worse than your usual garb.'

I'm just about to give a particularly scathing reply when Emma and Holly come clattering down, followed by James. I'm already in the front seat with my seatbelt on by the time they finish their hand-shaking and greetings. I briefly think about honking the horn at them. It is intensely irritating whenever Sam does it to me.

Sam loads Emma and Holly's luggage into the boot and after some goodbyes to James (I do mine through the window and I notice a definite chilliness between him and Holly, no kissing) we set off towards the M5.

Sam must be absolutely bursting with curiosity but he doesn't show it. Emma politely but firmly bats back every question Sam asks until his conversational gambits on everything from the weather to politics have all been exhausted. She then looks firmly out of the window to make it clear to everyone that she is unavailable for comment. We can't talk about what's been happening with Emma present so I plump for a neutral topic.

'How's Norman?' I ask.

'Still eating your father's pilchards. Sorrel thinks he's missing the sea so she keeps filling the bath and tipping in half a tonne of rock salt for him to bathe in. Norman, that is, not your

185

father. So now Norman spends half the day floating about in the bath. Enormously disconcerting when you're trying to have a pee with Norman watching you.'

'And how's *Calamity Jane* coming along?'

'Much like the title, I think. Rehearsals are full steam ahead. Barney and I went to one last night and your mother tried to rope me in as one of her extras.'

'Are you going to do it?' I ask.

'I will if you will.' He grins at me disarmingly.

I have been an extra for my mother on many occasions but the last time was when I was about fourteen and I was a Munchkin in the RSC version of *The Wizard of Oz* (my mother was the Wicked Witch of the West, a role she took to with great gusto). I have a startling allergy to avocados which makes my face swell up spectacularly. There must have been some lurking in my lunchtime sandwich because I made all the children in the front row cry. Funnily enough I have avoided being an extra since then.

'I'll think about it.' As long as I avoid avocados, it might be quite fun with Sally playing the lead. 'Has Barney been roped in too?'

'Ages ago.'

'How was the rehearsal last night?'

'Catherine was making moon eyes at the vicar. And Bradley insisted on wearing a cowboy hat for most of the evening. Then we all went back to your house for coffee and cake to be greeted by the sight of Norman chasing Morgan around the kitchen table. I

186

was hard pushed to know whose side I was on.'

I grin at this. I could nearly miss being at home.

Well, almost.

I glance at the back seat. Holly has fallen asleep and Emma has joined her. Sam surveys them both in the mirror.

'So what has been going on, Clemmie?' he asks quietly as we are now free to talk. 'Your mother was quite hysterical on the phone. What trouble have you got yourself into this time?'

'Why do you always presume it's me?'

'Because it is always you.'

'It was Holly this time,' I protest. 'I was an innocent bystander who got caught up in this miserable business.'

He snorts. 'You seem to get caught up in an awful lot of things.'

'The statistics are stacked against me,' I huff and look out of the window.

'I suppose I can't ask what all this is about?'

'I wouldn't tell you if I could,' I say childishly. I hope the suspense is killing him.

'Fair enough.' He looks annoyingly unmoved and goes on to talk of other things.

12

A welcoming committee is waiting to greet us in the kitchen when we arrive. I have never been so pleased to see my family in my life. The ratio of Emma to other people is now much higher, nowhere near the statistic I would actually like but definitely an improvement.

My mother's eyes widen with amazement when she clocks my orange bobble hat and brown suede jacket which I haven't managed to take off yet. 'Dear God, Clemmie. What on earth are you wearing?'

Holly breaks off from giving my father a hug to call over, 'She's in disguise.'

'Take them off, Clemmie. You'll frighten the locals.'

My father is more concerned with the welfare of his daughters and is murmuring something to Holly, whereas my mother has a sod-them-who's-the-interesting-stranger attitude as Emma steps through the back door, followed by Sam who is carrying a tonne of luggage.

'This is Emma,' I announce.

My mother steps forward and gives her two big kisses on each cheek. I wish she wouldn't do that to complete strangers. She is clearly absolutely goggle-eyed with curiosity but feels it is slightly beyond good manners to introduce herself and then ask for Emma's life story. 'Emma, welcome to Cornwall! My goodness, you must be so glad that Holly found you and thwarted the madman!' I quickly manoeuvre myself into a position to make faces at her behind Emma's back. 'I mean, Holly has always been wonderful at her job and I'm so proud she is really helping people.' I move on to more blatant waving, and Holly joins me while my father and Sam look on in amazement. 'I like to think of her as some sort — ' The back of Emma's head is looking decidedly frosty so I step in before any more damage can be done.

'Actually, em, Mother, the thing is that Emma didn't really want to be found . . . '

'That's right,' spits out Emma. 'The only reason I'm here is because Holly managed to actually lead the *madman*, as you so succinctly put it, to me.'

'But you had disappeared.'

'Because of the madman,' I put in, feeling that some sort of clarification is needed.

My mother opens her mouth and then shuts it again. She is rarely lost for words.

My father, always sensitive to the delicacies of social situations, asks Emma kindly, 'Would you like to see your room?'

'Thank you,' she says quietly, which is the best we've had out of her for the last twenty-four hours.

She and my father select her bag from the mound of luggage Sam has dumped on the floor and make their way upstairs.

My mother immediately turns to us. 'What on earth have you been doing?'

'It was all Holly,' I get in before any nasty retributions start.

'BUT SHE'S PREGNANT,' my mother mouths while indicating a huge belly with her hand.

'That wasn't Holly,' I say, just to make these things clear. None the less, I look at my mother in baffled amazement. How can she tell? Can she smell the hormones or something?

Barney comes bursting through the back door and leans forward with his hands on his thighs to catch his breath. 'What the hell have you two been up to?' he asks, looking between Holly and me without so much as a how-are-you.

'It's all Holly.'

'I doubt that,' says Sam from the kitchen table. God, he's eating a yoghurt already. It's another rhubarb one — I can spot a multi pack from a mile off.

'I have been dragged into this very much against my will,' I say with as much dignity as I can muster.

'Clemmie, you're never dragged into anything against your will.'

'Are you and James okay?' my mother asks Holly. 'He sounded pretty mad with you last night.'

'He is,' says Holly weakly. 'I'm just hoping I can make up for it somehow.'

Just at that moment we hear my father and Emma coming back down the stairs and we all shut up. My father is busy telling Emma all about the village and where she is in relation to the sea.

They come back into the kitchen and Emma's face is already a bit cheerier. She looks lighter somehow; my father can have an amazing effect on people.

'Thank you for the flowers in my room, Mrs Colshannon,' says Emma quietly. Flowers and my mother? Holly and I exchange a look. That must mean that my mother has been in the garden. She must be absolutely desperate for information.

'Please do call me Sorrel.'

Barney leans over and introduces himself. Emma can't have been expecting all these people and I almost feel quite sorry for her. Well, almost.

'Now, you must be starving. I've done some soup and sandwiches for lunch.' My mother glares at Sam, who is eating another yoghurt, and shoos him away from the table.

Barney and Sam move all the luggage upstairs before Morgan can pee on it and then we sit sedately down at the table. It feels like we're back at school again and we've just brought some friends home for tea. Everybody studiously keeps off the reason for Emma being here.

I glance over at Holly who has been really quiet for most of the morning. 'Are you okay?' I lean over and ask quietly.

She makes a so-so face.

'Is it James?'

'God, Clemmie. It's everything. I've made such a cock-up of everything, haven't I?'

Tears fill her eyes suddenly and I feel somewhat alarmed. I bite my lip and pat her arm rather uselessly. Luckily everyone else is looking curiously at the stranger in our midst and completely ignoring us. 'Well, it's not really your fault. Charlie was very convincing. He had me fooled and don't forget . . . ' I lower my voice to an undertone, ' . . . he had Emma fooled too.'

Holly nods slowly at this and looks slightly happier. 'But James is right, I should have checked my facts more thoroughly. And now I've messed everything up for Emma, may have lost my job and even James too.'

I am vaguely shocked at this. 'You and James will be fine though, won't you? Goodness, Holly, you didn't mean for all this to happen.'

'I don't think he quite sees things like that. I have put him in a pretty awful position.'

'He'll come round,' I say comfortingly. 'All we have to do is keep Emma safe and deliver her to those friends in one piece. How hard can it be?'

★ ★ ★

Holly and I are given an Emma reprieve as my father takes it upon himself to drive her up to Watergate Bay for a walk on the beach and some tea at Barney's café. God bless him, he should be canonised. Sam has to go back to work and my mother is clearly torn between eliciting some juicy gossip from Emma and having to breathe great lungfuls of fresh sea air but, after making my father promise to relate everything he learns (but I will not press her, Sorrel), she elects to stay at home and smoke cigarettes instead.

I'm expected back at Mr Trevesky's café

192

tomorrow so I make the most of my last day of freedom by lying on the sofa and reading a magazine. Just as my mother is attempting to extract the juicy details of the Emma story out of me, the vet calls to tell her she is late for an appointment with Norman that she has completely forgotten about and she has to rush off. Holly wanders in at teatime demanding attention and together we walk down to the village to see if Barney has started his evening shift yet.

Because both Holly and I refuse to go into Barney's house, we coax him into the pub for a quick drink. After all it is nearly four o'clock.

'So what news do you have, Barney?' asks Holly, sipping on a vodka and orange. At least I have made some sort of salute to the earliness of the hour by putting some soda water in my white wine.

'I've joined the cricket team,' he announces grandly.

We both look at him doubtfully.

'Do you play cricket?' asks Holly politely.

'Well, not really, but they're desperate.'

'They must be,' I put in. The last time I remember Barney playing cricket was when he was at school and he got smacked in the eye by the ball because he was too busy chatting to the other fielders. He had to wear an eye patch for a month and his eye changed colour. 'Have you got any whites?' I ask. I quite like those chunky cricket jumpers and am hoping I'll be able to borrow Barney's.

'I've got a white T-shirt,' he says.

'Barney, if you're going to impress this girl, I

193

really think you ought to at least get some whites. I mean, she's hardly going to be won over if you turn up in a white T-shirt and a pair of swimming trunks.'

'Do you think?' he asks anxiously.

'Maybe Sam will lend you his,' suggests Holly. Sam very occasionally plays for the village but only if it's a choice between Trevor the organist and him.

Barney looks cheered by this. 'I'll ask him. Will you come and watch me?'

Both Holly and I wince slightly. The last time we went to watch the village cricket match we were severely yelled at. The grass was slightly damp so I took a very handy round circle thing out of the ground to sit on it. How the hell was I supposed to know it was the ruddy boundary marker?

'When are you playing?'

'First game is this weekend.'

'Of course we'll come.'

'Will this girl be there?' asks Holly sneakily.

'She might be. She lives in the village. And that's all I'm going to tell you.'

'Any developments?' I ask.

He shakes his head gloomily. 'Nothing. She doesn't even know I'm alive.'

'God, Barney, is she really worth the trouble? You've got tonnes of girls running after you. Why do you want this one?' Holly asks.

'Because she's different,' he says defensively. 'And I like her.'

'She must be some sort of goddess!'

'I think so.'

'Who is she?'

'No, no. I'm not telling you that. You and Clemmie will moon around making faces behind her back and then Mum will find out and start chucking herself about and it will all get very embarrassing and out of hand. Anyway, enough of the spotlight on me, tell me about Emma. She's hardly full of the joys of spring, is she? What on earth have you two been doing to get her in that state?'

'It was all Holly,' I announce again.

Holly shoots me an evil look and then launches into our tale of woe.

'Bloody hell,' says Barney at the end of it. 'That Charlie doesn't sound like good news.'

'His real name is Martin. Martin Connelly.'

'Is he dangerous, do you think?'

'What do you mean, dangerous?'

'Well, would he do anything?'

'What? Like murder us all?' I question.

'Well, yes. I suppose I do mean that.'

'Put it this way, I'm not going to give him the opportunity to try. I am firmly in the don't-be-a-hero camp. If I see him at the window, I'll be the first person to shove Morgan out and call the police.'

'You might be better off shoving Norman out first,' suggests Holly.

'I'll shove them both out.'

'How long is Emma staying for?' asks Barney.

'Not long, I hope. Her father is supposed to be arranging for her to go and stay with some people.'

'I'll call James tonight and see if any

195

arrangements have been made,' murmurs Holly.

'He has probably forgiven you already,' I say brightly. She looks cheered by this and we finish off our drinks.

★ ★ ★

Since Barney is working this evening my mother recruits Sam to have supper with us. He arrives about six, still wearing his suit so he must have come straight from work.

'Sorry we've got to eat so early but Sorrel has a rehearsal scheduled for eight o'clock,' my father tells him.

He smiles at her. 'No problem. In fact, I might come down and watch tonight.'

'I'll come too!' I put in eagerly, anxious not to be left alone with Emma, who has been resting in her room since she returned from her seaside trip.

'So how was the afternoon?' I ask my father cautiously.

'Yes, what did she tell you?' my mother rejoins, obviously feeling utterly frustrated. She thinks she is the last in the family to be told Emma's story and it is clearly irritating the hell out of her. Not to mention the fact that my father has banned her from smoking in front of Emma because of the baby.

'She didn't tell me anything because I didn't ask her. People are entitled to their privacy.'

'Not in this house,' snorts my mother and lights up a cigarette. 'Someone has to tell me soon. God, it's not even as though I can ply her with drink. You must have found something out

196

during that car journey of yours, Sam.'

Sam loosens his tie. 'Not a thing, Sorrel. She slept for most of it.'

'Well at least tell me who the father of her child is, Clemmie. Is it someone terrible? Like an archbishop or something?'

'His name is Martin Connelly.'

My mother looks terribly let down that the reality isn't as exciting as her over-active imagination.

'He's the madman who has been chasing her.'

She looks rather confused by this. As well she might. 'So the madman found her?'

'Well, no. Not yet.'

'Then how did she get pregnant by him?'

I'm tempted to say via second class post and a turkey baster but firmly desist, for the purely selfish reason that I will completely confuse her and then never hear the end of it. 'This was before she disappeared.'

'Before he became a madman?'

'Well, he was always a madman.'

'So she slept with this madman?'

'Yes, but before she knew he was mad.'

'How did she find out?'

'Well, I presume she did one of those tests, you know where you wee on — '

'No, when did she find out that he was a madman?'

'He always was one.'

My mother puts a hand to her head and is about to attempt more questioning when Holly returns from calling James. She looks despondent.

'How was James?' I ask.

'Still mad. Emma is going to be staying with us for a few more days and then we're escorting her to meet these people her father is sending her to.'

'Doesn't Sir Christopher want to take her?'

'I think he's worried Martin will try to follow him or something. I suppose it's pretty important that this final destination stays secret. Besides, I want to try to show James that I'm making up for the trouble I caused. Will you come with me, Clemmie?'

'Of course,' I say automatically, feeling really sorry for her. I'm sure Mr Trevesky will agree to just one more day off. 'Where do they live?'

'In France.'

'France?'

'They're French.'

'In France?' I repeat again.

'That's where the French live, Clemmie,' puts in Sam. 'Awfully inconvenient, I know. Brighton would be easier but there you are. That's the French for you.'

I shoot Sam an evil look and then turn back to Holly. 'You said we would take her to France? How on earth are we going to do that?'

'James says that Sir Christopher will try to organise some flights for us.'

'But I'm not sure I can get the time off work. I thought you meant we would drop her in Suffolk or something.'

'Please, Clemmie,' says Holly pleadingly. 'I've already said to James that you will help, please come. It should only take two days; we might

198

even be able to get there and back in a day. Besides, you speak French and everything.'

'Couldn't we bung her on a plane here and let the people meet her at the other end?'

Holly looks miserable. 'I just thought we're morally responsible for her, and if James sees that I'm doing everything I can to help her then . . . '

'Okay, okay. I'll ask Mr Trevesky tomorrow. He won't be too pleased, although Wayne will be thrilled, but I suppose I can always get another waitressing job.'

'How exciting! Your father and I could come too, Holly. For moral support. We can pay for our own flights,' announces my mother. 'You know I adore France. Besides, I'm practically a local.' My mother can barely ask for a loaf of bread in French so I'm not quite sure what she is basing this on but I am very pleased to have them along nonetheless.

'What about *Calamity Jane?*' I ask.

'Well, we were going to have a few days off anyway. Catherine Fothersby is going for a walking holiday or something and I can leave Matt in charge.'

'Oh, thank you,' says Holly joyfully. 'I'll call James and tell him. We can all fly over together.'

'Whereabouts in France?' asks Sam.

'Down in the south somewhere. James didn't say where exactly. I'll go and tell Emma too. She'll be pleased that something has been sorted.'

13

Over dinner and a sneaky white wine spritzer that my mother manages to coax Emma to drink, she, my father and Sam hear Emma's story for the first time and I think they are suitably shocked. Well, at least Sam and my father are. In fact when Sam, my mother, Morgan and I walk down to watch the *Calamity Jane* rehearsal, Sam can talk of nothing else apart from how sorry he feels for Emma. Holly has opted to stay at home as I think she is feeling far too depressed about James to face the am dram society.

Emma didn't seem at all surprised that we're off to France so she must have been abreast of the plan all along. You know, I do feel really sorry for her. I think of how she was planning to marry the man she loves and then the next minute she's pregnant, her fiancé's turned out to be a lunatic and she's being packed off abroad. That's pretty tough. But then she does something really aggravating and all my sympathy evaporates within about a millisecond. For instance, she has taken an extreme dislike to all the animals. Now, I know this is hypocritical of me because I am hardly a founder member of the Norman and Morgan fan club but at least they are family and I have a completely legitimate right to dislike them. Emma has developed a nasty habit of snitching on them, so she'll squeal loudly that

Morgan has been jumping up at her when she has probably been baiting him with bits of bacon. I might have to tell her that Morgan will pee on her if she stands still too long.

I watch Morgan's baboon-like bottom as he disappears into the darkness in front of us. Yet again I have had to take charge of the torch because every time my mother wants to make a point about Emma and her story, she waves it madly around.

'My God, I wonder how she must feel about having his child,' Sam is saying.

'Well, I don't think Charlie, I mean Martin, is like Dr Crippen or anything. The child isn't going to inherit bad genes. If you know about the case then I think Martin had a really raw deal in all this.'

'I remember the case really well and I agree with you, I think the system was very harsh on him, but what he has done to Emma cannot be excused. How on earth did you and Holly get mixed up in this?'

'It was all Holly,' I announce again.

'Well, she is a reporter,' says my mother idly. 'I suppose it's an occupational hazard.'

'She probably thought she was helping,' Sam adds as an afterthought.

God, he has such a soft spot for Holly. He's always sticking up for her. The best you can say after he's finished with me is that I've never set fire to anything or run anyone over.

I open the village hall door rather grumpily and we all waltz in. The cast are waiting for us apart from the ever tardy Bradley. Catherine

Fothersby is looking angelic in a baby pink angora twinset and keeps making google eyes at Matt the vicar, whereas Sally is a far more welcoming sight in jeans and a tatty jumper that I think used to be Barney's. Matt looks absolutely thrilled to see us but then he has probably been stuck with Catherine's theological account of St John's scriptures or something. He strides forward to grasp Sam's hand.

'Sam, so nice to see you! I haven't seen you for weeks, have you been working too hard again?'

'No more than usual but how are you, Matt? Converted anyone lately?'

'Lord, no. I have problems enough with the ones I've got. We had a christening last week and the parents were adamant that I light this massive thirty-foot candle. Of course there were about a hundred little blighters running around who would insist on prodding it and I had to keep halting the service every time one came within about five feet of it. I found myself yelling 'DON'T TOUCH THE CANDLE!' every other second.'

I laugh, my humour instantly restored by this twinkly-eyed giant of a man.

'And how are you, young Clemmie?' he asks.

'Bearing up, Matt. Bearing up.'

'Family troubles?'

I try not to catch Sam's eye. 'Nothing more than usual.'

'I thank the good Lord every day that I'm not related to them.' He grins widely.

'Any time you want to take them on you'll be more than welcome.'

202

We smile at each other again and then I move forward to greet Sally who I haven't seen since I left for Bristol. 'How are you?' she greets me joyously. 'How was Bristol?'

I am sorely tempted to tell her exactly how Bristol was but Holly threatened the wrath of James if I told anyone about Emma. This is enough to keep me quiet.

'Oh, fine, fine. Holly has come back here for a few days and she's brought a friend.'

'Holly is back too?' The village grapevine is fairly voracious and so it will only be a matter of time before the news spreads; already I can see that Catherine Fothersby has overheard and looks very interested as she bustles over to us.

'Did I hear you say that Holly is home, Clemmie?' she asks.

'Yes, and she brought a friend back too. You should meet her, Catherine!'

Thankfully our conversation is cut short because my mother starts to round them all up for the rehearsal.

Sally walks halfway to the back of the hall with me. 'I really wish Catherine would just get on and shag Matt if that's what she wants to do. She is being such a pain in the arse at the moment,' she murmurs to me before she turns back to join them all on stage. You know, for someone in the choir, Sally can be really close to the bone sometimes.

Sam and I go to the back of the hall and sit down.

We sit in silence for a few minutes, watching as Bradley finally makes his entrance and then makes everyone switch seats as he says the draught from the door affects his voice.

'How's work?' I ask Sam hastily before we can begin another 'where Clemmie has gone wrong in the Emma affair' conversation.

'We're busy which is great.'

'Is it?'

'When it's your own firm, busy is always great. Stops everyone from sloping off to the pub.' He smiles at me.

'Why do you assume everyone slopes off to the pub? We don't all have that attitude to work,' I bristle.

'Oh, come off it, Clemmie. I bugger off to the pub if we're not busy. We can't all be pillars of society like your good self.'

Oh. I calm down slightly. Here we go again. I always presume he's getting at me somehow, and then I go on the defensive and he lapses into flippant mode. This is why he kisses Holly hello and not me. I make a conscious effort to relax and think of something innocuous to say. Sam gets there before me.

'Are you looking forward to your trip to France?'

'I'm looking forward to getting rid of Emma.'

'That's a bit rough. She's having a shitty time.'

'I know, but she keeps snitching on Morgan for jumping up at the table.'

'Since when have you and Morgan had any love lost between you?'

'That's not the point.'

'Actually, it is really annoying, and I saw her trying to make him jump up for some cheese tonight. But you have to make allowances for her.'

'I have to say that I'm glad my parents are coming with us.'

'Well, you couldn't have gone without your mum. She wouldn't have let you.'

'At least Morgan won't be with us,' I say, thinking of our last French trip.

'Barney or I will take him in.'

'There's Norman too, don't forget.'

'Well, I'll take Morgan then,' says Sam hastily.

'I just want things to get back to normal.'

'And what is normal for you, Clemmie?'

I look at him suspiciously. Usually this would be the precursor to a huge row, but he's looking at me in quite a friendly fashion and so I relax a bit.

'Work, family, I suppose.'

'Are you going to keep on at Mr Trevesky's café?'

'I might. I don't know. Why? What's wrong with Mr Trevesky's café?'

'Nothing, nothing. I just thought you might try to get back into the art business.'

'I can't seem to find anything.'

'Would you join another insurance company?'

I really wish he wouldn't keep saying I work for an insurance company but I make a magnanimous effort to rise above it. 'It's finding another firm, they're a bit thin on the ground. I might have to go to London and I think I would quite like to stay in Cornwall. I haven't really had a chance to look yet. Why?'

'I just wondered if you were still getting over

Seth and that's what was stopping you,' he says quietly.

There's a silence and I shift position in my seat. I feel vaguely annoyed by the presumption behind his question, as though he's trying to father me or something. I watch Sally and Bradley pretend to be madly in love with each other. Bradley, who is as gay as coot (my father's expression and I'm not sure exactly what he knows about coots), keeps trying to unhook Sally's bra so she is acting the entire scene with her arms pinned to her sides. I smile.

'Is it, Clemmie?' asks Sam again, gently.

'No, Sam. I'm not still getting over Seth. I really am looking for a new job.' I turn and look him squarely in the eye. I try to turn the tables. 'What about you? Do you prefer it down here in Cornwall? I mean, you weren't tempted to stay in London?'

I remember thinking how strange it was that Sam returned to Cornwall. He had been so adamant about going up to London, and we all wondered at the time whether this was because his parents had lived there. After all, Sam was only brought up in Cornwall by default; this was where his aunt was living at the time of his parents' car accident.

Sam looks down at his hands. 'Not really,' he replies shortly and looks straight ahead.

Hmm. There is something slightly intriguing here and I can't quite put my finger on it. Ha! Mr I'm-so-sorted-in-my-own-life-I'm-going-to-make-a-video-about-it. Sam had put his aunt's house on the market before he left, was about to exchange contracts with someone and then simply called the whole thing off. He never said a word about why he'd decided to come back. Seth thought Sam simply couldn't hack the pace in the big city.

'So why did you come back from London?' I press.

'I just didn't get on there.' He still doesn't look at me.

'But you'd only been in your job a few months,' I say, smelling blood. 'It was a really good job, wasn't it?'

'Yes, it was. It just wasn't for me. Haven't you done enough detecting for one week, Clemmie? Just leave it,' he says tersely.

I watch him for a couple more seconds and then think that he's right. I have done enough for this week, but one day I really would like to find out what exactly happened.

We sit in silence for a few minutes and watch Sally gamely throwing herself into a rendition of 'A Windy City' while Catherine sneaks looks at Matt when she thinks no one is watching. Morgan strolls up the aisle towards us, stops and stretches. He then looks at us as though he's never seen either of us before in his life and carries on with his inspection of the hall.

'Holly seems upset about James,' ventures Sam. 'Is he really that mad with her?'

'Have you met James?' I ask out of curiosity.

'He came down here with Holly a couple of times while you were away. I like him but I imagine he can be quite tough when he wants to be.'

'They were moving in together, which my mother doesn't know by the way, and it doesn't look like it's going to happen now. Holly said he might take his flat off the market. He's pretty mad with her.'

'I suppose Holly put him in a tricky position with his work.'

'Well, he said that Martin hadn't done anything wrong legally so it wasn't an actual case.'

'God, Martin Connelly must be extremely pissed off to go to all this trouble.'

I remember the scene at the *Gazette* just before we left Bristol. 'I think he is. Emma said her father received regular hate mail from him when he was in prison. Maybe he cooked up this little scheme then.'

'But he gets absolutely nothing out of it apart from pure revenge. No wonder James is mad with Holly for exposing Emma to him.'

'I think Sir Christopher has also been on James's case about Holly and . . . ' I'm about to say 'and me' but then realise that I don't really want my part in all this featured or preferably mentioned at all, 'about Holly. He wanted to sue her and the paper.'

'You didn't feature in any of this, did you, Clemmie?'

'It was all Holly,' I announce firmly.

'Hmmm. So you keep saying.'

★ ★ ★

The next day is Saturday and although I have only been away from Mr Trevesky's café for

208

exactly seven days, it feels like a lifetime. Returning to work isn't a completely unwelcome thought because at least I can get out of the house and avoid any nasty run-ins with Emma or Norman. Since Emma's story, or Emmagate as my father likes to call it, emerged last night, sympathy for Emma in the Colshannon household has risen considerably, and has tailed off for Holly and Clemmie.

It's almost as though the last seven days have never happened as I am immediately plunged into a spooky déjà-vu of last week. Over breakfast, as my mother feeds Norman sardines, she announces that we are all seeing Charlotte tonight.

'It completely slipped my mind to tell you, Clemmie, with Emma arriving and everything. She has invited all the family down for supper at her house to thank us for all the times she has eaten here.'

I am about to announce that she can have my share of the hospitality absolutely gratis when my mother sees my imminent protest and pre-empts me by saying, 'And don't think that you can get out of it, Clemmie, because I have already accepted for all of us.'

'But what about Emma?' I protest, trying to adopt the role of concerned hostess. 'Remember, she should have been getting married today so she might need some cheering up.'

'Sam called this morning and said that Holly and Emma are invited too.'

'They could go in my place?' I suggest hopefully. 'I mean, I don't want to upset her seating arrangements.'

'No, Clemmie,' says my mother firmly. 'Absolutely not. I think Sam would be most upset if he thought for a second that you didn't like her.' I don't think that Sam would care less either way. 'Besides, Charlotte took the afternoon off yesterday to cook for us all.'

'What about Barney?' I demand. 'Is he coming too?'

'Of course he is.' Bollocks. I was hoping Barney might be a very neat get-out clause.

I look despondently over at my father, who glances up from his newspaper and gives me a sympathetic smile. 'I hope she has cooked something decent,' I say gloomily.

'Let's put it this way,' he says. 'It'll be better than anything you would have got here, whatever it is.'

★   ★   ★

The day passes quickly and none too pleasantly when I have to ask Mr Trevesky if I can have a few more days off to deal with a family trauma (which is the politest way I can think of to describe Holly). I am told that it is the last holiday I can take for a while; in fact, ever. I am so thankful to be left with a job of any kind that I gratefully agree.

My poor feet and back are aching so much from my now unaccustomed labour that I simply have to have a bath instead of my customary shower when I get home. Besides which, even though my hair was tied back in a ponytail, I managed to dip it into a jug of white sauce which didn't make me, Mr Trevesky or the customer very happy at all, and now all the ends keep clogging together. I pour a little bath oil into the hot, swirling water in an attempt to cover up the awful cooking smells that seem to be permanently stuck up my nose today.

My bath isn't as satisfying as I would have liked because the bath oil turns out to be very sticky and leaves a very peculiar rim of oil around the bath. Feeling fairly disgruntled, I get out and start drying my hair, but there is still an unpleasant smell hanging around.

I wander downstairs in my dressing gown, still towelling off my hair.

'Bloody hell, Clemmie, what have you been doing at that café of yours?' asks my father. 'You smell like Norman.'

I freeze in my steps. My mother waltzes past en route to the sitting room. 'Clemmie, dear, if you're thinking of having a bath then do remember to wash it out first because Norman has been floating about in it for most of the afternoon.'

I stare at my father for a second. 'Was she feeding him sardines in the bath again?' I whisper.

He nods slowly. 'Straight from the tin.'

Why me? Why not Emma or Holly or even Charlotte? Why? Why? I run like billy-o upstairs and jump in the shower, where I scrub and polish until my skin and scalp are raw.

'Do I still smell?' I ask anxiously as I hurtle back downstairs and proffer my wet head towards my father. He sniffs apprehensively.

'Only slightly.'

'But I've scrubbed until my head is raw!' I wail.

'Well, you did bathe in fish oil. It is somewhat hard to get rid of.'

My mother is clearly experiencing one of her mad energy phases and she zooms back into the room at well over the speed of sound. 'Patrick, what on earth are you doing? There's no need to sniff Clemmie like that; I'm sure she doesn't smell that bad. Her hair has probably just picked up some of the cooking smells from the café.' She looks at her watch. 'I'd suggest you go and have a bath but you simply haven't got time.'

'I've already had a bath,' I say sulkily.

'Well, I hope you remembered to wash it out first.'

She looks from one to the other of us.

'I did tell you to wash it out first.'

One of us is looking very mutinous.

'You didn't wash it out first?'

Very mutinous indeed.

'Good Lord, you are going to smell. Never mind! No time for that now!'

She yells up the stairs for Emma, who is apparently having a quick rest, and then through to the sitting room for Holly, who has been lying comatose on the sofa since I got home from work. To add insult to injury, Norman then waddles in and makes his way straight over to the Aga, which my father lit a few days ago, and settles himself down on to his beanbag with a contented sigh.

'Why is he in here?' I ask crossly.

'Darling, it's too cold outside for him now.'

'Too cold? What about the millions of other seagulls out there?'

'Well, they can have a fly about to keep themselves warm.'

'He could jump up and down on the spot,' I retort.

'Now don't be mean to Norman. It's not his fault you forgot to clean out the bath.'

I look at Norman crossly and he stares back at me. Is he . . . ?

'Is he laughing at me?' I demand. 'He has a very funny look in his eye.'

'Don't be silly, Clemmie.'

Holly wanders, yawning, into the kitchen. 'What's going on?'

'Clemmie forgot to clean the bath out after Norman had been in it.'

Holly looks at me delightedly. 'Do you smell?' she asks, a large grin spreading across her face.

'Of sardines.'

Emma has, in the meantime, followed Holly into the kitchen. She is all ready to go and carrying her handbag. 'Did someone mention sardines? Goodness, I can really smell them now.'

'It's Clemmie,' says Holly. 'She took a bath after Norman had been eating sardines in it.'

'You used his old water? God, how disgusting!' says Emma in horror.

'No,' I snap. 'I just didn't know he had been in there.' I throw my mother an evil look but she's too busy putting lipstick on to notice. 'Can you really smell sardines?'

'Your sense of smell is always stronger when you're pregnant. And you stink.'

Oh good.

I run upstairs, deaf to my mother's pleas that we really should leave, and spray myself all over with perfume, throw on some clothes and then charge back downstairs.

'Have you got anything else to wear?' Holly greets me doubtfully.

I look down at my old cords. I've bunged my father's old beanie hat on, as well as a bohemian kaftan, in a vain attempt to hide the smell. 'What's wrong with this?'

'You look like some sort of old fisherman,' puts in Emma. Was I asking her?

'Of course, that might be the smell,' murmurs Holly.

'Too late to change!' cries my mother and hustles us all out of the door.

What a marvellous evening this is going to be.

14

'Do come in!' Charlotte's very distinctive vowels echo in the street. 'It's getting very chilly out.'

'Charlotte, *dear*, thank you *so* much for inviting us. *Such* a treat.' Holly and I look at each other and raise our eyes to heaven as our mother gives Charlotte a huge kiss on each cheek. 'Now tell me, what's the name of the *fabulous* perfume you're wearing? It smells *simply* divine. It must be terribly, terribly expensive.'

Charlotte blushes and leads the way in. 'Oh, it's rally sweet of you to say so but it's just essence of violet from Yardley. Honestly, I could drown myself in it for fifty pounds.'

'I could donate thirty quid,' I murmur to Holly, who giggles.

We all make our way into the house, and I reluctantly relinquish my hat and then make a beeline for the fire while my mother introduces Emma to Charlotte. It is rather chilly out, especially with wet hair.

As I am toasting my bottom, Sam comes out from the kitchen. My parents make me smile with the warmth of their greeting to him, he gives a wave to me, a kiss for Holly and then goes off to get drinks for us all.

Sam and Charlotte are entertaining at Sam's house because Charlotte's place couldn't fit eight people in for a dinner party. This is the place his aunt used to own and I actually don't think I have been inside it since she died so I look around with some interest. It is in a perfect position in the village, just far enough away for the church bells to sound peaceful and facing the small patch of grass we like to call the village green. Barney's cricket matches are supposed to be played there but the village tries to get as many away fixtures as possible due to the fact that a ball inevitably goes through someone's window. I can't imagine anyone who lives near the green will be very happy to hear that Barney has now made the squad.

Anyway, Sam's house is a very sweet affair. I am glad to see that he has made his mark on the place: out have gone his aunt's faded, chintzy sofas, to be replaced by a huge leather Chesterfield and two beautiful chairs. He has kept the pieces of old antique furniture and the occasional blue Wedgwood vase, but most of the ornaments have disappeared.

I smile up at him as he passes me a glass of champagne (ooh, lovely champagne, mustn't appear too excited at this and thus look as though I'm easily bought) and then offers me a smoked mussel drenched in lemon juice, olive oil and black pepper.

'I like what you've done with the place,' I say to him.

He looks surprised and then smiles back at me. 'Thank you. I didn't want to throw everything out though. Sentimental value and all that.'

We stare at each other for a second and

suddenly I want to ask him all manner of questions. I want to ask if he misses his aunt, if he remembers anything of his parents, if he has happy memories of this house. But Charlotte comes out from the kitchen, wiping her hands on a tea towel, and Sam moves on. Charlotte starts to look nervously around the room. She must be looking for Morgan; it's a pity we couldn't have brought him. It still amuses me that Charlotte won't keep still for a second around him — my parents are starting to think she has some sort of attention deficit disorder. Marvellous.

'He's at home,' I call out to Charlotte.

Her head jerks up at the sound of my voice. 'Hmm? I'm sorry?'

'Morgan. We didn't bring him. He's at home.'

She walks slowly towards me, frowning a little. 'No, it's not that. There's just some sort of . . . well, smell, I suppose. A fishy sort.'

Bugger. I thought I'd sprayed enough perfume on. My mother breaks off from her conversation with Emma. 'It's Clemmie,' she calls out and then goes back to her chat.

Dear God! Does she have to do that? Tell everyone that I smell as though I have a perpetual struggle with being whiffy and then just leave it at that? No I've-been-feeding-my-ruddy-seagull-in-the-bath-again.

'It's Norman,' I put in quickly.

Charlotte has another quick look around the room. 'But he's not here.' She clearly thinks I'm trying to pass my rather severe odour problem on to some poor unsuspecting creature who isn't even present.

'No, I know. But my mother was feeding him sardines in the bath this afternoon and didn't tell me, and so I took a bath when I got home from work. I think the oil has somehow stuck to me.'

There's a loud guffaw of laughter from Sam as he tops up Holly's glass. I look at him suspiciously but he now appears to be talking seriously to Holly about property prices.

'Oh,' says Charlotte, who is clearly at a loss as to how to reply to this. Debrett's obviously doesn't cover such incidents. 'Well. That clears that up then. I'm glad it's you because I thought something had died in here!' she says jollily.

'Really.'

She blushes a brilliant red and Sam lets loose another shout of laughter. We both look at him this time but he's still talking to Holly. Charlotte bustles off back to the kitchen and Sam goes to fetch another bottle.

I wander over to Holly, who is grinning at me.

'Well, so much for social etiquette. She just told me I smell like something that's died.'

'That's God punishing you for the perfume comment. I have to say that you don't smell good.'

'She'll probably make me eat outside.'

I can hear Barney's dulcet tones coming from the kitchen; he must have let himself in through the back door; a few seconds later he makes his appearance, grasping a glass of bubbly in one hand and several canapés in the other.

Holly and I give an involuntary gasp which makes my mother and father cut off their conversation with Emma and turn towards him.

He has had all his golden, blond locks cut off to a smart, short stubble. He grins at us all nervously and quickly shoves the canapés into his mouth.

'Hello,' he says through the bulges in his cheeks, and waves at us uncertainly.

'I think he's better looking,' murmurs Holly in disbelief. I take a long, hard look at him. I've never seen him without his hair. It's actually a couple of shades darker at the roots and his features seem more pronounced and angular somehow. The whole thing makes him look more grown-up. I can almost feel my mother getting a little tearful as she stands next to me but I think Holly is right. Barney is better looking for it which almost seems impossible.

'Do you like it?' he says apprehensively, glancing from one to the other of us.

We all loudly voice our assent and, looking more relaxed, he joins Holly and me at the fire. Luckily his sense of smell has been eroded by the state of his own kitchen and so he doesn't even pass comment on me.

'What on earth made you decide to do that?' asks Holly.

'I thought I would look more serious.'

'You do. The Scooby T-shirt and trainers ruin the effect a bit though.'

'Has this girl of yours seen the new haircut?' I ask in a whisper.

'Yes.'

'And?'

He shrugs. 'I don't know. I'm not sure if she liked it or not.'

'Of course she liked it,' I say fiercely. 'She must have done. She's probably playing her cards very close to her chest.'

'I don't think she's very impressed with anything I do. She just said she was pleased I was going to get a new job and that was it!'

'Sometimes, when someone doesn't like you in that way, there is nothing you can do about it.' I look at my dejected brother's face and my heart goes out to him. The poor boy simply doesn't know what to do because it's never happened to him before. Whereas it's happened to me aplenty.

Sam calls us through to the dining room for supper before we can ask any more questions and so I give Barney's hand a quick squeeze in lieu of any verbal comfort.

It's a peculiarly strange feeling watching Charlotte in Sam's house, taking over the kitchen, striding from room to room finding serving spoons and heatproof mats for the table. She has an old apron wrapped around her waist and the whole scene seems unbearably cosy. Sam is opening some wine in one corner and I feel quite possessive about him suddenly. After all, he is practically a member of my family, and I feel as though Charlotte is an intruder. I quickly shake off the feeling and drain the dregs of my champagne. After all, I daresay I would feel exactly the same if it were Barney.

Sam passes around the wine while Charlotte serves a starter of little onion tartlets. We all begin eating and I have to admit that she really is quite a good cook.

'So how long will you be staying with the Colshannons, Emma?' asks Charlotte politely.

Emma is still holding the fact that she had to pack in a bit of a rush against me and Holly, and my forever good-tempered mother has let her rummage through her own wardrobe (in which there are a fair smattering of designer labels from photo shoots and adverts). I did offer Emma the use of my own meagre wardrobe but she said she didn't want to because besides making her look like some sort of refugee, my clothes would be far too large for her. Considering she is pregnant and an inch taller than me, I take this as a fairly large punch in the face. Holly has lent her something for this evening because she desperately needs Emma's help to write copy for 'High Society'.

'Just a few days.'

'Have you and Holly been friends for long?'

'Oh, we're more than just friends. I owe Holly a lot.' She shoots a really nasty look down the table at us and Holly blushes.

'Oh that's nice.' Charlotte smiles prettily.

'Isn't it? I'm hoping to pay her back one day.'

'Sam is always telling me how generous Holly is, I mean in spirit.'

'Oh, she's definitely that,' affirms Emma.

'How do you know each other?'

'We work together at the paper. Holly is so popular there!' Goodness! Is Emma paying Holly a compliment? I glance over to Holly. Emma has the whole table's attention now. 'Yes,' she continues, 'Holly is quite a girl.'

'Oh really?' says Charlotte with interest. 'How do you mean?'

'Well, there are so many stories that I hardly know where to start!'

Holly sucks in her cheeks and looks absolutely thrilled.

'What sort of stories?'

'Well, do you remember that time, Holly, when Joe nearly had to get the police in because they thought you were dealing in drugs?'

There is a collective gasp around the table and Holly damn near falls under it. She quickly pulls herself together. 'I hardly think that a few vitamin C tablets can constitute a drug charge, Emma,' she says in a very careful voice. 'I was only joking and Joe just got the wrong end of the stick.' Holly looks round at all the anxious faces to make sure they are taking heed. 'The wrong end of the stick,' she says again, enunciating very clearly. My mother lets out a nervous giggle.

'Oh. Was that all there was to it?' says Emma with obvious disappointment.

'Yes. It was. You know how these things can get exaggerated.'

'Well, what about the time you were caught letting men into the office late at night to drink from Joe's booze cupboard? Was that exaggerated too?' Emma is making Holly sound as though she's some slapper who picks men up off the street.

'They were a few old university friends who were visiting for the weekend,' says Holly

222

through gritted teeth. I don't like the nasty glint in Emma's eye.

'Really, that's not what I heard. I heard that — '

In the meantime I have wolfed down the rest of my tartlet and put my knife and fork together with a loud clatter. 'Gosh! Well that was delicious,' I babble at Charlotte before Emma can go any further. 'You must give me the recipe for it.'

'Of course!' Charlotte smiles, suitably distracted.

'I mean right now. Do you have it in the kitchen?'

Charlotte looks at me in mystification. 'Em, yes. If you really want it, Clemmie.'

She daintily finishes her food and then bustles off kitchenwards for a recipe that I probably will never master nor will ever feel the inclination to, especially after a day at Mr Trevesky's café.

Holly and I help to clear the plates and take them through to the kitchen.

'Did you listen to Emma out there?' demands Holly under her breath so Charlotte can't hear. 'If it wasn't the day she should have been getting married I'd have stabbed her with the cheese knife. God, I wish I'd read a few more Agatha Christies. I'd finish her off in no time.'

'I wouldn't hold out too much hope of getting Emma to help you with 'High Society',' I murmur.

'And that's the least of my problems,' groans Holly.

I grimace slightly. 'We'll deliver her safely to

France and then everything will get better. It has to really.'

Charlotte has been busy rooting around in a recipe folder while we've been talking (does she keep them here? How domestic is that?) and she presses the recipe on me before I can object.

The next course is pasta with sun-dried tomatoes and pine nuts. Sam comes and sits between Holly and me while Charlotte sits up at the other end of the table with Emma and my parents, where my father will rein in the conversation if it gets out of hand.

'So have you sorted out the final arrangements for France yet, Holly?' asks Sam quietly, his eyes carefully watching Charlotte.

Holly's fork pauses midway to her mouth. 'Well, there's been a slight hitch . . . ' she says carefully.

This time my fork pauses midway to my mouth. 'What sort of hitch?' I ask.

'I've been talking to Joe today. He's pretty cross about things . . . '

'So?' I demand. 'So?'

'Holly needs to go back to work next week, Clemmie,' interjects Sam calmly, and he has absolutely no problems in getting his fork up to his mouth.

I look in horror at him and then Holly. 'You're going to leave me with Emma?'

'Mum and Dad are going too.'

'Much use they'll be if Charlie swings through the window with a knife between his teeth.'

'Well, I wouldn't be that much use either.'

'But you're leaving me at the mercy of her

rather unfortunate personality disorder,' I hiss.

'I'll go to France with you,' says Sam.

Holly looks at him in absolute delight. We still haven't managed to eat anything but Sam has nearly finished his plate.

'Would you, Sam?' The gratitude in her voice can't be disguised. 'I'd feel so awful just leaving them to it.'

'So you should feel awful. You can't make poor Sam take time off work.'

'Well, I do own the firm, Clemmie. It'll be good for them to do without me for a while and we're only talking a couple of days, aren't we?' Holly nods energetically at this. 'Besides, it has been worrying me what you would do if that Martin character turned up. I don't like the idea of you out there by yourself, Clemmie.'

'I am perfectly capable of looking after myself, thank you.'

'Oh yes, and what would you do? Stab him with a hair slide?' Actually I know how hopeless I would be if I were faced with Martin Connelly and that's exactly what I would do.

'I have taken a self-defence course,' I say haughtily.

'Well, I might just come along in case your hair slide plan doesn't work,' says Sam dryly.

I secretly quite like it when men come over all protective about me but I cannot betray my feminist principles. Still, it has been worrying me what I would do if Martin turned up, especially since I can't remember any of my self defence course. I would feel happier if Sam — a healthy, young, virile man — is with us but I don't see why Holly should be let off the hook this easily.

'But you got us into this mess, Holly.'

'I know, I'm sorry, but I think I might lose my job if I don't get back to the paper and make amends.'

'What are you all talking about down there?' calls Charlotte from the other end of the table.

'The village cricket match tomorrow,' calls back Sam.

'Super! I love cricket!'

'Barney is playing.'

Charlotte turns wide eyes of surprise on to our brother. 'You play cricket, Barney?'

'In a manner of speaking,' he says modestly. Well, it's certainly unique, there's no doubting that.

The spotlight now safely off us and on to Barney and his cricket, the three of us turn back to the subject in hand.

'What will you tell Charlotte?' I whisper.

'Something along the lines of the truth. But not.'

'So a lie, then?'

'Er, yes. Pretty much.'

'Do you think that's fair?'

'I don't think you can lecture me about lies, sardine girl. Holly has told me all about your part in this debacle.'

I glare at Holly. 'Please don't start calling me that.'

'Why? It might catch on.'

'Yes, that's exactly why,' I reply tersely and start to eat my now-cold pasta.

'Ooh,' says Holly suddenly. 'You're all going to

have a wonderful time. I quite wish I was coming with you.'

God, if looks could kill.

★ ★ ★

The next day dawns beautifully sunny for Barney's debut and I wander downstairs in my dressing gown. Norman is still nestled in his bean bag by the Aga and by the look of him has probably been there all night. How he has managed to escape the attention of my father thus far I simply do not know. My mother has probably been draping tea towels over him or something.

I help myself to cereal from the packet on the table and then munch away, trying desperately to wake up. My mother drifts into focus.

'Darling, Holly told me that Sam is coming with us to France now instead of her. Is that right?'

I'm still incapable of opening my mouth and so just nod.

'Won't that be fun?'

It's quite lucky that I can't open my mouth because otherwise I would tell her exactly what I think of the entire situation.

'Now, what are you going to pack? Holly says we're flying down to Nice and that these people live somewhere in Provence. Isn't that lucky? I'm so glad they live in the south. It must be simply boiling down there. And I've just spoken to that charming Sir Christopher McKellan on the telephone and he is absolutely insisting that he pays for all our flights. Even Sam. He says it's the least he can do for us having had Emma to stay down here. What a nice man.'

I make grumbling noises at her. It really is far too early to be talking about things like this.

'Your father and I might stay an extra day or so while we're out there. Would you be able to stay too? After all, I have left Matt in charge of *Calamity Jane* for the week and Barney has promised faithfully to look after Morgan and Norman.'

This brings a wry smile to my face. Norman is used to beanbags by the Aga and sardines fed to him in the bath. Staying at my brother's is going to be a short, sharp shock to his system. Norman probably won't want to even go near the kitchen there.

'I simply must get down to the shops before we go and buy some sardines for Norman.' She doesn't pause for a reply to any of these questions but simply sweeps off muttering about thank you notes to Charlotte and the such like.

Emma elects to stay at home for a rest while we all trundle down to the village green to watch Barney play. My mother says she has packed a picnic but Holly and I don't hold out great hopes for this. She is certainly carrying a picnic basket but this doesn't usually count for much. She simply sweeps anything she can lay her hands on between two slices of bread and calls it a sandwich. When any of us siblings were given a packed lunch for our school trips we tried to shove as much breakfast down us as possible and then went hungry. At least today Holly and I have stolen a march because we both have cereal bars shoved up our sleeves.

I have sort of forgiven Holly for leaving me to take Emma to France, mainly because I can't be arsed to hold it against her and we're having a very nice speculative gossip about who Barney's secret amour might be. We know she will be present at the match today.

The sun is shining after a wet night and the hedgerows smell gorgeous as we thump down the hill towards the village. Most of the residents are already gathered around the green. I don't think this is from any altruistic interest in the village community spirit but simply because this way they feel safer knowing that they can duck any balls heading their way.

My mother picks up Morgan lest he gets trampled underfoot and waves madly at a few people. She is hopelessly over-dressed as usual and is wearing a garish wraparound skirt with a frilly white blouse and huge hat. We spot Sam and Charlotte over in the far corner and start to make our way towards them, dodging through various groups of people. This is a slow business because they all want to say hello to Holly and gossip with my mother. My mother absolutely adores chatting to the locals now but I remember it was difficult when we first moved here due to their strong accents and their propensity to throw in the local rhetorical catchphrase of 'Look-see?' at the end of every sentence. My mother kept thinking they were pointing something out to her and spent the entire time turning around to look.

They are both already gossiping so my father and I give up and leave them behind.

'So,' I whisper to my father, 'you know this girl that Barney is interested in?'

'I am absolutely not telling you, Clemmie.'

'I'm really good at secrets.'

My father gives me a sardonic look. 'Clemmie, we both know that you would squeal at the slightest provocation.'

'Okay, okay. But how did you guess?'

'Some things are obvious.'

Er, not to me. 'Do I like her?'

'Clemmie, I am not playing those does-her-name-begin-with-D games with you.'

'Does it?'

'I'm not playing.'

'But is she here?'

My father lets his eyes sweep around the perimeter of the green. 'Yes,' he finally answers. 'And that's all I'm telling you.' And with this he marches off Sam-wards.

My eyes follow his route. So she's here. Who on earth can she be? For all the fuss that Barney is making she must be some sort of goddess. Goddesses, both external and internal, are surprisingly thin on the ground in the village so surely she should stick out like a nun in a nightclub.

Talking of nuns, Catherine Fothersby looms in front of me. An apparition in pale blue cashmere.

'Good afternoon, Clemmie.'

'Oh, hello Catherine. How are you?'

'I'm helping Mummy with the teas afterwards.' That's not what I asked but anyway. 'Matt tells me that Barney is playing?'

'Hmm. Yes. Loosely speaking.'

'Matt is captaining today.'

'Thank God for that. At least he'll put Barney a long way away.'

'Well, I hope he won't let the team down,' she says primly.

'Absolutely. It's all about the taking part, isn't it?'

She narrows her eyes at me as though she's not quite sure if I'm taking the piss and I gladly take my leave and move on to Charlotte and Sam. 'Hello!' I say. 'Thank you for a lovely meal last night.'

Charlotte smiles and tells me I'm welcome. My mother and Holly manage to make it over to us at last.

'Hello Charlotte, hello Sam. Isn't this just too, too exciting? One of our boys playing cricket. I do hope he knows how to play.'

She puts Morgan down, who immediately flops at her feet, and enthusiastically joins in a very disjointed smattering of applause that starts up as the two teams run on to the pitch.

I sigh to myself. This is what I hate about cricket. How on earth am I supposed to know which side is which? They all look the bloody same in their whites. I manage to pick out Barney and my heart swells slightly with pride. My father manages to stop my mother from waving and shouting 'Cooeee!' at him.

'You'd think the other team would at least be

wearing a different coloured top,' I grumble to Sam. 'How are we supposed to know who is who? I can barely recognise anyone from this distance.'

'Well, one team bats and the other team bowls and fields.'

'Is that supposed to mean something to me?'

Sam tries again. 'So only two members of the other team are on the pitch. The ones who are batting.'

'That seems hardly fair,' I object. 'All those men against two.'

'Think of it as just the bowler against the batsman.'

'Oh. Okay. Can Barney play cricket?' I ask hopefully.

Sam frowns. 'Well, we played a bit at school but then he got that cricket ball in the eye and after that they always made him go further and further out. He was fielding in the woods by the end.'

'But he knows the rules?'

'I suppose, but you know Barney and rules. They've never really got along. I don't really know why he wants to play for the village team. He's never shown the slightest amount of interest before.'

'Hmm,' I say non-committally. So Barney really hasn't said anything to Sam about this girl.

Unfortunately ruddy Charlotte seems to have been reared on a diet of cricket and we get non-stop jabber from her about leg-overs and balls under which my mother says all sounds fabulously vulgar. Barney has been put out to field and already I can see him chatting to some onlookers at the perimeter. I really hope he will concentrate.

Holly's mobile starts ringing mid-bowl, which attracts a few nasty looks from the cricket lovers, and she wanders off to answer it. With any luck it might be James.

I turn my attention back to the cricket but she suddenly appears next to me looking white-faced.

'Everything okay?' I ask in concern.

She looks at me dazedly. 'It's Martin Connelly.'

'What about him?'

'He's on his way down here.'

15

I stare at Holly aghast. 'Where? I mean, how?' I ask in confusion.

'I don't know. That was Ruth on the phone. She's on the Sunday shift today and apparently she was walking to work when this bloke fell into step with her and asked if Holly Colshannon worked at the *Gazette* and wasn't she the daughter of that stage actress . . . '

'But how on earth did he find that out?'

'I don't know. He must have done a bit of research himself.'

'Maybe he went to the library and looked up your old stories on microfiche. Our mother might have been mentioned there.'

'It doesn't bloody matter how he did it, he just asked Ruth if I lived in a village in Cornwall and she helpfully filled in the name for him.'

'She didn't!'

'She bloody did.'

'Oh my God.' I close my eyes briefly and really wish there was somewhere I could sit down. 'Didn't Joe tell people not to talk to anyone suspicious? Didn't she see him when he came into the office?'

'I know, I know. She said he was so friendly and nice that she thought he was a fan of our mother's. He just asked the one question and then ran off, and because she wasn't at work and looking for someone suspicious, she answered automatically.'

Sam, who has been looking at us quite suspiciously himself, comes over. 'Is everything okay?'

'Martin Connelly is coming down,' I blurt out. 'He found out the name of the village and he's coming down.'

'When? When did this happen?'

'About half an hour ago,' replies Holly.

I look at Sam admiringly. No hows or whys for him. How eminently practical he is.

'Come on,' he says after a moment. 'We need to get back to Emma.'

He smoothly gathers my parents from the crowd and then goes to speak to Charlotte, who nods understandingly. He's probably told her that Clemmie is a complete fruitcake and he's just going to pop off and have her committed immediately. We all start up the hill towards home.

'Why is Martin so desperate to find Emma?' asks Sam as he strides away. God, do we have to walk so fast? I know that a convicted felon is after us, but still. 'He must realise that her father knows who he is now.'

'I don't know,' I puff. 'What's he going to do though, Sam?' This thought has been playing on my mind. Maybe he's so furious that he's coming down expressly to kill me. My mind lingers unpleasantly on this picture for a moment. No, no, don't be so self-centred, Clemmie. Of course not. He'll kill Holly first.

'I don't know,' he mutters. 'I'm thinking.'

I leave him to think for a whole minute.

'Any ideas?' I venture.

'Still thinking.'

He's obviously gone into Pooh Bear mode, so I drop back to join my parents who are a good fifty metres behind. 'What's Holly doing?' I ask. She is another fifty metres behind us and talking on her mobile.

'Calling James,' answers my mother. 'Maybe he'll know what to do.'

Well, I'm all for taking a few supplies, popping Norman at the front door and disappearing to the cellar. The plan seems watertight to me.

We reach the house and all pile through the unlocked door into the kitchen. Just that realisation makes me feel quite faint. Our doors are always unlocked, we simply don't think anything of it. Martin could have walked straight in and up the stairs towards Emma. Maybe he is already here? I look around in alarm. Let's keep this in perspective, Clemmie. Someone spoke to him in Bristol about half an hour ago. Even Martin doesn't have supernatural skills.

'I don't think we should panic Emma until we know what to do,' says Sam.

'What do we do?' I ask.

'Er, I don't know yet but we have at least two hours. I think the important thing is that he doesn't see Emma. Even if her condition isn't that obvious, it would be awful for her. So we need to move her.'

'That's exactly what James says.' Holly has come in after us all.

'Is James coming down?' I ask hopefully.

236

Preferably in a large squad car with sirens and maybe a bit of back-up as well.

'No, he's not,' says Holly shortly.

'Could we call the local police?'

'And have the whole of the village know where she is? Besides, Martin still hasn't done anything illegal, Clemmie. And you might argue that he has a perfect right to know he's about to become a father,' says Holly.

'I don't think the moral issues are any concern of ours. You and Clemmie made a promise to help Emma and that's what we're doing,' interjects my father.

'We can either move her to Barney's house or mine,' says Sam. 'I think mine might be best because the fewer people who know the better. Any of Barney's housemates might be at home.'

'What about Charlotte?' asks my father.

'I might have to tell her.'

'Better her than any of Barney's blabbermouth friends,' I throw in.

I look over to my mother to see if she has any sage words of advice for us all but she looks so absolutely thrilled by the entire scenario that I decide it's best to leave her out of it.

'So we move Emma to Sam's house,' my father summarises.

This is all very well and good but I'm keen to move on to the next part. 'And then what?' I ask eagerly. 'We make for the hills? Pop off to Jamaica Inn for a drink?'

'No, I think the best thing is for us to face him.'

'Face him? You mean Martin Connelly? We are

talking about the same person, aren't we?'

'Clemmie, if we don't convince him that you and Holly have absolutely no idea where Emma is then he might keep hounding you. Even after we have delivered Emma to France. Which isn't illegal but difficult to stop.'

Good point. I don't like it much but it's a good point.

'Holly, I might just give James a call and have a chat with him. See if he has any ideas,' says Sam.

'I'll go and wake Emma and tell her to gather her things together now that we know where she's going,' says my father.

Holly hands her mobile over to Sam and he and my father disappear off in separate directions, leaving the three women and Morgan in the kitchen.

'Aren't Sam and your father wonderfully in charge?' breathes my mother. 'It's just too, too thrilling. Barney will be so disappointed to have missed all this. Do you think I should go and get him?'

'No! I think you should leave him where he is.'

'You're right. It might be dangerous.'

'The way Barney is playing cricket I think he would be better off facing Martin Connelly.'

'Holly, what do you think?'

'Why do you think Martin is so desperate to see Emma?' I cut straight across my mother and address myself to Holly. 'Sam's right. He must know the game is up.'

'I don't know. Perhaps he wants to rub it in, otherwise it's a bit of a silent victory for him, isn't it? Having gone to so much trouble, he probably wants to experience the end result.'

'And he was supposed to, wasn't he? They were going to get married and then go and surprise her father. Maybe he's pissed off that she has upset his plans.'

'Well, we certainly know that he's pissed off from his little scene at the paper,' agrees Holly.

'Now, what do you think I should wear?' says my mother.

★　★　★

My father is the first to rejoin us and informs us that Emma is packing. When Sam returns he at least seems to have some sort of plan. Not my sort of plan, but a plan.

'James and I think the best thing is for us all to be very surprised when Martin turns up. He only has the name of the village at the moment so he needs someone to direct him up here.'

'You will stay with us, won't you?' I ask suddenly in alarm.

'Maybe it's better if Sam isn't here,' says my father gently. 'After all, the least number of people that Connelly knows the better.'

'But I'll stay if you really want me to,' says Sam.

'Let's hear the rest of the plan first,' says my father firmly.

'Then when Martin turns up, Holly tells him that she dropped Emma off with her father and she hasn't seen her since.'

'IS THAT IT?' I roar. 'But he won't believe it!

What on earth is Holly doing down here anyway?'

'She'll say her editor was so pissed off with her over the story that he made her take a week's sabbatical while he decides whether or not to fire her. Naturally she came home for a while. And of course he won't believe Holly when she says she dropped Emma off at her father's. So at this point, Clemmie, you jump in and say something like Emma talked about staying with some friends of John Montague's in Birmingham. All clear?'

Er, no. Not really.

Sam stands up as though he's about to leave. 'Where are you going? I ask in alarm.

'I'm going to take Emma down to my house. Via the back entrance, naturally.'

'I'll come with you!'

'Don't be silly, Clemmie. You have to stay here. Besides, I need to see if I can get us on any earlier flights to France.'

'To France?'

'Yes, Clemmie. We still have to take Emma to France.'

'Why don't we set off now?' I clasp myself on to Sam's arm.

'Clemmie, it's all going to be fine.' Sam starts to prise my fingers off his arm, one by one. 'Everyone is going to look after you and then we're all setting off to France together. Thank God Holly isn't coming with us now, that really would look suspicious if he was watching us. At least we can say we're just popping off for a little holiday.'

240

'I'll try to inadvertently mention it, just in case he's thinking of coming back,' my father says calmly.

'I don't really have to be here, do I?' I interject. 'Couldn't I be somewhere else? He's really come to see Holly, not me.'

'You're essential to the proceedings.'

'Well, that's sweet of you to say so, Sam. But you might need some help carrying Emma's luggage.'

'I think I'll be able to manage Emma's luggage. You're needed here, Clemmie, because you're the weak link. Let Connelly throw his weight around for a bit, a few bully boy tactics, and then you hit him with the punchline. That you heard Emma on the phone and Birmingham is where she's heading.' Sam gives me a couple of slaps on the back and leaves.

This has got disaster written all over it.

★   ★   ★

By my father's reckoning Charlie should be here at five. We all arrange ourselves decoratively in the sitting room, complete with Sunday papers and the remains of some tea things. My father seems genuinely interested in the article he's reading whereas I can't even focus on the words long enough to take them in. I start playing the 'what if?' game. What if Martin instantly knows I'm lying? Do I just blab out that Emma is at Sam's house or hold my ground while he tries to throttle me? What if he simply doesn't believe us? What if . . .

241

'Clemmie! Will you stop sucking that cushion? We paid an awful lot of money for it and we don't need your dribble marks all over it,' says my father.

I nervously replace the cushion and pick up Morgan, who has been expressly asking to sit on my lap for the last ten minutes. I hope I'm not going to inadvertently start sucking him too. That really wouldn't be nice.

'Darling, just do what we do in the theatre,' says my mother soothingly.

'What's that?'

'Breathe,' she says, and waves a floaty arm in front of me.

'That's it?' I demand. 'Breathe? You haven't anything better than that? No drugs, no alcohol?' I go back to wringing my hands.

Please God, let Martin lose his way. I promise I'll start going to church. I'll start being nice to Catherine Fothersby. Maybe even Charlotte too.

God has clearly heard it all before. He certainly has from me because the doorbell rings and I nearly leap through the roof. Poor Morgan ends up back on the floor.

'I'll get it,' says my mother.

'Clemmie, just calm down or you're going to blow it for everyone,' hisses Holly in a none-too-friendly way as she gets up from the sofa. 'Sit!' She gives me a little shove. I can hear my mother breezily leading someone through; she is undoubtedly a very gifted actress. It's just a pity I haven't inherited any of her skills. I whimper to myself as I hear Martin's dulcet tones getting closer and closer.

'Darlings, there's someone here to see you. I'm

242

so sorry, I didn't catch the name. It was . . . ?'

'Martin Connelly,' he replies, and there he is standing before us. His eyes catch like Velcro on to mine and I hope I give a passably good impression of being surprised. I am certainly shocked to see him. It's peculiar to see someone who features in your worst nightmares casually standing before you. Like Hannibal Lecter or Freddy Kruger just popping in for tea.

'Hello Holly, hello Clemmie,' he says quietly.

Holly has risen unsteadily to her feet and stares at him for a moment. My father, who has also risen to his feet, says in his best paternal manner, 'Holly, perhaps you could introduce us?' She duly makes the appropriate introductions and the two men shake hands. 'Do you know Holly from work?' asks my father politely.

'Em, yes. You could say that.'

'What on earth are you doing here, Martin?' Holly smoothly interrupts. 'How did you find our house?'

He gives a mad sort of laugh. Well, it's probably quite a normal one but I have a slightly tainted view on Martin.

'You're not the only one with detecting skills, Holly. Now look, I'm not going to get angry, I'm sorry about that. I just want to ask you a few questions.'

'Won't you sit down, Mr Connelly?' asks my mother, gesturing to a chair which is so close to me that I think she must be going quite mad too. Does she want him to sit on my knee or something? I quickly sit back down and concentrate on making myself as small as possible. I curl my legs up under me and shrink into the back of the chair.

'Would you like a cup of tea? Martin did you say it was?' interjects my mother. Martin nods his assertion and she goes out of the room.

'So where do you know Martin from?' asks my father, looking from one to the other of us. Holly looks very convincingly shamefaced: she obviously has inherited some skills from my mother.

'I'm afraid it was that story I got involved in, Dad.'

'You mean the one you got suspended for?'

'Yes. Things weren't as I thought they were.'

'You've been suspended?' asks Martin.

'For a week, pending an inquiry.'

My mother returns with a cup of tea for Martin and he takes it, thanking her prettily. He still has some very nice manners.

He sips his tea for a second and then turns to me and says softly, 'Clemmie, where's Emma?' He clearly has spotted the very obvious chink in the armour here.

'I . . . I don't know,' I stammer. 'We took her to her father's house and left her there.'

'Look,' says my father. 'Holly has told me all about your situation. I take it you are Charlie? She did exactly as I would have done, she washed her hands of the entire affair. After all, there is no story in it for her now, and I have to say you used her in this nasty little game of yours. I am surprised you took the trouble to come all the way down here to ask them — one day later you wouldn't have found us because we're all going off on holiday. But I would have thought it was obvious that the girls simply don't know where this Emma is.'

Normally, my father should now turf Martin out, but things still have to be said, and parts have to be played.

'Well, you see that's where I think you're wrong, Mr Colshannon, because I believe that Holly and Clemmie do know where Emma is. In fact, I am so convinced of it that I travelled all the way down here to ask them. Now, things aren't going to get nasty, I just want to know where Emma is.'

'We dropped her off at her father's house,' Holly repeats.

'I'm not sure that I believe you.'

We are all quiet for a moment. I stare steadily at my knee.

'Look,' says my father quietly. 'Do you mind if we just look at this from their point of view for a moment? Holly starts on a story that she thinks she can make something of but during the course of her investigation finds out that the facts aren't what she thought they were. Her editor is on her case, Sir Christopher McKellan is threatening to sue her and there isn't a story any more. So what does she do? She dumps Emma back with her father. Why on earth should she do anything else? Yes, she feels guilty that she might have inadvertently led you to Emma but I'm afraid you have too much faith in her sense of responsibility. Quite frankly, all I'm worried about is whether Holly is going to keep her job or not.'

This is a long speech for my father and I can

see that Martin is quietly impressed.

'I'm really sorry about Holly's job.'

Luckily butt-clenching terror keeps me from snorting loudly.

'Hounding her and Clemmie and practically attacking them isn't going to help you.'

'I'm sorry about that too. I was acting kind of crazy that day.' All the same, it doesn't stop him turning to me. 'Clemmie? When you left Emma, did she mention what she was going to do next?'

I look wildly around the room, reeking of guilt, which is probably just the reaction I ought to be giving.

'Clemmie, you don't have to say anything,' says my father.

'Look, I just want to talk to her. Why else would I want to track her down so badly?'

'I told you,' I whisper. 'We dropped her at her father's house.'

'I know she's not at the house in Bristol or in Rock. I just want to tell her that I'm sorry I caught her up in all this. Please just let me have the chance to try to make amends.'

I don't believe him for a second but it's just the thing to make me spill my guts. 'All right,' I burst out. 'She said she might go and stay with some friends of John Montague's in Birmingham. She didn't tell me anything about them.'

Martin smiles a peculiar small smile. 'Thanks for the tea, Mrs Colshannon.' And with this, he places his cup on a small side table and gets up. My father escorts him out of the room and moments later we hear the front door slam and the hum of a car starting up.

16

'Right, the only thing I could get us all on is an overnight train to Nice.'

'An overnight train? I thought we were flying.' I'm sitting on the kitchen table ramming some random cake into my mouth. I think this whole episode might leave me with an eating disorder.

'Our flights weren't until Wednesday and Christopher and I feel we can't wait that long. It was the only thing I could get us on.'

'Christopher?' I query, spitting crumbs at him. Surely he's not referring to bloody scary Sir Christopher McKellan?

Sam looks at me strangely. 'Yes, Emma's father. You must remember him, Clemmie. The one you met.'

'Oh, I remember the one I met. He just doesn't bear any resemblance to the one you're talking about,' I mumble as I pop the rest of the cake into my already burgeoning mouth.

'We're leaving tomorrow night. I thought it might be best to make sure that Connelly isn't still hanging about somewhere. How was it by the way? Your father told me the bulk of it.'

I shrug and study my flip-flops for a moment. 'It was okay. I don't really know what to make of him.'

Sam comes over and sits next to me on the table. He puts a comforting arm on mine. 'Clemmie, you don't have to make anything of him. You shouldn't have been part of this dreadful business at all.' I look up hopefully at this glimmer of sympathy. 'It was bloody foolish to let yourself get involved in the first place.' Ah. Not really a glimmer at all. 'But we'll be rid of Emma in a few days. We just have to deliver her to these people in France and then the ghastly business will be finished.'

My lip trembles a smidgeon at his soft tone. 'What if Martin keeps plaguing us?'

'He's had his little revenge, Clemmie. He'll give up in the end.' The end of what? The end of time? Sam gives me a couple of slaps on the leg and slips off the table. 'You'd better go and pack. We've got to leave at lunchtime tomorrow.'

'Lunchtime?' I shout after his disappearing back. 'I thought it was the overnight train?'

'Overnight from London,' he yells over his shoulder.

That's the problem with sodding Cornwall. It takes you at least half a day to get anywhere. And what on earth is Mr Trevesky going to say?

* * *

Luckily Mr Trevesky doesn't say too much because he has his head in his hands for most of the conversation. He does manage to get out that if I'm not back in a week then I shouldn't bother coming back at all, and that I'm awfully lucky we're out of season. He wanders off muttering that Rick Stein doesn't have to put up with these problems.

I scramble home gleefully, relieved that he

248

didn't make me stay and work the morning. Holly is gloomily spooning cereal into her mouth in the kitchen.

'Hello!' I greet her. 'How are you?' We're dropping Holly back in Bristol en route to London this afternoon.

'Depressed.'

'Why? Because you don't get to spend the next few days in Emma's scintillating company?'

'Oh, it won't be that bad. You've got Sam.' I can't see why this is so marvellous but I let it pass. 'I've got to try to sort out work and James.'

'Is he still mad?'

'He's being pretty cool at the moment.'

I can't think of anything sympathetic to say so I pat her hand for a little while. 'I don't know what to pack,' I proffer.

Holly looks at me sardonically. 'I might lose my boyfriend and my job and you don't know what to pack for your imminent jolly to the south of France?'

Put like this, and sympathy for Holly aside, I actually start to feel a little excited. It's been ages since I've had a holiday (I don't think you can count my round the world trip of a few weeks ago) and although I will be saddled with Emma for a while, I get to see the French Riviera, have a swim in the sea and maybe sip something delicious while wearing just a T-shirt and a sarong. And although I absolutely love the rugged wildness of the Cornish coast, there is something supremely seductive about the sophistication of the Côte d'Azur. Oooh, and I can pack my new bikini too.

'I'll come and help,' offers Holly.

There is a huge rumpus going on upstairs. My mother is flying from room to room with great armfuls of clothes yelling 'Shit McGregor', while my father is sitting on their bed, sedately reading a map.

We try to ignore her and take a swift left into my bedroom. Holly strides over to the wardrobe and flings it open. I start to gather a few toiletries and put them on the bed.

'Things are looking a little on the sparse side,' comments Holly. 'I thought you dressed like that because you chose to.'

I look at her indignantly. 'I do choose to!'

'You and I really need to go shopping, Clemmie.'

'But things don't tend to look the same on me as they do on you.'

'Nonsense! You've got a gorgeous pair of legs. The fact that you could do with a small truckload of conditioner is neither here nor there but you have lovely wavy hair.'

'Is that what is commonly known as a shit sandwich?' I ask dryly.

'What exactly do you do to your hair, by the way? Do you dry it properly?'

'Of course I dry it properly.'

'How do you dry it?'

'I go to bed with it wet and by morning it's dry.'

'That must make for some interesting hairstyles.'

'Every day is different.'

'God, I wish I was coming with you, I'd soon

lick you into shape. You might meet some gorgeous Frenchman. Do try and make an effort.'

'I think I'm still a bit off men,' I mumble. 'I think Seth is the reason why I'm not very good with clothes. He used to buy me those designer dresses, do you remember? I thought he was just being kind but he simply wanted me dressed in the latest designer names when I was with him. I used to feel so uncomfortable and now I just don't know what suits me any more.'

'He eroded your confidence on everything, didn't he?' Holly squeezes my arm. 'We'll definitely go shopping when you get back. What are you packing in, by the way?'

'This?' I proffer my rucksack.

'I'll get you my wheely case,' says Holly despondently.

'Darlings, isn't it marvellous that we're going by this sleeper train?' says my mother as she whizzes by with yet more clothes.

'Is it?' I ask.

'Of course! Morgan can come with us now! His pet passport is all up to date.'

Oh goody. Morgan is coming too. Thank God they don't have passports for seagulls.

The next morning, after we've dropped Norman with his bean bag and several tins of sardines at Barney's house, we pick up Sam and Emma. Emma has been at Sam's since Martin's visit and I have to say that the atmosphere in our house has lightened considerably. Not that it made a great deal of difference to my parents because my mother is so thick-skinned that she

251

wouldn't notice an atmosphere if it came up and slapped her in the face (which is funny because she claims to be terribly sensitive to it), and my father is perennially good-humoured anyway (and has to be to put up with the aforementioned mother), but Holly and I have certainly rejoiced in her absence.

My father's Range Rover has a funny little child's seat which folds down in the boot and, since there are six of us, one of us draws the short straw. Emma is pregnant, Holly and my mother claim to get car sick (if only) and Sam is a bloke. So that leaves yours truly. At least I don't have to make polite conversation but get to pull faces at other motorists on the motorway.

We drop a very despondent Holly in Bristol. She lets me out of the boot of the car so I can take her place. I give her a big kiss and a hug. 'Thanks for the suitcase.'

'Promise you'll call me as soon as you get back,' she pleads.

'Of course I will!'

'Try and pump Emma for some details for 'High Society'. Joe is climbing the wall about it and I've got to write copy in a couple of days.'

'I'll try. Where will you be?'

'I might stay at James's flat for a while until Martin stops hounding us. If James will let me, of course.'

'Why wouldn't he?'

'I don't think he's that keen on moving in with me any more,' she mumbles and looks at her hands.

'Sweetheart, it's just a row. It'll blow over.'

Holly doesn't look so sure but she gives me another kiss and I climb in next to my mother, ready for a long journey to London.

★ ★ ★

It takes some time to get through passport control and the X-ray machines at Waterloo station due to the prolonged examination of Morgan's pet passport.

After a quick pit stop at Duty Free to feed my mother's appalling fag and gin habit we board the train for Lille, where we have to change for the night train to Nice. We spend a pleasant couple of hours playing cards and teaching Emma how to play Slam! (I suggested we play Slap! instead but no one agreed with me).

On the platform at Lille we take some seats to wait for the train and my mother and Morgan whizz off to see if they can find some whisky for my father, which they completely forgot to buy at Waterloo, and my father goes to change some money. Sam seems completely absorbed in the paper so that leaves Emma and me sitting in an awkward silence. I stare long and hard at my feet until eventually I feel forced to speak.

'Er, are you okay?' I ask Emma tentatively.

She deigns to give me an extremely withering look. No less than I deserve. 'I've been better.'

Hmm. So have I. I let another minute of silence pass before I try again.

'Still feeling sick all the time?'

'Yes. Still feeling sick.'

I try staring at Sam, willing him to stop

reading his paper and help me out. I must transfer some vibes to him somehow because he suddenly looks up and smiles at Emma.

'Are you sad to be leaving England?' he asks.

'Yes, a bit. I don't know when I'll be coming back.' Her face brightens a little as she speaks to him and I try to empathise with her predicament.

'Will your father come down and visit you?'

'Oh yes, as soon as he can. He needs to bring the rest of my stuff but just wants to make sure Martin has gone away for good first.'

'But you will come back to England eventually?'

'Eventually. I don't know when.'

'But Emma, the south of France won't be such a bad place. These people you're staying with are ex-pats, aren't they?' She gives a small nod. 'So they'll know other English people and you'll soon make some friends. There's usually quite a little community out there.' Sam looks at me and I nod encouragingly. 'Besides, it will be warm and you can swim in the sea for most of the year. Think of all that lovely French bread!' He gives her a broad grin and I find myself grinning too. 'And runny cheese and pâté,' I add on.

They both give me a look. What?

'I can't eat runny cheese and pâté,' says Emma.

'She's pregnant,' says Sam.

Bugger. I forgot.

'Yes, but you can after the birth.'

Well recovered there, Clemmie.

Sam pats Emma's hand. 'It won't be as bad as you think, I promise.' Emma looks at him and I can see her really believing in him.

'Thank you, Sam. You've been kind to me. All of you.' She looks carefully from Sam to my father, who has returned from his money trip and is now busy reading Sam's discarded paper, and studiously misses me out. Well, really. How long is she going to hold it against me?

'Thank God I managed to find some whisky,' announces my mother as she returns. This is one thing I like about my parents. They never travel long distances sober.

'Why are you carrying Morgan?' I ask.

'He tried to pee on an umbrella.'

'Oh God, we're not going to have too many of these incidents, are we?'

'He just didn't like the look of the woman, darling. He took a pathological dislike to her, actually.'

'So he tried to pee on her umbrella?'

'Well, she was rather shifty-looking.'

'Clemmie, we've got two double couchettes and one single booked,' says my father. 'Naturally Emma should have the single, so I think you should share with your mother and Sam and I will double up.'

'Darling, I do hope you've washed your hair again since the sardine incident,' says my mother. I look at her incredulously as they all laugh because it was her fault anyway and she talks in her sleep and Morgan snores so it's not as though she's drawn the short straw.

We are called to our train and with some

trepidation we haul our luggage aboard and start to look for our couchettes. Because of our late booking, they are dotted over three carriages. My mother and I install Emma in hers and then leave to find ours. Panting slightly, I haul my little wheely suitcase and my mother's bag, which she couldn't manage with her wheely suitcase and Morgan, down the very slim corridor until we find our number. With some excitement I peer in.

There are two sort of sofa things facing each other with a slim piece of floor in between. They must somehow convert into beds. A little cupboard houses a sink and some glasses and there are some string luggage racks hanging over the beds. It is very snug indeed.

Morgan's bottom and I are going to be in very close proximity until tomorrow morning.

'Darling! Isn't this fabulous?' enthuses my mother from about two inches away. 'Just like a doll's house. Shall we unpack?'

With a great deal of effort, I haul our bags into the cabin and, after a bit of manoeuvring, manage to close the door.

'There!' I say. 'We're in!'

We stand for a second and survey the luggage. I can't even see our feet and Morgan is already sitting on one of the sofa things. So I decide that it simply isn't possible for both of us to be in the cabin and unpack at the same time.

'I think I might just go and find Sam and get a drink.'

'Wonderful idea. Order a large G and T for me and I'll be along in a while.'

'I'll be in the restaurant car then.'

I knock on Sam's door on the way to find he is facing a similar problem with my father and gladly volunteers to accompany me. It's funny but this is the most amount of time I have ever spent with Sam alone. There is normally always Holly or Barney or my parents around and it feels strangely intimate.

The restaurant car is already filling up as we bag a table and, having ordered two large gin and tonics, relax into our window seats.

'This is quite exciting, isn't it?' I stretch out my toes and give them a little wiggle. A large gin and tonic and a few days off work. God, I am easy to please.

Sam smiles back at me and for once a desultory, half-sarcastic comment doesn't drip off his lips. He simply says, 'Yes, it is.'

Our drinks arrive and we silently clink our glasses together and take a very welcome sip. It has been a harrowing few days.

'So what did you tell Charlotte in the end?' I ask.

He shrugs. 'I had to tell her the truth. I didn't tell her that Emma is Sir Christopher McKellan's daughter though. But she would be really pissed off if she thought I was just going off for a jolly holiday with you lot.'

'Would she?' I ask in surprise.

He looks up at me. 'Wouldn't you be if your boyfriend went off without you?'

'I suppose so. I just think that you're part of the family so it seems entirely natural to me but Charlotte probably doesn't see it that way.'

'No, I don't think she does.'

With a jolt, the train starts to make its way out of the station, which distracts us for a minute as we watch the platform recede.

'Where's Emma?' asks Sam.

I shrug. 'In her couchette, I think.'

'Your parents will collect her on their way through, won't they?'

Don't know. Don't care. 'Why all this sudden concern for Emma?' I ask in slight annoyance.

'I just think she's had a rough time, and she's pregnant as well. Must be awful.' He takes a sip of his drink.

'Just because she's pregnant doesn't make her the bloody Madonna, you know. Nasty women get pregnant too.'

'Why are you so worked up about her, Clem? This isn't like you.'

I pause slightly. How does he know what's like me? 'She just annoys me. I've never really liked her. She doesn't have any eyebrows.'

Sam lets loose a guffaw of laughter. 'You can't judge someone on their eyebrows, that's absolutely ridiculous.'

I cross my arms, and look out of the window. Of course I don't dislike Emma because of her eyebrows. It's her whole attitude that's the problem. I take a sip of my gin and tonic and let the silence endure. I hope it's killing him.

'Talking of eyebrows, did you see Catherine Fothersby making eyes at Matt the other night?' says Sam.

I turn to him in delight, all manner of sulks forgotten. Now, this is just my tipple. 'Bloody hell, I thought they were going to pop out of her head!' I rejoin. 'Mrs Fothersby can't be all that pleased about Catherine being on the stage.'

'She'll be pleased if Catherine and Matt end up together.'

I frown. 'But they're chalk and cheese, Matt surely wouldn't be interested in her?'

'Oh I don't know, Clem. I think our Catherine might have hidden depths. I bet she can't wait to give up that job of hers and become the model vicar's wife. Tea parties and whist drives. She is undoubtedly her mother's daughter.' He pauses for a second. 'Talking of jobs, have you thought any more about work, Clemmie?'

God, do we have to bring up Mr Trevesky? I am desperately trying to forget about him.

'Well, I said I would be back within a few days and Mr Trevesky replied that if I wasn't then he would — '

'No, I mean long term,' Sam interrupts. 'What are you going to do long term?'

'I don't know,' I say in a small voice, my mood slightly deflating. I fiddle nervously with my glass. 'Why?'

'After our conversation the other day I just wondered if you should think about doing something else in the art world. I mean, St Ives has the Tate, and Padstow and other places have lots of galleries. Perhaps you could even open your own?'

I look at him thoughtfully. Work in a gallery. I hadn't really thought about that. Open my own gallery. Maybe. In time. But what a wonderful idea. I even start to feel a little excited. I could purchase works of art, light them properly, have drinks evenings and events.

'Thanks, Sam,' I say. 'That's a really good idea.'

He smiles and I notice suddenly that he has a really nice smile. It's warm and friendly and shows all his teeth. Great teeth too, white and gleaming. I haven't really clocked any of this before. How can you have known someone for over twelve years and not noticed their smile?

Before I can reflect on this any further, my parents come noisily into the carriage with Emma in tow.

'Emma said she wasn't hungry but we absolutely insisted,' says my father cheerfully. 'Can't have that baby of hers going hungry! Budge up, Clemmie!'

The tables are only designed for four but because my parents don't want to leave someone to eat across the gangway, they insist we can all manage to sit together. Luckily the seats are of the bench variety so we can squeeze up. Unluckily they haven't reckoned on the size of my arse.

Emma and Sam sit together and watch with some amusement as all three of us try to squeeze on. I end up with half a butt cheek on my mother's lap, feeling somewhat giggly.

'There!' says my mother. 'Beaucoup des gin et tonics, s'il vous plaît!' she adds to the waiter, who tuts slightly at our unconventional seating arrangement but quickly recovers his good humour when my mother turns her charming, infectious smile on him. We have that contagious *joie de vivre* of people just off on holiday and he's prepared to be magnanimous.

We have an absolutely marvellous evening. The wine flows and my good temper isn't even dented by the fact that Sam won't let any of us have pâté or runny cheese on account of the fact it would be unfair to Emma. In fact, the sacrifice is well worth it because Emma becomes positively good-humoured as we chug through the darkness of the French countryside towards the coast and her final destination.

17

We all cheerfully stumble back to our cabin for a quick nightcap without Emma, who pleads tiredness and the need for an early night. Morgan is pathetically pleased to see us and I notice someone has been in and made the sofas into beds. I sit heavily down on one of them and pull my feet off the floor so Morgan can't pee on them. My mother lights her first cigarette of the evening and draws deeply on it. She hadn't been able to smoke in the dining car because it is non smoking, which normally doesn't deter her but there was also Emma to consider too. Actually I'm quite sure these little couchettes are non smoking too.

'Whisky, Clemmie?' offers my father. 'Actually, it's all we've got unless you want neat gin.'

'Whisky will be fine, Dad. In fact, I think I'm developing a bit of a taste for it.' I push the blinds to one side and take a peek out of the window. It's dark and raining and not really what I had in mind.

'What temperature do you think it will be in the south?' I ask, thinking about my bikini.

'Definitely T-shirt weather,' says Sam.

I eye the rain doubtfully and then return to my huddled position. 'I hope Holly will be okay. There's an awful lot of people mad at her.'

'There's always people mad at Holly. She should make a career out of it.'

'I hope she won't lose her job though. She loves it so much,' I say wistfully.

'Joe won't sack her. He has a complete soft spot for her.'

'I'm not sure that James has at the moment.'

'I must call Gordon as soon as I can reach a phone,' says my mother. The wonders of modern technology are lost on her. She used to have a mobile phone but she didn't know how to use it, kept locking it inadvertently and could never hear it when it was ringing. I accessed her message service once and there were forty-six messages waiting. When she left it in a taxi, my father didn't bother getting her another one.

'Did you tell him you were going away?' asks my father.

'Yes, he's probably hoping the Channel Tunnel has caved in or something. I must also call Barney.'

'Why do you want to call Barney?' asks Sam.

'I want to make sure that Norman is all right, of course! There might be a frost so I do hope he remembers to bring him in tonight to sleep in the kitchen.'

'If Norman has any sense he'll be better off staying outside. He'll probably catch food poisoning in that kitchen of theirs,' says Sam. My father's eyes light up at this possibility.

'Barney is probably too busy mooning after that girl of his to worry about Norman,' I say, having just taken a quick swig of my whisky.

I stop mid-swig as everyone looks at me. It then occurs to me that the combination of gin, wine and whisky may have caused me to cock up.

'What girl?' asks my mother.

'Yes, what girl?' echoes Sam.

'Er, no girl. No girl at all.'

'You just said there was a girl,' demands my mother.

'Girl? I didn't say there was a girl.'

'Don't be silly, Clemmie. I heard you.'

I rack my brain for the name of an ex-girlfriend of his. 'I meant Lucy.'

'Lucy with the nasal problems?' says my mother.

'Nasal problems?' queries my father.

'Yes, she always had this large bogey on her nose. I kept trying to give her a tissue but she wouldn't take the hint.'

'We keep telling you, it was a nose stud,' I say.

'Darling, I really don't know the trendy slang for it, but in my day it was called a bogey.'

'But Barney hasn't seen Lucy for months,' says Sam in puzzlement. 'He finished with her and he's never mentioned her to me since.'

'Clemmie meant someone else, didn't you, Clemmie?' demands my mother. Dear God, the woman has just sunk a couple of gin and tonics and a bottle of wine. Can't she just leave it? 'Does Barney like someone?'

I carefully avoid looking at my father who I know will be glaring at me. 'He likes a girl, but he won't say who she is,' I mumble in a small voice, cursing my lapse. Barney is going to kill me. And then my father is going to kill me again.

The other two seem elated by this admission.

'I knew something was up,' says Sam. 'All this cricket stuff and talk of a new job.'

'Who on earth can it be? How absolutely thrilling! A secret amour!'

'ANYWAY,' says my father. 'Time for bed, I think. Come on, Sam.'

My mother doesn't really notice them leaving, she is too busy staring at me with her eyes aglow. 'So is this why he's joined the cricket team and cut his hair? To impress a girl?'

Now the rather ominous presence of my father has gone, I feel quite happy talking about it. It's not as though I know the identity of the girl, is it? Barney deliberately didn't tell me for this very reason. How very perceptive of him.

'I think the problem is that she doesn't like him.'

My mother looks at me in extreme horror. She seems to be taking this as a personal insult to her. 'Doesn't like Barney? What do you mean she doesn't like Barney? How can you not like Barney?'

'I don't know. She just doesn't like him in that way.'

'Well, really. Why on earth is he bothering with her?'

'He really likes her. Enough to cut his hair and play for the cricket team when he doesn't really like cricket.'

'I *knew* he didn't play cricket but I kept thinking I was mixing him up with one of your other brothers. Now who on earth do you think it is?'

'She lives in the village, whoever she is.'

My mother stares excitedly at me until the expression slowly dies from her face.

'What?' I ask. 'What is it?'

'I think I know who it is.'

'Who?'

'It's not good.'

'Who? WHO?'

'It's Catherine Fothersby, isn't it?'

'Catherine Fothersby? What on earth makes you think that?'

'Darling, it has to be. She doesn't like him back which can only mean one of the Fothersbys because EVERYONE loves Barney. He's doing all this self-improvement stuff to try to make himself more worthy of her. Dear God help us. It's bloody Catherine Fothersby.'

I stare at her in horror. Catherine Fothersby? Could it be? He certainly comes to quite a few rehearsals and he is quite defensive about her.

'But why?' I blurt out. 'Why?'

'I don't know, Clemmie. I dropped him on his head once when he was a baby. I've always been worried about that.' She puts her hand to her head. 'I think I might be getting a migraine. I simply must lie down.'

All in all it isn't a fun night. My mother insists on lying down which leaves me to take Morgan out to wee when we stop at various stations. The ruddy animal just refuses to do anything at all at the first two stations; as soon as we reach terra firma he simply flops over on to his side and pretends to be dead. I know he is doing this deliberately to annoy me because he wouldn't dream of doing such a thing to my mother, but

266

at last his bladder defeats him and he has to do his stuff, and I can get to bed. I lie, fully dressed, on top of my little bed, intending to have a think about things before undressing, but the swaying motion of the train has a soporific effect on me and I fall asleep with my boots still firmly attached to my feet like all good cowboys.

* * *

I dream that Emma is Barney's secret amour, but she in turn only loves Sam and nobody loves me at all. I wake up upset and quite confused until I realise where I am. I am in France and on holiday! All dreams forgotten, I immediately leap up and peer out of the window, forgetting that I didn't actually manage to get undressed last night. It feels as though I have been amputated at the knee — pesky, bloody cowboy boots — and I collapse in a heap on the floor. When I do manage to scramble to my feet, I look out at a wide expanse of bright blue sky. The landscape is desiccated, desert-like and mountainous with dry, dusty little bushes and trees dotted everywhere. This is definitely T-shirt weather. Hooray!

I just about manage to brush my teeth in the little basin but feel so grubby from sleeping in my clothes that I resolve to have a shower as soon as we reach our hotel. Our steward brings us a breakfast of brioche, orange juice and funny little biscuits, all of which my mother thanks him for in her pidgin French. She seems amazingly cheerful this morning; she says she is simply not

267

going to think about Barney and Catherine because she is positive that Barney will see the light, especially when she starts working on him.

'But you won't mention anything to him, will you?' I plead. 'He'll be cross that I told you and never tell me anything again.'

'Don't worry, darling. I'll be subtle. I am a mother of four . . . '

'Five,' I correct her.

She looks thoughtful for a moment as she mentally counts her brood and then says, 'Well, there you are. I'm a mother of five which makes me even better qualified to handle these sorts of situations.'

'I think that's what worries me,' I murmur.

'I won't say that you told me, I'll just pretend I found out from my mothering intuition.'

Barney simply won't buy this at all. My mother hasn't got any intuition, mothering or otherwise. 'You weren't being very intuitive when you forgot how many children you had.'

'I temporarily miscounted.'

Sam knocks on our door to ask us if we're ready and starts dragging some of my mother's luggage towards the exit.

'How was last night?' he murmurs to me.

'Morgan snores.'

'I mean your mother and Barney. Did she worry?'

I start to follow him down the corridor. 'She thinks it's Catherine Fothersby,' I whisper. He stops and turns towards me with a frown. We both gently sway on the still-moving train. 'She what?'

'She thinks it's Catherine Fothersby.'

'Is she mad? Barney doesn't like Catherine Fothersby!'

'Are you sure? Because he has been behaving quite strangely. Why wouldn't he tell you? He normally tells you everything.'

Sam frowns some more and we start our journey again. We reach the exit doors and he piles the bags up. 'You're right, it is strange that he hasn't told me. Why wouldn't he say anything?'

'Because he thinks you might not approve?'

'God, it can only be someone horrific.'

'Like Catherine Fothersby.'

'He wouldn't,' he says, staring at me in shock. 'Would he?'

'Hello!' says my father, making us jump, so entranced are we in our little world. 'Are we all ready for the off? I'll just go and collect Emma.'

We are soon all gathered on the platform in Nice with our pile of luggage and one grouchy dog. We haul the bags to the entrance of the station and Morgan and I sit on them while my father goes off to hire us a car. My mother is busy telling Emma all about her five pregnancies, which, according to her, were all dreadful, especially Clemmie, even though I am sitting right in front of her.

We seem to be sitting by the side of a particularly busy one-way system which spreads across three lanes and is criss-crossed with other streets. Horns blare at pedestrians who dare to try to cross the road, and the bright sunshine makes everything dazzle.

Eventually my father comes to collect us and we make our way to a multi-storey car park to locate our rental car. When we find it, I risk a look at Sam and feel an attack of the giggles coming on.

'It's all they had left,' says my father defensively. 'We hadn't booked.'

'Darling, you might as well have hired us all bicycles. Like the bloody Von Trapps,' says my mother.

I take a quick look at Emma's face which is absolutely devoid of any humour at all. I don't think the Von Trapps had Sulky Spice in their midst. My father starts to load some of the bags into the boot. It takes a grand total of two.

'Shall we put the luggage on the roof?' I ask tentatively.

'Get in the back, Clemmie,' says Sam firmly with a grin.

'Or perhaps we could trail it behind us?'

'In you go,' he says, starting to hustle me towards the door. 'I'll pile the surplus on top of you.'

Why are people always trying to put me in the back of cars?

'I could drive,' suggests my mother, clearly seeing that Emma, being pregnant, will immediately win the front seat.

We all stop where we are and look at her. My mother and driving are not natural bedmates. She once arrived home and casually dropped into the conversation that she had accidentally knocked part of the trim off the car while parking it. When my father went out to inspect the damage he found the whole bumper on the back seat.

'You're wanted for motoring offences in various countries,' says my father. 'Not least your own.'

'Darling, I did try to explain to the officer that it is terribly difficult to drive with Morgan on my lap.'

'And what about that man you knocked over on the zebra crossing?' asks Sam.

'I didn't knock him over, I playfully tapped him. He was from China and very charming.'

'You're not driving,' says my father firmly. 'In the back with Clemmie, please.'

Eventually we're all piled in with Morgan and the bags spread across the back and all I can say is I'm very glad Emma is in the front because this is very intimate and not something you could do with a relative stranger.

I think the rental firm must have felt a little bad about the situation because they have presented my father with five maps so we all have one each. Something I think my father now regrets as we all suddenly decide we are experts in negotiating the tricky one-way systems of Nice.

'Where are we staying, Sam?'

'A hotel in Cap Ferrat.' We all frantically consult our maps and start yelling directions at my father, who completely ignores the rest of us and only listens to Sam and his softly spoken instructions. I hate it when men bunch together.

We start off down the massively busy one-way street and then my father makes a right turn towards the sea front. We have a nasty moment as my father waves an elderly woman across a pedestrian crossing and then accelerates straight at her. She nearly has a heart attack on the spot but manages to make it to the other side.

'What the hell are you doing?' yells my mother.

'It's very confusing!' yells my father back. 'I don't know whether to stop for the ruddy pedestrians or mow them down.'

Eventually we start on the coast road towards Cap Ferrat, which seems to be situated on a little island outcrop with just one road leading to it. We climb and climb on a road cut out of the cliffs and I feel like I'm in a movie. Eventually we turn right and begin travelling back down towards Cap Ferrat. It is beautiful. Tall, expensive hedges hide wealthy houses, geraniums spill out from window boxes everywhere, sprinklers are turned on and the birds call loudly to one another. The colours seem to have been washed especially for us.

Our hotel is situated right in the centre of Cap Ferrat and my father has no difficulty parking in a tiny little space that the Range Rover would normally struggle to get a wheel into. My mother and I fall out of the back of the car, giggling madly and wildly excited by the exotic feel of the place. The bougainvillea is in full bloom, bright cerise paper lanterns adorn the doorway, the calla lilies gently sway in the sea breeze and there is the smell of fresh bread and sun lotion in the air.

We take a couple of bags each and then go to

the reception to check in. The people who are taking care of Emma are collecting her tonight at six from the hotel. My parents are staying a few extra days while Sam and I have vague plans to return on tomorrow night's train. However, after experiencing the bright sunshine and heady sea air Mr Trevesky has become a distant memory.

The hotel reception is very smart with a great display of flowers and lots of squishy Colefax and Fowler sofas. The manager is a large lady with short red hair and a rather unfortunate choice of cerise lipstick who asks me how our journey has been and then gives us our keys. Sam and my parents have rooms near to each other on the second floor whereas Madame obviously feels I need more exercise and bungs me up on the fifth floor. Since Sam sets the precedent by taking the stairs (my mother refuses point blank and she, Morgan and Emma get into the lift) I have to yomp all the way up to the fifth.

In my pretty little single room I swing open the shutters and survey the fabulous view. The sea is a startling blue and the land between us is dotted with extravagant villas. Unlike the mountainous region beyond, this area is lush and green and full of exotic plants that only the rich can afford to buy and maintain.

Feeling ridiculously excited, I unpack my suitcase, hang a few things in the wardrobe and take a quick shower. I am anxious to get on with the very serious business of enjoying myself.

18

I pack my little straw beach bag with some sun cream, my bikini and sarong and one of the hotel's towels. It's not quite hot enough for shorts so I settle for a summery skirt, a little T-shirt and some espadrilles that I found at the back of my wardrobe. These are a little mildewy but no matter. Shoving my sunglasses on top of my head, I'm too excited to wait for the lift and gallop down five flights of stairs to reception.

Sam is already waiting for us all and he is looking insolently continental in low-slung jeans with a polo shirt that's barely tucked into them and feet encased in Sebago loafers. His hair is still wet which means he's just come out of the shower too. He's talking urgently into his mobile but gives me a quick smile to indicate that he'll only be a minute. Needless to say my parents haven't made it down yet.

I plonk myself down on a squishy sofa and wait, content to just look around and soak up the atmosphere. However, Sam is true to his word and within a few minutes comes and joins me on the sofa.

'God, this is nice, isn't it?' he says as he throws himself into one of the corners and stretches his legs out in front of him. 'To be away from work for a few days.'

'Lovely!' I agree. 'When did you last take a holiday?' I ask idly.

'Not for ages. The business has never really been able to spare me. It's only now I feel able to leave the whole firm in someone else's hands for a few days.'

'How long is 'not for ages'?'

'Oh, I don't know. A couple of years maybe.'

'What? Before I went away?'

He looks at me thoughtfully. 'Yeah, that would be about right.'

I frown at him while I think back to the days when I was still going out with Seth. Sam was much more like Barney then, still serious about his work but more carefree somehow. Perhaps the strain of running his own firm has worn him down somewhat.

'You need to take a proper holiday,' I say seriously.

'I know, Charlotte wants to go away and maybe we will. I've just had other things on my mind these last few years.'

'I suppose building your own firm has been tough.'

'I've been lucky. At least I haven't had to pay a mortgage and I used the money I got from my parents to start up the firm.' He smiles at me and I think he would much rather have his parents back. 'But, it's not just been that,' he murmurs, fiddling with a bit of the sofa.

'What else has it been?'

He turns and looks me square in the eye. He opens his mouth to reply but then seems to think better of it. 'Ask me some other time, Clemmie.'

I'm about to open my mouth and insist that he tells me now and stops this infuriating

I've-got-a-secret-I'm-not-telling-you stuff when I hear my mother's dulcet tones echoing down the stairwell.

She arrives looking as though she has walked straight off the set of a Sophia Loren movie. Her huge floppy hat, which nearly takes out Emma's eye every time she turns to talk to her, is a vitriolic yellow, and is combined with her black Jackie O sunglasses and some sort of floral dress-cum-sun lounger. She is puffing dispiritedly on a cigarette and carrying Morgan under her arm.

'Darlings! Have you been waiting long? Your father seemed to take an age to get ready.' We all look absolutely disbelievingly at her, including my father. 'Now, what exciting thing shall we go and do?'

'I'd like a swim!' I announce.

'Well, let's go back to Nice for a swim and then perhaps drive along the coast for some lunch in Monte Carlo?' suggests my father.

'That sounds perfect!' trills my mother, and even Emma has a go at not looking altogether displeased. 'Can I make a call before I go?' she asks.

'Of course!' says my father. 'Madame will let you call from reception.'

He escorts her over to the reception desk. 'Who's she calling?' I ask my mother in a whisper.

'I think she mentioned someone like, em . . . oh, I can't remember. It was a plain, no-nonsense name.'

I sigh. We have to play these sorts of games

with her all the time. 'Will? Harry? Simon?'

She frowns, 'Noooo . . . None of those.'

'David? Richard? John?'

'John! That was it!'

'John Montague?'

'Yes! Montague. I remember thinking about *Romeo and Juliet*.'

'Who is he?' asks Sam with interest.

'The MP for Bristol. He's a friend of Sir Christopher's and Emma was staying with him when we found her.'

My father chats to Madame while Emma is on the phone and when she finishes, he gestures to us and we hand our keys back to reception and make our way out to our Legoland car. Emma gets to go in the front because she is still pregnant and Sam, my mother, Morgan and I pile into the back where I have to sit in the middle. Luckily our maps are still in place from where they were hastily abandoned earlier and we eagerly take them up again.

My father expertly negotiates the sharper corners and hills of the one-way system of Cap Ferrat and soon enough we find ourselves on the beautiful coast road back to Nice. The road climbs steadily for a few minutes before it opens out on to the fabulous vista of the Côte d'Azur. We can see for mile after glorious mile of beach and sea. We soon start our descent, however, and as soon as we have driven around Nice harbour, the road opens out on to the Promenade des Anglais. The famous dome of the Hôtel Negresco is in sight and we start to look for a place to park. I am desperate to get into the sea.

Once we are out of the car, my mother and father announce that they would prefer to take a stroll up the promenade with Morgan and maybe stop for some coffee at the Negresco. Emma elects to join them, so Sam and I indicate where we'll be for them to come and collect us when they're ready and then scramble down to the beach.

The beach is quite stony and the pebbles have absorbed the heat of the sun, so we scrabble over them to a free spot. Sam dumps his towel, which also appears to have been stolen from the hotel, and starts to pull his polo shirt over his head. I hastily avert my eyes and suddenly feel strangely embarrassed. Sam and I have known each other for years and it abruptly strikes me that I have never seen him in a state of undress. Not even a bare torso or anything because we always surf in wetsuits so we can stay in the cold Cornish water for longer.

I vaguely fiddle with my T-shirt and stare out to sea, trying to look as though I'm studying the form, or at least thinking about something immensely important.

'Come on, Clemmie! Get your kit off!' Sam says, standing before me with his swimming shorts on. He's smiling wickedly which suggests he knows I'm feeling embarrassed.

I stare fixedly at his face, without looking down. 'You go on. I've got to change into my bikini.'

'Do you want me to hold a towel for you?'

'No, no! I'll be fine. I'll just, er, you know. Wriggle into them.' I feel my face blush red.

Dear God! What on earth is wrong with me? I'm behaving like some sort of virginal teenager.

'Well, hurry up!' He turns and marches down to the sea and I cannot resist taking the opportunity to have a good look at him.

Bloody hell, he's gorgeous.

I clap my hand over my mouth.

This is Sam we're talking about, Clemmie. Just to remind you. Just to make things clear.

I continue to watch him with some sort of morbid fascination. He has a broad back with a large mole on one side. His hair is cut so short at the back that I can just see the shadows of little baby hairs in the nape of his neck. His legs are strong and powerful and I daren't even mention his bum. Really, I can't. I'm too embarrassed. I realise this is Sam but he is still gorgeous. He wades into the sea and then dives into one of the waves.

In a vague state of shock I start to drag my bikini out of my beach bag. I lug on the bottoms underneath my skirt, give a little wriggle and then awkwardly haul my arms inside my T-shirt and unhook my bra. I put my bikini top on while still wearing my T-shirt but it is distractingly tight. I peer down the neck of my T-shirt to check all is in order. My breasts are squashed absolutely flat. I did get the right size, didn't I? It definitely said size twelve on the briefs but I'm pretty sure this isn't a size twelve top. Not unless my boobs have unexpectedly metamorphosed. Oh bloody hell, what is wrong with me? Emma wouldn't have done this.

I glance up to see Sam standing with his hands

on his hips, up to his waist in water, staring at me. I blush again. He must wonder at this sudden fascination I have for my mammaries; he's probably been watching me staring down the neck of my T-shirt at them for the last few minutes. Does he think I'm admiring them or something? 'Come on! It's beautiful!' he yells.

I awkwardly take off my T-shirt and then adopt an arms-pinned-to-side with folded-arms-across-boobs stance as I stagger awkwardly on the pebbles down to the shore. At least I've remembered to shave both armpits this time.

Now and again I look ahead at the figure in the water. When did Sam become this attractive? Has he always been this attractive? Has he had a new haircut? Is it the heady sunshine of the south of France? As I make my slow progress across the stones, I can see more and more why Barney and he are best friends, as though it's never occurred to me before. They both have that casual insolence and those lazy good looks. Sam is much darker than Barney though. He has chestnut colour hair and brown eyes as opposed to Barney's fairness.

He is grinning broadly at me now, waiting for my arrival in the water. I am normally a tiptoe into the water sort of gal. An inch at a time, grimacing madly, but today I simply cannot afford to be. I need to get my torso underneath that water as soon as possible.

Sam is right, the water is absolutely beautiful once I have got over the initial shock of cold. I paddle out to him and crouch down so I can bob around.

'This has got to be worth any hassle from Emma, hasn't it?' he says. 'Do you want to swim out to that raft? What on earth is wrong with you? Why are your shoulders hunched up?'

'I think I might have bought the wrong size bikini top,' I say in a small voice. We both involuntarily look down at my chest.

'I think you might have done.'

'It was in the bargain bin.'

'I can see that.'

'The bottoms are the right size. I just didn't check the top.'

'It looks like a couple of eye patches sewn together.'

There's a slight pause as we consider the situation.

'So no underwater rugby tackles then?' asks Sam.

'I think even strenuous swimming might be out of the question.'

'I promise I'll keep my eyes fixed on your face at all times.'

'Even if you step on a crab?'

'Even if I step on numerous crabs.'

★　★　★

True to his word (and in my heart of hearts I am slightly disappointed at how easily he seems to be able to stick to it), Sam keeps his eyes firmly away from my top half while we mess around in the waves for the next half an hour. We float around, chatting idly about things, until I eventually decide to wade ashore to dry off while he swims out to the raft.

I quickly dry and re-clothe myself in my T-shirt, not caring if I have slightly damp patches, and then sit on my towel in my bikini bottoms with my sunglasses on, happily surveying the scene around me. It is absolutely blissful to be away.

'Cooo-eeee darling!' calls a particularly resonant voice. I turn around to see my mother waving from the pavement. There can be no mistaking her nationality.

I smile and wave back and then gesture to Sam, who is just exiting the water. I have no wish to blush at Sam any more so I hastily gather my things together, pop my skirt on and make my way up to my mother, stumbling on the hot stones underfoot as I go.

'Hello!' I greet them as I shove on my espadrilles. My father and Emma are just wandering up towards us.

'Darling. I have just seen Michael Portillo.'

'God, have you?' I say, absolutely thrilled at our first celebrity sighting.

My father is shaking his head behind her. 'On a moped, Clemmie,' he puts in. Ah. So maybe not our first celebrity sighting. 'Did you have a nice swim?' he asks.

'Lovely. How about you?'

'We had some coffee at the Negresco and then your mother made us look in some shops.'

'Did you get anything nice?' I ask my mother, thinking that it's a pity she didn't take the opportunity to entirely re-clothe me.

'I tried on some shoes. The shops are

fabulous, Clemmie!'

'You really should take a look, Clemmie,' says Emma, looking me up and down. She is in a position of superiority because she fits in completely with the style of the Côte d'Azur, but even so, I don't like the tone of her voice very much.

'I think I will.'

'Darling, you'll adore it!'

'Come on!' says my father, linking his arm through mine. 'Let's go and get some lunch. Will Monte Carlo be okay with you, Clemmie?'

'Monte Carlo will be just fine, Dad.'

* * *

After my mother has made a huge fuss about whether we need our passports in Monte Carlo, we park near the casino, which has many more glamorous cars than ours parked outside it and then wander down towards the famous marina. Emma, my mother and Morgan decide to take the public lift while Sam, Dad and I choose to walk. It's not that I fancy the exercise, it's just that where Emma is, I am not.

'It's amazing to see these streets after watching them on the Grand Prix, isn't it, Sam?' comments my father.

Sam makes some insightful comment but loses me after the first word or so because it's all formula whatever speak. So I'm left to my own thoughts, which involve looking in various shop windows and trying not to eye Sam's backside.

We eventually arrive at the marina and locate

my mother and Emma sitting outside an exclusive little restaurant. My mother is already in possession of a large gin and tonic, a cigarette and a bowl of water for Morgan.

I push my sunglasses on to the top of my head and pull out a chair to join them.

'How are you feeling, Emma?' I try to sound sympathetic.

'Sick.'

'Oh dear. And when will that stop?'

She gives me a withering look. 'Probably when the baby comes out. The heat isn't helping. Of course, it wouldn't be this warm in England.'

Ah. She's still holding that against me, is she?

'Let's get you something to eat,' says Sam kindly. 'You'll feel better with food inside you.' He signals to a waiter who presents us with five large menus.

My mouth waters greedily at the various descriptions but I have to spend the next ten minutes explaining the menu to everyone else and then trying to ascertain whether various cheeses are safe for Emma. The French don't seem to have heard of pasteurisation so we abandon that tack and take on the tricky task of finding something that Emma can eat. I'm just about to suggest some bread and butter might go down well, even if the butter isn't bloody pasteurised, when Sam mentions soup.

Whilst we all ponder our choices, my mother chats away to the head waiter in her pidgin French, entertaining him greatly. He chats back to her in his near-perfect English and together they seem to be getting on like a house on fire.

'What is zis 'Shit McGregor?'' he is asking.

'Il y a un bateau . . . ' my mother starts to explain. 'Clemmie!' she roars a moment later, making me jump out of my skin, 'what's French for Scotland?'

I'm sorely tempted to tell her the wrong thing because I once told her that the French for a cow is a squirrel and it still makes me giggle whenever she asks if the cheese is goat's or squirrel's, but this time I don't think quickly enough and end up telling her the truth. Damn.

I eventually manage to pass on our order to the head waiter, who is now walking round murmuring 'Shit McGregor' to himself, and relax back in my seat and take a sip of the ice-cold white wine that Sam has poured for me.

'So, Clemmie, what was the name of that art dealer? The one you brought to the Christmas party at the paper?' asks Emma slyly. This is the first time she has ever made any reference to meeting me before.

'His name was Seth. He valued art actually. Just like me.'

'I remember him because he refused to drink the wine. I don't blame him on that, of course, it was filthy. Are you still together?'

'No, we split up some time ago.'

'Holly said that was why you disappeared off around the world for a year.'

So Emma obviously knew that we had split up. I am going to kill Holly if Martin doesn't get to her first. 'Did she?' I say, trying to keep my voice light.

'I thought you just needed a holiday,

Clemmie,' puts in Sam. I flash a smile at him gratefully.

'Are you seeing anyone else?'

'No, I'm not.'

She looks at me pityingly and it's all I can do not to answer her back because it's not as though she has made a roaring success of her own love life.

'Do you think you'll go back to valuing art?' she persists.

'Actually, I thought I might open my own gallery,' I say bravely.

'Clemmie!' exclaims my father. 'What a wonderful idea!'

'Sam's idea actually,' I admit. 'But I like it.' This seems to shut Emma up, thank God, and we move on to talk of other things. Saying Sam's suggestion out loud seems to lend it some weight though, and move it slightly more towards a reality. It wasn't laughed off as a preposterous idea so maybe I could actually do it. My mind starts to think a little more about perhaps trying to find a job in one of Cornwall's many galleries when we get home. This might work out quite well as Mr Trevesky must have given up on me by now.

Some sort of resolution reached, I turn my thoughts to how wonderful it will be to see the back of Emma. Roll on this evening.

'I wonder how Holly is getting on?' asks my mother. 'Do you think James has forgiven her yet?'

'Of course he has!' I say staunchly, aware that Emma is listening intently. Holly and James are generally considered public property in Bristol since their get-together was documented by Holly in the *Gazette*.

'Did they have a row?' asks Emma eagerly. I know she has always been a bit jealous of Holly and now I have met James I don't really blame her.

'Not really a row,' I hedge. 'More of a discussion.' Of course, if any other member of the family had asked me then I would have been forced to tell them they'd had a humdinger of a row and I didn't know if they'd ever speak to each other again. 'Anyway they've made it up.' I cross my fingers under the table.

My mother distracts us further by shouting, 'Oh, darlings, do look! I think it's Tony Blair over there!'

* * *

When we get back to the hotel, Emma excuses herself and goes off to collect her belongings from my parents' room. The rest of us plump ourselves down in reception and wait for the Winstanleys, the people Emma is going to stay with, to arrive.

'Clemmie, darling, would you mind doing some lines with me for my new play later?'

'Not at all. What's the play about?'

'Well, your part is a bad-tempered old lady, embittered by some bad experiences in life.'

'And yours?'

'Beautiful ward fighting to follow the love of her life into battle, of course!' That figures. 'How was Charlotte?' she asks Sam. Sam called her on his mobile on the way back to the hotel.

I had a very quiet journey back as Emma was refusing to talk to anyone, Sam was sitting next to me talking to Charlotte on his mobile and my mother was on the other side talking to Barney on my mobile (but I had to dial the number for her because she kept pressing all the wrong buttons).

'She's good. She's taken a few days' holiday from work and has decided to stay in Cornwall.' I listen with interest as Charlotte has taken on a whole new lease of life in my eyes. Have I not warmed to her because I secretly fancy Sam? Is she pretty? I can't remember but Holly certainly seems to think so. And my parents seem to like her.

'She's seen Barney and Norman. Apparently Barney is spending most of the day trying to persuade Norman to take up flying again by tossing pilchards into the air. But of course Norman just waits until they hit the ground and then waddles over and eats them.'

'At least they're bonding,' I remark.

'When I spoke to Barney, he sounded as though he was enjoying having Norman to stay,' says my mother. I probably wouldn't go that far.

My father and Emma emerge from the lift together. My father is carrying her bag for her and he parks it by the sofa.

'All packed, Emma?' asks Sam politely.

'Yes.' She looks very downcast and I almost feel sorry for her.

My father perches on the arm of one of the

chairs next to her. 'Will your father be out to visit you soon?'

'He says he'll try to get out as soon as possible.'

'It'll be all right, Emma,' says my father gently. 'These things have a way of working themselves out.'

We all sit in silence for a moment until I remember my promise to Holly that I would try to glean some information from Emma for 'High Society'. This is my last chance.

'Er, Emma? I don't know if you know but Joe has asked Holly to write 'High Society' until the paper can find a replacement for you.' I'm hoping this will sound as though Joe has asked Holly to write it because she is so talented, rather than the fact that we made such a cock-up of things.

'Oh, really?'

'Yes. Have you got any tips for her?'

Emma glances over to my father. I know that she likes him and wouldn't want to appear rude in front of him and thus she has no choice but to help me. Ha!

'Holly isn't terribly au fait with the social scene, is she?' This is a rhetorical question and I glance over to my father to see how he is taking this thinly veiled insult. He is making a sort of true-true face. Damn him, he always thinks the best of everyone. It is an extremely annoying trait.

'No, she's not.' Holly would rather poke herself in the eye than have to swan around at various cocktail parties.

Emma relents. 'Tell her to take a look at some notes I was making for the next column on my PC.'

'Thanks, Emma.'

'But she really hasn't got the contacts to be doing it for any length of time. I have a firm following of readers and her stories from the local pub won't do for very long.'

'I'll make sure to tell her,' I say through gritted teeth, and just at that moment a man and a woman walk into reception. I know instantly that they are the Winstanleys. Amazing how you can spot your own countrymen from about a mile off. They look quietly distinguished and I notice, as they introduce themselves, that they speak very well. But then I wouldn't have expected anything less from Sir Christopher McKellan.

Emma says her goodbyes to everyone with a relative degree of warmth until she reaches me. 'Well, Clemmie. I suppose you've done your best in all this.'

'Yes, I have.'

'I know Holly can be terribly persuasive. People tend to like her so much that they'll do anything for her. So I know I might have acted as though I blame you for some of this but I don't really.' So she just doesn't like me then.

I open my mouth to defend my beloved sister but then think better of it. I simply cannot be bothered.

'It was all Holly,' I announce for the last time. 'Take care of yourself, Emma.'

She half smiles and then takes her leave of us.

19

Freedom! Or as the French would say: Liberté and er, something else. I feel liberty is the bit worth concentrating on though. We are officially Emma-free, a blissful state, one much taken for granted previously.

We wander out onto the hotel veranda for a drink. I leave them wandering and march in double-quick time to the bar, intent on ordering the largest drink ever. I might even ask them if they have any runny cheese and pâté too.

'Clemmie!' my father calls after me. 'Order Kir Royales!'

Ooh, yum. Champagne and cassis.

'Quatre Kirs Royales, s'il vous plaît!' I ask the waiter. My French isn't quite sufficient to add 'and make them whoppers' but I think he gets the general gist from my various hand gestures.

My parents and Sam settle themselves on some wicker chairs on the edge of the balcony looking out to sea. The sun is starting to sink, which bathes our little island outcrop in a mellow light.

'I think you've caught the sun,' says Sam as I approach them.

I immediately put my hand to my nose. 'Do I look red?' I ask anxiously.

'No, just freckly.'

'Oh God. How awful.'

'They're sweet!' protests Sam. But not sexy.

Not exactly alluring. Unlike Sam, who has managed to catch the sun and has a golden glow about him.

Must stop these impure thoughts at once.

They're unfortunately quite addictive though. Maybe when we return to England and normality then Sam's and my relationship will too. He'll go back to bored disdain and I'll go back to being annoyed about my rhubarb yoghurts.

'Are you two still planning to go home tomorrow?' asks my mother idly while feeding Morgan a pistachio.

Sam and I catch each other's eye. 'I suppose I ought to get back to work,' says Sam.

I droop a little with disappointment. 'I suppose I ought to as well,' I say half-heartedly.

'But on the other hand, there's no need to exactly rush back, is there?'

My spirits rise wildly. 'No rush as such.'

'I mean, it seems a tad rude just to abandon your parents, Clem.'

'Really rude. What on earth would they do without us?'

'Well, since you put it like that, I consider it my moral duty to stay and look after them.'

'Me too!' I grin widely at him and take a sip of my drink. Heaven.

'Well, you two will have to fend for yourselves tomorrow night because your mother and I have reservations for La Colombe D'Or,' interjects my father.

'Where's that?'

'In St Paul de Vence. It's usually booked up for

months but I called just before we left England and they had a cancellation, so I am afraid, my little chickens, that we are absolutely not missing that.'

'Oohh, I daresay we'll manage,' I say with a degree of composure, trying not to look too lecherous at the prospect of an evening alone with Sam. I look accusingly at my Kir Royale. Is it making me behave like this? Dear God! This is Sam you've developed a sudden yen for, Clemmie. Sam who you have never really had much time for before.

I take another sip of my drink and spear an olive thoughtfully while the others nonchalantly discuss what they might want to do tomorrow. I really need to think this through and not rush at anything because the whole episode could become fairly embarrassing. I don't want to seem as though I've developed a thumping great crush on him and then have to leave the room every time I meet him for the next fifty years. My eyes involuntarily glance at him. I even like the way he sits. His frame is thrown arrogantly back into his chair but he is leaning forward slightly, laughing at something my mother is telling him. Of course, one cannot ignore the fact that he is going out with Charlotte. But one small glimmer of opportunity remains. Charlotte isn't here and I am. Charlotte is a few thousand miles away whereas I am barely a few feet. Charlotte is an actuary whereas I . . . Yes, well, I . . . Actually, what am I exactly? Do you think he likes the whole actuarial thing? Should I play on the fact that I used to work for an insurance company a bit more? I frown to myself. This is a tad confusing. Maybe I shouldn't dwell on it. But here we are, in the seductive setting of the south of France, without a care in the world and the prospect of being alone together. If he didn't want it to happen then surely he would have beetled off home at the earliest opportunity? He would be leaving train timetables lying around with a few suggestions ringed and 'EXCEL-LENT TRAIN' written in red next to them.

'Clemmie?' questions my father.

I pause from my little soliloquy and look up. They are all looking at me warily.

'Are you all right? You were murmuring to yourself.'

'Hmmm? Oh yes, quite all right. Just thinking about something else.'

'You were saying something about actuaries?' queries Sam with a slight smile.

I colour slightly. 'Oh yes! Actuaries! I was wondering how Charlotte was getting on. With her being an actuary and everything.' Oh, well done, Clemmie. Congratulations. Just as we have been trying to forget about his girlfriend, you manage to carefully lob her existence back into his head.

Everyone looks a little taken aback.

'You were wondering if Charlotte was okay with being an actuary?' says my mother, looking puzzled.

'Well. Yes. I suppose I was. I mean, I think it must be quite stressful, er, being an actuary.'

'I didn't think you knew what one was,' says Sam with some amusement.

'No, no. Charlotte has explained it to me.'

'Did you understand her? Because those two statements aren't necessarily mutually exclusive,' puts in my father.

'Well, exactly,' I bluster. 'That's why it sounded so stressful.'

'Because you didn't understand what it was?' asks my mother, looking even more puzzled.

God, does she have to go on so? Have we not got anything better to talk about? We could be talking about Third World debt or the latest political crisis. Do we have to linger on this?

'Where are we going for supper?' I ask desperately. 'I'm starving! Morgan's looking pretty hungry too.'

Morgan has wolfed down about a hundred pistachios so I hardly think this is likely but he is always a neat distracting point for my mother.

'I thought we'd wander around the corner to the Royal Riviera.'

'Maybe I ought to go and change.' I look down at my sandy outfit and wonder what on earth I can change into.

'I suppose we all ought to,' Sam says lazily as I gulp back the remains of my champagne.

'Meet back down here?' queries my father.

* * *

Sam and I are the quickest to change. Myself out of pure lack of choice (I get to wear my other skirt and my flip-flops) although I do take the time to dry my hair straight. I leave it loose around my shoulders and then add some foundation to my rosy face, along with a quick lick of lipstick and some eyeliner. Sam is already waiting for me when I arrive back at our seats. Without asking he goes off and returns with another Kir Royale.

The evening strolls along very pleasantly. My parents join us and after the delicate supping (my mother) and guzzling (me) of a few more beverages, we go round the corner for some food. The heat of the day has subsided and become a beautiful, balmy evening. We walk down some steps to the tiny harbour and meander along the front looking at the boats until my father finds a restaurant he likes the look of.

After the consumption of several bottles of wine and lots of gorgeous food, I feel enormously content and at one with the world. I look over to Sam, who is listening intently to my mother as she tries to convince him that she has seen Gordon Brown wearing a Bermuda print shirt (I've noticed that for some reason all her celebrity spottings have been politicians). He has a slight smile on his face which tells me he is trying to take my mother seriously and not laugh. I wonder why I haven't noticed him in all these years. I suppose I have been rather busy with my own life. And Barney and Sam were extremely annoying when we were younger. I mean, they are quite annoying together now but back then they were positively enraging. Lying about on the sofa together, eating yoghurts and taking the piss out of me seemed to be their favourite occupation. None of it was particularly malicious because Barney simply hasn't got a malicious bone in him, but when I wanted to watch TV they would be playing computer games on it. When I had booked to borrow the car, Sam and Barney had already taken off in it without telling anyone. It's quite difficult to notice someone who has a long history of just simply aggravating you.

After the main course, my parents announce that they don't want pudding and they're going back to the hotel to have coffee there. I certainly do want pudding, I have a certain yen for crème caramel. I express this view to Sam after they've left.

'God, don't tell me that you're pregnant too, Clemmie.'

'Christ, chance would be a fine thing,' I say and snort unattractively. I immediately regret this and blush. Must stop drinking wine. Just as soon as I've finished this glass.

The waiter comes over and presents us with the menus. He gives me a stern look as I have already managed to set light to two menus by holding them over the candle on our table. The first one was laughed off with much hilarity until they presented me with a second one and I did the same thing almost immediately. Our candle was pointedly blown out and has remained so ever since.

'I hope Emma is okay,' says Sam as we make our choices and hand the menus back to the waiter. Bloody hell. She's only been gone five minutes.

'I'm sure she's fine.' I try to keep my top lip

from curling. 'Her father will look after her.'

'You don't like him, do you?'

'Let's just say I won't be visiting Rock for a while.'

'He's not as bad as you think.'

'Really?' I am unconvinced.

'I wonder what Emma will tell her child about its father.'

'Preferably not the truth.'

'You don't get to choose your parents.'

'I clearly didn't.'

Sam smiles at me but there's a slight wistfulness in his expression which makes me add, 'God, I'm sorry, Sam. I was forgetting. Do you miss them?'

'I suppose I do. I mean, my aunt did her best but it's not the same. Your parents have always been amazing to me.'

'Have they?' I say, knowing full well that they have.

'They didn't just let me practically live at their house, they let me be a proper teenager. I never felt like a guest who had to say please and thank you. They let me lose my temper, lie about on the furniture, and your dad even taught me to drive. That stuff means more to me than anything.'

I smile at him and suddenly forgive him for everything. Even the rhubarb yoghurts.

'Dad said that one of the reasons you went back to London was to find out some more about your own parents. Did you find what you were looking for?'

'Yes, Clemmie. I found it all right. But . . . '

He breaks off as he notices me staring absolutely transfixed over his shoulder. 'What? What's wrong?'

'I've just seen Martin Connelly walk past.'

20

Sam makes a huge 180-degree swivel in his chair. 'Where?'

'He has literally just walked past.'

'Are you sure it was him?'

'Absolutely positive.'

'Did he see us?'

'I don't think so. Oh my God. How on earth can he have found us?'

'Which way did he go?'

'Towards the hotel.'

'Come on! Let's follow him!'

Sam is upstanding in an instant and calling for l'addition. I struggle to surface from my alcoholic stupor and just about manage to scramble to my feet. Follow him? Why are we following him? Shouldn't we be trying to lose him?

Sam is already over with the maître d' and is frantically shoving notes into his hands. I try to hurry over to him in order to voice some very heartfelt concerns about this plan of his but some bugger has placed an inordinate amount of tables and chairs in my way like some sort of bizarre obstacle course. 'Pardon! Pardon!' I chirrup as I cannon off another unfortunate couple's appetisers.

Sam is by the exit now and peering in both directions while he waits for my arrival. 'Clemmie!' hisses Sam. 'Will you come on?'

'Sam, why are we following him? Shouldn't we be going in the other direction?' But my words are left hanging as Sam grabs hold of my arm and marches me out.

We exit into the balmy evening air, subtly scented with flowers, and I breathe in deeply. Big mistake. I nearly pass out with the heady rush of oxygen and have to cling on to a handy lamp post.

'Clemmie! Will you stop pissing about and come on! This is no time to start reading posters!' Sam doubles back and takes hold of my arm. I'd forgotten how bossy he can be. He marches me down the street at about a hundred miles an hour.

'Can you see him?' he asks me urgently.

I pretend to peer knowingly in front of me but in actual fact I am just trying to focus. 'Er, no.'

'What was he wearing?'

'A tweedy sort of coat. And he has chestnut coloured hair.'

We reach the main street and Sam peers in both directions. 'There he is! Come on!' He points to some pin-like figure in the distance. How can he even see that far? Damn the Côte d'Azur and their street-lighting policies. 'We need to catch him up a bit!'

'Em, Sam. Why are we following Martin Connelly?'

'Because we need to know where he's staying, Clemmie,' he says patiently. He's looking at me in a sort of 'duh' way.

'Again, I have to ask why? Why do we need to know?'

'Because if we know where he is then it makes our position stronger.'

I can feel Sam getting distinctly annoyed with all my questioning so don't feel brave enough to ask any more. But I do feel brave enough to have a petit pit stop, and sit down on a convenient bench.

'Clemmie! Come on!' says Sam, dragging me onwards. 'Jesus! Martin Connelly is here and you're . . . what's wrong with your face?'

'Hmmm?'

'Your face. What's wrong with it?'

I put a hand up to touch it. What does he mean, what's wrong with it? How rude is that? My features seem to be exactly as I left them, except . . . oh no.

'I'm swelling up!' I say in horror.

'I can see that but why? You didn't eat any of that avocado, did you? I did point it out.'

'What avocado? I didn't see any avocado.' My legs seem to have taken on a life of their own and are frenziedly keeping up with Sam. I do wish they would stop it.

'In the salad. I told you it was there.'

'I didn't hear you!'

'Too busy gassing with your face in your wine glass. Never mind that now, can you still see him?'

Can I see him? I'm having great difficulty seeing Sam, let alone anything more than a metre away. God, I can't believe I ate some avocado. I've only done it once since the Munchkin fiasco and I really can't remember how long it takes to calm down. Twenty-four hours? Surely it can't be any more. And that gassing/wine glass jibe really hurt.

'I simply can't believe it,' says Sam, his hand still has my elbow in a vice-like grip.

'I know. Nor can I,' I mumble, panting slightly with the sheer effort of everything.

'Maybe we should have anticipated this.'

'Yes, but the problem is that avocado is green, and the salad is green, so of course that makes everything green and then it's pretty hard — '

'Clemmie, forget your bloody avocado. I mean Martin Connelly. Maybe we've been too naive. I just blithely expected him to swallow your story and go on back to Bristol or Cambridge. It's my fault.'

Do we have to talk about Martin ruddy Connelly? My face is starting to look like a bull frog's and Sam is waffling about it being his fault. What is his fault is that once he'd noticed the avocado he should have been jumping up and down on the table until the waiter took it away.

'Quick! He's stopping! In there!' says Sam suddenly, and without so much as a ladies first he gives me a shove into the nearest doorway.

To ask my very frazzled nerves to make a split-second reaction and then actually get my feet to lift themselves over a step is beyond me. I stumble quite badly, fall through the open doorway, cannon at quite a speed on to a gleaming and highly polished glass floor and then glide gaily over to the reception of what seems to be a very posh hotel. I come to a stop with my nose pressed up against the front desk.

A man peers courteously over the bureau. 'Can I help you, Madame?' he asks politely in perfectly accented English. He makes a supreme effort not to recoil from my bloated face.

I look over to Sam, who hasn't made the same entrance as me. He stumbled over my falling body but managed to save himself and is now standing in the doorway, peering out into the street. He shouts, 'Back in a minute, Clem!' and then legs it. Marvellous.

I slowly uncurl myself and try to surreptitiously pull down my skirt. The man has come out from behind his desk and is trying to give me a hand up. 'Are you okay, Madame?'

'Em, yes. I think so.' The fall seems to have winded me somewhat so it is with some difficulty that I stagger to my feet. I've lost a flip-flop which the man retrieves from the other side of the room.

He nips back behind his desk, leaving me to straighten myself out. I look back up to find myself eyeball to eyeball with him.

'Can I collect your luggage for you?'

'Hmm?'

'Are you checking in?'

'Er, no. Not exactly.' He looks puzzled by this, as well he might. I was pretty eager to enter his hotel and now I'm pretty eager to leave it.

'What are you doing then?'

Good question. Well put. 'Em, just looking.'

'Looking?'

'Yes. At the decor.' I waft a hand airily towards the furniture.

'And the floor?' he asks with a mere soupçon

304

of derision. I blush bright red and start to edge towards the door.

'It's a beautiful floor. Is it, em, French?' Oh God.

'We're in France.'

'Yes. So, of course, that would make it French.' We both look down at it again and I take another few steps backwards. 'Well. Thank you. For letting me look.'

'It's been a pleasure,' he says, heavy on the sarcasm.

'Me too.'

I'm going to kill bloody Sam.

★ ★ ★

As I step out back on to the street, feeling decidedly more sober, I spot Sam striding down the hill and waving at me. I ignore him and start to walk sulkily back towards our hotel but he catches me up about halfway there, completely oblivious to the fact that I might be in a mood with him.

'I found him!'

'Oh goody.'

He ignores the tone of my voice. 'He's staying at a little B and B near the top of the hill.'

'And how, exactly, is that little piece of information going to help us?'

'We need to know where we can find him. And now we can!'

'Great,' I say betwixt gritted teeth.

'Are you okay? Did you hurt yourself?'

'I'm fine. Just fine.'

As soon as we get inside our hotel, Sam takes a swift left up the stairs towards my parents' room. I follow and he's already rapping at their door by the time I reach him.

We're duly admitted and find that neither of them have gone to bed. In fact they are sitting out on the balcony blithely sipping two brandies. My mother leans back in her wicker chair with Morgan on her lap and sucks hard on a cigarette.

'I thought you were going to bed?' I ask.

'Darling, I simply didn't have enough nicotine in my system so I just had to . . . what on earth has happened to your face?'

'It's swollen up.'

'Golly, I can see that. You didn't eat that avocado in the salad, did you?'

'So it would seem,' I say between clenched teeth. 'You didn't think to mention it, did you?'

'Sam told you it was in there. God, do you remember when you swelled up during *The Wizard of Oz* at Stratford? I always remember that poor little girl with ringlets who was sitting in the front row. She cried so hard, it was terribly distressing. Do you remember?'

'How can I bloody well forget? It was pretty distressing for me too, since half the children in the audience also started to cry,' I snap.

'But darling, I can't tell you how awful you looked. Really, I do feel that we, as the onlookers, got the raw end of the deal. And . . . '

Sam and my father have been talking urgently in the corner during this little interchange. And it's just as well my father interrupts because I

306

can feel myself about to say something really rude.

'Sorrel, Sam has just seen Martin Connelly.'

'Martin Connelly?' she asks in blatant bewilderment. Marvellous, isn't it? She can remember the child with ringlets in the front row many years ago but she can't cast her mind back forty-eight hours.

'The madman,' says my father patiently.

'The psychologist?'

'That's the one.'

'He's here?'

'Clemmie just saw him walk past the restaurant and then they followed him to a B and B.'

'Do you think he knows we're here?'

'I would imagine that's a good bet.'

'But how?'

My father looks towards Sam, who shrugs. 'Maybe he followed us to Waterloo. Maybe he found out from someone at the paper. But I should think he just didn't believe what Holly and Clemmie told him and stayed behind in Cornwall and watched us. Maybe he got suspicious when I mentioned our holiday.'

My father turns towards me. 'Clemmie, did you see anything that . . . what on earth have you done to your face? You didn't eat that avocado in the salad, did you?'

Why was this bloody avocado so glaringly visible to everyone except me? Was it daubed in fluorescent paint or something?

I try hard to keep my voice steady. 'Yes. I think I might have eaten a little.'

'I think it's got worse,' says Sam, peering at me.

I go through to the en-suite and have a good look in the mirror. A disturbingly familiar-looking stranger stares back at me. Little slitty eyes in a sea of red puffy flesh. I've lost my cheekbones, my chin and nearly my nose too.

'Should we get you some antihistamine or something?' asks my father as I return to the room and retire behind the curtain.

'No, it normally goes down by itself.'

'How long will it take?' asks my mother. I poke my head out from behind the curtain and glare at her. 'Now, darling, don't be like that. You don't have to look at you. Look, poor Morgan won't come out from under the chair.'

Back behind my curtain, I slouch to the ground miserably. I can hear them discussing how Martin might have found out our whereabouts and whether he knows where we are staying. Inevitably the conversation turns to everyone's concerns for Emma.

'We're going to have to warn Emma,' Sam is saying. 'We can't not.'

'Yes, we'll have to call Sir Christopher McKellan and get him to contact the people she's staying with,' interjects my father.

'That means we'll have to call Holly and tell her too.'

'Okay. You call Holly and I'll call Sir Christopher.'

They resolutely grab their mobiles and make for better reception downstairs. Silence reigns after they leave the room. It clearly isn't bothering my mother because I can hear her sucking on her cigarette and then exhaling deeply.

I stick my head out from behind the curtain.

'Oh, there you are, darling. I was wondering where you'd got to. Come and sit down.' She leans over and pats the seat next to her. I begrudgingly crawl out and sit down.

'Do you want to read some lines together? While we're waiting?' I ask.

'No, I don't think I could concentrate with your face looking like that. I spoke to Matt earlier.'

'How are they doing?'

'Well, Catherine has gone away for a couple of days . . . '

'Where's she gone?'

'Up to the lakes, I think. I don't know, I wasn't really listening. But thank God she's away because at least I know Barney is safe. They've only had Matt, Sally and Bradley at rehearsals but I think it's going quite well. Apparently Charlotte and Barney took Norman down to watch the rehearsal and he persuaded Charlotte to stand in for Catherine. I think we'll have to have a full rehearsal with all the extras when we get back. Will you be around for that? Gordon has promised to come down to give his professional opinion.'

Not sure I want to be around for that. 'Hmm, I'll try,' I say non-committally.

'Did you have a nice time tonight?' she asks. 'Apart from your face?' she hurriedly adds on.

'Yes, I had a very nice time.'

'You and Sam seem to be getting on well?'

I look at her suspiciously. Where exactly is she heading with this particular line of enquiry? Is it obvious that I fancy him?

'Hmmm,' I say again and fiddle with a corner of a cushion.

'You are getting on, aren't you?'

'We're certainly getting on better. Whether that constitutes getting on well, I don't know.'

'Sam has always been very much one of the family.'

'I know. It seems bizarre that I haven't really noticed him before.' What on earth am I saying? Does avocado have hallucinogenic effects as well? Or is this still the alcohol talking? One rule of our family is never confess anything to our mother. She has no idea of the meaning of discretion. It will be all over town by tomorrow morning. At the very least she'll be making faces behind his back.

Her lack of response makes me look up suddenly. 'What's wrong?' I ask. My mother being sensitive is a new one on me.

She blows out a cloud of smoke. 'I just don't want anyone to get hurt.'

God, it must be obvious that I'm practically drooling over him, and even more obvious that he's not about to return the favour. I'm glad the failing light hides my blushes.

'Because don't forget there is Charlotte to consider too.'

I know, I know. How ironic it now seems that someone I was so dismissive of has come back to bite me on the bum. Serves me right for being so superior.

I take my first official warning firmly on the chin. My mother is right. Sam does have Charlotte and it would be incredibly embarrassing for me to launch myself at him like some unguided missile only to be rejected in favour of someone who doesn't surf.

'I know,' I mumble.

'Darling, I only have your interests at heart.' She turns and looks at me. 'You're my only daughter.'

'We just dropped your other daughter in Bristol yesterday.'

'Darling, you're my only other daughter.' She looks at me thoughtfully for a moment. 'How long did you say it took for the avocado to wear off?'

My father comes back into the room, sits down and takes a sip of his brandy. In the end the silence gets to me. 'Well?' I demand. 'What did he say? What horrible task does he want us to do now? Does he want me to dangle myself as bait in front of Martin? Does he want me to permanently stand guard over Emma? Because I can tell you that I am getting pretty sick of this whole thing. I think we have done more than our fair share and Emma is no longer our responsibility. Let's just leave them to fight it out between themselves.'

'But Clemmie, I think it became our responsibility the minute you and Holly got yourselves involved in this dreadful affair. You don't know enough about this Connelly character for us to risk just walking away. He has

311

obviously spent a vast amount of time and effort orchestrating all this. What sort of hatred fuels that kind of commitment? As far as I'm concerned, apart from the fact that I would rather you and Holly had never got involved in the first place, I want this affair to be resolved one way or another because we have no idea what Connelly is capable of.' He looks at me fiercely and I gulp slightly. My father can be pretty forceful when he wants to be and even my mother isn't risking opening her mouth. 'What if he gets it into his head that you and Holly are accountable for his nasty little scheme failing? Is he going to follow you two around? And there seems to be a limit to what the police can do. So we are not leaving here until I know it's all been sorted out. One way or another.'

One way or another. I really don't like the sound of this.

'What does Sir Christopher want us to do?' I ask resignedly.

21

I'm just about to get into bed wearing my very
attractive striped pyjamas (my mother originally
bought them for Barney for a hospital visit but
he refused point blank to wear them), when I
start to think about what my father has said. I
don't like it. An ex-convict is out to get me! How
could I have overlooked such a thing? This is the
same ex-convict that I blatantly lied to and
intentionally misled. At this very moment he
could be considering how to get his extremely
large hands around my swan-like neck. Well, it's
not very swan-like at the moment but it will be
as soon as the swelling goes down.

I nervously chew on the sleeve of my pyjamas
and then creep out of bed and over to the
window. I twitch a corner of the curtain and peer
down into the street. Is he there? Watching and
waiting? Will I see a plume of smoke being gently
exhaled from behind a lamp post or something?

Oh shit. Shittyshitshitshit. And bugger.

Maybe Martin doesn't want to see Emma at
all, because now his little revenge plan is ruined
what would be the point? Maybe he's turned his
focus on the people who foiled his plan. Namely
moi.

I don't think I can stay in this room by myself
any more. I'll go and wake up my parents. They
won't mind me kipping on the floor. In one swift
movement I am across the room with my hand

resting on the door handle. I nervously peer through the peep hole. All clear as far as I can see.

I grab my room key from the dressing table and pull open the door before I can change my mind. I scurry along the corridor like the little scared mouse I am, down several flights of stairs and finally arrive outside my parents' door. I knock gently. I wait for a second and then try a bit louder. 'It's me,' I whisper at the door. I wait again. Absolutely nothing. In fact, if I listen hard enough I can hear Morgan snoring.

I knock quite loudly this time, and then look nervously around me. It's only just past midnight — reception is probably still open and Martin Connelly could walk straight in. I give up and make for two doors down.

'Sam!' I whisper. 'Let me in! It's Clemmie!' I knock again and then hear movement after a few moments. He opens the door looking sleepy and dishevelled. He squints at me. 'Clemmie, what are you doing?'

'Sam, I've been thinking and . . . were you asleep?'

'Get in the bloody room.' Sam grabs my arm and pulls me forward. He shuts the door behind us and turns on the light. He squints at me and rubs his eyes.

'Did I wake you?' I ask anxiously.

'No, no. I was up. Simply waiting for you to pop down here and call on me.'

I notice he only has a towel wrapped around his waist so I hastily pull my eyes up to his face and concentrate on keeping them there. Perhaps this wasn't such a good idea.

'I'll go,' I say hastily.

'You're here now. What's been worrying you?' He takes my arm and leads me to the bed. We both sit down. He looks at me in concern and puts his arm around me gently. I immediately feel reassured.

'I didn't want to be alone. I've been thinking about Martin Connelly and I'm scared. What if he hasn't come to find Emma at all? What if he — '

'Hang on. Is this about Martin Connelly?'

'Of course! What else would it be about? Do you think Martin Connelly has come here just to find Emma?'

'Why else would he be here, Clemmie?' asks Sam patiently, moving his arm away.

'Well, what if he's pissed off with someone else? What if he's decided to get back at the people who ruined his little plan? Because we know he's quite pissed off generally with life.'

Sam wearily rubs his eyes. 'You lost me somewhere after the first word. What's your point?'

'I think he's come down here to find me!' I announce dramatically.

Sam snorts with laughter. 'Come down here to find you?' he echoes. 'He hasn't come down here to find you, Clemmie. Don't be ridiculous.'

'But why else would he be here?'

'Martin is here to find Emma,' says Sam firmly. 'For whatever twisted reason of his own. He hasn't travelled a few thousand miles just to give you a good poke in the eye.' He squints at me for a second. 'Although, he'd have trouble doing that at the moment. Has your face gone down at all?'

My hand immediately flies up to investigate. Bugger. I'd forgotten all about it.

'I just didn't see the avocado. You know, restaurants really shouldn't be putting those things in salads, they're just plain dangerous.'

'You were pissed!'

Ooh. That hurt. Is it gentlemanly behaviour to remind a girl of a slight overindulgence? I get up and make towards the door. 'I'm going back to bed.'

'Well, remember to lock the door.'

This tiny show of concern stops me in my tracks. 'So you do think he might be down here to find me?' I breathe.

'No, but I wouldn't put it past him to come and knock on your door. So just remember to lock it. In fact, come on . . . ' He strides past me. 'I'll walk you back up there.' He pulls open the door with some force and speeds ahead of me.

As I trot along behind him, I keep my eyes firmly fixed on the little dimple at the bottom of his back, hastily realise that it is quite inappropriate and raise my eye-line to the back of his neck instead. We pass Madame on the stairs, who Sam gives a cheery, 'Bonjour!' to, and who I can't even look at. What sort of depraved bedroom antics must she think are going on? Especially with my swollen face and pyjama combo. When we reach my room, Sam takes the key out of my hand and opens the door.

'Would you like me to check underneath the bed, Clem?'

I open my mouth to say, 'Would you mind?' but see he is grinning wickedly at me. I wouldn't give him the satisfaction. 'That's quite all right. I'll be fine now,' I say stiffly.

'Are you sure? What about the wardrobe?'

'I can manage perfectly well, thank you.' God, he's annoying.

He beams in an infuriating kind of way, ruffles my hair and then turns on his heel. 'G'night!' he calls over his shoulder.

I expect to spend the whole night tossing and turning and so am ashamed to confess that I fall asleep almost immediately. In the morning, all my anti-Martin devices — my sarong twisted around the door handle and then wound around the wardrobe knob and my espadrilles rammed through the window latches — are still in place. I go through to the bathroom and check my face. Happily someone vaguely resembling me stares back at me. Thank God for that, I'm not sure if I could have faced going out today looking like a bull frog. As it is, I slather on some tinted moisturiser and mascara, pull on my skirt, which I only just notice has a hole in one of its seams, fail to locate one of my flip-flops so have to make do with my cowboy boots instead, and go downstairs where Madame informs me that my parents have gone to have coffee on the harbour front.

I exit into the gorgeous morning air and breathe deeply. The little village is starting to wake up and the tantalising smell of fresh bread is in the air. I jog down the steps towards the sea front and within a minute I round the corner to see my parents sitting in the morning sun. Sam is sitting at the table as well, much to my consternation.

'Anything going bump in the night, Clemmie?' Sam greets me. 'Any unexpected guests? Strange noises?'

'No,' I say with as much dignity as I can muster. I have to admit I am feeling a little ashamed of my rather hysterical claims last night. I can only put it down to the alcohol and having a face like a puffa fish. Which only goes to demonstrate the dangers of remaining sober for too long. I pull out one of the wicker chairs, sit down and help myself to some coffee from the cafetière.

'Dare I ask if anything should have been going bump in the night?' asks my father politely.

'Clemmie got it into her head that Martin Connelly had come all the way down to the south of France just to bump her off,' explains Sam.

'I didn't say I thought he was going to bump me off,' I protest.

'What *did* you think he was going to do? Ask for a best of three at tiddlywinks and then disappear back to Cambridge for good?'

'I thought he might be a bit cross that I've thwarted his plans. That's all. Besides . . . ' I turn to my father, ' . . . you're the one who put the idea in my head.'

He stares at me. 'I don't think he's going to kill you, Clemmie. I just think he might make a bit of a nuisance of himself if we don't stop him now. You didn't really think he might murder you, did you?' My father snorts with laughter.

'Well, vindictive people don't always have rational thought processes. Anyway . . . ' I add, anxious to get off the subject, ' . . . have you heard from Holly this morning? Have you told her what Sir Christopher wants us to do?'

'Holly was going to talk to James and get back to me this morning.'

My mother hasn't added a word to the conversation yet. She is sitting with her huge, dark glasses on, staring out over the view with Morgan on her lap. Mornings really aren't her best time. She hasn't stirred once since I arrived and I have a strong suspicion that she is asleep behind those enormous glasses.

My father pays the bill and then we all get up slowly and start to wander back towards the hotel, my father occasionally steering my mother in the right direction. Madame greets us as we arrive. 'Ça va?' she asks me.

'Oui, ça va,' I answer, looking up at her. She is looking deep into my eyes and smiling sympathetically. What's up with her? 'Et vous?' I ask politely back.

'Je vais bien,' she says gently and gives my shoulder a compassionate little squeeze.

'What's wrong with her?' I ask Sam as she walks back behind the reception desk.

'She probably thinks you've been crying,' says Sam.

'Me? Crying?'

'Well, your eyes are still a bit swollen and red.'

'What on earth would I be . . . ?' Bloody hell, the old nag thinks I've been crying about Sam. She saw him escorting me back to my room last night and probably thinks I was chucking myself at him or something and had been gently but firmly rebuffed. I feel the colour start to rise up my cheeks. Madame gives me a little smile from across the room.

'Right, who's going to kick off?' says my father. 'Sir Christopher is calling me again this morning. So I would rather stay here and take the call, and your mother is useless before noon anyway. It might be better if you and Clemmie head off by yourselves,' says my father. When he spoke to Sir Christopher last night, they both agreed it was strange that Martin Connelly was still hanging around. Surely if he had seen Emma leaving with the Winstanley family then he would have followed her. So the only conclusion we have drawn is that Connelly didn't see Emma go and is still waiting around here for some clues. So basically Sir Christopher wants us (if it isn't *too* much trouble) to stick around, keep an eye on Connelly and see if he really has found out where Emma is before Sir Christopher starts making new plans to move Emma again. And, as you know, my father is pretty keen to resolve this whole thing so he agreed to it.

'Clemmie and I will take the first shift if you like,' says Sam.

'So what exactly does this involve?' I ask.

'We're just going to go about the normal business of enjoying our holiday and see if we spot Connelly anywhere.'

'And what if we see Connelly?' I ask my father. 'What do we do then?'

'Absolutely nothing at all. Just keep track of him.'

'I'm not sure I'm going to be very good at this.'

'Clemmie, we're not asking you to be an actuary for the day.' I look sharply at Sam at this little jibe but he continues regardless. 'We're just asking you to sit around in some cafés and maybe have a swim. That sounds pretty much like what you do in Cornwall.' I narrow my eyes at him. What exactly is he getting at?

I turn to my father. 'And why is Sir Christopher calling you?'

'I'm hoping he might have thought of something. Either way, we need to decide what to do next. Your mother and I will take over after lunch. You might cave under the pressure if you think you're being shadowed by Martin Connelly all day.'

'And how are you and Mum going to take over? If given a choice between following you or me, he's going to pick me.'

'Not necessarily. You and Sam come back here at lunchtime and then your mother and I will go out. Hopefully he might switch to us.'

'If he's following anyone at all,' puts in Sam. 'Because he clearly can't have been watching when the Winstanleys picked up Emma, and he wasn't watching us last night when we saw him in the restaurant.'

'Okay, you're all doing my head in. I think we

should call Holly and ship her out here. It's all her fault we're in this mess in the first place.'

'And you had nothing to do with that at all, did you, Clemmie?'

'Absolutely nothing! It was all Holly.'

There's a small silence as Sam surveys me for a second. 'Boy, this is going to be a fun day out,' he remarks.

★　★　★

After I have collected my little beach bag and rescued my bikini from the washing line in the bathroom, I meet Sam in reception. He still looks disturbingly handsome and has changed into a pair of linen trousers, a shirt and a pair of loafers. Everyone in the world must have more in their wardrobe than me. That includes Madame, who is looking fondly at us both and smiling. Sam gives a cheery 'A bientôt!' and pulls me out of reception.

'Now, do not spend the entire day looking over your shoulder. Just act natural.'

Sam wants me to act natural. I am in the presence of someone I fancy but am not supposed to fancy while being followed by an ex-convict bent on revenge. My mother has also told me to keep an eye out for any more politicians as she is now convinced they are having some sort of secret summit over here. And Sam wants me to act normal.

'Get in the car.'

'Where are we going?' I ask.

'I thought you might like to visit an old hill

town; I asked Madame where to go and she suggested a place called Eze.'

'But Martin Connelly might not have a car. He might not be able to follow us.'

'Clemmie, I couldn't give a shit whether Martin Connelly can follow us or not. I would really like it if we could just go out and have a nice day by ourselves, without worrying about anything.'

He smiles at me and I suddenly relax and smile back. 'So if this is a hill town, is it a good bet that no bikinis will be needed?'

He grins. 'No bikinis will be needed. Now get in.'

I don't need asking a third time. I scuttle to the car door and get in with great alacrity. I get to ride up front this time too.

22

Sam looks quite ridiculous driving the car to Eze. The seat is back as far as it will possibly go and still his legs are around his ears. Back home, his car is an automatic so he keeps forgetting that he has to put the clutch in to change gear and this results in a great deal of swearing as the little car chokes and grumbles and occasionally conks out altogether. All I do is shout 'PASSENGER-PAVEMENT' every so often to remind him to keep the passenger side to the right as we have a tendency to drift over to the left-hand side of the road and come eyeball to eyeball with some unfortunate motorist driving the other way. Somewhere off the coast road to Monaco, we take a left into the hills and start an enormous sweeping zig-zag up this vast precipice with absolutely no barriers on the edge. So the first time we are really able to make conversation is when we arrive and park in the only car park we can see. I exit into the still-soft sunshine and breathe deeply. The mountain air is clean and smooth and even though it is still relatively early, the crickets have started singing in the dusty car park.

'God, that was a bit hair-raising, wasn't it?' I remark.

'You stamping on your imaginary brake every other minute did wonders for my confidence.'

'Sam, we were so close to that Renault that at

one point I thought I was going cross-eyed.'

'Of course, it didn't help you screaming 'Look out for that car!' every time one appeared on the horizon.'

'I thought I was being helpful.'

'I'll try to remember to be as helpful the next time you drive.'

'Do you think Martin was following us?' I ask.

'I have no idea. I wasn't about to take my eyes off the road. Besides, Clemmie, I don't want to think about Martin Connelly today.'

'Or Emma?'

'Or Emma.'

Sam goes over to the ticket machine and buys a ticket, which is lucky since I still haven't managed to get my hands on any euros.

'Sam, I haven't changed any money yet. Can I pay you back later?' I ask when he returns to the car, anxious not to appear like a freeloader.

'Don't be silly, Clemmie. You don't need to pay me back for anything. Let's go.'

We start walking up an incline towards what looks to be the town. 'I think this is right,' says Sam. 'Madame said that no cars are allowed.'

'Thank God for that.'

We reach the grey stone wall that encompasses the town and rises up like a giant, sheer cliff in front of us. To one side there is a wide, sweeping staircase and we start to climb it. Halfway up, the wall partly falls away and we can suddenly see for miles and miles down to the coast and out to sea. The still, oppressive heat is lifted by a breeze. Sam and I eye the view for a while while I surreptitiously catch my breath and try not to look as though I'm about to collapse.

We push onwards and upwards and soon emerge through a couple of archways to a small, cobbled street.

'This is gorgeous,' I breathe, looking around at the ancient stone buildings. Miniature, wonky mews houses with wooden front doors surround us. Some have window boxes overflowing with colourful geraniums, others still have their wooden shutters closed against the heat of the sun.

'Do you want to walk to the church?' asks Sam, indicating a little wooden sign on the wall which points in the direction of 'l'église'.

I smile and nod and we start the slow, gradual climb up tiny twisting alleyways and crooked steps. Now and then we glimpse a tiny rooftop garden or a Romanesque window.

We monitor each other's progress and give encouraging smiles until Sam breaks the silence by saying, 'So, did you ever hear anything more from Seth?'

The question takes me by surprise and I stop on my step and look over at Sam. He pauses a couple of feet ahead of me and leans against a wall.

'Em, no. I haven't heard from him since I left the country.'

'You know he tried to come and see you?'

I frown. 'No, when was that?'

'You'd just left for your trip.'

'What? Did he call?'

'He actually came up to the house. Barney nearly lamped him.'

'But Holly said Barney saw him in Exeter.'

'Barney doesn't know where Exeter is!'

'Why didn't anyone tell me?'

'We didn't think you needed to know.'

'Who is 'we'?'

Sam shrugs. 'The family.'

'Why on earth didn't I need to know? I might have wanted to see him.'

'Don't get your knickers in a twist, Clemmie. I'm only telling you because I thought you might want to know and Barney told me you seem to be well over him now. You're not still bleeding your heart out for him, are you?'

'No, I'm definitely over it.'

'He was hopeless, you know.'

'Nobody thought of telling me this at the time?'

'Come off it, Clemmie! You were so smitten! And he was so smug! I hated the way he always talked about how much he earned, he name-dropped for the Olympics. He was a pompous arse who treated you appallingly, so of course we weren't about to tell you that he was trying to get hold of you.'

The pompous arse bit stings. It feels like some sort of personal insult, which of course it is, as it implies that I am incapable of picking out a good man. Which of course I am.

I ignore the few people struggling to pass us in the narrow street. 'Since when did everyone decide he was pompous? I thought you liked him!'

'Oh, come on Clemmie! He would blind-taste a cheap bottle of plonk from Sainsbury's and rave about its virtues. And he would insist on cleaning his shoes every day. He even tried to get you to do it! It used to drive me nuts.'

'Is that why you kept stepping on his feet?' I demand.

Sam relaxes and grins suddenly. 'Did you notice?'

'Of course I did! I thought you'd lost all hand-eye coordination in some sort of freak accident.'

We stare at each other for a second and then we both laugh.

'Come on. Let's go and see this church.' We start our slow progress once more, pausing now and then to peer into shop windows.

The church is more beautiful than I could possibly have imagined. It is so quiet and cool when we enter that it feels like we're stepping into another world. The walls are painted with ancient murals and pictures of various saints. I slip into one of the pews and sit quietly for a while while Sam prowls around trying to read all the various inscriptions. I try my best to think of Godly things but fail miserably and end up in a lovely fantasy where Sam and I are actually going out together and have just popped down here to the south of France for a little holiday.

Eventually we feel cool enough to return outside and decide to push on up to the pinnacle of the village: *le jardin exotique*, which is apparently built on the site of the old castle.

'Has there been anyone since Seth?' Sam asks as we start to climb the steps again.

I shake my head. 'No one. Well, a couple while I was away,' I add hastily, not wanting him to think I have taken a vow of chastity. 'But no one important. I know Seth was pompous at the end but he was quite different when we first started seeing each other and I somehow managed to lose sight of that.'

'I know it was a rough time for you, Clemmie.'

We pause and I look up to meet his eyes. They're not mocking or probing but full of warmth and sympathy, which makes me want to open up a bit more.

'I just can't understand why I didn't notice how much he'd changed.'

'I think you're too hard on yourself.'

'But you're right! He did turn into a pompous arse and I did absolutely nothing about it. I didn't even acknowledge it to myself. He even started choosing my clothes for me! I suppose he was embarrassed. I have an eclectic taste at the best of times.'

'I love your taste!'

I beam at him. 'Do you really?'

'Of course!' His eyes take in today's outfit. It is a bit tatty and I squirm slightly. 'You can't say it's not individual. But I love the cowboy boots. Anyway, maybe deep down you did know about Seth but just wanted to avoid the storm for a while.'

I find this vaguely comforting. 'It was quite a storm, though, wasn't it?' I smile. 'I managed to lose my job because of it. I just wonder if I'd come to my senses earlier, would I still be working there and not living back at home and being shouted at by Mr Trevesky on a daily basis?'

'Maybe you needed things to come to a head before you could let him go. Besides, you wouldn't have done your round-the-world trip, and perhaps something better is waiting for you on the job front.'

I smile at him, feeling happier about the situation than I have done for a while. 'Maybe it is. So what about you and Charlotte?' I ask shyly after a moment. Sam pauses to look at some signs. My heart thumps madly in direct contrast to the slow and deliberate way I am looking at him.

'Charlotte is a really nice girl,' says Sam firmly and gesticulates towards the sign for the garden which indicates a left turn. This is not really the sort of information I am looking for. I am looking for something along the lines of I-thought-I-liked-her-until-I-spent-some-time-with-you but this is clearly not forthcoming. Perhaps I am barking up the wrong tree. Or maybe just plain barking.

We enter a beautiful garden full of exotic cacti. There are still more steps and when we reach the summit of the garden the views are absolutely breathtaking and well worth the climb. The crooked rooftops of Eze lie at our feet and the whole of the Côte d'Azur is spread before us. We sit for some minutes and survey the scene in silence.

'Tell me more about Barney's girlfriend,' says Sam after we have begun the climb back down again. 'You don't really think it could be

Catherine Fothersby, do you?'

'I bloody well hope not! My father knows who it is, but won't say.'

'How does he know?'

'I think he saw Barney and this girl together and guessed.'

'I can't think why Barney wouldn't tell me.'

'Maybe because he knows you would try and talk him out of it?'

'Not if I thought that's what he truly wanted.'

'Even Catherine Fothersby?'

'Well. Maybe her.'

'You see? It's got to be someone really awful if he hasn't told you. You're his best friend.'

'I'm going to talk to him as soon as we get back to Cornwall.'

I groan. 'Do we have to talk about going back to Cornwall? I don't want to go back to work.'

'Nor do I.'

'I think you work too hard.'

'I think I do too. I'm going to make a conscious effort to cut back. Are you going to find a new job when we get back?'

'I don't think I'll get a choice. Mr Trevesky will have definitely fired me.'

'Be the best thing for you. Just don't become an actuary. You'd be rubbish.'

I open my mouth to jokingly reply but then I glimpse a figure ahead. He does look like . . . I squint and bob my head from side to side in an attempt to gain a better view.

'What?' says Sam.

'I think that might be . . . ' I stand on tiptoe but people are obscuring my vision and he's disappeared. 'It looked like Martin Connelly.'

'Do you think it was?'

'I don't know. It looked like him.' I shiver as the sun goes behind a cloud. 'Let's get back to the hotel.'

Although my possible Martin sighting casts a shadow over the morning, I can't help but think how nice it has been to spend some time with Sam. I look over at him crunching gears and swearing madly. God, he is gorgeous. Is this one of the last times we'll ever be alone together? I feel a bit disappointed because if he had any feelings for me whatsoever then surely this would have been a good time to say something? Apart from the fact that he needs to concentrate on the road.

When we arrive back at Cap Ferrat, Madame looks absolutely thrilled to see us and greets us like long lost friends. She looks quite teary-eyed at the sight of us together and for a worried second I wonder if she is going to cry. I quickly ask her if she has seen my parents to distract her and she points us towards the restaurant.

We find my parents and Morgan there. They have ordered themselves lunch and they ask the waiter for some more menus. I sit down at one of the place settings and help myself to some bread and butter while we're waiting.

'Darling! Did you have a nice morning?' asks my mother. 'You'll never guess who I saw strolling past the window a second ago without a care in the world!'

'Another Cabinet member?' asks Sam.

'How did you know?'

'Just a lucky guess. Clemmie thought she saw Martin Connelly.'

'My God!' says my father. 'Did you really? Where was this?'

'At Eze. We were just having a walk round.'

'This is getting really out of hand. I'm not having this man following my family around. I'm going to call James again, see if there is something we can do.'

Just as my father says this, I hear a familiar voice in reception talking to Madame. I leap up and, still carrying my bread, walk out into the foyer.

There are Holly and James, standing with a little wheely case between them.

I let out a squeal of excitement and they turn around. I don't think I have been so pleased to see anyone in my life. I suppose it's quite nice that Holly's here too, but James is the one I'm concentrating on. All six-foot police officer of him.

I run over to them, give Holly a big hug and manage to smear butter on her shoulder. 'Ooh, sorry. I'm sure we can sponge it off,' I say as I wipe it with an oily finger. 'Hello James!' He gives me a kiss on the cheek. 'I am *so* glad to see you! Did you bring any back-up?'

'Do you count Holly?'

'No.'

'Well then, I didn't.'

He is distracted by Sam and my parents and strolls over to greet them. I link arms with Holly as we walk over to join them. 'Does he carry a gun?' I whisper to her.

'Er, no.'

'A knife?'

'No.'

'A truncheon?'

'I don't think so.'

'Oh. Did you fly over?' I ask out of sheer politeness a moment later.

'James decided we ought to come down. He thought the situation might be getting a bit out of hand.'

'Oh, it is. It is. What's he going to do?'

'Try and find Martin Connelly, I think.'

My parents chivvy everyone through to the restaurant because Holly and James booked on a low-cost airline and haven't had much to eat. Sam and my father pull up two extra chairs and we all sit down. My mother is thoroughly overexcited at seeing them.

'My darlings! I am so pleased you came down! Just think of all the fabulous things we can do now you're here!'

We all look at her incredulously. 'Sorrel, I think they're here to sort out the Martin Connelly situation,' says my father.

'Who?' I really think she has forgotten about him. I wish I could do the same.

'Martin Connelly.'

'Oh. The psychologist.'

'That's the one.'

My mother seems thoroughly bored by this and looks out of the window.

'Well, I have to say, James, that we are extremely glad to see you,' says my father.

'Sir Christopher called me and, combined

with your worries about the girls, I thought it was best that we flew out and sorted things once and for all.'

'So are the police involved now?' I ask.

'No, I'm officially on holiday.'

'How's everything at the paper?' I whisper to Holly as James starts to discuss things with my father and Sam.

'It's okay. Sir Christopher seems to have calmed down but Joe is still mad and I've got to file copy for 'High Society' by tomorrow.'

'How's it looking? Did you find those notes on Emma's PC that I told you about?'

'They are pretty thin. Just jottings really. Did you manage to get anything else out of Emma?'

'Em, no. Not really.'

'God, Clemmie. You've got to help me find something.'

'I'll try,' I say, looking doubtful. 'What sort of thing are we looking for?'

'Anything! Parties, fashion, that sort of thing.'

I pull a face at her and change the subject. 'It's good of James to come.'

'Dad has been so worried about the situation.'

'So you and James must be okay if he's flown out here to help?' I nudge her slightly.

'I think he's more worried about you than me, Clemmie,' says Holly dryly.

I smile and reassure her that it can't possibly be true. It is so nice to see her and I am incredibly tempted to tell her all about my rather sudden crush on Sam. I open my mouth to do so but James stops me by getting up.

'Where are you going?' asks Holly.

'I'm going to Martin Connelly's B and B to try to talk to him.'

Rather him than me.

★ ★ ★

None of us are sure how long James will be because he says that if Martin isn't there he will simply wait for him. So we hang about nervously in reception, undecided as to whether to go out or stay put.

Holly goes back to her room to make a phone call to the paper, and I am just about to pop upstairs to my room to retrieve a book when Sam, who has been peering through the glass doors at the entrance, suddenly says, 'James is coming back.'

'I suppose he decided not to wait after all.'

'No, I think Martin Connelly is with him.'

Oh God. I peer out from behind Sam, 'Oh shit. It is Martin Connelly. Why the hell is he bringing him here? Have we time to hide?'

'Don't be silly, Clemmie,' says Sam, grasping hold of my arm. 'I'd quite like to meet him.'

'I've already met him,' I hiss, but it's too late. James and Martin are already mounting the steps to the hotel.

I make an effort to release myself from Sam's hold but he's too strong for me and after a brief struggle we have to make out that we're holding hands as James and Martin swing through the door. Our knuckles are absolutely white but Martin probably just thinks we've got very firm grips. I plaster an over-bright expression on my

336

face. 'Hello!' I greet them jollily as though Martin is a long lost friend and I am extremely glad to see him.

James eyes me suspiciously. 'I met Martin in the street and we thought we would come back here.'

'Did you?' I say, sounding rather hysterical.

'Hello Clemmie,' says Martin in a strained voice. 'I take it you all know I'm here then.' He looks from me to Sam and I wonder fleetingly whether I should be introducing them or something.

'Yes, we saw you the other night,' I say quietly. Will he be cross that we've blown his cover?

'Shall we sit down?' says James, gesturing towards the normally very inviting sofas in the reception area.

I make to sidle away but Sam pulls me towards a sofa. Madame waves at me from behind the reception desk and I smile hopefully back. Will she come and rescue me? Sam obviously sees me looking in her direction and planning my escape as he heftily pulls me down off my feet and on to the sofa. Martin clearly thinks we are going out with each other as we have been pinned together since he arrived. We both smile in a forced manner.

'So, Martin. Do you want to tell me what's been going on?' says James in a dangerously friendly manner.

'I want to find Emma. I want to apologise to her. I know I've been acting crazy and I apologise for my behaviour, but I really want to make amends.'

337

'Do you?'

'Yes. I've treated her badly. Very badly and I want to say I'm sorry. I've become quite . . . fond of Emma over the last few months.' He hesitates.

'Go on,' says James. Holly returns, her eyes opening wide at the sight of Martin, but she sits quietly down on a sofa. She takes no notice of Sam and me, who are still holding hands and practically sitting on top of each other.

'Imagine me in prison. I was due to go to Oxford, you know. I had a great future ahead of me and it was all ruined because of one mistake.' He looks defiantly at us and I can suddenly see an arrogant schoolboy who fervently believes he has done nothing wrong.

'Your girlfriend died,' says James quietly. Please don't rile him James.

'She knew the risks and she paid the price. It was nothing to do with me.'

'Martin, I'm not here to argue about your case.'

'No. That's already been done for me and I lost because of McKellan. Day after day, month after month in that prison. My mum used to send me the *Gazette* to keep me up to date with the local news, what was going on in Bristol. Sometimes my old classmates were mentioned. And one day I noticed that those diary pages were written by Emma McKellan and I wondered if she was a relation of his. And then she mentioned him in those pages, some charity bash they had been to together. Her father. Sir Christopher McKellan. And that's when I started to think about how I could get my own back on him. Through Emma.'

I open my mouth to say something but Sam pinches me so hard that I'm forced to draw my breath in instead.

'Of course, you know what I did. It all went perfectly to plan at first, but then I started to grow fond of Emma. As our wedding day grew closer and closer, I realised I couldn't go through with it so I started to think of how I could call the whole thing off. I thought I could just leave her a note telling her I can't have children and that it would be too cruel to make her marry me, and then disappear so she would never be any the wiser. It would have been infinitely kinder than my original plan.' He gives a bitter little laugh and doesn't seem to notice the frozen expressions that have come over our faces.

'Can't have children?' says James lightly. 'Is that true?'

Martin looks up at him. 'Yes, it is, actually. Had mumps as a kid. I hadn't told Emma because I didn't want to give her a reason *not* to marry me. Ironic, isn't it?'

23

Can't have children? So who the bloody hell is the father of Emma's child?

I can't stop a little noise escaping my lips as we all stare at Martin. James notices the noise and looks at me sharply. 'Don't you have to be meeting your parents, Clemmie? Holly?'

'Hmm?'

'I think you should go now.'

He is clearly worried that I might let slip about Emma. And he's absolutely right because I think I might explode any second. I must be using up countless calories keeping my face absolutely rigid. I think my eyes are starting to water.

Neither Holly nor I move but James looks over to Sam and something unspoken passes between them. Probably something along the lines of get-these-two-gobmouths-out-of-here. Sam hauls me to my feet. When I don't want to stay he makes me, and when I don't want to leave he makes me.

Martin barely notices us leave. Sam escorts Holly and me over to the restaurant where my parents are still having coffee and releases us just as we step inside. I realise it's been quite nice to have Sam so close to me. But no time to think about that now, more pressing issues are at hand. We stand just inside the door and look open-mouthed at each other.

'But Emma is pregnant!' I say, rather stating the obvious.

'Not by Martin Connelly she isn't.'

'Bloody hell!' says Holly, neatly summarising everyone's feelings.

Still in a state of shock, we wander through to the veranda where my parents are sitting. My mother has lit up a cigarette and is trying to blow smoke rings. I sit down on one of the wicker chairs while Sam has a stab at trying to explain the sage so far. Just as I am thinking we could be here for quite some time, my mother surprises us all by grasping the concept quite early on.

'So who on earth is the father?' she asks.

We all look at each other.

'Holly?' I ask because, after all, she knows Emma the best.

Holly shakes her head. 'Haven't a clue. I thought she was supposed to be overwhelmingly in love with Martin.'

'Emma is certainly turning out to be very interesting,' says my mother.

'Do you think she knows that he can't have children? Does she know the baby isn't his?'

'He said he hadn't told her.'

'And Martin Connelly has been going to all this effort to find her because he feels sorry about what he's done?' asks my father disbelievingly. 'Are you sure this isn't just another plan? Maybe he knows she's pregnant.'

'I don't know. I don't think so. James is still out there with him.'

'Tell me what he said. Exactly,' says my father.

341

By the time we have repeated the whole of Martin's conversation word for word, and gone over it twice for my mother, James joins us.

'James, what on earth is going on?' asks my father as soon as he reaches the table. 'Do you really think he wants to apologise? It's not just another scam?'

'I believe him and he certainly doesn't know she's pregnant,' says James. 'Of course, we're not going to tell him where she is. I told him we haven't got a clue where Emma is and so I think you can be sure that he is going to stop hounding the girls. All he is interested in is finding Emma. To apologise. We can all go home.'

My father looks intensely relieved at this.

'I don't know how long he is going to keep trying for. Sir Christopher will have to decide whether he wants to move Emma again or not.'

'So what shall we do?' asks Holly.

'Obviously Sir Christopher will warn Emma that Martin Connelly is here, but I, for one, would like to find out what the bloody hell is going on. So I think we should find out where they live and go up there,' says James.

'Me too!' says my mother. 'We'll all come!'

'We can't all go!' protests my father.

'I think Emma at least owes us an explanation,' I protest. 'She has run circles around us. Holly has laid down her job and reputation for her. Mr Trevesky is extremely pissed off with me and even James is here trying to protect her. So I would quite like to hear her story first-hand. I'd like to see her wriggle out of this one.' I feel righteously indignant.

'We'll go tomorrow,' states my father firmly. 'Now I don't know about the rest of you but I am sick to death of this whole business. Your mother and I have reservations at the Colombe D'Or and we're going for a drink in St Paul de Vence first.' He gets up and holds his hand out to my mother, who looks as though she would much rather stay here and gossip with the rest of us but reluctantly takes it, scoops up Morgan, who was having a comfy little nap under the table, and off they go.

We all order another drink and Holly and I discuss the Emma situation in the only way women can. The fifth time we wonder who on earth the father of Emma's child could be, Sam and James start to look bored.

'All right you two. That's enough. Can we talk about something else?' says Sam.

'What do you want to talk about then?' I ask.

'I thought you were going to keel over when you saw me coming back with Martin Connelly, Clemmie,' grins James.

'I had to practically sit on her to stop her from bolting,' says Sam.

'When you said we should talk about something else, did it have to be this?'

'You make wonderful peanut butter and banana sandwiches,' says Sam comfortingly. True. True. 'Just the thought of them is making me hungry. Why don't we go and get something to eat?'

'I'd like to take a shower and change,' says Holly.

'Me too!' I agree.

'Shall we meet back down here in half an hour?' says James.

We all get up and move towards the door. I drag my feet unwillingly because much as it is lovely to see Holly and James, it also means that Sam and I really won't get to spend any more time alone together. Soon we will return to England, he'll marry Charlotte and that will be that.

'Clemmie, would you mind if James and I had a quiet supper by ourselves?' whispers Holly on the first landing as we lag behind the men. 'It's just that things have been a little tense lately and I think it would do us a lot of good to relax.'

'Of course! I don't mind spending the evening alone with Sam!' I say eagerly. The words 'alone with Sam' hang jauntily in the air. 'I mean, so you and James can mend ah, er, little . . . or patch things . . . ' I haven't a clue what I'm talking about but leave it at that and hope Holly doesn't misinterpret anything. 'You two slip off. I'll square it with Sam.' I nod encouragingly and hope I don't look too lecherous.

Madame has given Holly and James a room on the first floor (she obviously didn't like the look of me) so we drop them off there and Sam and I walk up the next flight of stairs together towards our own rooms.

'Holly and James want to have a quiet supper by themselves,' I say super casually. 'They've been having quite a rough time lately.'

'Okay.'

We climb in silence for a second.

'Well, would you like to go and find some food?' asks Sam.

'Only if you're hungry,' I say nonchalantly.

'Would you prefer an early night? There's been lots of stuff going on. Don't worry about me, I can pop out and get something.' Hmmm, maybe a little too nonchalantly.

'Er, no,' I say quickly. 'I could probably manage a little something.'

'I'll see you in reception in, say, twenty minutes?'

I nod, leave him on his floor and then indifferently meander my way up another flight of stairs until I am out of sight and then leg it to my room. Twenty minutes! God, you've got to give a girl a chance. Can I do what I have to do in twenty minutes?

I arrive at my room, thrust open the door and run to the wardrobe. The cupboards are bare. A brainwave occurs to me and I leg it down another four flights of stairs. At least I'm going to be fit at the end of this.

'Holly!' I hiss as I thump on their door. I don't care if they're jolly well having sex in there. Their relationship might be hanging on a thread but at least it's there.

Holly opens up. 'Clemmie, what on earth are you doing?'

'Erm, I was wondering if I could borrow something to wear.'

'Why? Didn't you bring anything?'

'It's all dirty. Freak accident with the sun lotion.'

'What's wrong with what you're wearing?'

God, what do I have to do to gain access to her wardrobe?

'Dirty too.' Holly's eyes wander down my outfit. 'Well, I feel dirty. Could I just borrow a little dress or something?' I plead.

'I suppose,' she sighs, begrudgingly opening the door. The shower is on so I presume James is in it. 'Just as long as you don't get sun lotion on that too. I want to wear it tomorrow.'

She goes to the open suitcase on the bed and unpacks a lovely little French Connection number, which is embroidered with huge circles in scarlets and orange and comes to just above the knee.

'Thank you!' I gasp, clasping it to me.

Back in my room, I try to remember all the things you're supposed to do before a hot date. I can only take inspiration from my in-flight magazine. So I hop into the shower and soap everywhere thoroughly, remembering to shave both armpits. I moisturise all over my body (this is crucial apparently but not sure why) but have to hold back from any nail varnish as my normal quick-drying method of wafting my hands above the toaster is not possible.

I arrive in reception with a screech about twenty-five minutes later. My espadrilles don't really go with the dress but other than that I have to say I am quite pleased with the results.

Sam is chatting to Madame in a mixture of broken French on his part and broken English on hers. They stop as I come over and Madame gives me a knowing look in light of our recent encounter on the stairs. I try not to blush and concentrate on Sam instead, who is looking devilishly attractive in jeans and a thin, black jumper.

'You look nice!' he greets me.

'Holly's dress,' I explain.

'I think we might have to go out and get you some clothes tomorrow. You seem to be very thin on the ground where your wardrobe is concerned.'

'Lack of funds. It's been about two years since I've bought anything.'

'I'll buy you some things,' says Sam firmly.

'No, you don't have to do that,' I say, feeling madly encouraged.

'To be honest, Clemmie, if have to see you in that ropey old skirt again, I might have to top myself. I'll be doing humanity a favour,' he says dryly as he turns on his heel and walks out of the hotel.

Hmmm. Not sure that's quite so encouraging.

'Where do you want to go?' he asks as we emerge into the evening air. 'I thought maybe we could get some French bread and pâté and a bottle of wine and go down to the beach for a picnic.'

How lovely! 'That sounds great.'

He grins at me and I nearly swoon with delight. Just remember, I tell myself firmly as I trot behind him into a little shop, he is going out with Charlotte who is a very nice girl.

The shopkeeper is trying to close up for the night but still has one stick of French bread left so we scurry around picking up some pâté, olives, a bottle of wine and a corkscrew. At the last minute I find some of those mini gherkins pickled in vinegar which I absolutely adore. Sam rolls his eyes at me. After we have paid for our purchases, we walk down the street towards the beach. 'So what do you think about Emma?' I ask, anxious for his take on it. 'How do you think Martin Connelly will react when he finds out she's pregnant?'

'Well, it certainly turns his revenge plan on its head. He thought he was the one doing all the duping.'

'Do you think she knows he's infertile and that's why she's panicking so much about seeing him again?'

'No, I think she thinks the child is his.'

'I wonder if they'll tell him now.'

'That's up to Emma and her father. It's absolutely nothing to do with us any more, thank God.'

'I don't think I have a massive amount of sympathy for her,' I say.

'Mine is fast running out,' agrees Sam. 'I think we should forget about her and just concentrate on enjoying ourselves.'

Oooh, yes please. I'm all for enjoying myself, I think greedily.

We walk in single file down the one-way street towards the beach because the roads are so narrow. It is a beautiful evening and the air feels heavy with birdsong and freshness. I have to make a conscious effort to stop clutching myself with pleasure. Please do not make a fool of yourself, I tell myself firmly. He merely suggested a picnic on the beach because we are stuck together for this evening and it's a nice thing to do. If he had been stuck with Holly then he would still have suggested a picnic on the beach.

We clamber down on to the stony beach. The sea gently laps the shore and we make our way towards a large rock and spread out our things. I try to sit down delicately but Holly's skirt isn't giving me much room for manoeuvre and I have to sort of crumple in a heap. I pull my legs daintily to one side and suck in my cheeks. By contrast Sam chucks himself down and then rummages in the bag for the wine and corkscrew.

'I'm afraid you're going to have to swig it from the bottle, Clem.'

'That's okay.'

He deftly opens it and then proffers it to me. I hand it back to Sam after taking a gulp and am happy to notice that he doesn't bother to wipe the top of it before he too takes a swig.

I don't know if it's because I'm having to drink from the bottle but it doesn't take long for me to sink into a pleasant state of inebriation. Sam leans back against a rock and we have an absolutely marvellous time. We talk about anything and everything and Sam's tone is distinctly flirtatious. I don't think I am imagining it. His hand occasionally brushes mine as we go about our little picnic and his eyes sometimes hold mine longer than is strictly necessary. Occasionally I have to pinch myself to believe the whole thing is actually happening and is not the result of my rather over-fertile imagination.

Eventually we decide it is too dark to stay on

the beach, gather our belongings together and meander back to the hotel. We don't speak very much on the way home but the atmosphere is heavy with intent. He glances at me, I glance at him — there is a whole lot of glancing going on.

Once in the hotel, we walk up the stairs and I hover uncertainly on the second landing, wondering what happens next. Sam takes matters into his own hands and says he'll escort me to my room. I start to feel incredibly nervous and run through a mental checklist: Have I brushed my teeth? (Yes, definitely.) Did I leave my clothes all over the floor? (Maybe. Can't remember.) Do I have a matching set of bra and knickers on? (Do I own one?)

We slow down to a positive dawdle until we reach my room. His chocolate brown eyes fix on mine as I lean against the door feeling like a foolish teenager.

'Where's your key?' he asks softly, still staring straight into my eyes.

I rustle about in my handbag and produce it. He starts to lean gently towards me. This is it! I close my eyes and wait for the blissful feel of his lips on mine. It's as though I have been waiting forever for this moment and . . . it appears I might have to wait a bit longer because out of the corner of one half-closed eye I notice that Sam has merely leaned forward in order to unlock my door. I hastily snap my eyes open and stare at him like a rabbit caught in headlights. Oh God! How embarrassing! Did he see me with my eyes closed, positively panting? I was so absolutely sure something was about to happen.

Sam is looking thoughtfully at his shoes, as though he is trying to find the words to say something difficult. Maybe he simply doesn't fancy me. After all, he does have a girlfriend, one he has admitted to being terribly fond of, so why on earth should he be messing about with me? I feel absolutely mortified. And there was I, puckered up and ready to go. Sam looks at me; he has obviously found the words he was looking for.

'Em, Clemmie. I think we need to — ' He breaks off suddenly and turns his head. I realise he is listening to voices on the stairs. 'Madame is coming and . . . ' He starts to listen more intently.

'What's the matter?' I ask.

'That's Charlotte's voice. Charlotte is here.'

24

Sam quickly moves away from me and starts to walk down the corridor to meet her. With a mixture of shock and apprehension, I half-heartedly follow him. Charlotte? Is he sure? What on earth is she doing here? A decidedly more male voice suddenly attracts my attention and I start hurrying after Sam until I round the corner.

'Barney!' I exclaim. 'What on earth are you doing here?'

'Oh hello, Clem. We were just coming to find you! How are you? You look nice, been out to dinner?'

'Em, yes. Sam and I just got back . . . ' I am watching Sam who is kissing Charlotte. I feel sick to the stomach. How could I entertain such notions about him when he has a girlfriend? 'Sam was just seeing me back to my room,' I say distractedly. 'What are you doing here?' I ask again.

'Well, Sam called and told Charlotte that there had been some complications and you were going to stay a couple more days. So we didn't see why you should have all the fun and caught the next flight we could out of Bristol. Aren't you pleased to see us?'

'Em, yes. Thrilled.' I try to give a passably good impression of a smile and feel quite, quite horrible. Sam and Charlotte have started to wander back down the stairs now and Barney and I follow them. We pass Madame on the stairs, who gives me the dirtiest of looks, and I feel unbearably awful. Barney thanks her politely and then puts his arm companionably around me. 'We didn't think we'd find you in, thought you'd be out painting the town! Madame has found me a single on the first floor and Charlotte has dumped her stuff in Sam's room.'

'Of course,' I say falsely as the situation starts to ram itself home. Right between the eyes. Charlotte will be sharing Sam's bed tonight.

Barney and I catch Sam and Charlotte up on the first floor.

'Clemmie!' Charlotte exclaims and kisses me on both cheeks. 'I haven't said hello! How *super* to see you! Barney and I couldn't bear to think of you all having such fun without us.' I studiously keep my eyes away from Sam. 'Can we go somewhere for a drink?'

'The hotel has a bar,' says Sam.

'You can tell us *exactly* what's been going on!' says Charlotte chattily as she links her arm through Sam's. 'We've been waiting *all* day at Bristol for a last-minute flight but at least it was cheap.'

They make to move down the next flight of stairs but I interrupt them. 'I'm going to go to bed, I'm all in. Sam will tell you both all the news.'

I will Sam to look at me, just to give me some small sign that everything might be okay, but he doesn't. He is clearly as embarrassed as I am. So with a slightly wobbly jaw, I bid them all goodnight and turn on my heel.

In my bathroom, I take a good look at myself in the mirror and lean my hot forehead against the cool glass. Is it possible to die of embarrassment? Because I wish the good Lord would take me right now if it is. My mind relentlessly plays the whole scene over and over again. My face puckered up, eyes closed, lips at the ready and Sam having to gently tell me that he wasn't really up for it as I am sure he was about to. Oh, the shame. Am I so out of practice that I can no longer judge a situation? Or do I fancy Sam so much that I am completely blind to all the pertinent facts? Such as his girlfriend. Or how about the fact we have known each other for years now and Sam has never shown the slightest romantic interest in me. Let's face it, he'd be more likely to fancy Holly than me. All that kissy stuff and constantly sticking up for her.

Tears fill my eyes suddenly and I bite down hard on the inside of my cheek. Please don't start crying, I tell myself firmly. You'll end up with a hideously swollen face and slitty eyes and you'll have to tell everyone you've been eating avocado again. Besides which, Sam will guess you've been crying and this will become even more embarrassing than it is now.

I step out of Holly's dress and hang it on the edge of the wardrobe. I stand for a second and survey it. It's beautiful and a fat lot of good it's done me. I would have been better off in my tatty old skirt and cowboy boots; at least that way I wouldn't feel as though I had deliberately set out to beguile Sam and I wouldn't feel so awful about Charlotte.

I wander over to my bed, lie down and try to think about stuff back home to take my mind off Sam. I expect to lie awake all night but to my surprise I start to doze, and then fall asleep dreaming of seagulls and French fries.

★ ★ ★

I sheepishly turn up at breakfast the next morning and am extremely pleased that the first person I see is Barney. He is sitting alone at the breakfast table and in front of him is a huge basket of bread. Madame is obviously in love.

'Morning, Clem! Don't you just love French bread? It was worth coming all that way just for breakfast. I could eat a whole loaf of it.' He looks down at his plate. 'Actually I think I might have done. How are you anyway? Been having a nice time? Sam told us all about Emma and Martin Connelly, that's a bit of a shock, isn't it?' Barney pauses to shove another piece of bread into his mouth.

I have been so absorbed by my own problems that I have momentarily forgotten about ruddy Emma. God, even she has managed to seduce two separate people in the last six months.

'Yes, it is, isn't it?'

'Do you know who the father is?'

'No idea at all.' Probably another Adonis she managed to ensnare with her squashed lemon expression and charming manner. Maybe I should think about an image change.

'Sam said James is going to see Emma today.'

'I'm going with him.' When I think what she's put me through in the last week or so, there is absolutely no way I am not going to be present when Emma tries to wriggle out of this one.

'Can I come too?'

'I think that might be a bit of a crowd, Barney. But I'll tell you all about it when we get back. Anyway, how's things with you?'

'Pretty good actually.' He beams his dazzling smile at me and liberally smears his bread with more butter.

I narrow my eyes and look at him. Something is up. I hazard a guess. 'How's that girl of yours?'

'Great! We managed to spend a bit of time together while you lot have been away!'

'And you've been getting on?'

'We're getting on really well.'

'So I take it that she has seen the error of her ways?'

'Well, I wouldn't go that far but it's been much easier to spend time with her while you lot haven't been around.'

'So what are you doing here then? Why aren't you back at home trying to seduce her?'

Barney's thirtieth piece of bread pauses en route to his mouth. He looks at me cagily. 'Because she's gone away too.'

'Has she?' My mind tries to elicit some valuable clue from this little piece of information. 'Where's she gone?' I ask suspiciously.

'On holiday.'

He looks at me warily and I suddenly

356

remember that little pertinent detail my mind has been searching for. Didn't my mother say that Catherine Fothersby was going away for a few days? The light of recognition dawns on my face. 'Oh Barney!'

He knows he's been sussed. 'Now, don't be like that, Clemmie!'

'How could you?'

'I know you don't like her much but I think she's wonderful!'

'Our mother is going to kill you.'

'Mum won't be so bad once she knows the full facts of the situation.'

'That won't change who this girl is!' I hiss back at him.

'I know,' he peers over my shoulder. 'Look, Holly is coming. Please don't say anything until I've sorted it all out?'

I look at his gorgeous, pleading face and my heart melts. 'Okay. But I warn you, no one is going to be very happy about it,' I whisper.

'Hello Barney! It's lovely to see you!' Holly leans over and gives him a big kiss. 'I met Sam on the stairs and he said you turned up last night. So they let you back into the country after the electrocution incident then? I thought you might have a police record. Who's looking after Norman?'

'I dropped him off with Sally yesterday, along with his beanbag and about a hundred tins of sardines.'

'Sally will look after him. More is the pity.'

My stomach lurches at the mention of Sam and I wonder if he will be coming down to breakfast. I'm not sure if I can face him and Charlotte just yet.

'What time are we going to see the Winstanleys?' I ask Holly, ready to make a quick exit.

'Oh, I don't know. James is sorting that out. What are you doing this morning?'

'I thought I might go into Nice and have a look around.'

'I think we might need to get you some more clothes. I tell you what, I'll buy you some!' She beams at me. 'I missed two of your birthdays while you were away!'

'That's really sweet of you, Holly, but — '

'No buts! You can be my new project!'

I look at her in alarm. These projects don't normally end happily. 'Maybe we should wait to see if Mum and Dad want to come?'

'Mum's useless in the mornings so they might not be down for hours! Let's sneak off before anyone else notices.' This actually sounds quite good — Holly and I can argue about the clothes in the car.

I am just about to leap to my feet when Charlotte comes into view. Damn it.

'Morning everyone!' she greets us cheerfully. 'Isn't it a *super* morning? I am *so* pleased we came! Aren't you, Barney?' I don't even want to begin to think why she is in such a good mood. 'Holly, how *are* you? It is so nice to see you. Now, tell me all about this 'High Society' thing that Sam says you have to write.'

I lean back in my chair feeling fidgety while Holly tells Charlotte the latest gossip from the paper. Charlotte is looking very pretty this morning. Has her hair always had such a glossy sheen? Is her complexion always so clear and peachy? I can't see why Sam could even vaguely bother with me with this creature in tow.

Holly has finished telling Charlotte the latest news and brings me out of my reverie by asking eagerly, 'Where's Sam this morning?' I groan to myself. Please don't tell me we're going have to wait to say hello to Sam.

'He's having a lie in.' I'm just breathing a small sigh of relief when suddenly a voice pipes up behind us, 'Charlotte, *darling*! Barney! How lovely to *see* you both!' God, this is all I need.

Charlotte leaps up in delight and they all kiss and hug. You would think my mother hadn't clapped eyes on Barney for years. My mother puts Morgan on the ground during all these greetings and Charlotte watches him anxiously and lifts her handbag off the floor. This makes me feel marginally better.

Charlotte starts to tell my mother about their trip out. ' . . . when Sam called me and told me you *all* wouldn't be back for a few more days, I was so *cross* at the thought of you out here that Barney and I just decided to fly out! So we packed a bag, got into the car, drove to Bristol airport and caught the next flight out! It was *such* fun!'

'What did you do with my darling seagull? I hope you didn't leave those friends of yours in charge. He doesn't like them very much,' my mother says to Barney.

'We took him down to Sally's.'

She beams at him. 'Is he eating okay?'

'They ran out of sardines at the shop so we had to try him on tuna.'

'How did he like it?'

Barney wrinkles his nose. 'I don't think he was that keen.'

'Well, was it in olive oil or brine? Because he only likes tuna in olive oil from Fortnums . . . ' She glances over to my father, who is looking at her sternly, and very wisely changes the subject. 'How are the rehearsals going? Did Sally say?'

'I've been at almost every rehearsal,' says Barney. With that harlot Catherine Fothersby. 'It's been going really well, I think.'

I watch as the family continue to gossip together. My father and mother seem quite genuinely fond of Charlotte.

'Clemmie and I are off to Nice for a couple of hours before we go to visit Emma so we'll see you all later,' Holly announces after a few minutes. She stands up decisively.

I follow suit. 'Okay. What about James though? Should we wait for him?'

'God, no! He'll be on the bloody phone all morning!' Holly seems utterly unrepentant that he'll be on the phone all morning sorting out the mess she caused but I have no time to pick bones with her. She grabs a couple of slices of bread and I do the same. 'Besides, he hates shopping and generally becomes highly irritable. We can take the car. Let's go! Bye all!'

She and James must be getting on better because her usual hyper energy has been restored. She drags me out of the breakfast room, shouting to our father as she goes that she'll have her mobile on.

'Now, what do I have to remember?' she says as she gets into their little Fiat Punto.

'Er, to drive on the left?'

'Or is it the right?'

Now she has me confused. 'Well, it's the opposite to what we do in England.'

'Which side do we drive on in England?'

'You don't know? I've been driving with you all this time and you don't know which side of the road we should be on?'

'Now, Clemmie, don't be like that. I normally just follow everyone else.'

Marvellous.

We finally have an opportunity to chat when we are safely on the road to Nice and following a French Renault that presumably knows which side of the road to drive on.

'So what are you looking so miserable about?' asks Holly.

I make a face and look out of the window. Telling Holly about Sam is one thing, but to have the evidence shoved in front of my eyes for the next twenty years or so with her knowing how I feel about him is quite another. And yet I can't not tell her. I think I'll wait for things to calm down a bit and maybe I'll see things more clearly.

Holly glances over to me. 'Come on. I can see something is upsetting you.'

The temptation to fall sobbing on her shoulder is almost too much for me.

'Tell me what it is,' she repeats.

'The girl Barney fancies is Catherine Fothersby!' I burst out. Well, Holly would have kept going until I told her what was wrong and faced with the choice of sacrificing Barney or myself I'm afraid Barney gets it every time.

Holly nearly runs over a couple of pedestrians as she turns to look at me. 'Noooooo!'

'Yes! He made me promise not to tell you. So you can't mention it to him.'

'How did you find that out?'

'He told me!'

'He told you? Why didn't he tell me?'

'Well, I sort of guessed so he confessed.'

'How on earth did you guess?'

'We started to think it must be someone really awful because he hadn't told Sam, and then I came up with Catherine Fothersby and he told me I was right.'

'Who's 'we'?'

'Me and Sam.' I blush at the mention of him.

'Sam knows too now?'

Damn. I'd forgotten that I hadn't seen Holly since I'd cocked that up too. 'Actually, they all do. They plied me with too much drink and made me tell them.'

'My God! It can't be true! Barney and Catherine Fothersby! Well, he's absolutely wasted on that sourpuss and I shall tell him so. I am not being related to that family. Catherine would be our sister-in-law.'

'Please don't say anything to him. He'll know I told you.'

'Well, I shall do everything I can to dissuade him.'

362

'Me too,' I say, wanting to get off the subject. 'When are you and James going home?'

'Oh, tonight. I'd like to stay longer but James could only take two days' holiday and I honestly think Joe will fire me if I'm away any longer than that. What about you?'

'I think I'll try and get on a train tonight. Mum and Dad are coming home tomorrow but I need to get back to work myself.' I try to sound jolly but my stomach turns over at the thought of going back to the café. My self-confidence seems to have taken such a knocking that all notions of working in a gallery fly out of the window. 'Anyway, how is work for you? Has Joe forgiven you yet?'

'He seems to have. Luckily Sir Christopher has sweetened up since you dropped Emma off with the Winstanleys so I think Joe has almost forgotten about it. He let me have a couple of days off to come out here because I said I needed to finalise some things with Emma for 'High Society'. I didn't dare tell him about all the trouble out here.'

'But you haven't got anything for 'High Society' and Emma is hardly likely to tell you now. Isn't Joe going to expect marvels from you for the first instalment?'

'Ahh, but I do have marvels! Mum told me she's spotted several politicians over here!'

'She hasn't spotted any politicians over here.'

'Well, as I see it, I have a reliable eye-witness who claims to have seen them and I believe her. It will be a fabulous first instalment for the all-new social pages! I intend to breathe new life

363

into them and then Joe will wonder how he ever did without me!'

'I take it that James has forgiven you and is responsible for this restored gung-ho attitude to life?'

'Don't be such a cynic, Clemmie. But yes, he has forgiven me.' She beams at me and I take it that they managed to patch things up last night.

Once we have found a parking spot, which is no mean feat in the centre of Nice, we start to stroll towards the shops. I walk behind Holly, dragging my extremely heavy heart along in her wake. As soon as the pavement becomes wide enough, she drops back to join me.

'Are you still upset about Barney?' she asks sympathetically.

'A bit.' Well, that's true. Just not as upset as I am about Sam.

'Come on! Let's blow the budget!'

'I honestly don't need much, Holly.'

'You must be joking. Besides, you can always pay me back. Let's try in here.' She points the way to an exclusive little boutique. 'I'll go in first because they'll probably think you're a gypsy and turn you away,' she says merrily.

I thought she was supposed to be cheering me up.

25

If I could have worn all my new things at the same time then I would have done. But as it is I settle for my new silk wraparound skirt, which is embroidered with little pink flowers, and a tight-fitting T-shirt, along with my new strappy sandals. I damn near break my neck in them on the stairs but no matter, at least I will die looking fabulous.

I meet Holly, James and my parents in the reception.

'Darling, you look simply marvellous!' my mother gushes. 'Thank God Holly took you shopping! I do hope you have thrown that tatty old skirt you insist on wearing in the bin.'

'I certainly won't be wearing it as much.'

'Shall we go?' says James. He is not really asking us.

Only the five of us are going. Barney was leading a campaign for him, Sam and Charlotte to follow us in another car but was easily distracted by the promise of a swim and some ice cream. Besides which, some of us have to remain behind so Martin Connelly won't think anything is amiss if he is still watching us.

James leads the way to his rental car, and we all clamber in. Yet again I draw the short straw and have to sit in the back between Holly and my mother, but I smile cheerfully because I am so grateful to Holly. Not only has she bought me great armfuls of clothes, refusing to even let me look at the price tags, but she has also given my self-esteem a large boost when it needed it. At least I'll be well dressed every time I come across Sam for, oooh, the next twenty years or so.

I haven't seen Sam properly since our little incident last night. The family has always been around and, of course, so has Charlotte. Everyone was right about that, by the way. She really is very pretty. When we arrived back at lunchtime she was wearing a very sweet pale blue sundress with a matching pale blue polka dot bikini underneath. She had her hair loose and looked as though she had walked straight off a magazine shoot. So you can see why I am so grateful to Holly for making me so much better equipped for the encounter. Sam gave me a couple of sympathetic little smiles but luckily I was able to hide behind my sunglasses. What on earth am I going to do back in Cornwall when we have no sun? Not to mention what I am going to do back in Cornwall if this little crush on Sam continues. It hasn't shown any signs of abating yet; in fact, I think it might have got worse. I feel as though I've been kicked in the stomach every time I so much as glimpse him. I glance over at Holly. I might have to talk to her before I explode, but just as I am thinking this my mother says something that brings me out of my reverie.

' . . . I have to say that I am looking forward to meeting him. When did you say he was flying over, James?'

'I spoke to him this morning, just before he

caught his flight. He said that if Martin Connelly was over here in France with us then he might as well fly over to check that Emma is okay.' James keeps looking in his mirror to ensure Martin Connelly isn't following us.

'Em, who's he?' I ask tentatively. I sincerely hope 'he' isn't who I think he is.

'Sir Christopher McKellan,' says my father from the front seat. 'Have you been listening to any of the conversation, Clemmie?' Of course, it had to be.

'Sir Christopher McKellan? We're going to see Sir Christopher McKellan? Nobody mentioned this. STOP THE CAR!'

James looks at me in his mirror, frowns and ignores my instruction. 'Don't be silly, Clemmie. I'm on a motorway.'

'I don't mind, I'll walk back or catch a bus or something.'

'Why don't you want to see Christopher McKellan?'

'Because he thinks I'm some sort of reprobate sent by Martin Connelly to find his daughter. He'll probably try to imprison me on the spot.'

'Clemmie, he's a barrister. Not a high court judge.'

'He's bloody scary and I don't want to see him.'

'Oh come on, Clemmie. I'm sure he's not that bad.'

'Don't come-on-Clemmie me. And you weren't there. He was that bad. And he must think I'm the spawn of the devil.'

'Well, he doesn't think I'm all that great,' says Holly.

God, this is turning out to be a really bad day.

★   ★   ★

After about an hour's drive and several enforced games of I-spy-according-to-my-mother, Sir Christopher McKellan doesn't seem so bad after all.

We started to climb up into the hills of Provence about half an hour ago and the scenery is beautiful. When we pull up at the house, I think it can't be a bad place to be exiled in. It is a large square villa with beautiful green shutters and a red tiled roof. We park the car next to a gargantuan blacked-out Range Rover and we all get out and walk towards a colossal front door. We wait in silence while my father pulls the bell.

I think the family must be expecting us because a sombre member of staff immediately opens the door. We follow in single file until another door is thrown open and we are announced, in a heavily accented voice, to the family. I am at the back, as usual, so it's not until everyone has shaken everyone else's hand and stepped to one side that I have a view. Naturally, Sir Christopher is the first person to step into my field of vision and much as I try, I can't seem to see anyone else.

He proffers his hand and looks seriously at me. 'Ah, it's the reprobate.'

Everyone laughs heartily as I nervously shake hands with him. Sure. Laugh it up. He's put people away for less. I then step to one side to reveal Holly, who is positively cowering behind me.

'Miss Colshannon. We have met a few times before but as always your reputation precedes you.' Holly laughs nervously and shakes his hand.

After the rest of the introductions are made, Mr Winstanley, who is a quietly distinguished man, gestures us forward towards a group of sofas in front of a large fireplace. He must see me looking at it because he says, 'It can get quite chilly here in winter, especially as the house is designed for hot weather.'

Emma is sitting in the corner of one of the sofas and my parents bustle forward to greet her. She must have some of her own clothes by now because she is in a beautiful strappy dress. James formally shakes her hand and Holly and I stay at the back and wave awkwardly at her.

We all sit down and the butler character who answered the door places a large tray of glasses and a huge jug of what looks like lemonade on the low coffee table in front of us.

Sir Christopher kicks off. 'Thank you for taking the time to come all the way out here, Detective Sergeant Sabine.' Is that James? I am quietly impressed and have to stop myself making a face at Holly.

It must be him because he replies, 'I came out here because Martin Connelly is starting to harass the Colshannon family and for their sake I would like to sort this mess out. I think they have done more than their fair share in helping Emma.'

Atta boy, James. You tell him.

'Whatever the reason, thank you for coming. Have you seen Martin Connelly?'

'Yes, I have. He is here and he is determined to find Emma.' I look at James with interest. Is he just going to announce Emma's infidelity?

'He didn't follow you up here?'

James looks witheringly at Sir Christopher and I make a mental note never to make him cross. 'No, I made sure of it.'

'I apologise if I appear to doubt your abilities but I love my daughter very much and I need to know that she'll be safe here.'

'There might be something that could guarantee her safety.'

Sir Christopher looks taken aback for a second and then leans forward eagerly. 'Is there? Do you know something?'

'I think I need to speak to Emma first. Privately.'

Sir Christopher looks none too keen on this idea but James stands up decisively and turns expectantly to Emma, who has added nothing to the conversation so far.

She stands up too, looking less certain, and says, 'We can go out by the swimming pool.'

She leads the way and James follows. We all hesitate for a second until my mother, Holly and I can bear it no longer. We unite in an I'll-be-buggered-if-I'm-missing-this group and all scurry after James. My father, being the extremely polite man that he is, stays to chat with the family.

Emma leads the way through French doors to a patio area next to a large, inviting, turquoise pool. She sits down on the edge of a wooden lounger and looks enquiringly at us all.

'Emma, I don't feel you have been honest with us,' says James. I might be mistaken but I think there is a very wary look in her eye.

'Oh really?' she says.

'Yes. You see, Holly and Clemmie have done a great deal for you. I know they shouldn't have got mixed up in this whole thing in the first place, but since they learned the truth I hope that you will admit that they have done their hardest to try and put things right. They have put their own necks on the line with regards to their jobs and personal lives in order to right what they acknowledge as a wrong. I am surprised, therefore, that you would prey on other people's good natures and lead them astray so badly.' Holly and I weren't actually very good-natured about any of it but I am absolutely with James all the way. 'You see, I spoke with Martin Connelly yesterday and was very surprised to find out that he is infertile.'

Emma looks puzzled for a moment and then her face clears. Far from being perturbed, she looks absolutely thrilled. 'You mean he can't have children?'

'No, he can't.'

'I don't believe it! Martin Connelly can't have children? So he's not the father?' she breathes. 'God, I can't tell you what wonderful news that is! Mr Colshannon said these things have a way of working themselves out and they have!'

'He is apparently sterile. He had mumps as a child. I take it you didn't know?'

'No, I didn't. But this is wonderful news! I'm not carrying his child! Does he know I'm pregnant? Do you think he's trying to find me because of that?'

'No, I don't think so. But if you tell him you are pregnant, and it's a decision you'll have to make with your father, I think he will leave you alone because you will have well and truly scuppered his revenge plan. He thinks you are overwhelmingly in love with him and yet all the time you were sleeping with someone else. Who is the father, by the way?'

Emma looks down at her feet. 'It's not as you think. I was very much in love with Martin. But one night we had a row, about my father and the wedding ironically, and I was staying in Bristol with an old friend. A very old friend. He didn't know anything about Martin, like all my friends who knew my father quite well. And I was upset. We had a bit to drink, he was trying to comfort me about something he thought had happened at work . . . ' She shrugs and looks down at her feet. 'One thing led to another. But I never dreamt he could be the father. I only slept with him the one time and Martin is so much younger than . . . ' She falls silent.

She can't just stop there. 'So who is it?' I demand. Emma glances up at me. 'I think you owe us that much, Emma. Just tell us.'

'I can't. He's — '

'Married?' enquires my mother eagerly. 'Gay? From Belgium? What?'

'No, he's quite well known. It wouldn't be right to tell you.'

I'm quite tempted to pin her to the ground and sit on her until she tells me but James gives me a look and I shut up.

'Just one last thing, Emma. I was curious when Holly told me how she found you. You had told Martin Connelly, the man you were going to marry, all about your family and friends?' Emma nods. 'So why hadn't you told him about John Montague? I presume you hadn't otherwise your father would never have hid you with him?'

'No, I hadn't told Martin about John.'

'Why not, Emma?'

A slow blush starts to creep up Emma's cheeks and she won't meet James's eye. I watch it all feeling slightly confused. Is James getting at what I think he is getting at? Has he known all along who the father of Emma's child is?

'John has actually asked me to marry him,' she says quietly.

'John Montague?' asks Holly, absolutely open-mouthed. 'The MP for Bristol? Are you going to?'

Emma lays her hand protectively across her stomach and then looks back up at us. 'I think I should, don't you?'

She starts to walk back towards the sitting room.

'I don't understand,' says my mother. 'Can someone explain exactly what is going on?'

26

It is good to be back in Cornwall. It is raining but it's good to be back nonetheless.

My mother made me promise that the first thing I would do would be to collect Norman from Sally's house. So after the taxi has dumped me and my wheely case at the house, I immediately start off down the hill to see Sally.

'So how was it? Did you have a lovely time?' she asks after she has squealed with excitement at the sight of me. I don't know if this is because she is pleased to see me or pleased to see the back of Norman.

I follow her into the kitchen. I notice Norman's beanbag in the corner. 'It was fun,' I say simply.

'You look different. Coffee? Tea?'

'Tea please. Holly bought me some new clothes.'

Sally pauses to look at me and tilts her head thoughtfully. 'No, I don't think it's that. You look different different.'

'Well, we've had a bit of a time down there.'

'What happened? Has something been going on? I knew something was up when your parents suddenly announced they were going away!'

I open my mouth to begin telling the story but realise that Sally is still in the process of making my tea and that I'm unlikely to get it if I start now.

'I'll make the tea. You sit down. I don't really know where to start. Do you remember that girl who was staying with us last week?'

★ ★ ★

Forty minutes later, I have drunk two cups of tea and eaten half a packet of Jaffa Cakes. Sally has two cups of tea sitting in front of her, both of which are completely untouched and stone cold.

'So you mean to say that you have all been out in the south of France protecting this girl?' she asks in astonishment. It makes me sound positively noble.

'Well,' I say modestly. 'Not exactly protecting her.'

'And this bloke . . . '

'Martin Connelly,' I put in helpfully for her.

'That Martin bloke was actually here in the village, looking for you?'

'On the day of the cricket match. In fact, he must have asked someone local where we lived in order to find the house.'

'My God, Clemmie. And tell me about this MP character, the one who got Emma pregnant.'

'Well, he's about twice her age and slightly bald. She's gone from the sublime to the ridiculous. Martin was, at least, completely gorgeous.'

'But totally cracked.'

'Yes, totally,' I agree, biting into another Jaffa Cake.

'And Emma is going to marry this MP?'

'So she says.'

'Did he ask her before he knew he was the father?'

'Yes! And before he knew that she could come back to England.'

'Well, he must really love her. So that's nice.'

'And as James says, she can go back to Bristol now because she doesn't need to be on the run from Martin Connelly any more. They're going to announce a hasty wedding between John Montague and Emma, Emma's condition will soon become apparent and Martin Connelly can put two and two together by himself. At least Holly has got something for her 'High Society' page now. Emma has promised her exclusivity if she doesn't reveal too many other details. And it couldn't have come a moment later, she had to file copy yesterday.'

'So where's everyone else?'

'My parents are coming back on the overnight train tonight. Morgan needed to have tick treatment or something so he could get back into England. Otherwise he would have had to have spent six months in quarantine.' More is the pity.

'What about the others?'

'Barney said he would try to catch a flight later today or tomorrow morning and I think Sam and Charlotte might spend a couple of extra days out there and fly back later in the week. I don't know, they didn't really say.' I keep my voice very light as I tell Sally this in order not to betray my feelings. Charlotte announced to everyone that she and Sam would be staying a few extra days and then she looked pointedly at me. And not for the first time I felt sick to the stomach at my behaviour. I had dismissed her as a boring, plain actuary who couldn't possibly be going out with Sam, whereas she's actually disarmingly pretty, charming and very intuitive in that she immediately picked up on the rather strained atmosphere between Sam and me. I really do think this is why I disliked Charlotte when I first met her — I was starting to like Sam. I know all these things but it doesn't seem to make the heartache any easier to bear. Sam didn't speak to me at all except when we were in general company, and it wasn't until Charlotte announced their plans that the penny finally dropped. Sam and Charlotte are perfectly happy going out together and any small flirting indiscretion had been a mere foolish act on his part.

'So you travelled back by yourself?' asks Sally.

I nod.

'Poor love.'

'Worse than that. I had to share a couchette with a female potato farmer from Scotland. Where's Norman, by the way?'

'Oh, he's out in the garden. I thought he might want some fresh air.'

'Any chance he might have flown away?' I ask hopefully.

'Absolutely none. I wondered if he might try to copy the other seagulls but he just sits on his beanbag and watches them.'

I look at her sternly. 'I do hope you haven't been indulging him, Sally.'

'Of course not! But I have noticed that he likes pilchards warmed through with a squeeze of lemon.'

377

'I'd better take him home, but I am not warming his food for him so don't be surprised if you find him on your doorstep tomorrow morning. I've got to get back because I need to see Mr Trevesky later this afternoon. How have the rehearsals been going?'

Sally looks down at her hands. 'Oh, pretty well.'

'Who've you had standing in for Catherine since she's been away?'

'Various people. Charlotte did it for the first few nights. She's lovely, isn't she?'

'Hmmm, yes.' Moving on.

'And then my mum did it but she wasn't particularly keen on the kissing scenes with Matt.'

'Ahh, how is our illustrious vicar?'

'Gorgeous as always.' Sally's eyes twinkle. 'In fact, neither Matt nor I were particularly keen on his kissing scenes . . . ' she says slowly.

'Sally, are you trying to tell me something?'

'Only that we're keen on our own kissing scenes.' She grins at me.

'You and Matt? Shut. Up.'

'No, it's true,' she giggles.

'When did all this happen?'

'While you lot were away in France, and Catherine was away in the Lakes.'

'He's the vicar, Sally!'

'He is single.'

'I suppose you are in the choir. Catherine is going to be gutted.'

'I don't think so. I met her mother yesterday and she said she's taken up with a highly undesirable youth in the Lakes.'

'Are there any undesirable youths in the Lake District?'

'Well, that probably just means he votes Liberal Democrat or something.'

I try to raise a smile but I'm thinking about Barney and how he is going to react to this news. It's great for the rest of us but I'm afraid that my darling brother might be broken-hearted. At least we can drown our sorrows together. 'Anyway,' Sally continues. 'Your mother wants Matt to organise a rehearsal for tomorrow night with all the extras. Will you and Barney be there?'

'Absolutely. I'm not sure I'll be able to look Matt in the eye, but I'll be there.' I grin at her. 'I'm really pleased for you. Are you happy?'

She smiles back and I wonder how I didn't notice her loved-up expression before. 'Yes, really happy. He's wonderful.' It chafes a bit against my own unhappiness but I love her so I'm truly thrilled for her. 'Sam is on my list of extras too. I take it that he won't be there?'

'No, Sally. I'm afraid he won't.'

★ ★ ★

After I have deposited Norman at home with his beanbag, several tins of fish and a squeaky toy which Sally has bought him, I get changed for work and then make my way up to Tintagel. But it turns out that Mr Trevesky has got someone in to replace me and only wants to give me my last pay cheque and a jumper I'd left behind. My replacement's name is Sandra, she doesn't mix up her side orders at all and Wayne seems positively besotted with her. Actually Mr Trevesky seemed quite upset to let me go but I daresay he'll get over it in due course.

So I am at a loose end for the rest of the day and don't quite know what to do with myself. I'm halfway home when Barney calls me on my mobile to tell me that he isn't going to be home until tomorrow. I feel unbearably fidgety so I turn the car around and drive down to Trebarwith Strand. I pace up and down the beach and for the first time ever, I actually wish that Morgan was with me. He quite likes pacing, you know, and he always loves swimming in the little rock pools.

My mind ranges over everything and anything. I think about Seth, I think about my trip abroad and I think about my job. But most of all I think about Sam. I look back over the years I have known him. I remember when Mr Jefferson from the local shop told me off once and made me cry, and Sam and Barney crept down in the middle of the night and let all of the air out of his car tyres. I remember when I passed my driving test and Sam took me out for lunch to celebrate. I remember all sorts of lovely things about him. I re-examine his past girlfriends and crushes and reflect on the fact that I haven't appreciated his presence at all. And now, just as we are all perched on the brink of branching off and making our own families, I realise how special he is.

The sun is starting to set as I drive back home. My mother wants me to make up the guest room for Gordon because he is coming down to talk to her about her new play, and he wants to watch tomorrow night's rehearsal as well. So when I pull into the driveway and see a strange BMW parked in front of the house, I groan to myself. God, he's a day early and that's all I need. Just when I want to collapse into a hot bath and watch some telly. My mother has clearly got her dates mixed up again, but Gordon will no doubt blame me and then proceed to lecture me on where exactly I have gone wrong with my life, all while I run around trying to cook him a half decent supper and taking swigs of the cooking sherry when he's not looking.

I get out of the car and walk very slowly round to the back door. But I am quite unprepared for the sight that greets me. Seth is sitting on the woodpile.

I stop dead in my tracks and stare at him.

'Hello, Clemmie, I'm glad it's you. I didn't know who would be back first.' He attempts a friendly smile but it comes out somewhat nervously.

'Seth, what on earth are you doing here?'

'Aren't you pleased to see me?' My God, the arrogance. He's only been here five seconds. 'I've been trying to get hold of you for ages. I've been calling you and coming by the house but your brother Barney told me you were away. You really need to speak to him, you know. He was unforgivably rude and told me to — '

'Look, Seth, I'm very tired and very fed up.

What do you want?' I interrupt him. It's ironic to think how much I had been dreaming of this moment but now I am simply not interested. I look at his urbane suit, neatly combed hair and highly polished shoes and only wish I could see Sam instead. How did I ever find him attractive?

'I came to see if you are all right, Clemmie. I feel bad about what happened and I've been trying to speak to you to see if you need anything. How's work?'

I hesitate. There is absolutely no way I'm going to tell him that I have just lost my job in a café where I was working as a waitress. 'I've only just got back from my trip abroad,' I hedge.

'Have you found any work yet? I know a lot of people now, you know. I could get you something.'

God, that would be nice, wouldn't it? A new job handed to me on a plate. It would certainly solve a lot of problems.

'Trying to appease your conscience?'

He looks down at his feet. 'Come on, Clemmie, try to be a bit grateful. I've travelled out here to the sticks to see you and it's taken me hours. I do feel bad about what happened, but one of us had to bite the bullet and it was better that it was you.'

'Only better for you.'

'Well, I can use my contacts to help you.'

'No thanks, Seth. I'm doing something by myself actually. I might be sending *you* an invite.'

'What to?'

'A gallery opening.' Blimey, if I said it then it must be possible.

'You're managing your own?' he says, looking suitably surprised.

'That's right. Cornwall is up and coming, you know. So no thank you, I don't need or want your help.' I fit my key into the lock of the door and open it. I turn round to look at him once I'm inside. 'And you finishing with me and me leaving my job was the best thing that's ever happened to me.' And I shut the door in his astonished face.

That felt good.

27

'Yee-haa.'

'No. Louder, Clemmie.'

'Yee-haa.'

'No, YEEE-HAAA!'

'Yee-haa.'

'YEEE-HAAA! . . . Let me hear you!'

'Yee-haa!'

'Clemmie, are you trying? I don't feel as though you're really getting into the spirit of things,' says my mother.

'Of course, I'm trying. Cowboy-ing does not come naturally to me.'

She tuts, dismisses me with a wave of her hand and moves on to the next extra. 'Right, Trevor! Let's hear you!'

I scurry away gratefully to the back of the hall where Barney is sitting with my old poncho on and a large cowboy hat covering his face while he has forty winks. It actually quite suits his golden looks. It's not a dress rehearsal but we all have been instructed by my mother to wear an item of clothing that makes us feel like a cowboy and my boots have come in handy. There are over twenty of us extras for the cowboy scenes and the hall is absolutely packed. Such is the force of my mother's personality that she has them all sitting as quiet as mice in orderly rows awaiting their instructions.

'Barney, wake up!' I nudge my brother.

'Hmm? Are we on yet?'

'No, no. Just fancied a chat. So, did Sam and Charlotte mention when they were getting back at all?' I ask nonchalantly, smoothing down the side of my dress. It's one that Holly bought me in France. I don't really need to wear it to this rehearsal but it makes me feel vaguely better. It's soft pink, buttoned all the way down the front and stops just above the knee.

'They didn't say.'

'Sam will pop in and say hello when he gets back, won't he?'

'Clemmie, I know what you are thinking and I do feel bad about it. Really I do, but I don't think there is anything I can do.'

Oh God. I am utterly transparent. He knows how I feel about Sam. I stare miserably at my feet. And if Barney knows, it is only a matter of time before Holly knows, and then my mother.

'You tell me what I am supposed to do,' he continues. 'Do you want me to tell Sam?'

I look at him in alarm. 'Lord, no. Don't do that.'

'Then what?'

'Can't we just keep it quiet?'

'And hope it goes away?'

'Exactly.'

'But it won't go away Clemmie. Can't you see that?'

'Well, I was kind of hoping that it would,' I mumble. With absolutely no resolution made, we sit in silence and watch the performers.

Barney nudges me. 'Look! Mrs Fothersby is on.'

Mrs Fothersby, absolutely panicked at the idea of her darling Catherine taking up with some lout from the Lakes, is determined to keep an eye on her and has therefore volunteered to take Sam's place in the extras line-up. I haven't actually told Barney about Catherine and her fabled lover and I'm not particularly relishing it. I decide to put it off no longer.

'Word has it that Catherine met someone on holiday. A young man,' I say casually.

'Did she?'

'But it probably doesn't mean anything at all.'

'Not if he's in his right mind.'

I frown. Is this any way to speak about your one true amour? 'How do you mean?'

'Poor sod will run a mile if he ever meets the Fothersby family.'

Oh I see. He's just jealous and trying to cover it up with a bit of snorting-at-the-in-laws stuff. 'I don't think they're that bad,' I say to him comfortingly.

Barney gives me a long, hard look. 'Clemmie, what are you on about? They're bloody nightmares.'

'Oh Barney, don't give up hope completely. I'm sure it's just a phase on Catherine's part.'

'Clemmie, what on earth are you talking about?'

'You and Catherine. I'm talking about you and Catherine.'

'Me and Catherine? What about me and Catherine?'

'Well, she's the girl. Your secret girl . . . isn't she?' I add on uncertainly.

'SHE'S WHAT?' Barney rises to his feet and elicits a furious 'shush' from the one and only Catherine Fothersby, who is watching her mother from the front row. 'Are you completely nuts?' he hisses and sits back down.

'Well, you said this girl had just gone on holiday and Catherine has just come back from the Lake District. And we all wondered why you wouldn't say who she was so we thought it must be someone awful. Like Catherine Fothersby,' I say quickly.

'Who's 'we'?'

'Oh, er, me and Holly. And Mum.' I say the last sentence very swiftly in the vain hope that he won't really hear me.

'AND MUM?' he half yells at me. This elicits another furious shush from the stage. 'Who told her?'

'Well, I might have done. But it was a complete accident.'

'How could it be an accident?'

'I talk in my sleep.'

'And they all think it's Catherine Fothersby?'

'Er, yes.'

'Well it bloody well isn't.'

'Who is it then?'

'It's Charlotte.'

'IT'S WHO?' This time it's my mother who calls from the stage. 'Clemmie, dear, could you and Barney take that very silly game outside?'

'It's Charlotte?' I whisper fiercely at him, ignoring my mother. 'You mean you have a thing about Charlotte?'

'I can't believe you think I fancy Catherine bloody Fothersby.'

'But what about Sam? He and Charlotte are going out.'

'Thank you, Clemmie, for pointing that out. I hadn't realised,' he says dryly.

'But he's your best friend.'

Barney looks absolutely dejected. 'I know. I feel dreadful. The first time I met her she was going out with Sam and I thought she was absolutely gorgeous. Well out of my league, of course, with her being an actuary,' he says gloomily.

'Don't be silly, Barney,' I say, still trying to recover from the shock. 'Surfing is a very worthy vocation. Not to mention the worm-charming. But you said you were getting on well together while we were in France?'

'We were getting on really well. She's never particularly looked at me in that way before, being Sam's best friend, but we really hit it off. Not that I would do anything, of course,' he adds hastily. 'I wouldn't dream of doing that to Sam.'

'So what was with the haircut and cricket stuff? Why bother with all that?'

'I know she likes people who make their own way in the world so I wanted to be worthy of her. I wanted a new job. I took up cricket because I know she likes it.'

'But you're rubbish at it.'

'I know, but I was sort of waiting in the wings because I didn't think Sam was particularly serious about her.'

'And now?'

'I don't know. They were pretty thick down in Cap Ferrat, weren't they? Kept sloping off together.'

My heart lurches at the thought of it. 'Yes, they were,' I say miserably.

'I only wish I had met her first.'

'So do I, Barney. So do I,' I say fervently.

'So everyone thinks I have a huge crush on Catherine Fothersby?'

'Er, yes.'

'Including Sam?'

'I'm afraid so.'

'But I thought you knew it was Charlotte.'

I think back to the conversation we had in France. I felt sure he had said it was Catherine but he can't have done.

'No, I didn't.'

'Dad knew it was Charlotte. Didn't you run the whole Catherine idea past him?'

'Em, no. I don't think we did.'

'So what was that conversation about?'

'What conversation?'

'The one we just had. When I asked you if you wanted me to tell Sam and you said you wished the whole thing would just go away.'

I look at Barney and bite on my lip. My brain just won't think quickly enough.

'Em, I don't know.'

'Clemmie. Tell me.'

'Oh, okay. I might have a very small, itsy-bitsy crush on Sam. But it's nothing. Barely there, in fact.'

'Sam? You and Sam? But he's going out with Charlotte!'

I give Barney a look.

'Sorry. I can't believe I just said that. Well, Clemmie, you're about two years too late.'

'How do you mean?'

'Sam used to like you. You know that.'

'Sam used to like me? No, of course I didn't know that!' My stomach turns to absolute liquid.

'It was perfectly obvious to anyone with half an eye.'

'Not to me.'

'Well, what about that time when Luke finished with you and you ranted on about it for four hours? He sat and listened to you throughout!'

'You'd tied his shoelaces to the chair! He didn't have any choice!'

'Ah, but he didn't know that until he tried to get up, did he?'

'But he's never said anything. Why hasn't he said anything? I never had a clue.'

'I think he was going to and then you started going out with Seth.'

'We've been finished for the last year and a half.'

'And what was he supposed to do? Leap on a plane on the off-chance that you might deign to spend some time with him? Bearing in mind that the only reason you went away was because you were so broken-hearted about Seth! Slimeball. I wish I'd got back yesterday, I'd have punched him. Anyway, Sam did the only thing he could. He got over you.'

'He got over me?'

'Clemmie, we didn't know when or if you'd ever be back. You might have met a hunky Australian and stayed out there. You can't expect Sam to stick around for ever, he hadn't taken a vow of chastity. He started going out with Charlotte. I really hoped it wasn't very serious at first but now I don't know.'

My mind starts to reel as I try to fit this information into every conversation I've ever had with Sam. 'Why did you think it wasn't serious between him and Charlotte?'

'Oh, only because of you, but I'm sorry, Clem, he and Charlotte seem to get on really well.'

'But she doesn't know him as well as I know him!' I protest. Surely if he liked me once then he could like me again? When you have a crush on somebody then you never stop liking them, right? Of course that's not true of Tom in year three but I didn't know about his Spiderman fetish then. Maybe Sam has discovered something about me he doesn't like?

'I'm sorry, Clem,' Barney repeats and squeezes my hand. My mother calls us up on stage and we reluctantly obey her.

It's the scene where Katie (played by Catherine) performs a sort of cabaret act in front of a packed saloon (us poor, overworked extras) so all I have to do is sit and watch and throw in the occasional yahoo.

It takes about twenty minutes for us all to get arranged on stage and I remark to Trevor, our deaf organist, that I can't see the play finishing before midnight. Of course, Trevor doesn't get any of this and I have to repeat it by shouting very loudly into his ear, which doesn't please my mother much.

We all kick off and I have to say that Catherine is simply marvellous. We all look at each other stunned because none of us know where this has come from. Catherine is dazzling; she is coquettish and brazen, then flirtatious and demure, and her mother doesn't quite know what to make of it but doesn't look altogether displeased at the spontaneous round of applause Catherine elicits at the end of her performance. This boy in the Lakes must have given Catherine a new lease of life.

The whole scene is repeated and my mother gets what she wants out of us this time because we're not so surprised by Catherine's performance. I don't know at what point he slips in but when I look over at the empty hall before us I see that Sam is sitting in one of the seats. I look quickly back to where Catherine is still performing, my heart going ten to the dozen, and then risk another look. This time he sees me and gives me a very casual smile. My heart still hammering, I smile back in what I hope is a non-delusional way and try to concentrate on what I am supposed to be doing which is absolutely nothing at all.

Thankfully my mother dismisses us for a short break and with feigned nonchalance I start to wander towards him, stopping to speak to a couple of people along the way. Everyone is still marvelling at Catherine's performance, which is lucky because I'm not particularly listening to any of them.

Sam, in the meantime, has walked down to the front and is speaking to Trevor. I make my way over. In true Sam style, he doesn't kiss me hello.

'You're back!' I say, stating the obvious and

completely uncertain as to how to behave with him. I want to tell him everything that has happened since I last saw him. I want to tell him about Mr Trevesky and Seth. I even want to tell him about Gordon.

'Yes, I'm back. How are you, Clem?'

'Oh, fine. Fired but fine.'

'Mr Trevesky finally decided you and Wayne should part company, eh?'

'Needless to say Wayne is thrilled. Did you have a nice time?' I ask uncertainly.

'You're back!' says Barney, stepping into our little group. They do a manly handshake and half hug.

'Just got in. Where's your dad?'

'Back at home.'

'I think I'll pop up and say hello. I'll see you all later.'

He smiles and walks away.

I feel absolutely deflated.

28

'Go after him!' hisses Barney. 'Go on!'

'I don't know what to say.'

'Just tell him that you like him.'

'Oh I can't, Barney. What if he's gone off me?'

'There's never been a better time to find out.'

I stand looking at him uncertainly, and then make up my mind.

I dodge through the rows of seats and run like mad for the door, just as Sam is opening it. 'Sam!' I call. 'Sam, wait!'

The figure stops and turns around. 'Clemmie? Did you forget something?'

I slow down to a walk as I approach him and feel my resolve about to go. Oh God. I haven't got a clue what to say to him. I just don't know where to start. I can't even see his face properly to gauge any reaction.

'Em, Sam. Can I talk to you?'

'Of course you can, Clemmie. What's up?'

This is awful. I simply don't know what to say. 'I want to talk to you about what happened in France.'

'In France? Now?'

'Er, yes.'

'Well, come and sit down then. We can't see a bloody thing out here.' He takes hold of my elbow and steers me back into the hall. It is the last place I want to have any sort of intimate conversation but I don't really have much choice. Perhaps he wants it here so I can't make any nasty, emotional scenes.

We go and sit down in the back row. The rest of the cast are wandering back towards the stage and being shouted at by my mother.

He sits to one side and faces me. 'What's up? Are you worried about Martin Connelly? Because I really don't think — '

'No,' I say hurriedly. 'It's not Martin Connelly.'

'What is it then?'

I really wish I'd had time to think this through. I glance up and see Barney watching us.

'Well, it's just that I thought we were, or . . . or might have been . . . But then I could be wrong . . . '

'Spit it out, Clemmie.'

'When we were in France together . . . '

'Look, Clemmie. I know what you're trying to say and I'm sorry about that. I really am.'

'Sorry about what?'

'I did have a girlfriend and I'm not such a bastard that I could simply just forget about her.'

'I know,' I say miserably.

'And I asked you to bear with me while I sorted it all out and I'm sorry that you didn't have the patience to wait a few — '

'You asked me to bear with you? When did you ask me to do that?'

'I slipped a note under your door. You did get it, didn't you?'

'A note under my door? I didn't get a note under my door. When was this?'

'The day after Charlotte arrived.'

Something vaguely stirs in my memory. 'You didn't write it on a receipt, did you?'

'Well, yes. It was the only bit of paper I could find at the time.'

I groan slightly and start to smile. 'I saw a bit of paper on the floor when Holly and I got back from our shopping trip. I thought it was a receipt that had fallen out of one of the bags as I came in so I threw it away.'

'So you haven't read it?'

'No!'

'I thought you were pissed off and simply ignoring me!'

'God, no!'

'You had those bloody sunglasses on all the time and wouldn't even look at me.'

'I was embarrassed.'

We look at each other properly this time. The first time in quite a few days. We start to smile.

I glance over to Barney, who is still watching us, and he also smiles encouragingly. In fact, quite a few people seem to be taking more notice of us than of my mother's instructions. Sam also clocks this and says, 'Shall we go somewhere a little less public?'

'Backstage?'

'Perfect.' He takes my hand and pulls me up. My heart bounds along quite foolishly at the simple fact that he is touching me. He doesn't let go of me as we walk down the hall and through the side door that leads backstage.

He pulls me towards some old packing cases and we sit down. 'So what has happened with

Charlotte?' I ask, starting to feel vaguely excited. 'I thought you were staying out in France for a holiday?'

'I just couldn't get the flights back and I thought it would be a bit callous to finish with her and then send her back on a plane while I travelled home with you on the train. I mean, she knew perfectly well why I was finishing it. She's not stupid.'

'Well, she is an actuary.'

'Clemmie, you told her that Morgan would pee on her if she stood still for too long. She told me.'

'Yes. Well. He might have done. I didn't want to see those beautiful shoes of hers ruined. So you've finished with her?'

'Yes. I didn't really want to do it in France but once I'd made up my mind I had to get it over with as soon as possible. I spent some very uncomfortable nights sleeping on the floor. The fact that I thought you were giving me the cold shoulder ensured those last few days weren't exactly memorable. So, can we take up where we left off?'

'And where was that?' I ask, just wishing he would get on with it.

He looks deeply into my eyes and smiles gently. 'Here . . . ?' He leans towards me. This is it! At last! I close my eyes and wait expectantly for the soft feel of his lips . . .

'Clemmie darling! There you are!' bellows my mother. I hastily open my eyes again. Am I destined never to kiss Sam? 'Where on earth have you been? We will need you for the next scene. I want you to do something.' What is she going to want me to do? Plunge naked from a burning stagecoach? Scalp someone with a tomahawk?

'Sorrel, Clemmie isn't going to be around for the next scene.'

'Why not?'

'She has a previous engagement.' He pulls me to my feet.

'How do you mean? You two aren't . . . ? You are, aren't you? Oh my darlings, how perfectly *sweet*. Don't let me stop you, just pretend I was never here. I must go and tell Barney, do you mind me telling Barney? It's just that I'll need him to do your bit, Clemmie.'

Sam makes a be-my-guest gesture. 'I think he already knows anyway, Sorrel.'

'And Gordon has just arrived, so are you sure you don't want to stay?'

'Quite sure.'

'Well then, you two just carry on . . . ' She stands and looks at us expectantly. 'Oh! Do you want me to go?'

'No, it's okay. We'll go.'

I follow him back into the hall. Everyone is on the stage and they watch delightedly as Sam leads me to the exit.

'So where is Charlotte?' I ask to cover the silence and my embarrassment. 'Will she still come down to the house?'

'Oh, I think so. She's gone back to London for now but she said something about coming to surf with Barney at the weekend. Typical, isn't it? They always end up liking Barney in the end.

She wants to go worm-charming with him too. That reminds me, I really need to talk to Barney about the Catherine affair.'

'Oooh, no need. I think that might have resolved itself. Probably best not to mention it at all, I think he's a bit embarrassed.'

'Really?'

'Yeah, he's gone off her.' I cross my fingers and grin at him.

He pushes open the exit doors and we emerge into the fresh, cold air. I have to pause for a few seconds until my eyes adjust. I shiver slightly; my dress isn't really designed for Cornish nights.

'Do you want my jumper?' asks Sam.

I hesitate. It's an automatic reaction to refuse anything from him and it's high time that I stopped it. 'Yes, please.'

He wordlessly hands it over and I snuggle down into it. It smells deliciously of him and I try not to look as though I'm sniffing it but just taking deep breaths of air.

'Was Charlotte upset?' I ask.

'A bit, but I don't think it was entirely unexpected. She knew I liked you.'

'Did you?' I ask in delight, overtly fishing for compliments. 'For how long?' I know damn well from Barney.

'Oh, more or less for ever. Or at least it feels like it. I came back from London for you, Clemmie.' This bit I don't know so I will want him to go over it at least twice.

'When? That Christmas?'

'Yes. I went to look at my parents' old house and to visit some relations. I thought it would help. I wanted to find out some more about them, my aunt never told me very much, but then I realised that all the while my real family and you were back in Cornwall. That's why I decided to leave London, I just didn't belong there. And I came back that Christmas to ask you out and there you were with Seth. Absolutely loved up.'

'Oh Sam. You should have said something,' I say. I'll save my news about Seth for later because for now I just want to talk about me.

'Well, I thought you would probably break up if I gave it some time. None of us really liked Seth. So I waited.'

'Why didn't you say anything when we broke up?'

'And when would that have been exactly? In the half hour between you splitting up and you getting on a plane?'

'You still should have said something,' I insist.

'But you were so broken-hearted. Should I have offered to shag you senseless? Let me give you a good seeing to and maybe you'll feel better?'

'But I didn't have any idea.'

'Most of the family knew. Barney, your dad and your mum.'

'Not Holly?'

'No, not Holly. She'd left home by the time everyone else guessed. She knows now though. I called her as soon as I reached Bristol to see if you'd said anything to her so don't be surprised to find a dozen messages on your mobile.'

'I never said a word to Holly about it. Didn't

400

want her nudging me every time you came into the room.'

'She says those social pages of hers have been really well received. Apparently everyone is rushing out to buy cowboy boots and wondering why the whole of the Cabinet has been having a secret summit in France!'

'I'm glad, she deserves it. Did you say my mother knew?' I ask suddenly.

'Yes, she guessed. She never mentioned anything?'

'No. God, that sounds far too subtle for her! She did try to warn me off you when we were in France.'

'I think she was trying to protect me. She knew how long I'd waited for you. Besides, they really liked Charlotte.'

'Well, I don't think they've seen the last of her,' I murmur. 'I thought you fancied Holly! You always kiss her and never me.'

'I hated touching you when I thought you didn't want me. I was just too uncomfortable.'

'Where are we?' I ask suddenly, looking around me. I have been walking in a daze.

'At my house. You didn't think we were going back to yours, did you? You must be mad. What with Norman and Morgan and god knows what else. Besides, I heard a vicious rumour that Gordon is coming to stay.'

'You're right, I'd rather be at yours.'

And this time, in the dark of the Cornish night, Sam really does kiss me. Properly. And just between you and me, he really does kiss rather well. Wave upon wave of beautiful kisses.

401

That is until Trevor wanders along and shines a flashlight in our faces.

'Bugger,' says Sam. 'We might have to go back to the Côte d'Azur to get some privacy. How do you fancy a little holiday, Clem? Just the two of us . . .'

We do hope that you have enjoyed reading this large print book.

Did you know that all of our titles are available for purchase?

We publish a wide range of high quality large print books including:
Romances, Mysteries, Classics
General Fiction
Non Fiction and Westerns

Special interest titles available in large print are:
The Little Oxford Dictionary
Music Book
Song Book
Hymn Book
Service Book

Also available from us courtesy of Oxford University Press:
Young Readers' Dictionary
(large print edition)
Young Readers' Thesaurus
(large print edition)

For further information or a free brochure, please contact us at:
Ulverscroft Large Print Books Ltd.,
The Green, Bradgate Road, Anstey,
Leicester, LE7 7FU, England.
Tel: (00 44) 0116 236 4325
Fax: (00 44) 0116 234 0205

Other titles published by
The House of Ulverscroft:

THE PARTY SEASON

Sarah Mason

Respected entrepreneur Simon Monkwell and party planner Isabel Serranti have known each other since childhood. He was a thirteen-year-old bully and she was the eleven-year-old whose life he made a misery. Now she's twenty-six, everything Isabel hears on the grapevine convinces her that Simon hasn't changed one little bit. So when Monty, Simon's father, asks Izzy to help him host a charity ball at the Monkwells' country estate, she has mixed feelings. However, Izzy is determined to put the past behind her — but she discovers that her childhood memories aren't quite as accurate as she thought they were . . .

PLAYING JAMES

Sarah Mason

Budding reporter Holly Colshannon thought things couldn't get worse than covering pet funerals. But then her boss at the *Bristol Gazette* hands her the poisoned chalice of a crime correspondent . . . Detective James Sabine is not happy to discover he is to be shadowed by a reporter: in fact, he wants his fly-on-the-wall to buzz right off. Holly, though, is not a girl to go lightly, especially when she has a daily column to write and an ailing MG to support. However, while relations between press and police continue to plunge, the reading public are starting to suspect that there's no spark without a flame.

TRUE BELIEVER

Nicholas Sparks

As the author of a popular syndicated column, Jeremy Marsh is regarded as an authority on debunking the supernatural. While nursing his wounds from the break-up of his most recent relationship, Jeremy receives a letter concerning ghostly apparitions in the small town of Washington, North Carolina. He sets off to uncover what he assumes is a hoax. But he hasn't anticipated meeting the granddaughter of the town psychic, Lexie Darnell, who is unlike any woman Jeremy has ever met. As he finds himself falling in love he is forced to confront secrets in his own past and to choose between the life he knows and a future that depends on his ability to do something he's never done before - take a leap of faith.